FIREBIRD

Also by Michael Asher

The Eye of Ra

FIREBIRD

MICHAEL ASHER

HarperCollins*Publishers*

This novel is entirely a work of fiction.
The names, characters and incidents portrayed in it are
the work of the author's imagination. Any resemblance to
actual persons, living or dead, events or localities is
entirely coincidental.

HarperCollins*Publishers*
77–85 Fulham Palace Road,
Hammersmith, London W6 8JB

www.**fire**and**water**.com

Published by HarperCollins*Publishers* 2000
1 3 5 7 9 8 6 4 2

A catalogue record for this book
is available from the British Library

Hardback: ISBN 0 00 225963 X
Trade Paperback: ISBN 0 00 710224 0

Set in Times New Roman by
Rowland Phototypesetting Ltd,
Bury St Edmunds, Suffolk

Printed and bound in Great Britain by
Omnia Books Limited, Glasgow

For Buzzo and Chumo

FIREBIRD

PRELUDE

ST SAMUEL'S MONASTERY, FAYOUM OASIS, EGYPT, WINTER 1995

A STORM WAS COMING. THE heat pulsated from a sapphire and ultramarine sky streaked with veins of blood-coloured dust among the foaming eddies of altocumulus. Professor Milisch Andropov smelt fire-ash on the air and frowned as he watched an Egyptian vulture plunge down like a stone, taking refuge in the branches of the tallest eucalyptus tree. He savoured the breeze, trying to calculate how long it would be before the storm struck, and reluctantly gave the gardeners the order to shut off the water-cocks. He lit a cigarette and watched the last of the water draining out of the feeders that took it among the olives, almonds, figs, oleanders, bougainvilleas and jasmine that filled the monastery garden. *Damn the storm*, he thought. In the twenty years he'd been coming to St Samuel's he'd seen the monastery transformed from a virtual ruin into a living, thriving religious community, and water had been the key to that change. He'd put in bores to tap the aquifers deep under the desert surface, harvested the occasional rains by turning every cloister and roof-top into a conduit, designed a reclamation system which meant that in a good year the place could exist in almost perfect homeostasis – the ecologist's dream. Andropov glanced up again and saw that the sky had darkened, the clouds coalesced into a single dark configuration that hung over the monastery like the claw of a giant. He shivered. It was a *ghibli* – the fearful southern wind that had been known to blind men and scour the paint off cars. The plants in the cloister-garden hadn't evolved in the desert, and a severe *ghibli* could wreck the place and set back his irrigation work by weeks. He stared at the vulture high in the eucalyptus tree, a hunchback shape with a piercing eye that glared back at him like a malevolent old witch.

It was a bad omen, he thought.

His reflections were interrupted by a high-pitched keening, and he looked down to see a procession entering the cloister through the main arch. The wind was whispering and sifting sills of dust across the quadrangle, and for a moment it seemed to him that the party had been blown in willy-nilly by the storm. Even from this distance, though, he could make out that the figures were Bedouin, and that they were carrying something among them on a makeshift stretcher. The stiffness and formality of their movements suggested to him a funeral cortège. A moment later the monastery's lay medical assistant, Da'ud – a grizzled Copt from Asyut with a permanent scowl – came shambling towards him. 'Professor, come quickly please!' he said breathlessly. 'Someone has been hurt!'

At the gate there were five or six sullen Bedouin in dirty *galla-biyyas* and turbans coiled tight around their heads against the wind. On the crude rope-bed they held what looked like a bundle of bloody rags from which the head of a boy protruded – a boy with blood-smeared hair, an ash-white face and fixed, staring eyes. A woman in black behind them wailed and screeched, *'Waladi! Ya Waladi!'* My son! My son!

'For God's sake, shut up, woman!' Andropov snapped in Arabic. 'To the infirmary! At once! At once!'

Da'ud led them across the square to the infirmary building, and Andropov trotted along behind, fumbling in his pocket for the key to the operating room. There was no incumbent doctor at St Samuel's and the Patriarch, Father Grigori, who normally supervised the sick, was absent. Andropov had been a medical student before he'd shifted to Earth Sciences, and though he'd never practised professionally he'd seen enough sickness and injury in his time to double as medic when he was staying here. He urged the cortège into the little operating room and the men laid the boy on the table. He washed his hands quickly, put on gloves and told Da'ud to set up the intravenous drip, then switched on the operating light. The Bedouin pressed around him muttering and the woman blubbered to herself. He gripped the oldest-looking of the tribesmen tightly by the arm.

'Get that woman out of here!' he said. '*You* – tell me what happened. The rest – out!'

Outside, the storm was swelling, pressing against the window with probing fingers. When the rest of the tribesmen had gone, Andropov peeled back the sheet and what he saw almost made him retch. Half the skin of the boy's torso had been flayed off and his genitals had been mutilated beyond recognition. There were lacerations on his legs, arms and shoulders so deep that in places he could see the arteries pulsing and glimpse the ends of shattered bones. The boy's breathing was laboured, and he was quivering in shock. Andropov drew a deep breath and explored the thigh wound gently. His first impression was that the boy had been slashed with a machete or cut with an axe, but on second look he realized the wounds were too ragged – they looked more like they'd been gouged with a rake, he thought.

'Well?' he asked the Bedouin who'd remained.

The man was old, with skin like tanned goat-hide, his face long and curved at both ends like a crescent moon, with outsized ears and an expression of such dolt-like blankness that Andropov knew it had to be false. He was a village headman, he guessed, probably from one of the settled tribes who claimed Bedouin ancestry but were actually peasant farmers. Andropov knew the monks despised them, because their religion was a hodge-podge of Islam, superstition and witchcraft. They had their own medicine men, he knew, and would never have come to the monastery if the boy hadn't been at death's door. The Bedouin's eyes were as cold and hostile as a fish's.

'I never saw it,' he said. 'Nobody here did. When we got there

3

he was already bleeding.' He stared at the floor. 'Probably a bull-camel,' he said, 'It's the rutting season. You stand in the way of a rutting bull-camel on heat and he'll rip you apart.'

'I've seen camel bites,' Andropov said, 'and this isn't one of them. Camel bites show signs of crushing, and this doesn't. It's almost . . . almost as if he was mauled by a leopard.'

'No leopards round here,' the old man said, lifting his eyes to Andropov. 'Used to be, maybe in my grandfather's time, but now there's only caracals and they beat it as soon as they get a whiff of *Bani Adam*.'

Andropov sized the man up again and noticed that he was carrying a big, greasy service revolver stuck in his belt. 'Why do you bring firearms into a monastery?' he demanded. 'Don't you know this is God's place?'

A cold smile spread across the Bedouin's wrinkled features. 'There's only one way of dealing with a murderous bull-camel,' he said. 'Besides, you never know when you might come across a blood enemy.'

Andropov stared at him for a moment. The tribes here were riddled with feuds that lasted for generations, and he wondered if that was what lay behind the boy's injury. Without knowing quite why he suddenly snatched the pistol from the man's belt and opened the chamber. It was filled with silver bullets. 'What's this?' he said, picking out a round and holding it up in the light to the medical assistant. 'Silver bullets? Da'ud, what in God's name is this about?'

Da'ud looked at the silver slug then stared at the boy's shattered body. An expression of terror slowly crept into his eyes. 'God protect us from the devil!' he gasped, stepping back from the operating table. 'Don't touch him, Professor! This is the work of a ghoul.'

Andropov glared at him. 'Ghouls? Witchcraft?' He turned to the old man with fury in his eyes. 'You tell me what's going on here,' he snapped, 'or I'll send for the police.'

The old man blanched, then nodded slowly and watched Andropov with bulging, sand-shot eyes. 'All right,' he said. 'It was a ghoul. God preserve us from Satan! Only silver bullets can kill a ghoul.'

'Pagan superstition!' Andropov said.

The old man's mouth curled into a crooked smile, showing a mess of yellow teeth. His eyes remained cold as needles. 'I know a ghoul's work when I see it,' he said. 'You said it wasn't the work of a camel – true, but it wasn't a leopard or a caracal or a hyena neither. There were tracks near the body – strange tracks. The man who found the boy said he saw a creature running into the desert – a hairy thing that walked upright on bandy legs. We tracked it out into the *khala*, and we'd have got it too if it hadn't been for the *ghibli*.'

Andropov shivered and turned his back on the old man. 'Very well,' he said, 'wait outside.'

There was a waft of fine dust as the door opened and the momentary drone of the wind. The boy was moaning softly, his eyelids fluttering. As the door closed, Da'ud stared at the patient again and backed away. He made the two-fingered sign against the evil eye. 'Leave him, Professor. The ghoul is within him. If it knows he's dying it will cross over.'

Andropov gave him a withering look. 'Shut up! Give me some morphine – quickly!'

The Copt fumbled in a glass cabinet and came out with a sterile syringe, a needle and a phial of clear liquid. The Professor grabbed them from his shaking hands, fitted the needle, then snapped off the top of the phial with calloused fingers. When he'd filled the syringe he held it up to the light for a moment and flicked it with his index finger. He was about to insert the needle into the side of the boy's buttock, when his eyes snapped open, his body convulsing wildly, his head writhing from side to side. The back of his hand caught the syringe and flipped it skittering across the floor. The Professor made a grab for him, and as he did so the boy grasped his wrist and gripped it with the strength of a drowning man. The look of horror in his eyes was so shocking that the Professor recoiled. 'What happened?' he asked. 'What was it?'

The boy stared sightlessly at the ceiling, his eyes bright with death. His purple lips moved haltingly. 'Ghoul!' he whispered. 'Ghoul!'

PART I

CAIRO, EGYPT, DECEMBER 1999

1

I DON'T CARE WHAT THEY say, I thought, *the head's too small for the body.*

I glanced up at the monster's inscrutable face, shading my eyes against the blazing light of the mid-morning sun, and felt a quaint thrill of fear – a thrill that had never quite left me no matter how many times I'd visited the Great Sphinx enclosure here at Giza. To me, this sculpture had always seemed the product of an alien mentality, and I knew why the Arabs called it Abul-Hol; 'The Father of Terror'. Its face was a frame without features, the face of a creature lurking at the cusp of reality and illusion – a shapeshifter's face. Or maybe it was just that I saw my own face there. The Egyptologists claimed that its features were those of Khafre, the Fourth Dynasty pharaoh who was also supposed to have built the second pyramid nearby. They said that the whole Giza complex – three large pyramids, six small ones, mastaba tombs, boat pits *and* the Sphinx – was constructed by a single dynasty of pharaohs around 2500 BC, and that each piece of the jigsaw was an integral part of a coherent whole. Something – call it intuition – told me that the Sphinx was much older, and even if it did have Khafre's face, that didn't prove he'd constructed it. Maybe it once had a lion's head, and Khafre simply had it recarved in his image. The experts disagreed vehemently, of course, but then I've never had much time for experts. They always seem to have a secret agenda of their own.

I adjusted my baseball cap so that the peak covered the nape of my neck, and wiped the moisture off my forehead with my cuff. It was unusually hot for December, and the met boys were tracking a massive sandstorm that they reckoned would hit the city in a couple of days. There were a few people about – European and Japanese tourists in shorts and sunhats, and the odd curious clump of locals – but the place was by no means crowded. On my way into the Sphinx enclosure I'd passed a film crew shooting a troop of men in ill-fitting leotards performing sweaty aerobics for a TV programme. Anywhere else it would have been beautiful young nymphets in costumes so tight they had to be poured on, but this was Egypt and we had to be content with pot-bellied bruisers. I knew they were still going at it despite the heat, because I could hear the half-hearted shouts of their instructor over the thick granite walls.

Amid the murmur of foreign voices I picked out footsteps behind me, and I knew at once they were out of place. The tread was too heavy and deliberate for a tourist – sight-seers here trod at a leisurely pace. Instinct told me the steps were heading towards me, and I felt discreetly under my old leather jacket for the handle of my .380 Beretta in its quick-draw shoulder-rig. It was just a precaution. The last thing I needed was a shoot-out under the eyes of the Sphinx, but in my few years as a Special Investigations detective I'd made some enemies, and I couldn't afford to be casual. I still had the scar on my rib-cage from the time we'd staked out the Shadowmen's stronghold in New Cairo and they'd been waiting for us with rocket-launchers and God knew what hi-tec shit. There was still flotsam of the Shadowmen about, and any one of them had a good excuse to stiff me if he had half a chance. Even before I'd turned, though, I'd recognized the tread of Colonel Hammoudi – the measured pace I'd grown used to over the years. He eased his bulk up beside me and squinted sideways at Abul-Hol.

'Can't leave this junkyard alone can you, Sammy?' he said in a low voice. 'Not even in your spare time.'

I snickered, relaxing my grip on the Beretta. It *was* kind of pathetic that a eligible young police lieutenant like me had nothing better to do on his day off than stare at the Sphinx alone. But I had no wife, no children, no girl, no social life outside the police and no friends apart from Hammoudi. Home was a spartan apartment at the top of a block on Roda. Some people said I was a hermit, socially awkward, or even a closet gay, but I wasn't. It was just that until I'd completed my job here, that was the way it had to be.

I smiled at the Colonel. 'Half the police budget goes on guarding our glorious heritage,' I said, 'so I reckon there ought to be at least one cop who knows what it is we're protecting.'

Hammoudi grunted. 'Our glorious heritage,' he repeated, rolling the words around his mouth as if trying to suck some kind of meaning out of them. He was a good nine inches taller than me – six-three at least – and he wore a faded dark suit that must have felt like chain mail in this heat. His white shirt was frayed at the collar, and he wore a dark tie and black shoes that had been polished so much the uppers had begun to wear through. His shoulders looked almost impossibly broad, and I knew it wasn't padding. His head was a dome, his hair receding, streaked with silver at the sides, and his face, hacked out of granite, was as aggressive as a bulldog's, its cradle of intersecting lines emphasized by a neatly clipped moustache.

'How'd you know I was here?' I asked.

'Call it empathy,' Hammoudi said, a wolfish crease spreading between the corner of his mouth and left eye.

I stifled a rude snort. OK, Boutros Hammoudi had many gifts, but I wouldn't have numbered empathy in the first ten. He still ran the Special Investigations Department with the same rod of iron he'd earned a name for years ago as a parachute sergeant in the Yemen. Then, he'd led a unit called the Night Butchers who'd operated at night behind enemy lines, bringing back the penises of their victims as trophies. Now he was sixty and nearing retirement age, but he still worked out with weights four nights a week, and could pack a wallop. I once saw him hit two slime-balls with a volley of snap punches that dropped them as clean as steel bolts through the skull. The sound of his knuckles on their flesh was like gunshots. Empathy? *Bukra fil mishmish*, I thought.

Hammoudi grimaced impatiently as if following my cerebral processes. 'You told me days ago you were overdue for a trip to Giza,' he said. 'This is your first day off in weeks, so I guessed you'd be here.'

That was nearer the mark, I thought. 'Well I hope it's strictly social,' I said, 'because like you say, this is my day off, and every time I've had a day off in the past three months something has come up!'

The Colonel gave a feral grin and drew a flattened pack of Cleopatra cigarettes from his side pocket. He flicked one out, stuck it in his mouth and lit it with a disposable lighter. He breathed out smoke and stared with apparent interest at the front paws of the Great Sphinx. 'Isn't there supposed to be a stela or something in there?' he asked.

I screwed up my eyes against the sun and turned my baseball cap the right way round. 'Yeah,' I said, 'you can just see the top of it from here, but it's crumbled and unreadable now. They call it the dream-stela of Thutmose IV, the Eighteenth Dynasty pharaoh who ruled before the heretic Akhnaton.'

Hammoudi raised his eyebrows and spewed out smoke. 'Akhnaton!' he said. 'Seems that guy got his ugly snout into every damn place.'

'Sure, but they weren't exactly classmates. Story goes that one night Thutmose crashed out under the head of the Great Sphinx and dreamed he was about to become pharaoh. Like dreaming you were going to win the lottery. Anyway, the guy *did* become pharaoh, and he had the stela stuck between the paws to commemorate the dream. Funny thing was that in his day the Sphinx was half-buried in sand – only the head showed. According to the stela he ordered the whole thing dug out, but no one knows why.'

Hammoudi blew smoke and brooded thoughtfully for a moment. 'It's hotter than hell,' he said. 'Let's go grab a soda.'

I nodded. He didn't have to twist my arm. I was sick of gawking at the Great Noseless One anyway.

We tottered back through the Valley Temple with its great pillars and architraves bending the sunlight into blocks of light and shade. We paused there in an island of shadow for a moment while Hammoudi stubbed out his cigarette, both glad of a moment's relief from the heat. 'Freak heat,' Hammoudi commented. 'They say a storm's gonna strike in a couple of days.'

I sniffed the air. 'They're wrong,' I said, 'it'll be here tomorrow.'

'Why don't you run the met office?' Hammoudi chuckled.

I shrugged and ran a hand along one of the temple's massive limestone blocks. As always, I marvelled at its hugeness. The two temples at the foot of the Sphinx – the Mortuary Temple and this one, the Valley Temple – are only forty feet high and haven't attracted the same attention as the much more impressive pyramids nearby, yet they are real wonders of engineering skill. 'You know these blocks were quarried out of the Sphinx pit itself?' I asked Hammoudi.

'No,' he said. 'Big buggers, though, aren't they? How the hell did they lift them?'

'That's a good question. Some of them are reckoned to weigh two hundred tons – that's nearly three times as much as most of the blocks used in the Great Pyramid. Even a modern gantry-crane – the type used in shipyards – can only handle about a hundred tons.'

Hammoudi looked unimpressed. 'And don't tell me,' he said, 'they didn't have gantry-cranes in those days. Come on, let's get out of this garbage lot.'

We went out through the exit, past a couple of tourist police asleep on their chairs. The aerobics team had gone and the TV crew were packing up their cameras and reflecting mirrors. We walked down the hill towards the bus-park in the blistering heat.

A knot of tourists in white sunhats was queuing to embark on a luxury coach, anxious to be back in its air-conditioned interior. They looked depressed, I thought. A few touts pestered them listlessly, holding up stuffed camels and soapstone models of the pyramids. In years past this place would have been packed with foreigners on a Friday, but the tourist trade was in the doldrums. It had been that way ever since the last terrorist massacre at Luxor when the Militants had shot and mutilated a bunch of foreigners – men, women and children, whose only crime was that they'd come for a looksee at the ancient ruins. What a débâcle that had been, I thought. The foreign press didn't know the half of it. The Militants had even shot up a couple of police stations and only a handful of troopers had had the guts to shoot back. The few wounded on the terrorist side had been topped by their own men to stop them squealing, and the Anti-Terrorist Squad had been unable to identify any of the stiffs, or even to say for sure whether they were Egyptians. You couldn't blame the tourists for not wanting to come here, but the decline in the industry had hit the country hard. Of course, things were slowly getting better. There were more cops on the street, and more visitors were arriving as confidence was regained, but everyone knew that one more stroke like the Luxor fiasco would put the mockers on the business for ever.

It was good to get under the awning of a soft-drinks stall. We were the only customers there, and we sat on stools right up against the ice-box while the barman dipped into it and brought out two bottles of Canada Dry so cold the stuff was almost frozen. I sipped the drink and gasped at its coldness. In a few seconds the liquid had worked its way to the pores, soaking me in sweat. Hammoudi drank half the bottle in one go, burped, then wiped his mouth with the hairy back of a hand. He lit another Cleopatra. I sipped and waited for his gambit, but he concentrated on his cigarette and ignored me until I caved in.

'You didn't come here just to quiz me about ancient history,' I said.

He made a wry face, the big, marble-smooth features shattering and reforming. 'No, I didn't. Something has come up.'

I almost choked on my soda. 'I knew it!' I said. 'What the hell is it this time?'

'Something quite interesting.'

'Look, unless it's got at least one donkey's foot, I'm not interested. I've been sidetracked too many times, and this is my day off, all right.'

'All right,' Hammoudi said, adopting a sympathetic tone that I'd learned to be wary of. 'I just wondered if you'd ever heard of a guy called Adam Ibram, that's all.'

'You mean *Doctor* Adam Ibram, the American-Egyptian egghead who worked for NASA. Sure I've heard of him. I read in the paper a few days back he was over here for a visit.'

'Yep, his final visit. Some assholes shot him dead in a coffee-shop in Khan al-Khalili this morning.'

I paused in the act of sipping my drink. 'The Yanks won't like it. Wasn't Ibram a big wheel in the States?'

'That's right. Born in Egypt but brought up and educated in the USA. He'd become a real big honcho. Advisor to the US president, no less, on environmental issues, and almost every other damn issue. You name it; he was boned up on it. The US ambassador bent our minister of the interior's ear as soon as the body was found, demanding to let his FBI office run the investigation. The minister OK'd it, but on the understanding a senior Egyptian detective would be top dog. His Excellency probably thought it would be just a rubber stamp job, but the minister told me he wanted someone who would put Egypt's interests first, and had naturally thought of yours truly. I was flattered, actually. You know how much I appreciate the Yanks.'

I horse-laughed openly this time. Hammoudi knew well enough that I was the product of a short-lived fling between my Egyptian mother and the American father who'd dumped me as a kid, leaving me to grow up hard as a street-boy in the bazaars of Aswan. It was water under the bridge to me now, but I guessed secretly that the Colonel had added it to the list of grudges against the Yanks he'd been compiling for years. Hammoudi was well known for his patriotism and his dislike of foreign meddling in Egypt's affairs. That was one reason he'd been tolerated for so long despite his remarkable and almost unique inability to lick the asses of his superiors.

'Why me?' I asked. 'What happened to your duty assistant?'

Hammoudi looked at me with feigned indignation. 'You know I can't trust anyone else on the squad,' he said. 'Remember the Shadowmen? I still reckon someone on the team tipped them off. You're all I've got.'

It was a sad admission, I thought, for someone who'd spent most of his life as a cop, but it was probably true. Hammoudi was a member of the despised Coptic minority, and had had to work his way up by sheer ability and devotion to duty. Any other man as good as he was would have been a general by now, but first he was a Copt, then a Sa'idi – a southerner – and to cap it all there'd been an enquiry a few years back about a subversive leader he'd allegedly allowed to escape. I happened to know the allegation was true, but I doubt anyone else on the force did. Hammoudi had kept his trap shut and in the end there'd been no evidence. Anyway, the Colonel was too smooth an operator, too obviously loyal to the country and too successful at what he did to be got rid of that easily.

'What if the FBI don't want me?' I asked.

'Sod them, Sammy. Their official brief is to "assist" local police on cases involving American property, interests or citizens, that's all.'

'Yeah, but those guys are mavericks. Plenty of times they've arrested suspects in foreign countries without the government's approval.'

'I know. As it happens, the FBI boss has already assigned a detective to the case.'

'Shit.'

'Yeah. Shit. That's why I want to get down there now, before the FBI have stomped over every bit of evidence that might be of value. Let's make damned sure we get the truth, even if we have to keep it under our hats.'

I swivelled my baseball cap round and scratched under it with my free hand doubtfully, knowing I couldn't refuse. If I had been any other officer on the team, Hammoudi would just have ordered me to hit the street on the double and that would have been it. But he and I had a special understanding. Ever since I'd finished police training school, Hammoudi had appointed himself my guardian angel – a sort of father-confessor and back-up rolled into one. He'd taught me more about detective work than all the training-school instructors put together. I'd never stopped being amazed at the information Hammoudi had at his fingertips – the big man's sources had got me out of tight spots more than once, not only with punters but also with the top brass. I guessed that he'd chosen me as a sort of personal successor – almost the son he'd never had. Hammoudi always said he hadn't had time to get married and have children, but women found him attractive, and I'd always been staggered how easily he seemed to find willing partners.

He cocked an inquisitive eye at me. 'Well?' he said, glancing at his watch.

I finished my Canada Dry. 'OK,' I said. '*Yalla binna.*'

'Good man,' he said, draining his soda, 'I'll make it up to you.'

'No you won't. You never do.'

I stood up and passed a hand through my hair. It was long overdue trimming, and I knew there was a three-day stubble on my chin. Apart from my leather jacket and baseball cap, I was wearing a black sweatshirt, jeans so ancient they might have been designed by Fred Flintstone, and a pair of trainers only slightly less venerable.

Hammoudi watched me for a minute, chuckling. 'Don't worry if you're not dressed for dinner,' he said. 'After all, it's only the FBI.'

We sauntered up to Hammoudi's unmarked Mercedes diesel, parked badly near the sidewalk. Mercifully, the Colonel had remembered to put up a cardboard sunshade on the windscreen, and the seats were still cool. As I settled in and clicked the seatbelt, Hammoudi nursed the big car into the street, his oversize hands gripping the wheel like he wanted to wrench it apart. Traffic was sparse. From Al-Malik Salem Bridge the Nile looked blue and calm – cool enough to dive into – and as we crossed the stream I looked up to see a silver shape dropping out of the sun. I realized suddenly that it was a grey heron, and I watched fascinated as it spiralled towards us on the thermals, its crested head haloed in sunlight as though it was on fire. As a kid in the south I'd spent hours lying on the riverbank watching herons. I loved the way their necks curved into an almost perfect 'S', the disdainful way they shook their wings when you approached them, the way they waited like statues for ever in the shallows, moving one leg almost imperceptibly forwards until the spiked beak flashed down like an ice-pick, and came up with a silver fish impaled on it, shimmering in the sunlight. I watched the bird now, the uplifted wings picked out in flame and thought of the Winged Disk that you found almost everywhere in ancient Egyptian inscriptions. Suddenly a phrase drifted into my head unbidden, and I heard myself muttering, '*I have gone forth as the phoenix, in the hope of life eternal.*'

'What?' Hammoudi asked, but I shrugged and he didn't press it. He was well used to my irrational outbursts by now. I looked ahead to see a traffic cop with a dirty white band on his cap, who was waving us on with whistles and languorous movements of the hands. When I glanced back the heron was nowhere to be seen, and whether I'd imagined it I was no longer certain.

After that I rode in a kind of daze as we followed the line of the Roman aqueduct, skirting around the stark dust-coloured sugar-loafs of Muqattam, on which the citadel of Mohammad Ali stood, with its array of castellations, onion-roofs and pinnacles like a image from Walt Disney's *Aladdin*. The streets were crowded here with family groups, some of them sitting in corners sharing food set out on newspapers. Giza had been almost deserted, but half of Cairo, it seemed, was spending its day off at the old fortress. It was only when we reached the twin mosques of Rifai and Sultan Hassan, rising sheer out of the maze of streets like the walls of icebergs, that I snapped out of it and tweaked my head into some sort of reasoning mode. 'What time was the incident?' I asked.

'Body was found at nine-thirty,' Hammoudi said, 'in the back room of a kebab-joint-cum-coffee-house, with a bullet wound smack in the middle of the forehead, and others in the chest and legs. Eye-witnesses said three men were involved, but the only one who saw the actual shooting was a waiter who happened to be coming out of the john. They got him too, but he survived. A plain-clothes officer from National Security who'd been mingling with the crowds went through Ibram's pockets and found his US passport, wallet and credit cards.'

'No theft motive then?'

Hammoudi chewed his lips silently. 'Who knows?' he said. 'The perps were disturbed, of course.'

'Anyone identify them?'

'No, they were wearing *shamaghs* across their faces, and some onlookers claimed they were carrying submachine-pistols.'

'Sounds like a terrorist job.'

'SSSH!' Hammoudi hissed. He glanced at me urgently. 'Whatever you do, don't mention the dreaded "T" word. You want to give the minister a coronary thinking of those thousands of dollars that won't be pouring into the economy from petrified tourists? This is strictly an SID investigation with a little help from our friends. The Anti-Terrorist Squad haven't even been tasked.'

I concentrated on the road and said nothing, but I knew there had to be more to it than he was letting on. I'd worked with him long enough to know he hadn't come all the way to Giza to get me to investigate a simple homicide.

2

IN SAYYIDNA HUSSAYN SQUARE THE police had rigged up a wall of yellow and black striped crash-barriers to keep out tourists and nosey-parkers, and a squad of blackjackets with red bands on their berets stood on guard outside with pump-action shotguns and kalashnikovs. The square was famous as one of the entrances to the bazaar of Khan al-Khalili, the sprawling warren of shops and artisans' workshops that had been the heart of the walled city of Cairo in medieval times. It was named after a man called Jarkas al-Khalili – a fourteenth-century prince who'd set up a huge khan or caravanserai here where Persian merchants could hole up and sell goods shipped by camel-caravan from as far away as India and China. That must have been an amazing joint – the Hilton of its day, and then some. While the traders found rooms on the upper floors, their camels were stabled in the courtyard below. The precious merchandise – rare stones, pearls, perfumes, porcelain, carpets, cottons, spices and silks – was stowed safely in tiny warehouses built into the ground-floor walls. The Khan's courtyard doubled as a bustling market where the merchants erected stalls and bargained with their clients over mint tea. Eventually the trading had spilled over into the area outside the walls, which had grown into a sprawl of crooked dark alleys where anything and everything could be bought and sold. By the time the Turks made their successful take-over bid for Egypt in the sixteenth century, Khan al-Khalili had become one of the most important trading centres in the whole Middle East.

A young lieutenant in clean black cotton combats and jump boots waved the Mercedes to a halt, and crossed his palm with a finger, silently demanding our ID. While he inspected our cards I glanced round at the small crowd that had gathered outside. Two TV teams were already setting up their gear from the back of vans, one Egyptian state TV, and the other CNN. A local TV reporter pushed through the crowd and pressed a bulb-shaped microphone right into the car's open window. 'Is it true this is a terrorist murder, sir?' he demanded.

'No comment,' Hammoudi growled. He snatched back the ID cards from the lieutenant, who saluted smartly as the car pulled into the square.

Sayyidna al-Hussayn Square was named after the nineteenth-century mosque whose austere stone edifice bounded the whole of its northeastern side. The northwestern side was a solid row of teashops and kebab joints stretching to the corner of the famous al-Muski alley, broken off-centre by a shadowy tunnel that opened into the depths of the Khan itself. Patrol cars and unmarked mini-buses were parked haphazardly around an oblong area in the centre of the square, where strong steel railings need-lessly defended a few metres of sun-blasted shrubs and dead grass. Normally the square was packed with tourists, shoppers, bootblacks, beggars and touts, just as it had been for centuries. Today, though, there were only clusters of stern-faced men and a few women in sombre suits and black uniforms, hanging about listlessly as if waiting to be told what to do. As I closed the car door, the heat slammed me like a hammer. It was just after midday. The body had been found at nine-thirty, so the wheels had got in motion pretty sharply, I thought. That was the Yanks for you. The teahouse where Ibram had been shot was pretty easy to spot – the whole place had been surrounded by yellow incident tape on weighted stands – American incident tape, I presumed, since it formed an oblong of almost perfect right-angles. The place was called Gahwat az-Zahra – Flower Coffee-shop – and there was nothing much to distinguish it from the rest of the row, except, I noticed, that it had a public telephone sign outside and a notice in English and Arabic reading *You Can Telephone From Here*. There were bare tables and chairs in the street for the tea- and coffee-drinkers, and inside tables spread with checked tablecloths for customers eating. As we approached, a black-uniformed captain separated himself from a huddle and saluted Hammoudi.

'Good afternoon, Colonel,' he said. 'Good to see you on the job.'

'What's going on?' Hammoudi growled.

'The Americans have taken over, sir,' the captain said. 'They won't let any of our boys through the tape.' He gestured to a tall, massive American with a craggy face and spectacles, who was standing at the tape barrier holding a clipboard and a pen.

'We'll see about that,' Hammoudi said. He assumed his most truculent expression and strode straight up to the FBI man. I tagged along behind. 'What's this about not letting my men into the incident area?' he demanded in passable English. The American just grinned at him sleepily. He was almost as tall as the Colonel and wore a pistol in a black shoulder-holster over a white shirt that was damp with perspiration. A heavy walkie-talkie hung in a pouch at his belt, and an ID card with a photo attached to his shirt pocket read 'Special Agent Craig, FBI'.

'Sorry,' Craig said. His voice rasped like he'd eaten sandpaper. 'No can do, buddy. Legat's orders. No one but FBI goes through the wire until the chief investigating officer arrives.'

'I *am* the chief investigating officer,' Hammoudi said, holding up an ID card inscribed in both English and Arabic. 'And I am a full colonel, so you can call me sir.'

The FBI man looked at the card but remained nonplussed. 'OK...*sir*,' he said, 'your name's on the list.' He glanced at me, taking in my antediluvian jeans and sneakers. 'But who's this guy?' he asked. 'Is he a cop?'

'This is Lieutenant Sammy Rashid of the SID,' Hammoudi said, 'my investigating detective on this case.'

I presented my ID, but the FBI man scanned the list and shook his head. 'Sorry. The Legat only specified one local officer. Your name isn't on this list. I can't let you in.'

Hammoudi fixed the agent with a ferocious stare. 'OK, Special Agent Craig, or whatever you call yourself. This is Cairo, not Chicago, and I'm in charge of the case. I have shown you my ID. You have exactly ten seconds to stand aside and let us both through your bloody ''wire'', otherwise – you see those men over there?' He half-turned and gestured to the platoon of black-jackets at the barrier. 'I will order them to get in here, take your tape apart and use it as toilet paper. And you can explain *that* to the Legat. Let's not forget you are guests in this country, and believe me, those men will do as I say.'

I had to admire the agent's cool. 'Sir,' Craig said, 'I must advise you we have a Tactical Unit deployed for protection. There are powerful scopes trained on you right now. Anyone who threatens US personnel or property will be taken out.'

Hammoudi didn't turn a hair. 'In that case,' he said, 'you will be committing an act of aggression against friendly government forces in their own country. I'm sure President Clinton will be pleased to hear about it. I am still ordering my men in, and you still have ten seconds.'

For the first time the big American looked uncertain. He shook his head slowly as if dealing with unreasonable savages. 'OK,' he said finally, picking his walkie-talkie out of its pouch and flicking the 'send' button. 'Hello, sir,' he rasped in his buzz-saw voice, 'this is Craig.' I wondered why Americans always seemed to shout. With a voice like that, the guy hardly needed a radio anyway. 'Sir,' Craig went on, 'there's a guy here says he's the CIO – a Colonel, er . . . Hammoudi. He's on the list and his ID checks out. But he's got this kinda doohickey-looking sidekick with him claims he's the investigating detective. Got ID but he's not on the list. I told him he couldn't pass the wire, but it looks like an incident might be brewing, and there are TV cameras out here.'

The FBI man released the 'send' switch and held the radio to his ear. I could just make out the low crackle of a voice. Finally, Craig said, 'Got it, sir,' and slipped the walkie-talkie back into its sheath. 'The Legat's inside there with a bunch of forensics and photographers,' he said. 'You can proceed, but I have to ask you both to log on.'

We signed the sheet on the clipboard and the agent stood aside. As we ducked under the yellow tape, I asked, 'Who is this Legat guy, anyway?'

'FBI foreign station-chief,' Hammoudi said. 'It's one of those slick words the Yanks make up because they're in too much of a rush to say ''Legal Attaché''. Legat is a cushy number given to FBI officers who've proved themselves – this one is a guy called Marvin. Used to be FBI Assistant Director for Special Operations.'

I nodded and looked around the teashop. From outside it had seemed small and claustrophobic, but inside it was surprisingly deep, and obviously older than you would have judged from the exterior. The ceiling was high and criss-crossed with Moorish-style vaulted arches painted in black and red stripes. Beyond the tables was a bar of hardwood carved with ancient Egyptian symbols – ankhs, Wedjet eyes, falcons and cobras. I followed Hammoudi through the open door to the back room, where a knot of FBI men in suits or white lab-coats was grouped around the body.

Doctor Adam Ibram lay on the floor staring upwards with wide eyes that were partly obliterated by pools of coagulated blood. The blood had soaked into his shirt and dark suit so completely that they had become an almost solid mass. Blood was liberally spattered over the floor and walls. There was a gaping hole in the middle of Ibram's forehead, and other, smaller wounds scattered over his chest, stomach and thighs. One of his shoes was missing and lay in a corner nearby. There was a nauseating butchery smell in the air – flies everywhere – and I struggled to stop myself losing my breakfast. I'd seen dead bodies before, but I'd never got accustomed to it like Hammoudi, who looked about as concerned as a man weighing up the quality of steaks in a meat market. A telephone swung from its coinbox near the body, and at the far end of the room I saw the open door of an Arab-style squat-toilet. A few steps beyond the WC there was an entrance arch, covered with a baize curtain, and beyond that I saw a fan revolving slowly, set into a niche in the main wall.

'Now we know why Ibram chose this teashop and not the others,' I said.

'You mean to take a dump?' Hammoudi said, grinning.

I smiled. The Colonel's black humour seemed an affront to propriety, but I had long ago realized that it was a defensive mechanism. If you stayed too grim in the presence of death, the horror could overwhelm you.

'No, I mean to make a phone call. This is the only joint on the street with a public phone. There's a big sign right outside. Ibram had to get in touch with somebody urgently, and that phone call cost him his life.'

At the sound of our voices, one of the FBI men glanced up. He was tall – taller than me, anyway – and he looked muscular, with a gymnast's chest and beefy arms and legs. His face was creased with lines that looked like they'd been gouged in with a cut-throat, the hair a honed-down silver mat. His eyes were deep-set and guarded, his mouth turned down at the corners giving you the feeling that he could be a very mean son-of-a-bitch indeed.

'Colonel Hammoudi?' he said, holding out a hand. The accent was clipped – probably New England, I thought. 'I'm Thomas Marvin, Legat to the US embassy here. I run the FBI team. Glad to have you aboard.'

Marvin smiled with his mouth, but his eyes stayed cold as permafrost, and he spoke down to Hammoudi as if he was a new kid on the block. The American gave me the same condescending once-over, and I realized that my ragged jacket and jeans were hardly a match for his lightweight Armani suit. 'Who's this?' he asked.

27

'Lieutenant Rashid, my investigating detective,' Hammoudi said.

Marvin fixed his piercing eyes on my prehistoric trainers. 'We already have an investigating detective.'

'Not a local one,' Hammoudi said.

Marvin frowned nastily. 'This is an FBI case. My ambassador and your minister agreed that there should be only one local officer – a senior detective who was to act as liaison. That's you, Colonel.' He shot me a glance as cold as an ice-axe. 'And with all due respect, this is a job for hardcore professionals.'

'I don't believe in rubber-stamping reports,' Hammoudi said, 'if that's what you expected. My instructions are that I am in charge of this case. I can appoint whom I like.'

'I'm going to have to talk to my ambassador about this.'

I ignored the bickering and knelt down to examine the body. The limb and torso wounds formed a pattern, I saw, and the size and colour of the entries told me the shots had been fired from a few metres away, probably from the door. They'd also been fired from submachine-guns, because there was a burst pattern on the body, moving down the chest, to the abdomen, to the legs, and all submachine-guns tended to pull down. The head wound was quite different, though. The flesh around the entry was black with powder burns, showing that it was a hard-contact wound – the muzzle of the weapon had been laid flush against the skin. I lifted one of the limp hands gently. It was cold to the touch, and as I held it between a thumb and two fingers, I suddenly felt my senses twinge. My skin was tingling – a sure sign that I was losing control – and my heart began to thud. It was as if a chasm had opened in the fabric of the universe and I was falling inside it, slipping over the edge of darkness. I fought against it desperately but it was too strong. A wave of nausea engulfed me. The hubbub around me subsided, and the room went out of focus until I was suspended in a void where the only sound was the eerie soughing of the desert wind. At once, I started to get glimpses – faint disjointed images of a sphinx, constellations of stars with Orion's belt burning brightly,

28

the sun rising over the desert like a giant orange balloon. I saw a vast underground structure filled with huge pillars like giant trees, and a woman with the head of a lioness. I saw images of Doctor Adam Ibram running through a maze of dark alleys, of his face emerging into the light, of a man in a black suit lurking in the shadows. I saw a tall woman in Bedouin clothes with a veiled face, saw Ibram tearing up something with the help of a blunt knife. The last thing I saw was a strange shadow-creature with projecting, spidery limbs, whose eyes burned like beacons from beneath a shroud of darkness. I began to shake uncontrollably. Someone – it must have been Hammoudi – shook me suddenly and hard, and I opened my eyes to let real time come flooding in. I knew that only seconds had passed, but in those moments I'd been completely out of it, and I thanked my lucky stars Hammoudi was there to cover up for me as he had done so many times in the past. I stood up, sighing, shaking my head and blinking rapidly to bring myself round.

Marvin was watching me with wide eyes. 'You having a fit?' he demanded.

'No,' I said, gulping air. 'Just a bit giddy.' I paused and took more breaths, and Marvin swung round on Hammoudi accusingly.

'Like I told you,' he said, 'this is a job for hardcore professionals. This guy never saw a stiff before or what?'

'Lieutenant Rashid's one of the best detectives on the force,' Hammoudi said.

Marvin whistled. 'Jesus,' he said, 'what are the rest like?'

'I don't see any rounds or ejected cases,' I said, ignoring him, trying to strain the shake out of my voice, 'so I assume you got them. The perps must have fired at least thirty rounds.'

'You're supposed to be the star detective,' Marvin said sullenly, 'work it out for yourself.'

'Oh I have,' I said, breathing deeply through my nostrils. 'Three gunmen were chasing Ibram. He ducked in here to call someone for help. He was shot by at least two men from close range while he was on the phone. The first shots were probably fired from submachine-guns, but the last shot – to the head – was fired from a pistol at point-blank range. Street grafters? I don't think so. They wouldn't have chased a man through busy streets in broad daylight, even with *shamaghs* over their faces. Grafters work at night. We know he wasn't robbed, and that *could* have been because they were interrupted, but then why bother with the headshot? He couldn't have identified them. What we're left with, Mr Legat, is first-degree murder meditated and planned – a Mafia-style contract killing or a terrorist job. But I think you know that.'

Hammoudi cast me a worried glance and Marvin stared first at the Colonel, then at me. 'All I know is that Ibram's dead,' he said, 'and this homicide is officially non-political.' He brought a tiny cellphone from his pocket. 'I'm going to call my ambassador right now.'

Hammoudi laid a huge hand gently on his arm. 'Look,' he said, in his most diplomatic voice, 'if we're going to work together on this, Mr Marvin, I think we should . . . how do you say? *Level* with each other. We know Ibram was a big noise in the States. We can't rule out a political motive. The important thing is that anything we discover stays under wraps. I don't think either of our governments wants undue publicity, but we need to know what this is really about.'

Marvin looked thoughtfully from the Colonel to me, and put the phone back in his pocket. 'OK,' he said, 'I'll buy it for now. But if one shadow of a whisper gets to the press, I'll make you wish to God you'd kept your noses the fuck out of it.' He sighed and shook his head. 'This is one hell of a mess. Ibram was over here for a meeting of your Giza Millennium Committee.'

'Oh yeah,' I said, 'the committee's planning a huge shindig at the pyramids for the turn of the century. Big opera by Jean-Michel Jarre to be broadcast worldwide on TV with over a thousand singers and musicians. Even the president's attending. There's going to be hundreds of thousands of visitors here. The flights and hotels are already fully booked, and the government's hoping to revive the tourist industry in one go.'

'That's right. There's a lot of careers riding on it – and a mega infusion of cash from the States. That's how come a US citizen like Ibram got to be sitting on the board.'

'The Militants are already talking about putting the kibosh on the celebrations,' Hammoudi added. 'New Year's Eve falls in Ramadan, so the fundamentalists aren't going to be impressed with a lot of champagne-swilling foreigners on the rampage. Security's going to be a nightmare.'

'Exactly,' said Marvin. 'If it happens, the century's biggest party could turn into the biggest security fiasco of the millennium – something the Hate Groups will be crowing about for the *next* thousand years.'

Hate Groups, I thought, so that was what they called them now. It was only partly right. It always seemed to me that the Militants' biggest motivation was fear. They were frightened silly of a universe they couldn't control or understand, and had invented a set of phoney certainties to cling to like a drowning man clings to a floating spar. And they were prepared to kill anyone they thought was going to take that spar away from them. But perhaps hate and fear were just two different words for the same thing, anyway.

'You think Ibram's murder is related?' I asked.

'He was a member of the board,' Marvin said. 'Now he's a stiff. This could be the opening gambit.'

'What about the waiter?' Hammoudi asked. Marvin pointed to a yellow chalk mark in the shape of a stout human body by the toilet door. 'A big guy,' Hammoudi commented.

'Pavarotti lookalike,' Marvin said. 'Guy must weigh three hundred pounds, but it's all horizontal. Hit in the thighs. Out like a light when your men got here, but they managed to stop him bleeding to death. He's in our embassy medical facility in Garden City. Guy called Fawzi Shukri.'

Fawzi Shukri, I thought. The name went off like a buzzer in my head, but when I tried to listen it faded out. Marvin pointed to a stitch-pattern of bullet-holes on the lower part of the toilet door, and I went to examine them. 'They got him cold as he came out of the john,' Marvin said, 'but they didn't finish the job. When your footsloggers appeared, seems they beat it through that curtain. There's a flight of stairs behind there up to a corridor that takes you back into the bazaar.'

'I'm going to have a look at it,' I said and before Marvin could say anything I moved towards the curtain.

3

I BRUSHED IT ASIDE AND found a flight of bare stone steps leading up between mud-coloured walls from which plaster had fallen out leaving pustules of brilliant white. It was dark on the stairs, and at the top I found a long arched tunnel leading down to what was probably the external door. Shafts of light shot into the gloom from tiny flower-patterned windows. I took a pencil flashlight from my pocket and searched the ragged carpet carefully. It was thick with dust, dead flies and fragments of plaster. No one had cleaned the place in weeks. At the far end of the corridor I spotted an object on the floor and bent down to pick it up. It was a sealed pouch of uncured leather not more than an inch square, fixed to a short string. I had just stuffed it into my jacket pocket, when the door banged open and a blonde-haired woman stood there, thrusting the muzzle of an SIG 9mm automatic at me with both hands. I'd only just realized what was happening when she stepped forward again and without letting her aim waver even a fraction, slid her left hand under my jacket and picked out my Beretta, hooking her middle finger through the trigger-guard like she was hooking a fish.

For a fraction of a second I was completely fazed. On the streets of Aswan where I'd been dragged up you were either fast or you were dead. I'd seen some pretty swift moves in my time, but this was so slick it was almost supernatural. In a split second the girl had clocked where I wore my weapon and how, and disarmed me at the speed of light. I didn't know if she'd been born a human flash or if the move had been practised over and over, but one thing I was certain of: she was a pro.

'Who the hell are you?' she demanded. 'And what are you doing in a restricted area? This is FBI only.' Two heavy weapons are a bitch to handle when you're trying to keep a bead on someone, and I watched with professional interest to see what she was going to do. She didn't bat an eyelid – just drew out the magazine with one hand and dropped both pistol and magazine coolly into the Gucci handbag she wore over her shoulder. I was miffed that I'd been caught with my pants down, but I was also impressed. I almost expected to see her empty the shells out one-handed, too. I kept my mitts loose and looked her up and down.

She was early thirties, probably, and dressed in a green Lacoste shirt, white chinos and solid rubber-soled boots. She was very slim and long-legged, but all in proportion and the Lacoste shirt bulged satisfyingly at the front. Her features were twisted up in a 'don't-underestimate-me-just-because-I'm-a-woman' sneer, but I guessed that they were normally quite even, except for her tantalizingly erotic lips which were so full they gave the impression of a permanent pout. She had eyes as blue as hard crystals, smooth skin the café-au-lait colour of someone used to sunshine, and her blonde hair was tied out of her eyes in a long sensuous plait. There were two kinds of women, I thought – the kind who looked good in clothes, and the kind who looked good without them. They weren't necessarily the same thing. I'd known girls who'd looked ravishing until the moment they took their clothes off, and others who never drew a second glance until they put on a bikini and suddenly knocked you out. I couldn't help wondering whether this woman's mannish clothes were actually disguising a magnificently feminine figure. I'd have bet money they were.

I felt in my pocket for my ID card, and she stiffened. 'One more move, mister.' she said. I looked into the barrel of the pistol and grinned, seeing puzzlement come into her eyes.

'It's my ID,' I said. 'If you damn Yanks are going to pull guns on me in my own country, I've at least got the right to show you who I am.'

'OK, but you take your time.'

I slid my English-Arabic ID card slowly out of my pocket and dangled it in front of her eyes. 'I'm Lieutenant Sammy Rashid,' I said, 'Special Investigations Department, assigned to the Ibram murder enquiry. Now do I get my piece back?'

She looked at me with eyes narrowed. 'You don't look like any cop I've ever seen.'

'So what?' I said. 'Can I have my weapon back, please?'

She glanced at the ID again then looked me straight in the face. 'You've got green eyes.'

'It's not my fault. I was born that way.'

'Gyps don't have green eyes.'

'Yeah, well here's one who does. Now, gimme back my hardware.'

She frowned and let her SIG drop. She fished in her bag for the Beretta, and slapped it into my open hand. 'Hem,' I said, 'aren't we missing something? A gun is damn-all use without its ammunition and that was a full clip.'

She locked my eyes and sighed again, handing me the magazine. 'What were you doing sneaking around like that?' she asked.

'I wasn't sneaking, I was making a search. I'm the investigating detective.'

The girl opened her eyes wide in surprise. 'In your dreams, mister. I'm the investigating detective. This case belongs to the FBI.'

'You'd better ask my boss about that. He's the chief investigating officer on this case, and he's right downstairs now, talking to your Legat. Now I've told you who I am, how about returning the compliment?'

The girl pointed to the ID pinned to her ample chest, which read 'Special Agent Daisy Brooke, FBI'.

'Wow,' I said, 'I didn't know they let Barbie dolls into the FBI.'

I suppose I was still feeling a bit peeved that she'd worked me over so fast. I wanted to needle her, and I knew right away I'd pushed the right button. The girl's features turned even more vinegary and she gave me a shrivelling look.

'I've seen the way you people treat your women,' she said, 'and as far as I'm concerned you're a bunch of Neanderthals who belong in caves. And while we're on it, I didn't know they let freaks into the SID.'

I chuckled, slid the mag into my pistol and replaced it in its shoulder-rig. Then I followed her through the dimly lit corridor and down the stairs into the light. Ibram had already been transferred to a body bag, and someone had drawn the outline of the body on the floor in yellow chalk. The forensic team were packing up, and though Hammoudi and Marvin were still locked in discussion, I sensed that the atmosphere was more relaxed.

Marvin glanced at us as we appeared. 'So you've met?'

'Sir, this man says he's the investigating detective,' Daisy said. 'Could you please tell me what he's doing on an FBI case?'

Marvin grimaced. 'It's OK, Daisy, it's all been straightened out. Colonel Hammoudi here has overall authority and he's assigned Lieutenant Rashid to the case.'

'But I've already been assigned to it, sir. I haven't even had a chance to look at everything yet.'

'No one's taking you off the case, Daisy,' Marvin said, 'and if it's any consolation, I sympathize. But I've just been on to the ambassador, and he's anxious to avoid tension between the law enforcement bodies. We're on the same side, after all.'

Daisy stared at my baseball cap, a size too big, and pouted like a bad-tempered child. 'So now we're assisting kooks and weirdos,' she muttered.

A ghost of a smile played round Marvin's downturned mouth. 'The ambassador says let it go, and we agreed that the best thing is to let you two work together, sharing data. You'll be reporting to the Colonel here, and I'll be acting as liaison with the ambassador.'

'What?' Daisy gasped incredulously, 'you mean partners? With that space cadet? Holy Jesus.'

I groaned. 'Do I really have to do this, Colonel?' I asked Hammoudi. 'I knew I should have stayed at Giza. I'm going to be the laughing-stock of the team, working with this Barbie doll.'

'How long have you been in Egypt, Miss Brooke?' Hammoudi enquired.

'It's *Special Agent* Brooke,' she said, 'and I've been here a week.'

I groaned again. 'That's all I need,' I said, 'a greenhorn Barbie.'

'Actually I'm a counter-insurgency specialist.'

'Yeah?' I said. 'Am I supposed to do a jig, or what?'

'Sir, I don't need this,' Daisy said, appealing to Marvin. 'This guy's a kook.'

'You wouldn't believe it,' I said, 'but I still keep my eyes open, *Special Agent*.' I brought out the leather pouch I'd found upstairs and held it up for inspection.

'You missed it, and so did your forensic team. I think one of the perps dropped it when he ran.'

'Jesus!' Daisy said. 'That's pure speculation!' But she looked embarrassed, I noticed. Marvin took the pouch and examined it with interest, turning it over in his hands.

'What is it?' he asked.

'It's an Islamic amulet,' I said, 'containing a verse from the Quran written by a holy man or *faqi*. The verse is inscribed on a tiny piece of paper that is sealed inside the pouch. Believers say the amulet's got magic properties, and this type is supposed to give the wearer protection against knives and bullets. Now, I've seen a few of these things in my time, and as it happens I recognize this amulet. See the inscription on the side there? This thing belongs to a fundamentalist Islamic sect called the Sanusiya Brotherhood. The Sanusiya originated in Libya in the 1830s and

37

became one of the most powerful organizations in the whole of North Africa.'

All eyes were on me now. I could tell this was news, even to Hammoudi. 'Go on,' Marvin said, 'this is hot stuff.'

'Actually it's not so hot,' I said. 'The sect was disbanded some time around the First World War. This amulet's a museum-piece. As far as I know there haven't been any Sanusiya Brothers around for eighty years.'

4

OUTSIDE, THE AREA BEYOND THE barriers had already become a media circus. Gaping citizens were five deep, and local and foreign reporters had homed in like hyenas and were busy chatting up anyone who looked like he might have something to say. You could almost hear the word 'terrorism' humming like a mantra, and I knew if someone didn't put the dampers on it pretty soon the incident would be blown up into another Luxor massacre. Hammoudi surveyed the scene grimly and marched up to the local TV camera like he fully intended to kick it over. The reporter – a young, hip Egyptian in jeans, suede boots and a cowboy shirt – thrust a microphone at him like a sword and the crowd closed in for the kill, knocking the barriers aside. Videos and tape-recorders whirred, and cameras popped. 'Sir,' the TV reporter said, 'isn't it true that the murdered man was Doctor Adam Ibram, the former NASA scientist, who was over here for a meeting of the Giza Millennium Committee?'

'Yes,' Hammoudi said, 'Doctor Adam Ibram – an American scientist of Egyptian origin – was murdered in the early hours of the morning by unknown assailants.'

'Unknown assailants?' the reporter repeated, smiling. 'Isn't it possible that Doctor Ibram was murdered by Militants, who have already threatened to disrupt the millennium celebrations?'

Hammoudi refused to be drawn. 'As far as the police can

ascertain, terrorism is not involved. I repeat, terrorism is *not* involved. The police Anti-Terrorist Unit has not been mobilized, and we are treating it as a criminal case.'

I shifted nervously behind him, ignoring the microphones jabbed at me, and tried to keep my face out of the picture. A little way off, Marvin was surrounded by another school of media sharks, talking to a CNN camera – probably telling the same pack of lies.

'Why's the FBI in on this?' the reporter asked Hammoudi. 'Is this interference in Egypt's affairs acceptable?'

'The FBI team is attached to the US embassy here,' the Colonel said. 'Its function is to assist the local police with their investigation into the death of an American citizen.'

Suddenly another reporter wearing a dark suit, a beard and a white turban elbowed his way to the front of the crowd and shoved a portable tape-recorder almost into Hammoudi's face. 'Is it true that champagne is to be served at the so-called millennium celebrations?' he demanded furiously. 'Is it also true that there is to be an orgy of eating and Western pop music at a time when most Egyptians are fasting during Holy Ramadan? Is it true that tickets are to cost four hundred dollars each – a year's salary to many Egyptians?'

'You'll have to ask the organizers,' Hammoudi said.

'The year 2000 is a Western invention,' the reporter went on, ignoring him. 'It is meaningless to most Egyptians, both Muslim and Coptic Christian. Doctor Ibram was a Muslim – wouldn't it be understandable if a fundamentalist sect decided he ought to be punished for his part in this desecration of Egypt's heritage?'

Hammoudi's face stayed deadpan. 'I told you terrorism is not involved,' he said again, voice cold as a guillotine, 'and that's really all I have to say on the matter right now.'

He turned on his heel and together we strode back to the teashop, where Daisy was waiting. I noticed her gaze falling on my right ear, and I reached up instinctively and covered the blemish there with the rim of my cap. That was a mistake. Her eyes fixed on the place and never left it until we were right in front of her.

'That's about it as far as the crime-scene business goes,' Hammoudi said briskly. 'I know this isn't an ideal situation for any of us, Special Agent, but believe me, we *are* on the same side. As Mr Marvin said, you'll both be reporting to me, and your orders will come out of my office. And watch your mouths with the press. Those boys are squealing for blood as usual. I'm going back to the office now to make my initial report. I'll leave you two to get to know each other.'

'I think we should go talk to the waiter,' Daisy said, 'he might be able to give us a lead.'

'An excellent suggestion,' I said, 'only there remains the little matter of communication. Since you don't speak Arabic, how're you going to talk to him anyway?'

'*Min gaal lek ana mush 'arif 'arabi,*' she said, her blue eyes flashing suddenly. 'Who said I don't know Arabic? Actually, I speak it fluently!'

My mouth must have aped a goldfish. 'You said this was your first time in Egypt?' I protested.

'Maybe you hadn't noticed, *sonny,*' she said, 'but Egypt's not the only Arabic-speaking country in the world. I've worked in Saudi Arabia, Kuwait, Bahrain, the Emirates, Oman, Israel and the Yemen. I have a master's degree in Middle-Eastern studies from Berkeley. I speak some Hebrew too.' Her full lips pouted so antagonistically that for a minute I thought she was going to add: 'And put that in your self-opinionated pipe and smoke it.' Somehow I wouldn't have blamed her if she had.

Actually, I was still smoking it when I sat down in the passenger-seat of her dinky little white Fiat Punto. 'So,' I started lamely, as we drove through the police barrier, 'where're you from?'

'Monterey, California. It's a small town – I guess you've never heard of it.'

'I've been to California,' I said, 'and I know where it is, thank you very much.'

41

'You mean they let you people out of your cages?'

'From time to time. As it happens I've been on attachment with the San Francisco Police. And I tell you what – your California is the most racist, sexist society I've ever met.'

'We've still got to go some to beat you boys.'

'OK, so what's a nice girl like you doing in the FBI?'

She gripped the wheel with slender hands and pouted again. Her lips were so opulent that they gave an almost elongated look to the face that was amazingly expressive. I watched them fascinated as they formed and broke, and she saw me looking and flicked her plaited hair sideways with an angry snap of the head.

'For a start, I'm not a "nice girl",' she said. 'For a second, the FBI takes women these days. More than ten per cent of Bureau officers are female.'

'Ten per cent! Am I supposed to be impressed?'

'Listen, to you Arabs women are second-class citizens, and you're scared brainless of them. In Saudi they won't even give women driving-licences! I had a friend in Dubai whose fifteen-year-old daughter, a beautiful blonde, was out horseriding when a carload of Arab youths spooked the horse till she fell off, then beat her up. A fifteen-year-old kid! She wasn't badly injured, but it was still one of the weirdest things I'd ever come across. I mean, rape I could have understood, but there was no sexual assault involved. It took me a long time to work out that they were so scared of the kind of power she had over them that they had to attack her. That's how terrified you are of the "inferior sex", and that's why you keep your women veiled. It's a kind of control.'

'The veil is optional in Egypt,' I said, 'but a lot of women like it. They don't want to be seen as sexual objects except by their husbands, and the veil earns them a lot more respect from men.'

'Because men don't find a shapeless lump as threatening as a beautiful blonde girl riding a horse.'

'It wouldn't happen here.'

'Like hell! I've had my butt pinched so much in the past week I'm black and blue.'

'Maybe you should try wearing a veil, then.'

She flicked her hair aside again, and bared her lips over very white teeth as if she'd have liked to take a chunk out of my neck. 'Don't get clever with me, buddy-boy,' she snapped. 'As far as I'm concerned you forced your way into this investigation. It might go down hunky-dory with my chief, but I want to make it clear that I still regard myself as the investigating detective, and that I'm working with you under protest.'

'Hey!' I said. 'If you think I want to waste my time escorting a greenhorn of the ''inferior sex'' you're crazy. I can't think why they chose you for the case.'

'Because I'm the best they've got. I passed out top of my class at Quantico, which was ninety per cent men, and because I know more about the Arab world than all the other special agents here put together. Probably more than you, too.'

I clapped my hands silently. 'Congratulations!' Why should Egypt tremble with heroes such as these to defend her!'

Daisy set her lips into brooding mode and the effect was stunningly attractive. She squeezed the wheel till her knuckles paled, and I could see she was forcing herself to concentrate on the road. 'Go to hell!' she said.

5

There were US marines in full-dress blues at the entrance to the embassy hospital facility in Garden City, and I had to concede that they belonged in a whole different ballgame from our blackjackets in their ill-fitting cast-off uniforms and dirty unlaced boots. If things had worked out differently, I thought, I might have ended up as one of these men. If my father had married my mother. If he'd taken us back with him to the States. *If. If. If.* Your life seemed to turn on a pattern of conditionals, but I knew that was just how it appeared. Part of me had realized even as a kid that anyone who could abandon a child as my father had done wouldn't have been worth growing up with anyway. I knew I'd been lucky. And I'd been doubly lucky, because I'd escaped the fate of an Aswan street-rat, the slow inevitability of turning from petty theft to drugs, extortion and murder, and got myself a life. I knew whom I had to thank for that, and I knew where my real loyalty lay.

The first thing I noticed about the marine corporal behind the desk, though, wasn't his immaculate uniform, but his politeness. At least, I thought, these guys didn't need to act macho to prove how tough they were. Almost as soon as we'd shown our ID and signed the book, a male nurse in a starched lab-coat arrived to escort us to Fawzi's room.

'How is he?' Daisy asked.

The nurse looked like the marine corporal in another guise – young, tall, clean-cut, crop-haired – then again, I thought, perhaps he *was* a marine corporal. You could never tell in a place like this. 'He's off the critical list. The danger of gunshot wounds in the thigh is that a whole bunch of main arteries run through there. Getting shot in the thigh is one of the easiest ways of bleeding to death. All you have to do to stop the victim pegging though, is hold a cloth over the wound. This guy can thank his lucky stars whoever was first on the scene realized that.'

'Is he lucid?' I enquired.

The nurse laughed. 'Lucid, I don't know, but he's been gabbling in Arabic to anyone who came near him for the past two hours. For a while there we even debated giving the guy a tranquillizer shot just to shut him up!'

Our footsteps were almost silent on the rubberized carpet that curved interestingly between walls of clean, unfaced stone. This place was state-of-the-art, I thought – a little oasis of modern Western medical practice in the middle of North Africa. Closed circuit TV cameras shifted angle slightly as we passed, almost invisible air-coolers kept the internal temperature stable, fire doors opened automatically before us. Fawzi's room had a sterile viewing window, through which we saw a stout, balding man lying in bed on starched cushions. His face was plump and sallow, and his eyes looked like peepholes buried in a mass of red and purple bruise-tissue. Like Marvin said, he must have weighed more than three hundred pounds. A saline drip was attached to his arm and monitoring electrodes to his chest and the bridge of his nose, but despite all this he was apparently rambling to an attractive young nurse who was taking his temperature and trying her best to ignore him. At one stage he even tried feebly to pinch her bottom.

'Now, you can tell that guy's a Cairene,' I chuckled, 'a couple of hours ago he's on the critical list, and already he's pinching behinds. You've got to hand it to them – you just can't keep them down.'

Daisy brooded. 'Cave men quickly revert to their old habits,' she commented icily.

'Excuse me, Special Agent,' the male nurse said suddenly, 'we searched the patient's clothes as a matter of routine when he was admitted. We found these little babies in his pockets.' He held out five inch-and-a-half-long cubes the colour of gravy browning, covered in cling-film.

Daisy cocked a knowing eye at me. 'So our friend makes a little something on the side,' she said.

I picked up one of the cubes. It was Lebanese Red – the best quality grass on the streets. Then suddenly it made sense. 'I should have remembered the name,' I told Daisy. 'Fawzi Shukri – I've heard of him. Small-time grafter who peddles dope to tourists. My team's picked him up a couple of times, but he always had something interesting to say, so they let him off with a warning.'

'A ten-dollar snitch?'

'You got it, only here they come cheaper.' I flashed the nurse a grateful smile. 'Thank you,' I told him, 'these little guys here are going to make it very difficult for Mr Fawzi to withhold the truth.'

'He's still a patient,' he said, 'and I have to ask that you don't overtax him.'

'Oh I won't,' I said, pushing through the glass doors, just as the female nurse inside was leaving. The fat man didn't move – probably he couldn't anyway, but his slit eyes followed my progress towards the bed.

'Lord help us,' he whined feebly, almost to himself, 'I smell SID. I should have known the fuzz would turn up. I'm a sick man, Your Presence. I haven't done anything.' His half-closed eyes fell on Daisy as she slipped in behind me. 'Help me, miss,' he stammered, 'this cop is going to kill me!'

'It's all right, Fawzi,' I said, 'you're not under arrest. You're a hero. Tried to save a foreign visitor from the thugs.'

Fawzi's mouth formed a big 'O' of surprise. 'Me?' he said. 'I was in an accident. I didn't see nothing.'

'Don't you want to help us nail the men who shot you?' Daisy asked softly.

'You're a cop too?' Fawzi said. 'An *Afrangi* woman cop! That's all I needed!'

'What happened?' I demanded.

'It was an accident, Your Presence. I don't know anything. Born and bred in Khan al-Khalili, that's me. We go by the Law of Silence there, you know that? If I was to blab they might finish me off next time.'

'Don't give me that Law of Silence bullshit,' I snapped. 'They didn't finish you off when you blabbed to the SID officers who picked you up for dope-peddling, did they?'

'That wasn't me, Your Presence, that was another Fawzi. It's a dirt-common name in Cairo.'

I opened my hand and showed Fawzi the five cubes of hashish. 'Down to selling five-pound deals now, Fawzi? Not exactly big-time, is it?'

'They're not mine.'

'They were found in your pockets.'

'Someone must have put them there, Your Presence. I don't know nothing about it, honest. I don't know nothing about anything.'

Daisy and I exchanged glances. Only minutes ago we'd had our knives out, but this was business, and we were both professional enough to know it was time for the good-cop-bad-cop routine. Daisy sat down on the chair next to the bed and leaned over Fawzi, smiling sweetly, showing her white teeth. 'Look Mr Fawzi,' she said, 'you're in a US government facility. This officer can't touch you here. You're not under arrest, just like he said. Now, tell us what happened in the back room of the teashop. Tell us all you remember and I'll persuade this guy to forget the dope, OK?'

Fawzi shifted his eyes painfully from Daisy to me. Then he grinned weakly. '*Bukra fil mishmish*,' he said. 'Tomorrow in the apricots.'

Daisy looked at me, mystified. 'What the hell does that mean?' she asked.

'It's a expression they have in Cairo,' I said. 'Loosely translated, it means "pull the other one".'

'Look, Mr Fawzi,' Daisy said, 'anything you say stays between us. No need for anybody to know.'

'I'm saying nothing.'

'You owe it to the dead man.'

'Owe it? The guy did nothing for me. I don't even know who he was.'

Daisy sighed, bowed her head and cupped it in her hands sorrowfully. It was a lovely act, I thought. 'If you go on like this, there's nothing much I can do for you,' she said.

She slapped her hands back into her lap and stood up as if she'd suddenly come to a difficult decision. I was rapt in admiration.

'No, wait,' Fawzi pleaded, 'don't leave me with him. I know S I D. I know what they do. They string people up naked and poke electric cattle-prods up their arses. Don't go. I'll tell you what happened.'

Daisy sat down again. 'All right,' she said, taking a notebook and pencil from her handbag. 'You're a good guy, Mr Fawzi. No one's going to poke you with a cattle-prod while I'm here. Let's start with what you were doing in the john.'

Fawzi giggled. 'What does anyone do in a john?' he said.

'But you weren't answering nature's call, were you Mr Fawzi?' I glanced at her in surprise, knowing instinctively that she was right but wondering how the hell she'd been so sure. I realized suddenly that it was intuition – the kind only the best detectives have – and my admiration increased.

'OK,' Fawzi said, 'but it goes no farther than here, right?'

'Right.'

'OK, see, I went in there to cut this grass I'd just scored from a dealer. It's good Red Leb – the very best. All right, I'm not big-time, but a man's got to make a farthing to feed his wife and kids.'

I had to suppress a guffaw. I'd have bet a tenner that Fawzi wasn't even married. 'See,' he went on, anxious to talk now, 'a lot of tourists come to Sayyidna Hussayn after they've toured the bazaars, knackered, and sit down at the teashops for a rest. A lot of them ask to smoke a hubble-bubble. Most haven't done it before, and they think it's sort of romantic – the mysteries of the East and all that baloney. Of course the teashops only serve tobacco, but when I see a likely type I sidle up and whisper to them that it's not the real thing. If they want to have a real experience, I say, they should try a cube of hashish with it. Some are horrified, but it's surprising how many go for it.'

'Right, so you're in the john carving up your deals, and what happened next?'

'Well I hear the connecting door bang open and then footsteps, and of course, I'm all of a jitter. I wonder if it's the rozzers come to nab me. So I shove the dope in my pocket and crouch there sort of holding my breath. Then I realize that the guy who's come in is panting real heavy – kind of sobbing, you know. Sounds like he's having a stroke or something – puffing and groaning real bad, he is. So I think, well if this is the fuzz it's a bloody good act. It can't be. If they knew I was there they'd have smashed in the door by now. But then another thought strikes me. What if this geezer *does* drop dead, and the fuzz arrive and try to pin it on me? Better make a run for it now. Then there's the click of the phone being lifted and I hear the guy dialling. "So that's it!" I think to myself – "he's calling an ambulance"! I hang on just a second more to make sure this isn't some set-up, then I hear a coin drop and this wheezy voice saying, "Monod, is that you?" in English. I'm no English speaker, of course, but in my line of work you're bound to pick up a smattering. That's exactly what it sounded like: "Monod, is that you?" I relaxed a bit then. The guy's a foreigner, probably a tourist, and he's made contact with someone. Now's the time to make a run for it. I slide back the bolt, open the door, and see this old guy on the telephone with his back to me, chest heaving, gripping the phone like he's trying to crush it. I'm just about to sneak past, when the door busts open and there's three hooded guys standing there with these little submachine-guns, sinister like. Perfect timing, I'm thinking. The pigs set me up good and proper this time. I'm about to give myself up, when they start shooting at the old geezer on the phone. Funny, the guns made this kind of whizzing sound, like electricity. Hardly any noise at all. Surprise, Fawzi! It wasn't you they was after! Then everything happened so quickly. The old guy pitches over, sort of scrabbling at the air with his hands, trying to scream. The old throat's working overtime but nothing's coming out, see, and there's blood spurting all over everywhere, including me. Then, just as he hits the floor, the old boy grunts, "firebird". Just one word, "firebird" – like that.'

'You sure about that, Fawzi?' I cut in. *Firebird. Phoenix*, I thought. *I have gone forth as the phoenix in the hope of eternal life*.

'That's what it sounded like,' Fawzi groaned, 'I mean it's a pretty simple word, isn't it? Fire and bird? You don't need to have studied English at some fancy school to recognize it.'

'OK,' Daisy said. 'What happened then?'

'Well suddenly I feel like someone's just whopped me in the legs with a barbell, and crump! Next thing I know I'm lying on the floor near the old guy, who's still wheezing away. Suddenly this thug in a *shamagh* waltzes over cool as a cucumber to the old geezer, slips out a pistol and lets him have it right in the head. Wham! Almost blew my eardrums out. Then the gunman's looking at me in this beady way, and I remember thinking, "I'm a gonner. Forgive me Lord for all my sins!" Suddenly there's a shout of "Police!" and a rumpus outside. The gunman sticks the pistol in his belt pretty niftily, and the three of them scarper out through the curtain and up the stairs as quick as you like. Bloody good job they did, too, else Fawzi wouldn't be here talking to you. The next one to get it in the head would have been me.'

'OK,' Daisy said, almost purring. 'That's excellent, Mr Fawzi. You've been really helpful.'

Fawzi moaned suddenly. 'You know, the Khan used to be a pretty peaceful place. OK, there's always been street grafters, but nothing real serious. But just lately there's been a whole bunch of weird things happening. Take the ghoul, for example.'

'What ghoul?' I asked quickly.

'The one as has been haunting the Khan at night. Every few months you hear that another kid has been pounced on and all the blood sucked out of his body. I met someone who'd seen it – a great spider thing he said it was, with one leg like a person's and the other like a donkey's. They reckon it hides out in the Underworld until it gets hungry, then it comes up thirsting for blood.'

Daisy looked at me and raised an eyebrow. I rolled my eyes in response. 'OK,' I said, 'we can go into that another time. Right now I have just a few questions. Then we'll leave you in peace.'

'What about the dope?'

'I don't think we'll need to worry too much about that.'

Fawzi grunted. 'What do you want to know?'

'These three guys,' I said, 'how were they dressed?'

'They had *shamaghs* wrapped round their faces, but they weren't ordinary ones. Most *shamaghs* are red or black. *Hajis* wear bright green ones, but these were olive-green like the army wears in the desert. And that's not all. These guys were dressed exactly alike in those waxed coats – you know, with the flaps over the shoulders. All black. Looked spooky, like a bunch of undertakers. Oh, and the one who gave the old fellow the farewell shot in the nut had like a little leather box tied to his arm – an amulet like the old-time holy men used to wear. I remember thinking it looked way out of place on the guy.'

'I glanced at Daisy. 'Would you recognize any of the killers again?' she asked.

Fawzi closed his eyes for a moment, then opened them. With the mass of swellings around the eye-sockets he looked almost like one of those teddy bears that closed and opened its eyes when you tilted it over, I thought.

'They were hooded, like I said,' Fawzi continued, 'and I never got a look at their faces –'

51

Suddenly the swing-door opened and the male nurse put his head in. 'Sorry, Special Agent,' he said, 'but you'll have to wind it up. The patient's lost a lot of blood, and you've already had too much time.'

Daisy put her notebook away and got up. She tossed her long plait of blonde hair backwards and pouted at him with her wonderful lips. She had a way of setting her mouth as if she was actually smiling through the pout, so that you couldn't tell if she was mad at you or giving you the come-on. It was a look so enticingly feminine that for a moment all of us – even the male nurse – watched her fascinated. A wave of raw yearning washed over me, so quick and powerful that I couldn't prevent it. I felt a hotness growing in my groin and I struggled to forget how long it was since I'd actually had a woman. In some lights, I told myself, Special Agent Brooke might be not only pretty, but very, very attractive indeed.

'Well, goodbye, Mr Fawzi,' she said, 'and thanks.'

'But it goes no further than you,' Fawzi whispered, 'and you forget the dope, right?'

'Right.'

After Daisy had gone, I laid the five deals of hashish on Fawzi's counterpane.

'Here, my friend,' I said, 'a present from the SID. *Enjoy.*'

When we drove out of the gate in the white Fiat, I caught a glimpse of a tall Arab woman dressed in loose black robes from head to foot, standing in the shade of the concrete walls. She stared at me through holes in a vampire-like mask of the type some Bedouin tribes wore, and in a flash I was reminded of the woman I'd seen in the vision I'd had while touching Ibram's dead hand. Then I was distracted by the buzz of Daisy's mobile, and when I looked again, the woman was gone.

6

'I T'S FOR YOU,' DAISY SAID, flipping the mobile into my hand, 'Colonel Hammoudi.'

I fumbled with the controls cursing, and finally put the speaker to my mouth. 'Sammy here, Colonel.'

'Good.' Hammoudi's voice came back at me, metallic with rasping bass notes. 'The US embassy's just released the information that Ibram was staying at the Mena Palace Oberoi at Giza before he died. I want you to get up there and see if you can get anything from the staff, and find out if he left any baggage.'

'Sir, I could do that job alone,' I said. 'It's nearly five. I'm sure Miss Brooke here needs her beauty sleep.'

'Oh please!' Daisy said, her voice loaded, 'and it's *Special Agent* Brooke to you.'

'Nice try, Sammy,' Hammoudi said, 'but you work together. Those are the best terms I could get with the US ambassador.'

'I read you, sir.'

'Any joy with Fawzi?'

'Said the gunmen were wearing long black coats and military-style *shamaghs*, and he confirmed that one of them was wearing an amulet. It's sounding more and more like a Militant hit-job.'

'No shit?' Hammoudi said, impatiently. 'Anything else?'

'Two things. Ibram was on the phone to a guy called Monod when he was stiffed. That name mean anything to you?'

'Not off-hand. I'll run it through records. What was the other thing?'

'Ibram's last words. According to Fawzi he said "Firebird" just before he died.'

'What in hell is that supposed to mean?'

'Could mean anything or nothing. Ibram was coughing up blood at the time and in my experience that can lead to some *very* erratic behaviour. Anyway, the only Firebird I know is an American car. Maybe Fawzi got it wrong – the guy's not exactly a fluent English speaker.'

'OK, keep me posted.'

I handed the phone back to Daisy, who put it away in her bag one-handed still doing sixty along the Corniche. Suddenly a whole family – mother, father and two small kids – made a kamikaze rush across the road in front of us, and Daisy slammed on the brakes. She'd been driving one-handed and for a second I thought the car would go out of control, but it simply skidded with a squeal of tyres. For the second time that day, I was impressed with Daisy's speed. I was about the world's worst driver, and they'd run in front of us so abruptly I was certain I'd have ploughed straight into them.

'Jesus H. Christ!' she said. 'Don't you have subways here?'

'A little item neglected when they planned this great city,' I grinned, 'I suppose they thought no one'd have to walk anymore.'

'So what does the great Hammoudi have to say?' she asked, inching the vehicle forward again.

'Our orders are to hit the Mena Palace Oberoi hotel,' I said. 'That's where Ibram holed up before he died. It's at Giza, right at the foot of the pyramids – about a half-hour drive from here.'

'Oh boy! So I get to see the pyramids at last!' She looked so pleased with herself and so childishly enthusiastic that I almost felt sorry to disillusion her. Almost.

'Not today you don't, sweetheart,' I said. 'It'll be nearly dark by the time we get there, and anyway they close the site at four o'clock.'

'Just my luck,' she said, 'and I'm not your sweetheart.'

She pouted and was about to accelerate again when a motor-cycle cut in front, carrying another family – a man and a woman and no less than three children, the tiniest of whom was sitting happily on the fuel-tank. 'Will you look at that!' she gasped. 'Five people on a motorcycle! Is that legal?'

'No, but who cares!'

'I've had it with this traffic,' Daisy said, 'this is like Dante's *Inferno*!'

Earlier the streets had been almost empty, but now every motor vehicle in the city, it seemed, was either heading out for the evening or heading home. In Tahrir Square the cars were almost bumper to bumper and the air was heavy with gasoline fumes drifting nauseatingly in the heat. Cairene drivers like to drive at breakneck speed, and there was a deafening cacophony of motor-horns as they vented their frustration on each other. I saw a whole bunch of them sticking their heads out of their windows, waving their arms, and carrying on a running battle of abuse.

Past Tahrir Square the traffic freed up and as we circled slowly back into the sun on to the Corniche, a shaft of light shone directly into my face, blinding me. 'By the way,' Daisy said, staring at me suddenly, 'how *did* you get those green eyes?'

'Crusader genes,' I said. 'Result of all that raping and pillaging your ancestors did here. Specially the raping.'

'Come on. That's bullshit.'

'OK, maybe it is. If you want to know, my father was a Yank.'

'I don't believe it!'

'Believe what you want. I have to live with it. My father was a USAF sergeant over here on some kind of attachment – I don't know what. Mother was only sixteen when she met him and he was sort of brawny and handsome. She really fell for him. She lived in Aswan, and every time he came back he'd bring her presents. Swept her off her feet. It was frowned on by her family and the neighbours – big scandal, and even bigger when she got pregnant and I was born. Dad set us up in a flat and lived with us part of the time, but Ma was regarded as a whore and ostracized by the community. She didn't care, she said, because she loved him so much. Then Dad's posting came to an end and he pissed off and left us. He always promised Ma he'd come back for us, but he just dumped us without a cent. It was a long time afterwards that Ma got a letter explaining that he was already married and had three kids at home. He'd been married all the time. That killed Ma. They said she'd died of cancer, but I reckon it was a broken heart.'

I sighed and looked at the road, wondering as I'd always wondered whether that was the whole story. I'd been very young when my father had left, but I still remembered how he'd sat me on his knee and tousled my hair, saying 'I'll come back for you Sammy, if it's the last thing I ever do.' The truth was that despite my mother's later claims, I remembered him as a kind and considerate man who'd loved me. I could even remember the big sad face at the window of a train in Aswan station the day he'd gone for good. In the States I'd tried to find him again, but no one, not even the USAF Records Section, seemed to have heard of a Sergeant Desmond Redfield. He seemed to have disappeared without trace, and the wife and three kids he was supposed to have had – my half-brothers or -sisters – had vanished too.

'So now you hate Americans?' Daisy asked.

'I don't hate Americans,' I said, 'I just hate hypocrites and people coming over here telling us our jobs. There's good and bad everywhere.'

'What happened to you in the end?'

'It was bad enough to live with a woman who had no money and who everybody said was a whore. But after she died there was no one to look after me. No one wanted me, I belonged to no one. I wasn't even an Egyptian – not full-blooded anyway. I went wild, drifted on to the streets, mixed with all the other rejects. I became a regular street-rat – I mean I was smoking dope and drinking neat araki before I was ten. Got initiated to a gang and into everything – mugging, pick-pocketing, burglary, fights – I carried a shiv as long as my arm. Always in the shit with the cops – I mean if it hadn't been for my mother teaching me to read and write I'd have had no schooling at all.'

'Quite a transition – street-rat to SID officer.' She glanced sideways at my sleazy jacket. 'Though perhaps not. Street-gangs – that explains the pierced upper ear, right?'

I fingered the upper fold of my right ear self-consciously, probing for the perforation I'd received at the age of twelve – the brand that would always make me different from others. I'd been right about her spotting it, and I'd have bet money she'd clocked the dagger I wore on my left arm, too. The woman was sharp as a needle. She'd disarmed me in a split second by reaching out for my pistol with a confidence that seemed almost psychic, and a speed that defied logic. Damn Hammoudi, I thought: why the hell had he agreed to this? Daisy had what the Bedouin called *guwwat al-mulahazza* – an extraordinary perceptive ability. That and her unbelievable speed was a dangerous combination. Given half the chance she would blow my cover, and that was one thing Hammoudi and I couldn't afford. If we were going to work together over the next few days, I'd have to watch my step.

I pulled my cap down firmly over the pierce-mark. 'Every gang has its own rituals. The earring in the upper right ear was ours.'

'You should get yourself a bigger cap,' she said, 'or grow your hair longer. That's what they're designed to hide, isn't it? Why not just have plastic surgery – it wouldn't be much of a job these days. I mean, if you're so ashamed of it, why keep it?'

'Let's say it's because it reminds me of where I came from and who I really am.'

'And that blade you're wearing on your left arm. That a souvenir from your street-kid days, too?'

I smiled and slid the razor-sharp, double-edged stiletto from under the cuff of my sweatshirt, showing Daisy its bone handle, intricately and beautifully carved. 'How'd you guess?'

'All the time I had a bead on you, you remained completely confident. Most people – even the most macho types – go apeshit when they look into the muzzle of a firearm they know could blow their brains out. But you behaved as if you still had the jump on me and that had to mean you'd got another weapon on you. Then I clocked a bulge in the leather of your jacket above the left wrist. Whatever was there was too small to be a gun, so it had to be a knife. That's a pretty unpolice-like weapon. I never knew a cop who wore a knife before.'

'Welcome to Egypt,' I said, putting the blade away again. 'It always helps to have a back-up.'

'You reckon you're pretty fast with that stinger, huh?'

'I could have stuck you any time, gun or no gun.'

'Maybe we should try a contest sometime, for real.'

'Sure. Didn't you ever see that film *The Magnificent Seven* with Yul Brynner? There's the scene where the cowboy challenges the knife-thrower, saying he can draw his shooter quicker than the guy can nail him with his blade.'

'Yeah, I saw it. The way I remember it, the cowboy won.'

By the time we reached the stone lions at the entrance to Tahrir Bridge, the traffic had already thinned out. The heat of the day had melted away and the sun was a rose-coloured globe spinning gigantically between the skyscrapers over the Gezira. The Nile had become a red river with enough colours dancing around its edges to give you the feeling that it was as diaphanous as a rainbow. Even in Cairo, I loved this time of day. The light was so crystal-clear that every object it illuminated seemed larger, more real, more intense. It gave me an odd, vaguely spiritual feeling that I wouldn't have revealed to anyone in Cairo, not even Hammoudi, and certainly not Special Agent Hard-Ass Brooke of the FBI. I could understand how the ancient Egyptians had felt about the sunset. They saw the sun as a boat – the Bark of Millions of Years, they called it – which crossed the sky every day carrying the sun-god Ra. The sunset was a gateway into the Underworld – a terrifying dark land where Ra and his crew had to fight battle after battle with demons and evil spirits in order to emerge victorious next morning at sunrise. Sometimes, I thought, I knew exactly how that felt.

We crossed al-Gala'a Bridge and entered the built-up streets of western Cairo, where lights were already firing up in the apartment buildings. At the end of the great boulevard of Tahrir Street a huge, multi-coloured flyer was stretched across the road, with writing and an emblem picked out in the last of the sunlight. 'Phoenix Insurance International', it read, 'World Conference, Cairo, 1999'. The emblem, I noticed, was the scarlet image of a phoenix in cameo, rising from a ring of flames.

'Phoenix,' Daisy said suddenly.

'Arizona?' I said.

'Jesus Christ!' she snapped, mumbling something under her breath that I suspected was insulting. 'The phoenix is a mythical bird that the ancient Greeks believed would erupt into flames every millennium or so, and renew itself from the ashes.'

'So what?' I said, playing dumb but knowing she'd hit the nail right on the head.

'So the phoenix was known as the *Firebird* – and that was the last thing Ibram said, right?'

I have gone forth as a phoenix, in the hope of life eternal.

I paused, then looked at her, wondering whether it was worth continuing with the pretence. I decided it wasn't, and relaxed. 'OK,' I said, 'I know about the phoenix, except that that part of the myth is ancient Greek. The Firebird story is actually ancient Egyptian and existed millennia before the Greeks were even heard of.'

Daisy squinted at me suspiciously. 'You told Hammoudi the only Firebird you knew was an American car!'

'OK, so I was being a little obtuse for your benefit. You expected a cave-man, so that's what I was giving you. Actually, I know about all this stuff because I did a course in Egyptology

59

with the Tourism and Antiquities police. I'm also an enthusiast. If you're interested, I passed out top of my class.'

'No shit. I'd have said you couldn't string a sentence.'

'Thanks. In ancient Egyptian myth, the Firebird was called the *Bennu* bird, and it was supposed to represent the soul of Ra, the sun-god. The story went that the universe was originally a void of dark waters – the Waters of Nun, they called it – through which a mound of earth one day appeared. They called this the Primeval Mound and the Firebird was the first thing to land on it at dawn on the first morning, giving out this ear-splitting cry which was supposed to have set Time in motion. You could say the Firebird was a sort of ancient Egyptian version of the Big Bang'.

'OK, but what does the Firebird have to do with Ibram?'

'Odds are Fawzi got it wrong, and what Ibram really said was "bye-bye" or something. Our only solid clue at the moment is the Sanusi amulet – one scrap of evidence that links the killers to a fundamentalist sect, even if it is a bit out of date. If it *was* the Militants, they scored our own goal on this one, though, because Ibram was almost an Egyptian folk-hero – a poor boy who made good in the USA.'

'Sounds a good motive for whacking him,' Daisy said. 'Maybe in their eyes he'd done a Salman Rushdie on them. Maybe they considered him a Muslim who sold out to American imperialism and all that. I mean, he was a *very* big wheel in the States – I've read his FBI file. Born in the slums of Alexandria, but emigrated with his parents to New York in the 1950s. Learned fluent English in two years, and raced past his classmates. Harvard graduate, Professor of Earth Sciences at Cornell, won the NASA Medal for Exceptional Scientific Achievement – twice. Science advisor to the US president, consultant to NASA and an expert on the environment – especially desertification, the ozone layer and all those green issues. In on the Mars probe and studied the Martian landscape. He reckoned the nearest thing on earth to it was the Western Desert of Egypt – even wrote a paper on it. He was also on the National Research Council, the Medical Advisory

Board of the Atomic Energy Commission, and a consultant for the National Security Council.'

'On what?'

'I don't know, that part of the file was highly classified.'

'Maybe the Militants just bumped him off because they were jealous of his lifestyle. Or maybe we're right off course, and it was a grudge killing going back to his Alexandria days. Maybe it's as simple as that.'

'Hey look!' Daisy cried out suddenly. She pointed along the road to where a peak of stone stood out above the roofs of hotels and houses – a single polished facet glowing like a jewel in the sun's last embers.

'That's the Great Pyramid,' I said.

'Okaaay!' Daisy said, beaming. 'So I got a glimpse of it after all!'

7

THE MENA PALACE WAS ONE of the oldest and most famous hotels in Egypt – a rambling mansion of *mashrubiyya* windows and Turkish-style archways standing not more than a hundred metres from the Giza plateau. Before Cairo had expanded up the Pyramids Road it had stood out in desert, and was used as a hunting lodge by Ismael Pasha – the son of the great Mohammad Ali – in the early 1800s. Later it was bought as a private house by a British couple, Hugh and Ethel Locke-King, who'd eventually turned it into a hotel. In the old days it had had a famous golf course, and in 1915 the British Prince of Wales is supposed to have driven a ball on to the green from the top of the second pyramid. Daisy drove the Fiat under the arch and into a garden full of the perfume of bougainvillea and oleander. The main entrance was set beneath an elaborate portico where a barrel-chested commissionaire in Ottoman dress – fez, baggy trousers and an embroidered waistcoat – opened the car-door for Daisy, took the keys and parked up the Fiat. Only one of the entranceways to the lobby was functional, and inevitably there was a metal-detector beyond it. We were both armed, so we flashed our cards at the blue-blazered security men and sidestepped the detector frame.

The decor was marble and brass, the reception curving around beneath a gilt-encased ceiling towards a passage that contained a row of shops – a jeweller, a bookshop, a T-shirt boutique. There appeared to be almost no guests about. An exceptionally polite young Egyptian in a dark suit hurried off to fetch the front desk manager as soon as we showed our ID. The manager was a dapper man called Abd al-Ali, who wore a spotless suit of precisely the right shade of grey, and shoes so highly buffed you could have used them as mirrors. He bowed slightly as he shook hands with me, but gave Daisy only the ghost of a nod. Then he ushered us unctuously to a brass-topped table in the lobby bar. 'May I offer you a beer, coffee, a cocktail?' he asked. 'Won't you try our fresh lime-juice? It's highly recommended.'

'No thanks,' I said, 'I'd like to get down to business. We're here to enquire about the disappearance from this hotel of Doctor Adam Ibram.'

'Ah, such a tragedy,' Abd al-Ali said smoothly. 'I learned of Doctor Ibram's murder on the afternoon news. Is it true that terrorism is not involved?'

'Not as far as we know,' I said, pursuing the official line, 'we are treating it as a criminal investigation.'

The manager nodded seriously, but I noticed a twinkle in his eyes. 'I'm glad to hear that,' he said. 'These days every puff of wind is put down to terrorism, and the tourist trade suffers as a result. The Mena Palace used to be one of the most popular hotels in Egypt until all the brouhaha about terrorism started. Now it's all we can do to fill half the place on a regular basis. I try to tell them that Egypt is actually one of the safest countries in the world, and incidents occur once in a blue moon. It's blown up out of all proportion. Did you know . . .' he turned and gave Daisy a sour look, 'that statistically you are twenty-five times more likely to be murdered in the USA than in Egypt? I'd appreciate it if you'd keep the name of this hotel out of the press. Things are bad enough – this'll only make it worse.'

'I think we can promise that,' Daisy said, giving the manager her sweetest 'good-cop' smile. 'When did you first notice Doctor Ibram's disappearance?'

The manager shifted his gaze from me to Daisy, then back to

me. He raised an eyebrow at me interrogatively. 'It's OK,' I told him, 'This is my partner. You can answer her questions.'

Abd al-Ali made a camp frown at us. 'As far as I have been able to find out, Doctor Ibram hadn't returned to the hotel for the past two nights. People like to . . . well, enjoy the attractions, and of course, there's no law that says a guest has to return to his room every night. It's enough that the bill is paid – but even in a hotel like this we do get guests who flit without paying. You'd be surprised, actually. I've had people who you would have said were the soul of respectability just slip out leaving their baggage behind them. One guest even left an expensive stereo system. Not that a lovely man like poor Doctor Ibram . . . well, anyway, I let myself discreetly into his room. His baggage was all there – washing and shaving things laid out in the bathroom. He had some very nice things, actually – clothes very chic – probably Bloomingdale's. Anyway, I waited until this morning and when he didn't come back I thought I'd better refer the matter to the tourist police. This afternoon I saw that hunky detective on the news saying Doctor Ibram had been killed, and that was that. Awful tragedy – and he wasn't even that old. Well preserved, I should say.'

'Did Doctor Ibram do or say anything unusual before he disappeared?'

'I talked to Viktor, one of our commissionaires. He's a nice man – strong, silent type – who knew Doctor Ibram well. Said he had looked very worried in these last few days. Apparently he asked Viktor if he believed in ghouls. Viktor said yes, and that they were hairy and had one foot like a donkey's. I must admit it was a bit of a joke with the staff at the time.'

'And what did you do with Doctor Ibram's baggage?' Daisy asked.

'Well we couldn't just leave it, you understand,' Abd al-Ali said, 'I mean, we might have needed the room. When it was clear Doctor Ibram wasn't about to come back, I had it packed up and placed in the store-room.'

'You had no right to do that,' Daisy said.

'Oh yes I did,' Abd al-Ali said, smiling, apparently pleased with himself for having contradicted her. 'I can't be caught out there, miss.' He drew a folded letter from inside his jacket. 'That's a letter from the Giza Tourist and Antiquities Police,' he said with some satisfaction, 'whose station is just across the road. They gave me permission to move the baggage.'

I scanned the letter, and saw it was genuine. 'OK,' I said, 'I want to see the stuff now.'

'But the others are already examining it.'

'What others?'

'Some American gentlemen – very brusque types, if you ask me. Acted as if they owned the place. Forgive me, but I assumed you were part of the same party. They had ID cards similar to yours. I believe they're in the store-room right now.'

Daisy and I exchanged a glance, shoved our chairs back and stood up abruptly.

'Show us,' I said.

Abd al-Ali shrugged, got to his feet and stopped. 'There they are,' he said, pointing to the passage lined with small shops, off the main concourse.

I looked up to see a group of three men in almost identical grey suits, dark ties and black shoes advancing up the passage in line like a military patrol. The man in the centre was carrying a charcoal-coloured Samsonite suitcase, which might have been chosen to match his suit, and the other men were riding shotgun in front and behind.

'That's Doctor Ibram's suitcase,' the manager said.

We made a beeline for the procession and stood holding up our ID cards, blocking the way. 'Where do you think you're going with that?' I demanded. 'You have no right to remove evidence.'

The little party came to a stop, but the one carrying the suitcase didn't put it down. The guy in front was a broad-faced, sullen-looking type, with brooding eyes, and a walrus moustache that drooped around his mouth. 'Get out of the way,' he grunted, through gritted teeth, 'we have diplomatic immunity.'

'Like hell,' I said, nodding towards Daisy. 'This lady is the investigating detective on the American side. Put that damned suitcase down.'

I crossed my right hand inside my jacket and was about to whip out my Beretta, when a cold, hard rod was suddenly poked against the side of my head. 'Forget it, Lieutenant,' a bass voice said, and I saw Daisy's eyes flicker. I realized that someone had actually managed to slip up behind, unnoticed by me or even Miss lightning-hands Special Agent Brooke. Whoever did that had to be good, I thought.

'Like the man said,' the voice growled, 'we have diplomatic immunity. Let them pass.'

The cold metal was taken away, and I spun slowly to see a fourth man in a grey suit, holding a 9mm SIG pistol in his left hand. The man was middle-aged, very tall but with spidery long legs and arms that seemed to swing in simian fashion, a tad too long for the body. His face was dark with lines and pock-marks, making it look like it had been steeped for years in pickling fluid. His head was small – a lump on bony shoulders – with no hair but a long fringe at the back which turned outwards like a crest. His nose was long and high, and his eyes were close together giving the impression of two deep wells, impossible to see into clearly. There was a poised, almost brooding quality about him – a feeling that there was something very nasty and very dangerous here waiting to erupt.

'Shit,' I said, 'that's twice I've had a Yank pull a gun on me today! Don't you people know what the penalty is for pulling a piece on a cop in this country? I could have you inside for twenty years.'

The spidery man made a dry retching sound that passed for a laugh and stuck his pistol inside his jacket. 'I doubt that very much,' he said. The words came out slow and in an odd rhythm, I thought.

'Lieutenant Rashid,' Daisy cut in suddenly, 'this is Jan Van Helsing, the CIA's head of station here in Cairo.'

'CIA? I thought this was an FBI case.'

'So did I,' Daisy said, pouting at Van Helsing, and I realized suddenly that her face was white with anger. 'It would have helped if you'd informed me, sir,' she said.

Van Helsing made a sound as if he was sucking grit. 'I'm not answerable to you, Brooke,' he said. 'The CIA takes priority.'

'Sir,' Daisy said, 'you're making us look a pack of assholes in front of foreign law-enforcement agencies. I'll have to report this to the Legat.'

Van Helsing sneered, and I suddenly remembered where I'd heard the name before. Van Helsing was the hero of Bram Stoker's *Dracula* – the guy who'd hammered stakes through vampires' hearts.

'Watch your mouth,' the CIA man snapped. 'You cross me, Brooke and I'll have you stripped of your badge and thrown out into the streets to fuck spics and niggers. And don't think your daddy will stop me. I can take care of him, too.'

For a moment, my hair almost stood on end. It wasn't so much what the guy had said – though that was bad enough. It was the way he'd said it – that thick, uneven voice larded with deep-set hate. Van Helsing hadn't got the right name, I thought – Dracula would've been more appropriate. I watched the CIA man, realizing that I was almost shaking with resentment, feeling the kind of impotent rage I'd felt as a street-boy in Aswan, feeling the same need to smash out. I gritted my teeth and clenched my fists tight to prevent myself.

'Now piss off,' Van Helsing added, 'before I get riled up.'

Daisy's eyes blazed at him, and for a moment I thought she'd retaliate. Instead, she just touched my arm. 'Let them get on with it,' she said. 'Let's go.'

$$\boxed{8}$$

W<small>E SAT IN</small> D<small>AISY'S</small> F<small>IAT</small> in the Mena Palace parking lot and stared for a few silent moments into the night. In the yellow beam of a car-park lamp, Daisy's face looked beautiful and vulnerable for an instant, and I laid a hand on her shoulder. 'That was rough,' I said.

She hesitated a moment before shrugging my hand off, and when she rounded on me I saw Miss Hard-Ass had returned with a vengeance. 'So what?' she snapped, 'I'm a big girl, OK. I'm an FBI Special Agent, in case you hadn't noticed. I don't need to be patronized by a Neanderthal.'

'Neanderthal!' I said. 'Listen, I'm the one who got a loaded SIG in the ear, remember? And like I said, that's twice you Yanks have pointed pieces at me in one day. If I'm a Neanderthal, that must make your CIA guy there fucking *Australopithecus afarensis*. I thought the CIA was supposed to be the world's Great White Hope, but judging by Van Helsing it's just a bunch of foul-mouthed, ignorant cruds.'

'Van Helsing's a creep.'

'And that's putting it mildly. Who *is* that guy?'

'He's the top CIA man in Cairo. I've seen him around the embassy, that's all.'

'He seemed to know you well enough. What was that remark about your father supposed to mean?'

'Daddy's a US senator. Used to be a general – a real soldier, though, not a desk-man. He was captured and tortured in Korea, but never cracked, and came back a war-hero. Led a battalion in Nam, too – got wounded a bunch of times, and cited for bravery more than once. Daddy's dedicated his life to the States – it's a family tradition, you could say. My grandfather was a general in World War II, and my great-grandfather in the first one. Among the Brookes service goes back to Washington. I had ideals of loyalty and duty drummed into me before I could read.'

'Poor little rich girl,' I said, my spark of sympathy now completely extinguished. 'But I bet you had everything you wanted too – horses, servants, fast cars, motor-launches, exotic foreign holidays, swimming pools, big parties on your birthday and at Christmas.'

Daisy gazed at me – wistfully almost, I thought. 'Yeah, I had all that,' she said, 'but it never meant much to me.'

'Oho,' I said, 'well it would have meant a lot to me when I was a street-rat in the Aswan bazaars.'

'Look, I'm sorry about your pa, OK, but the world's a tough place. I'm sorry you were brought up dirt-poor, but you're still who you are despite that, and I'm still who I am.' She drew in her breath and looked out into the night. 'Daddy's an idealist,' she said. 'You couldn't find a more honest guy. He got into politics because he thought he could do some good, but it's full of sleaze-balls and hoods. You know what the military-industrial complex is? Yeah, well they rule the world – not only the States, but everywhere. It's like a secret government. They make the deals, and the rest of us are just cannon-fodder. Daddy was never part of it, not even in the army. He really believes in the Star-Spangled Banner and all that. He's not alone, but he's one of the few.'

I considered her sceptically, remembering the quip about power corrupting. 'Do you think Van Helsing could really mess him up?' I asked.

'I'd say no – I mean, he was just trying to make me back off. But when you think of it, who knows what the CIA can do?

They're the most powerful intelligence agency in the world.'

'And the military-industrial complex rules the world. Doesn't that make the CIA the cat's-paw of the ''secret government''?'

Daisy shot me a curious look. 'My first impression of you was spot on,' she said, 'you don't sound like a cop at all.'

'You know something, *Special Agent* Brooke? Neither do you.'

She sighed and yawned. 'Weren't you going to report to Hammoudi?' she said.

I took her mobile phone and struggled with the controls for a second time. 'Damn thing!' I said at last. 'You need a degree in astro-physics to operate it.'

'Let me,' Daisy said, taking the phone and punching in Hammoudi's contact number.

She handed it back to me. 'Yes?' came Hammoudi's gruff bass voice. 'Sammy? How did it go at the Mena?'

I described the encounter with the CIA, and Hammoudi swore. 'So much for the efficiency of the great US of A,' he spat, 'where the right hand doesn't know what the left's doing. The ambassador never breathed a word.'

'Probably didn't know,' I said.

There was a moment's silence, and I imagined the Colonel thumping the desk with his big fist, fighting down the fury. 'OK,' he said at last. His voice was controlled but I could hear the heavy breathing, 'Don't worry about it. The CIA's business is US national security, which includes papering over the cracks when well-known personalities go haywire. It's probably nothing more than half an ounce of hash or some dirty pictures in Ibram's suitcase they're concerned about.'

'But how the hell can they get away with sequestering evidence in a foreign country?'

Hammoudi snorted. 'Because this country gets millions of dollars in subsidies from the States, and because Cairo has the biggest American embassy in the world. It's as simple as that.'

Hammoudi rang off. 'OK,' I said, 'let's move it.'

Suddenly, she seemed reluctant to start the engine. 'What's up?' I asked.

She frowned. 'I don't know,' she said, and took a deep breath. 'I think he was lying.'

'Who? Van Helsing?'

'No, the front desk man – Abd al-Ali wasn't it?'

At that moment there was a tap at the window and a face was suddenly flattened against it. I had my Beretta halfway out before I realized it was Abd al-Ali himself. I flashed a curious glance at Daisy, swung the door open and jumped out. 'Don't do that!' I told him. 'Somebody might get blown away.'

'Sorry, Lieutenant,' he said, and I noticed he was holding what looked like the carrying case of a laptop computer, done in some kind of synthetic material with a shoulder-strap and a zip. 'Forgive me,' he said, 'but I observed that well ... somewhat embarrassing scene ... with the American gentlemen in the lobby. Very bad taste if I may say so. I'm only glad there were no guests around, otherwise it would have been a PR disaster. Actually, I felt quite guilty about it, Lieutenant, I did really. If I'd known, of course, I wouldn't have allowed them to take the case, but they had their ID and naturally, I assumed that it was all on the up and up.'

I sighed. 'Look, Abd al-Ali,' I said, 'you weren't to know. It happens. Now if you'll excuse me, I've had quite a hectic day.'

'I'm sorry to trouble you, Lieutenant,' he went on persistently, 'but if I may say so, I do despise these foreigners who come over here and think they can sort of run things. I mean, they're so arrogant sometimes, and this is Egypt after all ... all due respect to the lady, of course.'

'Yes,' I said, 'well thank you.'

'No, you don't understand,' he said, 'I would have said something to you earlier but I didn't quite know how to approach the subject.'

'Abd al-Ali, whatever you have to say, say it.'

'All right. Well, you see the case the Americans took wasn't the only one.'

'What?'

'There was another case – this one.' He held up the small computer case. 'I kept it aside from the other, and when the Americans asked if there was anything else, I must admit I told them a little fib. I don't know why I did that. Just something in their manner which I didn't like.'

He handed the case to me. 'Where did you find it?' I asked.

'It was in his room with the other baggage. Of course, I never looked inside.'

'Thank you, you've done the right thing. And if anyone comes asking about Doctor Ibram again, no matter who it is, you give the SID a ring first. OK?'

I watched Abd al-Ali walking back towards the hotel entrance, then I got back in the car, closed the door and locked it. 'You were right about him,' I said. 'He just brought us a present from Santa Claus.'

Daisy eyed the case dubiously. 'I once saw a marine sergeant kick an empty briefcase that had been left outside the US embassy in Beirut,' she said slowly, 'only it wasn't empty. Santa Claus had left a little something inside just for him. Took his foot off. Now they use metal-detectors.'

I put the case down on my knee and switched on the overhead light. 'I haven't got a metal-detector,' I said, 'but I've got intuition. Trust me.'

'That's what the marine sergeant said.'

I winced inwardly and unzipped the case. There was no booby-trap, only two documents. The first was a sketch map of some kind with hills and wadis marked on it, but no names, scales or coordinates. I examined it carefully and passed it to Daisy, who held it up to the light.

'That's useful,' she said. 'Could be anywhere. There's a half-circle on the left edge that might be significant but . . .' She ran her hand along the edge and her eyes opened slightly in surprise. 'It's been cut off,' she said, 'with a blunt knife, probably. This isn't the full thing – it's only half the map.'

72

I took it from her and felt the rough edge with my thumb. 'You're right,' I said, 'but you're also wrong. This couldn't be just anywhere. There's no rivers, streams or standing water. This is a map of the desert.'

'Great. Isn't the Sahara supposed to be nine million square kilometres in area? And it might not even be the Sahara.'

I grunted, placed the map back in the case and took out the other document. It was a sheaf of photocopies, and on the top was a blurred image of a lion-headed woman sitting on a throne. The woman was seen in profile, her ferocious lioness-head capped by a pharaonic headdress, and bearing the sacred sun-disk of the ancient Egyptians with a cobra emerging from it – the Uraeus, a symbol of kingship. She was big-bodied with thick limbs and a single breast shaped like a torpedo. In her right hand she held the ancient Egyptian ankh cross – a symbol of life – and in the other a sacred staff. Below the image, someone had written in English:

> Let the Eye of Ra descend
> That it may slay the evil conspirators.

I shivered and Daisy stared at me. 'What is it?' she asked.

'Sekhmet,' I said, 'the lion-headed goddess. The ancient Egyptians regarded her as the Bringer of Devastation. She was the daughter of Ra, the all-powerful sun-god, and represented the destructive power of the sun. In another guise she was the Wedjet Eye or the Eye of Ra – Ra's secret weapon. He once sent Sekhmet down to earth to destroy all human beings, but it didn't happen because Ra took pity on them. That verse is from the *Hymn to Ra* which tells the whole story. Sekhmet was a real bitch.'

I flipped the page up and examined what lay underneath. It was a report by two Dutch geophysicists called Blij and Neuven, reprinted from some scientific journal, on core samples taken at the Greenland icecap in the 1970s. I passed it to Daisy, who raised an eyebrow. 'Very topical,' she commented drily. She began to read, moving her well-manicured index finger down the centre of the page, then flipping it over.

'Hey,' I said, 'are you reading that, or just skimming?'

'Speed reading,' she told me. 'Something they teach you at Quantico.'

I left her to it and stared into the night for a few minutes until she closed the last page. 'Well?'

'Well, illuminating if you're into ice-cores,' she said, grinning. 'Seems these guys analysed cores going back as far as 100,000 BC, and were able to pinpoint years when there'd been some kind of atmospheric disturbance – say from volcanic eruptions, meteorite storms, sunspots – that kind of thing.'

'And?'

She opened the pages again and showed me some lines that had been highlighted in yellow marker. 'Those are the only lines highlighted in the whole report,' she said. 'There was a major disturbance in about 2500 BC. Anything significant about that date?'

I thought about it for a minute then shrugged. I took the report and placed it with the map in the case and zipped it up. 'Well, like you said, "illuminating". Half a map of nowhere in particular and a report on the icecap. Great. Let's get out of here.'

I switched off the light and Daisy gunned the engine. 'All that shit with Van Helsing,' she said, 'and I never even saw the pyramids. Not up close and personal, anyway.'

'I tell you what,' I said, 'why don't you meet me there – at Giza – at ten tomorrow morning and I'll show you round.'

She glanced at me doubtfully. 'We've got work to do.'

'It's relevant after all – Ibram was a member of the Giza Millennium Committee.'

Daisy grunted. She and I had worked together well with Fawzi – fallen into the good-cop-bad-cop routine without even exchanging a word. But now she was wondering how far could you really trust an ex-street-kid – especially one who still carried a razor-sharp stiletto up his sleeve.

'OK,' she said, 'I'll chance it.'

'Good. Ten o'clock, at the Great Pyramid. I'll wait for you there.'

*   *   *

The boulevard to the city centre was a stream of headlights and streetlights like strings of pearls stretching into the night. As Daisy pulled out of the arched gate of the hotel, I saw a woman in dark Bedouin robes standing in the orange glow of a street-lamp. She was unusually tall and wore a slitted vampire-like mask whose pattern was somehow familiar. 'Stop!' I yelled at Daisy. She looked around in alarm and stepped hard on the brakes. I wound the window down, but was just in time to see the robed figure melting away into the deepest shadows. 'Did you see that?' I asked.

'See what?' Daisy said.

9

THE GIZA PLATEAU WAS ALMOST as deserted as it had been the previous day. Standing on the western side of the promontory overlooking the desert, I noticed a roil of dust on the western horizon that could only be an approaching sandstorm – the one the experts had predicted would strike tomorrow. Like I said, I've never had much time for experts – I'd told Hammoudi it'd be here today, and here it was, right on cue. It would hit Giza in about ninety minutes, I calculated, and I didn't want to be on the plateau when it did.

As I waited for Daisy I walked around the base of the Great Pyramid, scenting the familiar chalk and flint smell of the desert, with that trace of fire-ash that heralded the simoom. I passed the old museum rest-house – a half-derelict building in red sandstone standing at the eastern corner of the Great Pyramid – and saw that a boom-style crane sprouted from its yard. I watched the crane operator climbing up the steel ladder to his cab as deftly as a gecko. He seemed to know his job, but all the same I wouldn't have envied him up there when the storm broke. I wondered what a crane was doing in the rest-house yard anyway. Actually, the place hadn't been a rest-house or a museum in years – it was a base and guard-post for the Tourism and Antiquities police. Today, besides the crane, there seemed to be a lot of activity there – minivans, cars, squads of policemen coming and going through the broken-down gates. I leaned on the railings of one of the excavated boat-pits nearby to watch what was going on and suddenly realized that the police squads weren't police at all. They wore black uniforms like the police all right, but they were much smarter than the ordinary blackjackets, and in place of black berets with scarlet stripes, wore the royal-blue berets of the *Guwat az-Zaiqa* – the Lightning Force – Egypt's elite army commandos.

I watched the dust haze gathering on the horizon, and breathed in the bittersweet desert scents. I narrowed my eyes and let my memories unwind for a moment. Out there I could see only sand, but inside I saw figures on the landscape – figures that were tiny pools of dark, like scarab beetles, at home in the bigness. There were other smells – camels, woodsmoke, uncured hide, and sour milk, oiled leatherwork, jerked meat. I felt a longing so intense that it almost doubled me over, and I saw a younger me out there, in a *jibba* and headcloth, dyed the colour of the desert, struggling across dunes and drum-sand with a caravan of camels on our way to find grazing at the Jilf. There were four boys with me, all younger than I was, and if we'd been more experienced we'd have known a big *ghibli* was on its way. I remembered how we'd looked at each other when the earth started to shake like Set was beating on it with a hammer, and 'Ali had whispered, 'Raul's Drum.'

It had come with terrifying speed, running at us like some giant invisible creature in vortices of dust thousands of feet high, creasing into us like a shockwave and almost bowling the animals over. We'd jumped off their backs and couched them, squatting in their lee with our headcloths over our faces. I knew we couldn't go on doing that – *ghiblis* could blow for days, even weeks, and if we tried to stay where we were we'd be parchment within forty-eight hours. I don't know how I found the nerve, but I forced myself back in the saddle and turned my camel into the eye of the storm. 'Come on!' I said. 'Get back on your camels! Let's go!' I still don't know exactly what happened. It seemed like a barrier burst in my mind, spilling out all kinds of things

I didn't know were there. It was like rays of sunlight bursting through a gap in dark cloud. Somehow I had a map in my head, or rather part of me was in a place where tracks from the past, tracks into the future, merged into one. For two days and two nights we trekked through a terrifying wasteland of noise, where demons ripped at our senses, where visibility varied only from black to grey. But always there was a brilliant light on the edge of my inner vision, a beacon whose strength never faltered. When we arrived in the camp, so dehydrated we couldn't speak, the Old Man hadn't even seemed surprised about what I'd done. I always suspected afterwards that he'd set it up as a test – sent me and the boys out into the *khala*, knowing a *ghibli* was on the way. Still, after that I was always known among the tribe as Nawayr – 'The Little Light'.

'Hey!' Daisy's voice shouted in my ear. 'Anybody there?' I blinked rapidly to dispel the memory, and saw her standing in front of me. Today she wore dark glasses, a loose-fitting red and blue cotton kaftan and jeans. Her braided hair had been coiled up and pinned under an elegant panama hat, and she wore flat, thick-soled shoes. She swung her Gucci handbag easily from her left shoulder, with the flap unfastened. 'Okaaay!' she said, whipping off her glasses and craning her neck at the Great Pyramid, whose peak towered more than four hundred feet above us. I wasn't looking at the pyramid, though, but at something that struck me then as far more wonderful – Daisy's profile. The slim hips and neatly curved breasts looked perfect, and I had to clench my teeth to control a waft of desire that ran through me like a tsunami. 'I've seen pictures of this thing so many times,' Daisy said, 'I thought it could never live up to them, but I was wrong. Now that is really *something*!'

And she was really something else, I thought. You can look at a woman, even find her attractive, but it takes a little time before it sinks in that she's just about the most beautiful creature you've ever seen. I smiled back at her, yearning for her, knowing there was no chance. Upper-crust girls like Daisy didn't go for ex-street-kids like me. She was the sort of woman that as an urchin in Aswan I'd always dreamed of having, but knew I never could. She was about as high above me as the Great Pyramid itself. 'You know there are more than 2.3 million blocks of stone in that heap?' I said, swallowing hard. 'Each one of them weighing about two tons or more. Some weigh as much as eighty tons.'

'That's incredible.'

'You've got it. The whole thing's unbelievably accurate, too. The length of the base is 756 feet but the maximum difference in length among the four sides is only one and three-quarter inches. It's almost completely level – less than a one-inch variation in the whole base. That's more accurate than most modern buildings – the kind of precision that even today you only find in machine shops. In the past it was a whole lot more impressive than it is now, because it was encased in brilliant white limestone that was stripped off later, and the whole place was surrounded by a twenty-five-foot wall. There was only one way of getting inside the compound – through a temple that's disappeared.'

'What about the apex?' Daisy asked, craning back again and shading her eyes. 'It looks kind of flat to me.'

'Yeah, that's a mystery,' I said, 'there obviously *was* a capstone there, but it's gone AWOL. No one knows what happened to it. They reckon it might have been covered in gold.'

'Wow! And to think the Pharaoh Khufu built this thing just as a tombstone! Now that's what you call megalomania!'

'Who said Khufu built it?' I asked. 'And who says it was a tombstone?'

'Come on – it's well known.'

'It's what the experts say, sure,' I grunted. 'But personally I've never had a lot of time for experts. They make out they're dealing in truth, but actually they're dealing in theories. Somebody once told me that the pyramids are actually older than they say, and when you think of it, if the Pharaoh Khufu did throw up this pile of rocks, why doesn't he or anyone else ever mention the fact? I mean, tombstones are supposed to have names on them, aren't they? These ancient Gyp bigshots weren't known for being backward at coming forwards, and believe me they usually laid it on with a trowel. But this guy's name isn't mentioned anywhere on the pyramid, inside or out. In fact, there isn't a single piece of sound evidence that links Khufu with it.'

'Isn't the Sphinx supposed to have the face of Khufu's son, Khafre?'

'Tell you what, you look at the Sphinx's face and then swear to me you can make positive ID of anybody at all. A couple of years back a New York Police Department artist who was an expert at doing facial reconstructions did a job on the Sphinx comparing the face to a statue known to be Khafre. His conclusion was that there was no resemblance at all.'

'OK, Mister Smart-Aleck, if Khufu didn't build the Great Pyramid, who did?'

'I don't know, but I just have this feeling that it's older than they say and that it couldn't have been a tomb. The ancient Egyptians built tombs to a pattern, and it doesn't fit. It's an *oopart*.'

'A what?'

'An *oopart* – ''out of place artifact'' – what they used to call an anachronism.'

'Hey, look, what difference does it make, anyway? I mean what's so all-fired important whether this thing is a tomb or not?'

'Flip the question round the other way. Why is the establishment so goddamn insistent that it was a tomb, and that it was built by Khufu? Why do they assert that they know all the answers, when there isn't one real shred of evidence to support their case?'

'Where did you get all this stuff from, Sammy? I don't believe they taught you this on any antiquities-police course.'

She was watching me speculatively now, and I knew I had to make some sort of response, no matter how lame. 'Like I said, somebody I once knew told me that there's a lot more to ancient Egyptian history than the so-called experts want to believe.'

'Who?'

'It doesn't matter. Just somebody I knew and respected. Why?

Can't a cop have views different from the establishment?'

'Cops exist to support the status quo. I just can't work out why a guy like you is a cop.'

'What about you? Oh, I forgot. Duty to the Star-Spangled Banner wasn't it?'

We walked around to the southern side of the pyramid, from where we could see the second and third pyramids bathed in light, and beyond them the desert, flowing on and on until it merged with a smoky horizon. Daisy gazed around, her blue eyes shining, entranced. 'Can we go inside?' she asked.

'Why not? Wouldn't be much fun if we didn't.'

We walked along the base of the pyramid, our hands skimming the great hewn stones that were visibly warped by time. A muffled woman sitting in the lee of one massive block offered us bottles of cola from a steel bucket. There was a sudden buffet of wind, which sent a flurry of wrappers, crushed cardboard packets and flimsy plastic bags across our vision, and a waft of unexpected cold. Daisy shivered.

'Sandstorm coming,' I said. 'Shouldn't be here for an hour or so, though, and we'll be long gone.'

'How does a street-rat like you get to be an expert on sand-storms?' Daisy asked, holding her head to one side in mock suspicion.

'I'm not an expert,' I said, 'I just have intuition.'

I pointed to the broken aperture, about twenty feet up the pyramid's wall, where a lone blackjacket stood on guard with an automatic slung round his neck. Thirty feet higher there was an even larger orifice through which giant corbelled blocks could be seen. 'The higher one's the main entrance,' I said. 'There probably always was a door there, right back to when the place was built, but when the Arabs tried to smash their way into the place in the ninth century they missed it, which suggests it was invisible to the outside. The lower, smaller entrance is the place they forced their way in. They only found the real door later when they stumbled on the passage that led away from it. Now, why would a tomb need a door? The ancient Gyps sealed their tombs for eternity, but a door suggests they wanted to mosey in and out. Why not just block it up for good?'

'But wasn't there a sarcophagus inside?'

'They found a thing that *looked* like a sarcophagus, sure, but there was nothing in it. It was just a big stone box – in a different context, it could have been anything.'

We climbed the twisting concrete steps that led us up the side of the pyramid to the platform where the guard waited. Close up, though, I saw that he wasn't an ordinary policeman, but another trooper of the Lightning Force – smartly turned out in blackjacket and royal-blue beret. He wore skiing glasses over a sharp moustache and carried a Heckler and Koch rifle that looked new. 'You can't go in,' he said as we passed the top step, 'It's closed.'

I drew out my ID. 'Lieutenant Rashid,' I said, 'SID.'

The trooper weighed up my jeans and sweatshirt and frowned blankly. He paused, then gave me a brisk salute. 'Sir,' he said, 'my orders are that no one's to go in, not even SID. The place is completely out of bounds.'

'What are you Blue Berets doing on the job? This is Antiquities Police turf.'

'Special assignment duty,' the trooper growled.

'What the hell is going on in there?' Daisy demanded.

'Renovations,' the Blue Beret replied, 'for the millennium celebrations. They're trying to clean it out a bit, improve the air supply, that kind of thing. There's going to be a big knees-up here. They tell me they're even going to put a new capstone on the thing – a golden one – and it's going to be lowered by helicopter.'

'Oh, yeah,' I said, 'I read about this. It's caused a lot of controversy. Last month a member of the President's Advisory Council called Sekina Fuad declared they shouldn't be messing around with antiquities.'

The Blue Beret shrugged, shifted his feet and tapped the stock of his rifle impatiently. 'It's closed,' he said again. Seeing we would get nowhere, we turned and walked down the stairs.

10

THE STORM CHASED US ALL the way down the Pyramids Road to the Nile, and by the time we were crossing the bridge the sky had turned an angry ochre red and currents of sand were streaking down the centre of the carriageway. Khan al-Khalili was protected against the storm by the massed buildings in the city centre, but the light was as dim as dusk, and the alleys were full of long shadows that seemed distorted and unnatural. To get to the address Hammoudi had given us we had to pass through tunnels clogged with rubble and effluent – old newspapers, flimsy supermarket bags that rustled like trapped birds, flattened milk cartons, empty cigarette packs. The buildings seemed to have been created in one continuous organic mass, and a lot of them were lopsided, leaning on each other like invalids. Liquid ran in trickles down the teetering masonry, forming sordid pools in the dirt. Flea-bitten cats darted about underfoot, beggars lurched from doorway to doorway, and streetwalkers congregated under the saracenic arches, leaning languidly in the half-light, puffing waterpipes spiked with hash. From the outside it was impossible to tell how big Sanusi's house was. There were no windows at eye-level, only small iron grates placed too high for anyone to see through without a ladder. Above them I glimpsed a bunch of upper floors with projecting balconies supported by quarried blocks. The door looked as though it had been made to resist a siege. It was heavy teak, weathered almost colourless, perforated by huge brass studs and decorated by a symmetrical flower-design with the words *Al-Khalig, al-Baaq* – 'The Creator, the Everlasting' – carved inside. There was a huge iron lock and a rusty knocker, which to my surprise seemed to be an effigy of a huge serpent – an odd contrast to the Islamic inscription. I tried the knocker and found it jammed so I rapped on the coarse wood with my knuckles. A moment later it creaked open to reveal a tall, almost cadaverous figure in a long grey *gallabiyya*, whose gaunt face was lit up weirdly from below by the beams of an oil-lamp hanging from his long fingers. His unkempt beard reached almost to his chest, but failed to cover an Adam's apple almost the size of a marabout stork's pouch. His bushy eyebrows were knitted together over piercing eyes – encased in half-moon glasses – and a hooked kedge of nose, which gave him the look of an ayatollah after a bad day's haranguing.

'Yes?' he demanded, holding up the lamp. 'What do you want?' The voice was pedantic, with an edge of barbed wire.

'Are you Doctor Sid'Ahmad as-Sanusi?' I asked.

The gaunt man ignored me and took a step out into the street, his eyes flicking left and right nervously. 'Did anybody follow you?' he demanded.

'No,' I said. 'Like who for instance?'

His eyes bored into us, and he drew a long talon over his lips, beckoning us into a dim tunnel that smelt of lamp-black and dust. 'Jinns,' he said, 'they come tapping at your door and creep in when you're not looking. They lie in wait.' Daisy rolled her eyes at me as the old man closed the door with a skeletal hand. He held the lamp up so that Chinese puppet-shapes fled across the walls. 'Follow me closely,' he said. 'It is dark. The lights have been cut.'

'Must be the storm,' I said.

'Ah!' he wheezed. 'That's what they want you to think!'

We passed a couple of turns and he stopped us before another door. 'Permission oh ye blest!' he yelled, so loudly that Daisy and I almost jumped out of our skins.

When the door opened I half-expected to find someone waiting inside, but there was nobody, only a hexagonal courtyard where heat thumped down from a six-sided section of sky high above us. There were three or four storeys to the house and looking upwards was like looking up the sheer sides of a deep well. There was a trace of fire-ash on the air, I noticed – the scent of the storm – but the yard was so deep that you felt no wind at all. The flagstones were intricately marbled in abstract Islamic patterns, and in the centre water sluiced from the head of a grotesque, scaly seamonster-fountain and poured into a large marble pool. The place was crammed with interesting artifacts. There was an Islamic lion that might have been taken from the Alhambra, a polished wooden oil-press, an Egyptian coffin from the Ptolemaic era with the remains of a man's face painted on it, and copies of much more ancient figures – aardvark-headed Set and falcon-headed Horus on either side of a stela inscribed in hieroglyphs. Set into the niche of a granite slab was the lion-headed goddess Sekhmet, a brooding eminence that seemed to lend a dark feeling of foreboding to the place.

Daisy let out a gasp of surprise. 'This is fantastic!' she said, in English. 'You'd never guess it was here from outside.'

The gaunt man sucked in his breath and grimaced. 'Ostentation is not the Arab way,' he said, in perfect English. We both turned to stare at him. 'What you see outside does not necessarily reflect what is inside,' he went on. 'It's the old battle between surface appearance and underlying form. You have a saying in English that goes "don't judge a book by its cover", do you not, Miss Brooke?'

'How do you know my name?'

The old man grinned through curls of beard. 'Colonel Hammoudi was good enough to let me know I might expect you. Otherwise I should not have let you in. I have to be on my guard. They're always tapping at my door, begging and pleading to be let in, but I won't have it. Oh no, I keep my defences up. You won't believe what creatures lie in wait out there. In one week I have seen seven men with their left eyes missing. Seven! I have seen five men with no left arms. I have seen a hunchbacked man with red hair, and two albinos. Why, I've even seen a ghoul sitting on the roof of the Badestan Gate, chewing bones.'

'A ghoul?' Daisy said.

'Yes. And that is precisely my point about outward appearance and underlying form. A ghoul is a creature that can take on almost any guise. In his natural state he is a human spider with one good leg and one like a donkey's. But he is a shapeshifter. He can be a dog, a cat, a goat, a ram, a man or a woman, a Christian, a Muslim, a Jew or even a heathen. He can assume the form of anyone, living or dead, with all their memories and idiosyncrasies. You might see him, but he looks ordinary and you don't know who he is. He can change into a king or a beggar. He can be a Negro or an Indian or an *Afrangi* – sometimes you will see him as a modest-looking man with a long beard and a brown cloak. He could be the man standing next to you in the bazaar, the man – even the woman – walking behind you on the street. He could be the one you are talking to right now. At night he roams the alleys, looking for helpless men and women to prey upon, and in the daytime he walks the endless corridors of the Underworld – right underneath the city. He knows its secret exits and entrances and how to deal with its serpent-guardians. He sneaks about changing his appearance, going invisible, hiding behind gates, sitting on roofs, passing through walls, dressing up as a beggar, mixing with all races and all religions as one of them. He's a dirty shapeshifter, and a shapeshifter can't be trusted.' He watched me carefully, unsmiling for a second, his small eyes steady behind the glasses. 'But then you already know that, I think, Lieutenant Rashid?'

I started, not expecting the question, and nodded too vigorously, not really grasping what he meant. 'Did Colonel Hammoudi tell you why we wanted to talk to you?'

'He mentioned the amulet,' Sanusi said, eagerly, 'I must have it back. It's part of my defences.'

'You mean this?' I said, bringing out the Sanusi amulet, now neatly parcelled in a polythene bag.

The transformation in Sanusi's features was sudden and dramatic. His eyes lit up and a tic activated in the corner of his left eye. The lines around it lurched skywards. 'My amulet!' he beamed. 'It *was* the one Hammoudi mentioned!' He put out his lean hand to take it, but I held it back deliberately and returned it to my pocket.

'You say it's yours?' I asked.

'Yes. Yes. It was stolen from my collection a week ago. But I explained all this to the Colonel.'

'Anything else stolen?' Daisy enquired.

'No,' Sanusi said, 'but that was enough.' He paused and peered at us through his half-moon glasses, muttering under his breath like someone used to going for days with nothing but his own company. Then he drew a large bunch of keys from the pocket of his grey robe. 'Come,' he said, gesturing towards one of the doors opening off the courtyard, 'let me show you my collection.'

The door was another solid hardwood piece with iron studs, a radiating chrysanthemum design in the centre, and flowing Islamic calligraphy on the lintel. The door creaked and we entered a long, narrow room – a small museum of sorts, with plaster walls covered in sepia-tinted photographs, framed documents and antique weapons – scimitars, breech-loading Martini carbines, daggers with weird and wonderful double blades, spears and shields. Pride of place in the room, though, belonged to the glass cabinets, one of which contained silver jewellery in complicated designs. Daisy stopped to stare at it. There were ornate necklaces of flat trapezoids, rectangles and plaited strands, and headdresses of silver hoops, nests of balls and dangling cylinders, with chains ending in what looked like tiny hands. Some of the pieces incorporated amber and carnelian, and others contained tiny boxes inlaid with finely worked gold or mother-of-pearl.

'Good grief!' Daisy muttered. 'Some of these things must weigh a ton! How did they ever wear them?'

'They didn't,' Sanusi said, 'these things only *appear* to be headdresses. They are Bedouin things, and to the Bedouin anything that is not mobile is useless. Isn't that so, Lieutenant Rashid? These things were really the tribe's mobile assets, which would be sold off in famine times – a reserve for when the going got tough.'

'But they must be worth a fortune,' Daisy said. 'Why would thieves break in and leave them?'

'Who said anyone *broke* in?' Sanusi snapped. 'I let the thief in, may God forgive my folly. The only thing broken was this.' He pointed to a cabinet standing in the centre of the room, whose glass had been shattered and was now patched up with tape. 'I haven't got round to repairing it, yet,' he said, apologetically. The cabinet was full of artifacts, and I saw that it contained a lot of amulets like the one I had in my pocket – tiny leather boxes, some of them delicately inlaid and inscribed.

'You're sure there was only the one missing?' I asked.

'Yes. And it's not even the most interesting or the most valuable – though it is entirely unique to the Sanusiya Brotherhood. This type of amulet is known as a *hejab*. It contains a verse from the Quran written by a holy man – some of the verses in these amulets were actually written by my ancestor, Mohammad bin Ali, the Great Sanusi, almost two hundred years ago. Such charms would protect them from knives and bullets. Psychic defences. They would no more have thought of going into battle without such protection than a modern labourer goes on site without his hard hat.' He led us aside and gestured to a lithograph of a saintly-looking man with a white beard. 'This is my ancestor, Mohammad bin Ali,' Sanusi announced, as if giving us a guided tour. 'He was not only a mathematician, theologian and astrologer, but was also gifted with tremendous organizing abilities. At the height of his power he was able to muster 25,000 Bedouin tribesmen to his banner. The amulets he gave to these tribesmen were absolutely effective, as long as they themselves continued to have faith. And faith is what counts.'

Daisy looked at him dubiously and I saw her choke back a comment. 'You say you know who stole the amulet?' she asked.

'Yes,' he said, 'I had a premonition, of course. I knew

something was about to happen. Seven one-eyed men, five one-armed men, two albinos and a hunchback – all in a week. Then the ghoul. I saw him sitting on the Badestan Gate, crunching bones, and next thing I knew he was tapping at my door, asking to see my amulets. Oh, he appeared to be a man, of course. He even had a name. He called himself Sayf ad-Din Ali, and said he was from the World Council of Islam. Gave me an address in the United Arab Emirates, but I knew he wasn't a native of the Gulf. He appeared a tall man – wore a thick beard, Mecca-style turban and a *gallabiyya*. Oh yes, he wrapped himself with the odour of sanctity all right, but I knew what he was. I smelt the Devil.'

Daisy giggled and Sanusi gave her a hard glance. 'You seem to find this amusing, Miss Brooke,' he said. 'Perhaps you think ghouls don't exist?' He moved to a side table and picked up a battered red scrapbook. 'This book is full of reports about them, I've been compiling it for years.' He flipped through the thick pages and I saw they were crammed with pasted newspaper clippings, some of them yellow with age. Sanusi stopped at a certain page and held the open book out to Daisy. 'Look here!' he said. 'You read Arabic?'

Daisy perused the page briefly and passed it to me. The clipping pasted on to it was from *Al-Ahram* – the most respectable of Egypt's newspapers – and was dated two weeks previously. *Ghoul Strikes In Khan al-Khalili?* the headline ran. I looked at it but only pretended to read it. I'd seen it before.

'A young tailor's boy was found in an alley one morning, just round the corner from here,' Sanusi said. 'When the corpse was examined it was found that part of the skin had been flayed off and all the blood had been drained from the organs. In fact, the body was no more than a shell. There were strange marks on it too – marks which couldn't have been made by any known animal.' He took the scrapbook from me and scrabbled through more pages with his talon fingers. 'Look at all these!' he said. 'It's happened before. Six reports since 1995, all in the Khan al-Khalili area, all of men or women disappearing only to be discovered in the streets with their blood sucked out of them, and the marks of some creature in their flesh. And the deaths occur in a regular pattern – once every six months. Now if that's not a ghoul, what is it?'

'Every six months?' Daisy repeated. 'Sounds to me like a serial killer with some sick MO.'

'Then how do you explain the loss of blood, and the animal-like marks?'

'Stranger things happen where I come from, believe me. You want to try visiting California.'

Sanusi closed the scrapbook and slapped it down on the table hard. 'I've been to other places,' he said, 'I just want to remain who I am. The worst thing that can happen to a man is to lose touch with who he is. There was a time in my life when I forgot who I was, you see.' He looked around as if there might be someone else listening, then he suddenly grabbed hold of my arm tightly. His eyes seemed to start out of his head, and his mouth trembled slightly. 'I tell you these ghouls aren't from this world at all,' he whispered, 'and they're planning to take over. Oh yes, they covet the earth all right, and only our psychic defences will protect us. No one believes me. They all think I'm mad. But I tell you – be prepared!'

I disengaged my arm and took a step backwards. 'OK,' I said, 'this er ... Sayf ad-Din character you claim took the amulet. You said he came from the World Council of Islam. What's that?'

Sanusi swallowed and his eyes dimmed for a moment. Then he seemed to recover himself. 'I've never heard of any such thing,' he said. 'He told me it was a new organization whose objective was to disseminate Islam in the nations of non-believers, especially Africa. He said he'd read all about the Sanusiya and wanted to know more – especially about the amu-lets. I showed him my museum and he asked if he could make notes. I said yes, of course, and I had to leave him for a moment. When I came back, the case was smashed as you see it now, the amulet had gone and so had the man. I did report the theft to the local police at the time, who searched the place, dusted the cabinet for fingerprints, and will no doubt have made a voluminous and incredibly tedious report on the subject. I told them it was the work of a ghoul, but they just laughed. Now, dear me, I am failing in my duty as a host. If you are finished here, may I offer you a glass of tea?'

11

THE SALON SANUSI SHOWED US into was furnished Arab-style. There were no high tables or chairs, but low divans and nests of richly embroidered cushions on the floor, calf-high tables of carved wood set on costly Persian carpets. In this room there were no clocks, no machines, no ornaments, only a low shelf of books – most of them large-format pictorial works on Islam and ancient Egypt. Everything else seemed entirely functional. Sanusi stuck the oil-lamp into a niche in the wall, and settled gracefully into a set of cushions, ringing a silver bell that stood on the nearby table. He removed his sandals and placed them out of sight. 'Please,' he said, as I stooped to pull off my trainers. 'I know old habits die hard, but don't bother, Lieutenant.'

That was his third or fourth shot across my bows, I thought. I was tempted to grab the crazy old man by his scrawny beard and demand what the hell he meant by it, but I checked myself and was about to plump down in some cushions when Sanusi shrieked, 'No, please, not there! No, that's where my Mamluk is sitting!'

Daisy looked startled and gazed around her. 'What Mamluk?' she asked.

'My Mamluk – a Circassian soldier from the time of Moham- mad Al Pasha. He was shot dead in this house, and his spirit has never left it. There he is, lighting his pipe. Can't you see him?' His eyes widened as he goggled at something invisible between us.

'No,' Daisy said, shifting uneasily.

'He doesn't speak,' Sanusi said, 'but he's always there – watching. It would be a mistake to annoy him though. You know the ancient Egyptians believed that each human being had a *ka* or ghost, which haunted his tomb after death. That's one reason they were afraid of entering tombs. My Mamluk is a *ka*.'

Daisy raised her eyes silently to the ceiling and we sat down side by side in another corner. The old man stared at us accusingly. 'So what have you come to see me about if it's not to return my amulet?'

'Have you ever heard of Doctor Adam Ibram?' I asked.

He beamed humourlessly at nowhere in particular, but he didn't seem surprised. He flipped off his glasses and placed them on the table, screwing up his eyes. 'Yes,' he said, 'I read about his murder in Sayyidna Hussayn Square yesterday. Muggers, wasn't it? The paper said that terrorism definitely wasn't involved.' He halted and rubbed his eyes vigorously with the palms of his hands. 'But what has this to do with my amulet?'

I pulled out the amulet again and laid it on the carpet in front of me. Sanusi's eyes were suddenly riveted on it. 'I'm glad you asked that, Doctor Sanusi,' I said, 'because your amulet was found at the scene of Doctor Ibram's murder.'

Sanusi looked genuinely astonished, and his tic suddenly began to work furiously. He stared at me, shaking his head. 'It must be a mistake,' he mumbled.

'It's no mistake,' Daisy said. 'Have you any idea what it was doing there?'

The old man's mouth beneath the grey curls formed a moue of sullen fury, and suddenly he stood up, breathing hard, with eyes blazing. 'Just what are you suggesting?' he shouted. 'Huh? That I had something to do with Ibram's death? Why, I ought to call my lawyer this minute!'

'That's your right,' I said, 'but we're not accusing anyone.

We just want to find out how the thing got there. Please, Doctor Sanusi, sit down.'

Sanusi considered it for a moment, then his dark eyes focused on me and he slumped down on the cushions. 'I told you,' he insisted, 'it was taken by a man who called himself Sayf ad-Din. That's all I know.'

'So there's no chance that the Sanusiya Brotherhood has been revived?' Daisy asked.

The old man looked as if she'd just given him a left hook in the ear. His eyes popped and his skeletal features ran the gamut of surprise, indignation, derision and finally full-blooded mockery. '*Revived?*' he repeated incredulously. Then his face twisted up as he let out a barrage of punch-like guffaws, growing faster and more intense until it sounded as if he was having a heart seizure.

'Jesus!' Daisy said. 'You all right, Doctor Sanusi?'

'Yes,' he wheezed, bringing out a silk handkerchief and holding it over his mouth. The guffaws dissolved into braying coughs as he tried to control himself. Then they burst out anew. 'I see it all now,' he gasped between bursts, 'oh, no, I see it all! I see what it is you're getting at!' He broke down again, and held the handkerchief to his lips. 'You think Ibram's murder is connected with the Sanusiya! That rot about no terrorism being involved was all hogwash, wasn't it?'

'Not necessarily. Let's say we're examining all possibilities.'

He stopped laughing suddenly, and pinned me with a stare of absolute contempt. 'You belong in the madhouse, the pair of you,' he said, 'to even suggest such a thing. Before coming here, barging in without a by-your-leave, wasting my time, you ought to have done a little bit of homework. I mean, do you actually get paid for such incompetence? I ought to get on the phone to Colonel Hammoudi this minute. Are you sure you're police officers? No wonder the world's in such a mess if it has folk like you looking after it.'

Daisy and I watched him and said nothing.

The old man banged the table. 'I'll have you know I resent this,' he bawled, 'and I resent it hotly! Why, suggesting the

Sanusiya could be involved in a political murder is as ridiculous as accusing the Red Crescent Society or the Rotary Club!'

'We're not accusing anyone,' I said, 'but let's face it, when the Sanusiya was going it was a militant fundamentalist brotherhood, not a benevolent society.'

The old man sat back aghast. 'The Sanusiya was a perfectly respectable organization,' he said, a shaky edge to his voice. 'It never was militant in the way you mean it, anyway, and if there is a sect at all it's all within these walls. I am the Sanusiya and all that remains of it and I can assure you I had nothing to do with Ibram's murder. I wasn't even aware of his existence until yesterday.'

'Yet you keep the memory of the old order alive.'

'If I don't, who will? But a memory is all the Sanusiya is now. If you'd done a soupçon of background reading, you'd know that the Brotherhood was crushed by British forces at Salloum in 1916. That's more than eighty years ago, if you hadn't noticed. Actually, the British massacred hundreds of tribesmen and took others prisoner. My great-great-uncle, As-Said Ahmad, who was then chief of the order, was picked up by his allies, the Turks, in a submarine and shunted off into exile in Istanbul. That, Lieutenant Rashid of the SID, was the end of the Sanusiya – until the dirty British set up my father as King of Libya, when they kicked the Italians out in 1942.'

'Your father was King of Libya!' Daisy said. 'Does that mean you should be running the place today instead of Gaddaffi?'

Sanusi chortled. 'Can you see me ruling Libya, Miss Brooke? Hardly. I never had the inclination to be a British puppet. I was brought up in a palace by private tutors, and never mixed with my peers. I knew I was odd – different from other children, but I didn't care. Over the years I grew so accustomed to my own company that I started to like it. I lived in my own world. I had the best teachers and I studied everything – history, theology, ancient civilizations, ancient religions, the Kabbala, alchemy – every esoteric field came under my scrutiny. I became an expert in Egyptology before I ever set foot in Egypt. Our exile from

Libya in 1969 put a stop to my private studies, of course, but I found I was well enough qualified to earn a living as an Egyptologist.'

'But you're still a Muslim?'

'Despite what you Americans may believe, madam, the word Muslim is not a synonym for terrorist. Yes, I have remained a Muslim out of deference to my forebears, but if you're looking for an extremist you've picked the wrong fellow. Islam means ''submission'', Miss Brooke, and it is a peaceful, compassionate religion, perverted by extremists into a militant political ideology. Perverted, I say! The Great Sanusi himself was never a fanatic. He believed in individual responsibility rather than blind obedience. That's why he fell foul of the Islamic authorities of his day.'

'OK,' I said, 'but the fact remains that the amulet was found at the scene of Ibram's murder, and an eye-witness claims that one of Ibram's murderers was actually wearing it. How are we to explain that?'

Sanusi shook his head and eyed us distastefully. 'I'd have thought, Mister Detective, that there would be one obvious explanation,' he said.

'Oh, what's that?'

'That the man – the creature – who called himself Sayf ad-Din was involved in the ... er ... incident. If you could find him, you would learn a great deal, perhaps.'

He stared at us both defiantly, and at that moment the door opened, and a thin woman shuffled in carrying three glasses of mint tea on a brass tray. The woman walked haltingly as if she had some sort of wasting disease and the tray shook so much in her hands that the tea spilled. She put down the glasses roughly on the low tables on silver saucers, and more tea slopped over. Instead of going out she turned to Sanusi. 'Where's my money?' she demanded in a whining voice. 'Where is it? Now you've got your important friends here you don't care about my money. You've cheated me out of my inheritance, and now you keep me like a prisoner. I want my money back!'

Sanusi flinched and stared at her. 'Not now, Salma,' he said, his voice pleading, 'I've got company. I promise you I'll deal with it as soon as they've gone.'

The woman whimpered like a lost child, but she didn't move. Then, without warning there came an abrupt transformation. She stopped crying, stood up straight and fixed Sanusi with a glare of murderous hatred. 'Bastard!' she said, in a voice so deep that I jumped. It was as if someone else was speaking out of her mouth – as if the frail woman had been replaced by an altogether more vicious entity. She turned and stared at me and I was shocked to see that her face had become a mask of loathing, her eyes burning, her nose hooked down over bared, toothless gums. 'He sits here telling you his lies,' the masculine voice spat, 'and you drink them all in. All the shit. He had me when I was a girl. I was pretty then and he took me as his fancy bit. It was all sweet words then, but now he treats me like a slave!' She turned back to Sanusi and he sank deeper into the cushions, trying to turn his face away. 'You are a damned liar and you'll come to a bad end,' she said. 'Oh mark my words! Death is too good for those who traffic with Satan!'

Sanusi caught his breath and went pale. He sat stock-still, and for an instant I thought I saw a flicker of real fear pass over his features. 'Salma!' he said. 'Remember where you are!'

At the sound of his voice Salma seemed to collapse. Her hands started trembling again and she dropped her gaze to the floor. 'Go!' Sanusi said. '*Itfaddali!* If you please!'

Salma sidled out and Sanusi beamed at us nervously, and pointed a finger at his head. 'Poor Salma,' he said, 'classic schizophrenia. Should be in an asylum. I took her in off the streets thirty years ago. She's got it into her head that she's the child of rich landowners and I've fiddled her out of everything. The truth is she was an orphan street-child with nothing at all.' He sighed and gestured towards the tea. 'Taste it,' he said. I took the glass and sipped the tea while he watched my face with apparent concern. 'Is it up to desert standards?' he asked.

I frowned at him. For a moment I wondered idly what he

would do if I dashed the stuff in his face. I crushed the impulse, and drank more tea. It was a trifle sweet but otherwise perfect. 'Excellent!' I said.

The old man smiled with satisfaction. 'As I suspected, an expert,' he said. He picked up his own tea from the table, and Daisy did the same.

We drank in silence. When Daisy was finished she put her glass down reluctantly as if something was troubling her. 'Doctor Sanusi,' she said, 'what does the word "Firebird" mean to you?'

The old man looked astonished, as though she'd caught him off-guard. I felt like shouting at her that she was sticking her neck out and giving the whole show away, but I remembered her intuition with Fawzi, and kept my mouth shut. Sanusi's pupils dilated and his tic began to pulse rapidly. His hands trembled slightly and there was a sudden and unmistakable pallor to his face.

'I don't know what on earth you're talking about,' he stammered, 'or what you're suggesting! Get out! Get out this minute, or I'll have you thrown out!'

'Steady on, Doctor Sanusi,' I said. 'The Firebird was the Bennu Bird of ancient Egyptian mythology. It was supposed to be the soul of Ra, the sun-god, and it was there at the First Time – Zep-Tepi – when the cycle of Time itself was set in motion. Miss Brooke wants to know what else you can tell us. She's just asking you to put on your Egyptology hat.'

The old man took a couple of wheezing breaths and watched us carefully from behind his camouflaging whiskers. 'I never wear hats,' he said acidly, 'only skullcaps and turbans. Hats are considered the work of the Devil by good Muslims. You know, you really do have the effrontery of Iblis! You come here, insult me and my forebears, and now you have the gall to quiz me on ancient Egyptian mythology! Well, for private tutorials I charge fifty pounds an hour.'

'We don't want a seminar,' Daisy said, 'just tell us what you know,'

Sanusi knitted his bushy eyebrows and tugged on his beard.

He sighed and eyed us derisively. 'What has this to do with my amulet?' he demanded again.

'Nothing,' I said, soothingly, cursing Daisy's impetuosity. I knew we'd have to tell him the full works now, or he'd clam up. 'It's just that ''Firebird'' might have been Ibram's last word. It may mean anything or nothing, and it might not even be what he said at all.'

Sanusi's screwed-up features had disbelief written all over them. He seemed calmer now, though, and I guessed he was torn between total denial and the desire to play the great authority. At last he sighed and eased himself to his feet. He put on his glasses and pulled a leather-bound volume from the nearest shelf, flipping through the pages and muttering. 'Here,' he said eventually, 'take a look at this.'

He laid the open book on a table and we crouched around to peer at it. Sanusi pointed a spiky finger at a full-page engraving of a heron with a human eye, perching awkwardly on the very apex of a cone. 'This is the Firebird,' he said, 'also called the Bennu Bird, or Phoenix. The ancient Egyptians often envisaged it as a grey heron, probably because herons were common in the Nile marshes in the summer and migrated somewhere else in winter, but always returned.' He paused suddenly and cocked an ear, listening. A faint scratching noise seemed to be coming from the walls. 'What's that?' he said, almost to himself. I listened. The scratching sound came again.

'Rats,' I said, 'you're bound to get them in old houses.'

He cocked his ear once more. 'No, not rats,' he whispered. He turned on us accusingly, with round eyes. 'Are you sure the *Jinns* never followed you?'

'Yes, I'm sure. But even if they had, how could they get into your walls?'

He ignored me and turned to listen again. The scratching was getting louder, and I had to admit that if it was rats they must have been monsters. Sanusi's eyes were almost popping out of his head. '*Jinns*,' he hissed. 'Every time I have company they come to haunt me. I'm sick, sick, sick of this accursed torment!'

He turned and began banging on the wall with the side of his fist, so hard that the oil-lamp wobbled in its cavity. 'You hear me,' he bawled suddenly, 'get out! Get out I say! I'm sick of your lousy persecution! Get out this minute! I seek refuge in God from the stoned Devil!' He paused, his fist held ready to hammer again, but the scrabbling had ceased. He stood listening for a moment, then, seemingly satisfied, he turned his attention back to us. 'The swine!' he said. 'They always try to make a fool of me. I've exorcized them more times than I can count, but they follow my visitors and when the door opens they take advantage and sneak in. It's not the scratching and scrabbling I mind so much as when they start throwing things about. They even trip me up, can you imagine that? I've been black and blue before now thanks to those accursed creatures.' His eyes suddenly filled with fury again and he glared at the wall shaking his fist. 'Get out and don't come back!' he yelled. 'You hear me!' I suppressed a grin. Since arriving we'd had ghouls, *Jinns*, and ghosts – what Hammoudi would have called 'the full head-banger's repertoire'.

'Now, what were we saying?' Sanusi said, looking round at us.

Daisy shifted nervously and rearranged her hands on her lap. 'Why was the Firebird central to ancient Egyptian cosmology?' she asked.

Sanusi chewed the end of his glasses, put them back on, and cocked his head to one side, as if pondering the question carefully. 'When the Firebird cranked things up on the first morning,' he said, 'the era known as Zep-Tepi – the First Time – started with a bang. That was when gods like Osiris, Isis, Thoth, Horus and Set walked the earth as real beings. Afterwards the bird returned to its home in the Isle of Fire – a place among the stars, where gods were born and regenerated.' He pointed at the engraving again. 'Now, you see this cone thing the Firebird seems to be perched on?' he enquired. 'That's the Benben Stone, which was closely linked with the Bennu Bird – Benben – Bennu – the words come from the same root, meaning ''to procreate''.

The Stone was the most sacred relic in ancient Egyptian mythology – it was thought to have cosmic origins. They said it had fallen out of the sky and thought of it as the Firebird's "Egg". The Benben Stone was the central artifact of the whole ancient Egyptian religion and the cult symbol of the Ra Brotherhood.'

'The what?' Daisy asked.

'The Ra Brotherhood – an order of high priests initiated into all the secrets of their culture. The Brotherhood goes way back, probably under different names, to the First Time, Zep-Tepi – a kind of secret college working behind the pomp and circumstance, giving form and continuity to a culture that remained basically unchanged for thousands of years. The Egyptians believed that their civilization had been created by a small group of gods – the Neteru – who arrived on earth in the distant past, and whose age culminated in the rule of Horus. This era was succeeded by that of the Sages, the so-called Shemsu-Hor, or Horus-Followers, half-divine beings who transmitted the secrets of the gods across time to the fully human pharaohs. The Shemsu-Hor were probably the original Ra Brotherhood, who initiated the first historical pharaoh, known to us as Menes, Narmer or "King Scorpion". Thereafter it was the Brotherhood who kept the whole thing on the rails. They were the most powerful men in Egypt, and they were the guardians of the Benben Stone, which was originally kept on top of an obelisk in the Temple of the Firebird at Heliopolis – a temple that no longer exists.'

'I'd love to take a look at the Stone,' Daisy said. 'Where is it now?'

Sanusi beamed at her coldly. 'I wish I knew, Miss Brooke,' he said. 'It went missing about 2000 BC. No one has seen it for at least four thousand years.'

12

When Sanusi escorted us to the yard door it was already night. Someone – probably the maid – had hung another oil-lamp in the musty corridor, and our shadows were pallid ghosts lurching along its walls. We shook hands at the street door. 'What about the amulet?' Sanusi said. 'It is a valued part of my psychic defences and I should like it back.'

'Right now it's police evidence,' I said.

'But what will you do with it?'

'We still haven't explained how one of Ibram's killers came to be wearing it,' I said. 'With all due respect Doctor Sanusi, I've got to check your story out. It's a sensitive case, and I have to make sure you're really what you seem.'

It was provocative, I knew, and I didn't have to wait long for a reaction. His eyes turned to ice and tiny pink circles appeared in the centre of both pallid cheeks. He snatched off his glasses and I saw that his tic had gone berserk. His hands shook slightly. 'Nothing is ever quite what it seems,' he said. He drew in a deep breath, trying to hold himself in check. 'The world is full of shapeshifters. Ghouls disguised as men, men disguised as women, people who appear to be something but are really something else. Take you, Lieutenant Rashid, what are you really? A police officer? And who is she?' He pointed his talon finger suddenly at Daisy. 'A faceless woman! A lurker in the shadows!'

A shiver ran down my spine suddenly and I broke out into a sweat. I wished I'd kept my mouth shut. The old man turned his hawk-like gaze back to me.

'I've met plenty of policemen in my time,' he said, 'but I've never heard of a Hawazim detective. The Hawazim have too long a history of persecution by governments for that.'

'I never said I was Hawazim.'

He snorted and put his glasses back on. 'No, you didn't,' he said, 'but the upper right fold of your ear tells a different story. It's pierced, and the Hawazim are the only tribe I know of who have their ears pierced in that place. Now, didn't the Hawazim have a lot of trouble with the police a few years back? I heard police troopers were killed. Curious that they should accept a member of a subversive group in the SID.'

So that was what the veiled comments were about, I thought. All that talk of appearances and underlying form, the rubbish about removing my shoes, which was a Bedouin custom, and his comment about the tea being up to 'desert standards'. I should have been on my guard. I fixed the old man with my most intimidating stare, suddenly aware that Daisy's eyes were glued to my face. 'I don't know anything about the Hawazim,' I said, 'I grew up as a street-kid in Aswan. The gang I ran with all had their ears pierced there.'

'Ah,' Sanusi said, 'is that so? Then what's that lump under your jacket on your left arm? Eh? You are wearing a blade. I never knew a policeman to wear a knife, but I do know the customs of the desert Bedouin well, Lieutenant. Many of my ancestors were Bedouin. Now, the only tribe I know who wear blades on their left arms are the Hawazim. A coincidence, perhaps? Your street-gang happened to have had that little quirk too!'

Daisy was laughing to herself quietly when Sanusi closed the door behind us, and I wondered if the old man had blown it. 'What was all that stuff about Bedouin tribes?' she asked me.

'Guy's as nutty as a fruitcake,' I said.

'Maybe, but did you see the way he jumped when I mentioned Firebird – nearly had kittens. Then he realized it was a question about Egyptology and calmed down. The guy is scared.'

'Yeah, scared of ghouls and *Jinns*.'

'Didn't Abd al-Ali say that Ibram had asked the doorman at the Mena about ghouls? Fawzi mentioned it too.'

'Look, I know all about that stuff. It's peasant superstition. Sanusi lives in cyberspace – he probably just imagined it.'

'That why you went so quiet when he was talking about it?'

'I've had to live with this kind of trash since I was a kid, that's all. Ghouls, ghosts and things that go bump, and all that bullshit about knowing who you are. I know who he is, he's a bloody sicko.'

'Yeah, but those were pretty damn big rats we heard. Or was that a figment of the imagination too?'

In darkness the Khan felt humid and oppressive. Heat radiated from the ground and the stonework, unleashing smells of stale urine and uncured hide. We walked in silence along an endless series of dark tunnels where sandpaper voices followed us, mingled with demonic laughter, and mysterious, disjointed groans. Shadows drifted past in long caravans like chains of slaves. Lights flickered momentarily from high windows, and the yellow eyes of cats seemed to glare malevolently from every cranny. 'I hope you know your way out of this place,' Daisy whispered.

'Why the hell are you whispering?' I said.

'I don't know. It just feels like I should.'

At the corner of an alley a crabbed old man with a face like Mr Punch was cooking sweet potatoes on a contraption that looked like a miniature locomotive mounted on a barrow. An oil-lamp hanging from the barrow cast a radius of yellow light, like an island in the darkness. 'Watch out!' the man told us as we passed, 'there's a ghoul about. Killed a boy near here only a couple of weeks ago.'

We left him cackling in his little circlet of light. 'How come you didn't know about that?' Daisy asked. 'OK, it's got to be a serial killer, but isn't that scary enough?'

'Not when you're packing a .380 Beretta and you're a crack shot,' I said, 'or when you're with a Special Agent who passed top of her class at Quantico which was ninety per cent men. Why should Egypt fear?'

'Leave it out,' she said, but I noticed she was giggling now.

'As it happens I did know about the kid's death,' I told her. 'I didn't want to contradict Sanusi at the time, but I read the autopsy report. The boy died of some rare blood disease, and the scratch marks on his body were probably caused by street-dogs, cats and rats, that chewed the stiff before it was found.'

Daisy shivered, and I hoped she was satisfied, even if I wasn't. What I didn't tell her was that I knew every inch of this bazaar from the hundreds of hours I'd put in over the past four years, trying to track down a monster that left its victims mutilated and drained of blood.

We passed through an arch that looked like the open jaws of an enormous lion, and beyond it we found ourselves in tomb-like silence. Beams from high latticework windows fell across our path in dapples and brindles. We passed under another series of moresco arches that faced each other at such regular intervals that you felt like you were walking inside the rib-cage of a giant beast. Occasionally we caught glimpses of side-alleys illuminated for a moment in ghastly fluorescence. In one of them a hooded figure sat motionless on a chair, apparently staring at some grotesque stains on the wall as if trying to read them. In another I glimpsed two nun-like women gliding away from us, carrying in their arms dead chickens whose limp, severed throats dripped blood. Human shadows passed briefly behind shutters like cinema screens, and disjointed human eyes seemed to leer at us from high niches in the walls. In one place a giant fan set into the wall creaked disturbingly as it revolved, and in another I made out a set of life-size murals – rat-headed Set, hawk-headed Horus, jackal-headed Anubis – the Guardian of the Underworld.

We walked in silence for what seemed like hours, then Daisy whispered, 'You sure this is the right way?'

'You're whispering again,' I said.

'Yeah, so what?' She stopped suddenly. 'What's that?' she hissed. A cat yowled. Flying shapes flitted past, and I felt the waft of their wings against my face.

'Bats!' I said, now whispering myself.

'It's not that,' she said, 'someone's following us. I swear it. Someone who's stopping every time we stop.'

I heard nothing, but I looked around. The street was a tunnel of blacks and greys, with the occasional spangle of illumination, and I had a sense of sheer ebony walls reaching up on either side like enormous cliffs, and of some malign presence crouching there in the darkness. We inched forward, and now I could hear it too. Soft footfalls behind us, keeping pace.

I jerked on Daisy's arm and we both stopped abruptly. The footsteps halted. I turned and looked behind again, and my scalp prickled. I had a momentary sensation that we were being followed by some huge, dark, spidery creature whose giant body reached up into the night.

At night he roams the alleys, looking for helpless men and women to prey upon.

Then the sensation passed, and I caught a fleeting glimpse of a figure dodging into a doorway. We started up, and I listened intently. There was the soft pad of feet again. I felt for the pencil torch I kept in my pocket, whipped it out and spun round, screaming, 'Stop! Police!' as loudly as I could. For an instant the feeble beam pinpointed the head and torso of a Bedouin woman – an exceptionally tall Bedouin woman – in dark robes and a vampire-like mask.

He could be the man standing next to you in the bazaar, the man – even the woman – walking behind you on the street.

The woman stood petrified in the light for a moment before she turned and bolted into the shadows, her rubber sandals making an eerie slop-slop sound as she ran. I exploded forward gripping the flashlight in my hand. She was surprisingly fast, but there were no convenient side-turns. She made for a covered entrance way, tried the door without success, then turned to face me snarling. I closed in recklessly, going for my Beretta. Before my hand connected with the handle, though, something that felt like a battering ram crashed into my jaw, and I staggered, seeing a host of red planets whizzing round inside my skull. I struggled to stay on my feet, putting up a hand to defend myself, when another battering ram – even harder than the first – slammed into me just below the ear. A comet with a fiery tail blitzed across my vision and I felt myself falling down a deep ravine into gentle dark waters that closed above me like curtains.

When I opened my eyes it wasn't night any more, and although I was still in a dimly lit alley it wasn't the same one, in fact it wasn't even in Khan al-Khalili. It was the Aswan bazaar, and I was a ten-year-old kid dressed in a torn T-shirt, hand-me-down jeans and flip-flops, slapping a baseball bat nervously against my palm, and pressing myself into the shadow of an archway. Across the alley, Furayj and Mikhael were almost invisible in the shadows – all I could see of them were the whites of their eyes, almost popping with tension. There was an old man shambling towards us, and though he was dressed like a townsman you could tell a mile off he was Hawazim. They sometimes came into the souk, exchanging their russet-coloured *jibbas* for long *gallabiyyas*, but they couldn't disguise their walk – that springy cameline gait, full of vitality – or those drill-bit eyes that seemed to look right through you. I didn't want to rob a Hazmi. I knew they were poor and they were supposed to be good fighters. But Furayj and Mikhael were watching me, and I knew I would be the butt of jokes for ever if I didn't have a go.

The old man was almost up to us now, and giving no sign that he'd spotted anything. Then suddenly he halted in his tracks – just stood stock-still. I saw his lean face come up, sniffing the air like a hunting dog, and in that moment I noticed that he was wearing a tiny silver earring on the upper lobe of his right ear. I stepped out in front of him with the baseball bat raised, then

I froze. The old man's eyes seemed to burn into me like lasers, and I suddenly recalled that I'd seen him before. It was the strangest sensation I'd ever had – a feeling that I really *knew* this guy, that I'd been here before many times, standing in front of him like this. It was more than the ordinary sensation that you've seen or done something before – more like an absolute blinding certainty that this had all been meant to happen – that the old Hazmi had actually come here *looking* for me.

The next instant Furayj and Mikhael came hollering out of their corner with big butcher's knives, and suddenly a stiletto appeared like magic in the old guy's hand. He seemed to erupt into a blur of movement you'd have thought impossible for such an old fellow. The stiletto flashed – only twice or three times – and I saw blood splash across the ground. There were sickening screams from Mikhael and Furayj, and I saw their knives drop into the dust as they fled down the alley, holding their arms, crying like babies and dropping big spatters of blood behind them. The old Hazmi turned slowly back to me, his eyes blazing, gripping his little stiletto and I started to shake uncontrollably, my eyes rolling, my breath coming in great gasps. It wasn't because I was afraid, but because I suddenly remembered where I'd seen him before. Ever since I could remember I'd been dreaming about him – always the same dream of myself standing in a featureless desert with the wind spinning ghost-devils along the emptiness. In the dream I'd see a figure riding towards me on a camel – just a black exclamation mark at first, with shimmers of light playing around it – but becoming more and more distinct as it drew near, until at last it stopped, and I saw this dark figure slip out of the saddle. Then the dark figure would pull the *shamagh* off his face, and it would be this old guy.

He smiled sadly, shaking his head. 'So I found you at last,' he said, 'the boy with green eyes. I've seen you in the Shining.'

'I know you, too,' I said.

The old man slid his stiletto into a sheath hidden under the sleeve of his *jibba*. He looked at me again. 'The city is poison to the soul,' he said. 'Where are your mother and father?'

'I have no mother and father.'

'Then come with me. The tribe will be your mother and father. You belong with us. We need you.'

I just dropped the baseball bat in the dust and burst into tears. It was that word 'need' that did it, I think. He put a hand on my shoulder and we never stopped walking till we came to the tumble-down archway at the exit of the bazaar. For me it had been a doorway into another life.

When I opened my eyes again, Daisy was slapping my face with her open hand.

'Ouch!' I said. 'That hurts!'

My ears were ringing like dinner-gongs, and my jaw felt like I'd just swallowed a full-sized football. 'Jesus Christ!' Daisy said. 'Who *was* that bitch?'

'I don't know,' I said, 'but whoever she was, she packs a punch like a fucking steam-hammer!'

13

WHEN DAISY DROPPED ME ON Roda Island, I told her I was
going home, but I didn't. I picked up a taxi, and had it
take me to the Scorpion Club on the Gezira, where I knew
Hammoudi would be waiting. We'd agreed secretly that I'd make
a nightly report to him, and if I didn't show he'd know something
was wrong. The place didn't look much from the outside – a
steel door at the bottom of a flight of steps on a street of half-
derelict houses and crumbling masonry. The entrance was
watched by a Turkish strong-man, an ex-pro wrestler called
Bakhit, who weighed about two-twenty and had a scar running
the entire length of his face from hairline to jaw, passing right
through the centre of the left eye, which was totally blank.
Another one-eyed man to add to Sanusi's list. When I entered
he turned his good eye on my swollen jaw, and appraised the
bruise professionally. He didn't make any comment, though,
and he didn't bother patting me down for hardware. He knew
Hammoudi and me. The Scorpion was still a hangout for pimps,
pushers, local gangsters and creeps of all kinds, but once it had
been much worse. When I first arrived in Cairo it had been a
meeting place of the Shadowmen – the mob who'd run the local
hard drugs scene, and who'd had several key politicians in their
pockets. It was Hammoudi who had busted them, with a little
help from me, of course. We'd tracked some of the capos back

to their derelict hideout in New Cairo – the Gallery it was called – and then moved in with the Special Ops Squad. Problem was, someone in the know had snitched and the Shadowmen were ready for us. That was the day I'd copped a 7.62 short kalashnikov slug in the ribs – a shot that had been intended for Hammoudi. He never talked about it much, but I could tell from the way he treated me that he'd never forgotten. Anyway most of the Shadowmen bosses were either inside or feeding the Nile perch now, but we'd never pinned anything on the politicians or found the snitch. The Scorpion itself was under new management, but stabbings and fistfights still occurred there almost on a nightly basis. Bakhit's scar was the result of one such brawl, and he would have been pushing daisies by now if Hammoudi and I hadn't been there to cover his back. That's why Bakhit never minded having us around. It helped to know a couple of SID officers were there packing in case of real trouble, but otherwise keeping their noses out. Hammoudi always said he felt right at home here.

Actually, the place was the cellar of a demolished warehouse and it was big – all alcoves and vaulted ceiling arches, lit with violet strips and little table lights done like miniature versions of Aladdin's magic lamp. There was a bar running half the length of one wall – a glitter of bottles and stainless steel, and barmen whose faces and hands were shadows, and whose white shirts stood out so stiffly in the ultra-violet it looked like you were being served by an animated shirt. Pipe music uncoiled sensuously out of concealed speakers and the atmosphere was thick with cigarette smoke and the fumes of apple tobacco, hemp, and smouldering incense. There was a carnival feel to the place. It was a hubbub of voices, groups of men and women in cameo, a shock of faces distorted in the flickering light – women with the black eyes and snouts of wolves, women like Pekineses, and men with bloated cheeks and upturned nostrils like pigs. Or maybe the fact that my jaw was killing me just made it seem like that. In one corner a small crowd was gathered round a snake-charmer, a shaven-headed guy in a multi-coloured dervish-cloak, who was swaying drunkenly to the music, holding a hooded cobra in his hands. Even from where I stood I could see the snake's forked tongue flicking out angrily, and as a rose-coloured spotlight turned on him, I saw the guy stick the head of the thing right into his mouth.

There was an 'ooh-aah' from the audience. I shuddered and turned away, finding Hammoudi where Bakhit had said he'd be – sitting at a table in one of the secluded alcoves, drinking araq with a girl about thirty years younger than him, holding her hand across the table. My first impression of the girl was that she was overdressed. She was nut-brown in the light of the table-lamp with heavy, gypsy-like features and rich black hair that cascaded down her shoulders, almost to her midriff. She wore a loose-fitting robe of some velvety stuff that fell all the way to the floor, and her neck, wrists, fingers and ears were weighted down with jewellery that wouldn't have disgraced Sanusi's museum. She stood up as I arrived and extended a smooth hand. She smelt of sandalwood and strong musk. 'Your Presence,' she said, bowing slightly, before hurrying off into the shadows.

I gazed after her admiringly. 'Sorry to break up the party,' I said, sitting down opposite Hammoudi. The girl's musk lingered.

'That's Nadia,' Hammoudi said, lighting a cigarette, 'she's an *'Alima.*'

'Ah,' I said. Now I understood the robe, the overdone make-up and the heavy jewellery – an *'Alima* was a professional singer, one of a caste who could trace their ancestry back to the legend-ary Baramikah – the entertainers of the Caliph Hiroun ar-Rashid of *The Thousand and One Nights.*

'Is she any good?' I enquired.

Hammoudi winked. 'She's on later,' he said, 'wait and see.' He pushed a clean glass in my direction and poured half a measure of araq then topped it up with water from an earthenware jug. I watched the stuff turn cloudy. 'Drink!' he told me.

I toyed with the glass, smelling the aniseed. 'I shouldn't drink this stuff,' I said, 'does funny things to me.'

Hammoudi topped up his own glass and held it out in a toast. 'Your health!' he said. I touched glasses, downing the slug in one go, hoping that at least it would stop the throbbing in my jaw. I stroked the bruise gingerly, and Hammoudi noticed it for the first time. 'Jesus and Mary!' he said. 'You and Miss Special-Agent-of-the-Year already had a bust-up or what?'

'Nah,' I said, glancing round at the tables and alcoves, islets of light, the hunched cameo figures wreathed in smoke and raucous laughter. The snake-eater had almost finished the *entrées*, I noticed – the cobra's tail was now hanging disgustingly from his mouth, flipping ineffectually. 'I had a fight with a Bedouin woman in the bazaar,' I said. 'Actually it was more like a mass-acre. She got away.' Hammoudi looked at me, amused. He stubbed out his cigarette and sipped more araq, narrowing his eyes reverently as if it were fine wine. At the far side of the room lights had come up on a small platform, and a traditional orchestra of musicians in striped *gallabiyyas* and loose white turbans were setting up instruments – lutes, tablas, flutes and viols, and a zither-like stringed instrument called a *qanun*.

'You must be losing your touch,' Hammoudi said. 'Yesterday you get disarmed by Miss Butter-Wouldn't-Melt, and today you get nailed by some granny in the souk. Who the hell was *she*?'

He poured more araq into my glass and topped it up. Warmth was already spreading through my body from the first one, and the ache in my jaw had diminished. I sipped the araq and attempted a lopsided smile. 'Had to be a tail,' I said.

'Who?' Hammoudi asked. 'CIA? Militants? FBI watchers looking out for our favourite Special Agent?'

'Could be anybody. Bloody woman had a punch like steel.'

Hammoudi stared at my jaw again and chuckled. The band were sitting down now, tuning up their instruments and an expectant hum had fallen over the audience. I drained my araq and felt my jaw again. It was numb – the ache had magically disappeared. Hammoudi filled both our glasses and ordered another third of a litre from a passing waiter. 'Drink!' he said. 'You'll feel better.'

'I shouldn't,' I said, picking up my glass.

'So you and Daisy got on all right?' Hammoudi asked.

'She's got the speed of a snake, never saw anyone so sharp. And she doesn't miss a thing even if she doesn't let on.'

'She missed the Sanusi amulet.'

That was a point I hadn't thought about.

'What about Sanusi?' Hammoudi asked.

'Scared of something, but I don't know what. He almost had a fit when Daisy mentioned Firebird.'

'Ah, Ibram's famous last word. Like I said, nothing came up on that or the name Monod, but I've already briefed Halaby. Said he'd look into Sanusi and Monod pronto and meet you here tomorrow night.'

'Good. If anyone can dig up the dirt it's Halaby. Anyway, Sanusi confirmed that the Sanusiya's been out of the picture since 1916 when the British kicked their arses with machine-guns at Salloum. He got real shirty when we suggested the Brotherhood might have been reactivated.'

'What about the amulet?'

'Reckons a guy called Sayf ad-Din took it. Guy who turned up disguised as an Arab and said he was working for a thing called the "World Council of Islam".'

'Never heard of it.'

'Neither had Sanusi. Reckoned it was all bogus. In fact, he claimed this Sayf ad-Din was a ghoul. Funny. Fawzi talked about a ghoul too, and apparently Ibram asked the doorman at the Mena whether he believed in them.'

Hammoudi smirked grimly. 'You know I never believed in hocus-pocus,' he said, 'but I just had a feeling about this case. Somehow I felt it might open up the whole can of worms.'

'It's a tentative connection, Boutros. Sanusi's wacky enough to have imagined it.'

'Maybe, but you know as well as I do there's something nasty on the loose in the Khan, whether it's a ghoul or whatever you want to call it.'

He was right about that. I'd damn near caught up with it two weeks ago, the night it got the tailor's boy. Could it be coincidence that Fawzi, Ibram and Sanusi had all mentioned the ghoul? Hammoudi's intuition about the case must have been more powerful than I thought.

'I tell you Boutros, I saw it that night – something that looked like a human spider – a sort of insect head and legs that were jointed the opposite way from ours. It was just a fleeting glimpse in the shadows, but a few minutes later I found the boy. Sanusi was all boned up on it, and Daisy caught on. I had to tell her the boy died of a rare blood disease.'

The Colonel loosened his massive shoulders uncomfortably and brooded for a moment. I swallowed araq. 'By the way,' I said, changing the subject, 'you get the ballistics report on Ibram's death?'

Hammoudi looked relieved. He was on safer ground talking about bullets and trajectories. 'Yeah,' he said, 'FBI lab confirms the shells were 7.62mm short – those are standard Russian military issue. Also confirmed the weapons used were Klobbs – a handheld machine-pistol, normally issued to Russian Special Forces. The *coup de grâce* came from a different weapon, though – a Browning 9mm pistol.'

'Not much there we didn't know.'

He grunted in agreement and flicked a cigarette from a flat packet. He placed it cockily in his mouth, brought up his lighter, then halted in the act of lighting it. On stage, the musicians were sitting down on stools and lifting up their instruments. 'Any minute now she'll be on,' he said.

'Known her long?' I enquired.

He pretended to look hurt. 'It's not that way at all, I'm like a father to her.'

The waiter brought the third of araq and another jug of water. I poured myself half a glass and topped it up. Like a father. *Bukra fil mishmish*, I thought.

'There's something wrong about that shooting,' Hammoudi said, lighting his cigarette at last. 'This *coup de grâce* business. That's not Militants. It's a kind of ritual thing – the Sicilian

Mafia does it, but it's never been a Militant trait. And those Klobb machine-pistols. They're special weapons – I mean you could buy them easily enough on the black market, I suppose, but they're not the kind of thing any idiot could use. Not like the trusty old AK-47 that's completely grunt-proof – just point it in the right direction and squeeze. No, the Klobb's a pro's weapon. And think of the coolness of the op. Broad daylight. In front of spectators. These guys were professional hit-men, not politicals. Either ex-military or a Mafia hit-team, I'd put money on it.'

I drank again, probing my jaw. Hammoudi sipped araq and glanced expectantly at the stage. The musicians were waiting in silence. Nadia walked gracefully up to the microphone, her heavy robes swinging, jewellery catching the light. She tossed her luxurious hair, and addressed the audience in a clear, musical voice that held just enough shyness to make it incredibly inviting. I was feeling more relaxed and comfortable now. Too comfortable. The knots of people around us no longer looked like wolves, dogs and pigs, but like hyenas and full-blown vampires. The floor seemed to be rippling slightly, like liquid, and I had the distinct impression I saw one of the snake-charmer's cobras wriggling under a table. Hammoudi was watching the stage. The spotlights were on Nadia, transfixing her in a rainbow of colour. 'By the way,' he added in a faraway voice, 'that talk about ghouls reminded me. I've got some new information.'

'Oh,' I said. 'What?'

But it was too late. Nadia had picked up the microphone and the audience had gone quiet. I turned to look. Suddenly the music started, went straight into a rocking beat without any build-up, a snapping rhythm of tablas and castanets that had your feet tapping wildly and made you want to rock to and fro. The strings led the music on subtly, building up inside the clashing beat in an intricate, spiralling pattern that stirred visions of rivers flowing, sands blowing, and gave you the feeling there was something here as ancient as the hills. Then Nadia's voice came in, quavering in high contralto, as clear as running water yet not overpowering or dripping false emotion like the classical singers. The voice was laid back, a virgin's voice, not dominating but complementing the music, as if holding a dialogue with the instruments. Nadia sang as if in a trance, swaying only slightly to the beat, then turned abruptly away from the microphone to let the music take over, with a new crash of percussion and swirl of pipes. The rhythm built up and up and the audience began to clap in time.

Hammoudi watched with sparkling eyes. When Nadia turned back a moment later, I saw she'd picked up a tambourine, and now she stood with her feet apart, shoulders angled passionately as she slapped the skin on her instrument, and began to sing. This time the voice was more forceful and energetic, as if Nadia had suddenly lost that shy, virginal character of the first round. The music became faster and faster, the musicians leaning into their instruments, lost to the world, their hands working in a blur of movement. Nadia began to sway more rapidly, as perspiration tracked down her make-up, and her movements became increasingly sensuous as she rotated her full hips and thrust out her breasts under the velvety robe. She paused again from singing, and now the music had gone wild. She danced about the stage with her head up, stretching her neck as if oblivious to anything but the beat. She caught the last bars of a phrase and joined in again, her body moving frenetically, the contralto voice lilting up and up, until it reached a soaring climax. She turned her back on the audience again, and the viols and *qanun* assumed the part of the human voice, running down slowly, as the instruments seemed to explore variations of the melody. The music grew quieter by degrees until it faded out. Then Nadia turned shyly again and bowed to frenzied applause.

Hammoudi slapped his great palms together deafeningly. 'Well?' he said.

The music had done something to me. Or maybe it was too much araq. I had sunk an inch into my chair and the top of my head felt like it was coming loose.

'That's what I *call* an *'Alima*!' I said. My voice came out slightly slurred, I noticed. 'A perfect performance!'

Hammoudi beamed proudly and poured us both another araq.

'Hey,' I protested, 'that's enough. Any more and I'll have to be carried out.' But Hammoudi wasn't paying attention. He was watching Nadia taking her leave, saying she'd be back later.

He lit another cigarette. 'Knew her mother,' he said, 'beautiful girl, like her. Used to be an '*Alima* too. Father was a real lowlife, though. Small-time heel grifter like Fawzi. Only the guy got himself mixed up with the Shadowmen pushing heroin. Started packing a Colt .45 and thought he'd hit the big time.'

'What happened?' I asked. 'You run him in?'

'No, I shot him. Right here in the club.'

'Shit. And she still holds your hand!'

'Why not? The guy spent most of his time beating up on her. After he'd driven the mother to suicide, that was. Did her the biggest favour of her life when I shot him.'

I looked around, catching a glimpse of a wriggling shadow on the floor, sneaking under one of the tables. 'Hey!' I said. 'You see that?'

'What?'

'There's a cobra on the loose!'

Hammoudi grinned. 'You're right,' he said, 'you've had enough.'

'Yea,' I said. 'Now, what was it you were going to tell me?'

Hammoudi scratched his chin. A new performer had started up in a corner – a magician with a strange conical hat like a Tibetan monk. He was choosing volunteers from the crowd and pouring something into their hands – some kind of divination, I supposed. 'Oh yeah,' Hammoudi said, 'Records came up with a name. Professor Milisch Andropov. Ever heard of him?'

'No.'

'He's a specialist in Earth Sciences – Ibram's field. Right now he's a professor at 'Ain Shams University, but he worked with Ibram for a long while in the States. They were real pals at one time, but ended up having a set-to and weren't on speaking terms any more. Now Andropov happens to have been on the Millennium Committee too.'

'He isn't any more?'

'You guessed it. This morning – a day after Ibram gets whacked out – Andropov resigns from the committee. He then applies to his university for a six-month sabbatical and skips town.'

I tried to sit up. The floor was spinning, and there was more than one cobra wriggling under the tables. I lurched slightly and gripped the edge of my chair to steady myself. 'Where'd he go?' I asked slowly, making a great effort to enunciate the words.

'Now that's the most interesting bit. His faculty says he's at St Samuel's Monastery in the Fayoum having a "retreat".'

I looked at him in dumb surprise. St Samuel's was where the first reports of the ghoul had come from – the reports that had set my people on its track in the first place.

'They tell me he's been going to the place for twenty-odd years. I phoned the monastery up, and they didn't want to tell me at first, but I laid down the law, and in the end they admitted he was there. I think you should make St Samuel's a priority, Sammy.'

'Yes, I will. Sure. But Boutros – Fayoum's a whole day's drive from here.'

Hammoudi had suddenly undergone fission – there were two Hammoudi clones now, both of them smiling crookedly. 'The FBI's got a chopper available,' he said.

'Nah – the bloody Yanks wouldn't give us priority!'

'Try sweet-talking Miss Daisy Brooke.'

14

I STILL HAD THE HANGOVER when the unmarked FBI Jetstream swooped in over St Samuel's Monastery near the Fayoum. From a thousand feet it looked like a wedge of interlocking boxes set in a tiny patch of green that was almost lost amid scarps of salmon-coloured rock and sheets of amber sand. The pilot – a grizzled US veteran with about five gold bars on his shoulder-straps – put us down with perfect precision on a landing-strip between shelter-belts of pencil cedars, eucalyptus and mesquite. We waited till the rotors stopped whizzing, then jumped out to meet a heavy-set monk, who was waiting for us beside a limousine. 'Brother Paul,' he said, bowing slightly. His beard was like a dark fan round his face, and he wore silver glasses and a black pillbox hat that went with his black soutane. He shook hands coldly. 'This is most irregular,' he told me, 'the retreat is sacrosanct. The Patriarch is very disturbed about it.'

'Sorry,' I said, 'but this is a murder enquiry.' My head was hurting and my stomach felt queasy after the helicopter ride. I was in no mood for niceties.

'Couldn't it have waited?' he demanded.

'Ask the murderers.'

He shrugged, ushered us into the car and sat next to the driver in the front. We rattled through acres of olive and almond-groves, through palmeries and vineyards that looked greener-than-green against the desert's pastel hues. 'Must be a lot more water here than there seems,' I commented.

'Water's a problem,' the monk said without turning round. 'It's also a priority. We have some of the best engineers and environmentalists to help us. We have deep-bores, but some of them are brackish – in this season we rely on our irrigation tanks. Professor Andropov is a dry-land specialist and he has been most valuable to us.'

Now I understood. Andropov was more than just a guest – he was a benefactor of the monastery. That was why they were so cut up about our disturbing him.

I looked out of the window and suddenly noticed a string of Bedouin riding fast on lean camels along the roadside. They wore ragged *jibbas* and layered headcloths the same hue as the desert itself, their features knapped down by generations of thirst and desert winds into their irreducible core. They looked as if they lived in another dimension, and to prove it they ignored us disdainfully as we roared by. It gave me a sudden surge of nostalgia to see them so unexpectedly.

'Who are those guys?' Daisy asked, staring back after them as they faded into the distance. I could have told her, but I left it to our host.

'They are Bedouin of the Harab tribe,' he said, 'people of the desert fringes. They have served the monastery for generations. Without them we could not have survived.' I was going to add that they had probably plundered the place periodically too – for Bedouin serve no one but their tribe – but I was distracted by the appearance of the monastery itself, looming suddenly up out of the trees. It was a huge rambling mass of high walls that had the same look as the tribesmen we'd just seen – honed down by the erosion of sand and wind over centuries into a form that had somehow established a kind of truce with the environment. The stone blocks were sun-scorched and blackened, and the walls were riddled with eye-slits and openings and strange little over-hanging trapdoors. The car passed through a long arch and up a tree-lined avenue that spoke almost audibly of water-richness, towards the newly whitewashed edifice of a church with twin towers. To the left was an ancient block building with external pillars and raised verandahs, which the monk told us doubled as the infirmary and museum. 'Our monastery has an interesting history,' he said. 'Please take a glance in the museum before you leave.' There was a tiny graveyard outside the building, I noticed, and an old man in a torn *jibba* and turban was working on the plot with a hoe.

'Stop!' I said suddenly. 'I'll take a look right now.'

The driver stopped the car and the monk turned on me with a puzzled frown. 'Didn't you say you were in a hurry?' he demanded.

'Yes, but there's something here I want to see.'

I walked over to the graveyard, and Daisy followed me. The monk sidled up behind us. The old man stopped his work as we approached, leaned on his hoe and felt his back.

'Peace be on you?' I said.

'And on you.'

He watched me in silence as I studied the graves. Most were marked with a cross and seemed to be the graves of Christian lay workers who had served the monastery. One, though, was clearly an Islamic burial, marked with an oval of stones around a mound with headstones at either end. A crude wooden inscription read, 'Mohammad Fustat. 1995.'

'Who's the sheep among the goats?' I asked Brother Paul.

He swallowed. 'An unfortunate affair,' he stuttered, 'I mean . . . he died in the infirmary. Actually he'd lost so much blood . . . an accident in the desert.'

'The boy was killed by a ghoul,' the old man piped up suddenly. 'Everybody knows it. He was looking for a stray calf in the Cave of the Owls. They told him not to go there, and when he didn't come back after two days they went looking. Found him still alive, half torn to shreds – and one of them saw a creature running off in the distance.' He made the sign of protection against evil spirits, and lowered his voice to a whisper.

'They said it was a hairy beast with one leg like a donkey's.'

'That's nonsense,' Paul said, looking daggers at the old man, 'just primitive superstition. He'd had an accident – been bitten by a bull camel – he'd almost bled to death. There was nothing we could do.'

'It was the *Afrangi*,' the old Bedouin blurted out suddenly, 'the *Afrangi* doctored him. You know . . . Androboff – the water-man. He's not a doctor at all.' He made the two-fingered sign for protection against the evil eye, and Brother Paul caught his hand, wrenching it down savagely.

'That's enough!' he bellowed, 'I'll have no paganism in the monastery. You can collect your wages and go back to your hovel!'

The old Bedouin threw down his hoe. 'I'll go!' he said. 'Curse your father, and a curse on all *Afrangis* and Christians!'

Paul went red in the face and took a step towards him, but the old man refused to be intimidated. 'There's evil here in the monastery,' he growled, turning to me, 'the ghoul was in the boy, that's why they wouldn't take him in the Muslim burial place. The ghoul crossed over – and it's still here.' He gave Paul a contemptuous glance and spat suddenly and venomously on the ground in front of him. Then he swirled his headcloth across his face, turned sharply, and was gone.

15

THE CAR HALTED BY ANOTHER arch, and we got out and walked through into a wide cloister – a central square full of oleanders, figs, wild olives and brilliant purple bougainvillea. You could hear the constant trickle of water down tiny feeders and here and there were miniature rainbows where the drops of moisture were momentarily penetrated by the light. Monks walked around the covered paths silently, lost in their own thoughts, and there was an almost palpable sense of contemplation to the place – a feeling that here was an unchanging haven of peace in a malevolent world. Brother Paul strode along in silence for a few moments, no doubt brooding over the little altercation with the old Bedouin. After a while, though, he turned round. 'I'm sorry about that scene,' he said, 'It's just that one gets so tired of local superstition. What with the storms and the drought everyone's been on edge lately.'

'I understand,' I said, 'but is it true that Professor Andropov doctored the boy who died?'

'The Professor has some medical experience, I believe, and if I remember rightly the Patriarch was away when the . . . accident occurred. Perhaps you had better ask him about it yourself.'

We walked a little further, looking around. 'This is the heart of St Samuel's,' Paul said, pointing to two very ancient-looking buildings opening off the cloister. 'Those structures have been here since the beginning. The one on the right is the chapel founded by St Samuel himself. He was a hermit, you know, who lived in a cave in this region, and who was tortured by the Muslims and sold into slavery by the Bedouin. He escaped eventually and made his way back here and built this church with his own hands. It's no longer used, of course. For centuries it has been a mausoleum containing the remains of all the Brothers who have served the monastery. There are thousands of skulls in there – a memento of the continuity of purpose our church possesses. Men who lived from generation to generation dedicated to the same end. Would you like to see them?'

'Maybe another time,' I said. 'What's the other building?'

'That's the library,' the monk said. 'In medieval times it was one of the best in Egypt. Had manuscripts in Coptic, ancient Greek, Latin, Arabic, and Hebrew – even Syriac. European adventurers bought a lot of them, though, in colonial times, when the monks had no choice but to sell. Today it's only a shadow of what it once was.'

I swallowed. There was a message here too – outsiders had continued to sack the place right up till modern times, even if was by filthy lucre rather than the sword.

He led us through a doorway, up a staircase and along a dark stone corridor supported by massive granite buttresses and lined with antique darkwood chairs and plain carpets. We halted before a heavy, studded door with a curved lintel. He knocked reverently.

'What's this?' I enquired.

'The Patriarch's office,' he said, 'Professor Andropov is in there.'

A reedy voice shouted, 'Come!' and we marched in to find ourselves in what was little more than a cell. It was spartan in the extreme, with only a mahogany desk carved in baroque style with angels and cherubs, some straight-backed chairs that looked like they'd been designed for doing penance, and a single beautifully carved crucifix on the wall. The windows were a series of slits, glassed with diamond panels, which allowed light to fall in golden ingots across the bare stone floor. The Patriarch was seated behind the desk, and Andropov sat on a hard chair in front of it as though he was being interviewed for a job. Both of them stood up to greet us. The Patriarch was a small, bent man whose face looked as if it had been scoured by abrasive sands into troughs and channels. He wore a badly stained and patched soutane with a thick leather belt, a velvet pillbox hat and a tiny silver cross around his neck. His beard was thin and moth-eaten, and his eyes beneath his thick-lensed glasses were full of irritation.

Andropov was an interesting-looking figure, I thought – almost oriental. In different clothes he might have been taken for a Mongolian tribesman. But he was dressed mundanely in a loose cream suit, with open-sided shoes, and his silver-coloured hair was pulled back from a skull that was pickled red in colour, and tied in a tight pony-tail against the nape of his neck. His grey goatee beard formed a dense ovoid shape around the lower section of his face, and his eyes were set in high Slavic cheekbones which gave you the impression that his face was frozen in a permanent condescending smile. His hand felt cold, soft and clammy like a mozzarella cheese, and there was an aloofness to his manner that made me feel he regarded us as ants that ought to be squashed. The Patriarch waved a hand towards some upright chairs and we sat down. There was an odd distribution of power in the room, I sensed. The body language of the two monks was subtly deferential to Andropov, as if he were the real Patriarch.

'I'm sorry, Father . . .' I said.

'Father Grigori.'

'Father Grigori. Before I talk to the Professor, I'm afraid I'll have to ask you to give us some privacy. This is a murder enquiry.'

The little man's cheeks turned bright red, and he fumbled in the pocket of his robe, and came out with a packet of Cleopatras and a box of matches. He struck match after match, but his hands were trembling so much that each one expired long before the cigarette was lit. Brother Paul rushed to help him but Grigori waved him away impatiently. 'I'm all right!' he snapped. Finally he steadied his right hand with the left long enough to light the smoke and took a deep drag. Only then did I notice that his fingers, teeth and beard were stained yellow with nicotine. 'You are police officers,' he said heavily, pronouncing each word carefully, 'you should know the right channels. These things should be set up through the highest authorities – the commander of your division should have approached the High Patriarch. Professor Andropov is a good friend of this monastery and he is a man of the finest moral character and the highest credentials. Without Professor Andropov this monastery would have collapsed years ago for lack of water. I have to say that I object to this bullying from the State, I resent this intrusion into the holy retreat of our honoured guest, and I repudiate implications of dishonourable behaviour against Professor Andropov.' There were a few moments of silence. Father Grigori drew in more smoke and blew it out.

'I'm sorry you feel that way, Father Grigori,' I said, 'but a man has died – a colleague of Professor Andropov. This is an urgent enquiry and we had no time for bureaucracy. I'm sorry we have to intrude, but . . .' I strung out the word for emphasis, 'a quiet word with the Professor here, in private, is surely better than a show of force.'

Father Grigori looked at me sullenly and his eyes found the pierce-mark on my upper right ear. He pursed his lips. Then he took a last, infuriated glance at us and stormed out of the office, followed by Brother Paul. Daisy and I exchanged a silent glance. I wondered why the hell Father Grigori had looked so scared.

16

'I F I MAY SAY SO, that was most uncalled for, Officer,' Andro-pov said. It was the first time he'd spoken and his voice was calm and steady – almost bored in fact. There was a touch of the pedantic academic there too, as if he was dealing with people who couldn't possibly be expected to understand the exquisite construction of his mind.

'Lieutenant.'

'Lieutenant. I am a guest here, you understand.' For a second he looked at Daisy and his eyes focused on her legs, encased in tight jeans. She felt the gaze and crossed them instinctively. I stood up, walked over to the door and turned the key in the lock. He watched me with the same haughty expression.

'So you think it was uncalled for?' I said. 'Well, two days ago, a former colleague and friend of yours, a fellow member of the Millennium Committee, was murdered in cold blood in Khan al-Khalili. Saturday – yesterday – you resign from your post and hoof it out here. You don't think you have any questions to answer?'

Andropov shrugged fleshy shoulders and looked at me plac-idly. 'What has it got to do with me?' he asked loftily. 'I wasn't close to him – haven't been for years.' He shook his Mongolian head wearily. 'Poor Adam,' he said, 'his death was a loss to the scientific world, a great loss, but I am not involved, and I can't tell you anything at all.' His eyes seemed to beam at us. Maybe it was the high cheekbones, but despite the well-chosen words his whole manner seemed to be saying, *Ibram had it coming*.

'No?' Daisy said suddenly. 'Then why *did* you leg it down here so soon after Doctor Ibram was murdered? Are you saying there's no connection?'

Andropov shrugged again. 'OK,' he said. 'I was bored with the Militants and their hit-list, and bored with the millennium celebrations. When it all comes down to it, it's just petty politics.'

'So you think it was Militants who killed Doctor Ibram?'

His eyes twinkled slightly and he looked at me as if I was a complete bumpkin. 'Naturally,' he said, and I'd have sworn he was about to yawn, 'they've been threatening me ever since I agreed to sit on the committee. I've had filthy letters, people spitting at me in the street, rocks through my windows, death threats, obscene phone calls – even a letter bomb. Adam's death was the last straw. I'm bored with it. I resign.'

For a guy who'd suffered all that he seemed amazingly unperturbed, I thought.

'You have proof that you were threatened?' I asked.

He looked up, his eyes momentarily hooded with anger. 'Of course I have proof,' he said evenly, 'you think I'm lying?'

Daisy took the cue and smiled encouragingly. 'You're Russian, Professor Andropov?' she asked.

'Not really – never been near the place in my life. My father was a White Russian civil engineer who worked in Iran during the Shah's time, but I was born and brought up in Tehran and I studied in London and Vienna.'

'And you specialize in dry-land ecology? That's how you've been able to help the monastery.'

For a moment Andropov looked gratified. 'My specialization is rainwater harvesting,' he said. 'You see, rain falls at some time even in the most arid places, although the showers may be rare and slight. The secret of good irrigation is to make sure you collect every drop of water and conserve it. If that water can be channelled even into a few hectares of fertile ground the product can be incredible. And a few productive plots can keep a community going for months.'

'And you have practised these techniques at the monastery here?'

'Yes, I mean theoretically this place shouldn't exist – the desert here is as arid as anywhere in the world – two hundred times drier than California's Death Valley. But even here by carefully husbanding resources you can survive. Under my supervision, the monks have built extensive cisterns all channelling water to a single point – even the roofs of the building are cisterns, linked by a complex system of drains to the internal plumbing, the sewers – everything is re-channelled and re-purified and recycled. When it doesn't rain we use deep-bores which are sunk into the water table, where the water is constantly replenished. True, we do often supplement the supply with Nile water, but in a good year the monastery works in pure homeostasis – a closed system.' He was beaming proudly now. 'In ecological terms,' he added, 'that's a great achievement.'

'Congratulations,' I said. I understood enough about moisture conservation to know he wasn't exaggerating, and I admired what he'd done here, but we had to get down to brass tacks. 'So did Doctor Ibram share your enthusiasm for rainwater harvesting?' I enquired.

Andropov sat back in his chair and sighed, as if the question exasperated him. 'Adam was always fascinated by the desert,' he said. 'He had been obsessed with it since he was a child in Alexandria. We first met when we were doing postgrad work on environmental studies at Harvard. Our fields were very close and we often worked together. I was studying the irrigation methods of the ancient Nabataens – the people who built Petra. They were so advanced that even today their techniques cannot be equalled. The object of my study was to develop an efficient water-conservation system which could be used for greening arid lands today. Adam was equally enthusiastic, because it was his dream that the whole of Egypt – even the whole of North Africa in time – could be turned into the vast garden he believed it once was.'

'And you agreed with him?'

'Without reservation. We spent a long time studying ancient rock-art – pictures of elephants, giraffes, hippos, rhinos and antelopes apparently living in places where today nothing can survive. We studied landsat images which revealed that there were once rivers and lakes lying under what is now only sand-dunes – images confirmed by rock-pictures showing people fishing and hunting crocodiles in boats where there is now not a hint of moisture. We collected all the archaeological and geological data and proved quite conclusively that the whole of the Sahara desert had once been green and fertile. That much was indisputable. The next questions were closely linked – why and when? What had created the world's most extensive desert – nine million square kilometres of arid land – and when had it happened? At that point Adam began to study ancient Egyptian records. He even taught himself to read hieroglyphics and got caught up in the whole ancient Egyptian thing. He started referring to it as his "destiny". That was when I began to have second thoughts, I suppose. We were both scientists and I felt he was beginning to lose his scientific detachment. After a while Adam came up with the theory that the ancient Egyptian Old Kingdom – the so-called Golden Age, when the pyramids are presumed to have been built – collapsed because of a sudden change in climate, from fertile to arid.'

'And you disagreed on this point?' I asked, interested now.

'No, I thought his reasoning was fairly sound. It does seem certain now that some time around the middle of the third millennium before Christ – that is about 2500 BC – the climate of North Africa tipped over the fragile balance between desert and fertility. The rainfall belt retreated south, and the land started to become desert. The Nile Valley was badly affected, and for the first time we have records of famine. There is a block from the Unas Causeway at Saqqara, for instance, showing emaciated men women and children, strikingly similar to the famine scenes from Ethiopia and the Sudan we saw a few years ago on our TVs. It seems also that great dust-storms blew up from the south – there are references to the sun being occluded, and of arable land being buried under shifting dunes. The whole social system collapsed – the pharaoh was discredited, the kingdom broke into petty feudal states, bands of armed men wandered up and down the Nile searching for food, plundering less badly hit communities. There are even accounts of cannibalism. In fact, though the civilization recovered, it was never quite the same again, and Adam traced this whole thing back to a climatic upheaval that had taken place some time around 2500 BC.'

'What was his proof?' I asked.

Andropov beamed over the high cheekbones. 'You're a stickler for proof, aren't you?'

'Aren't you?' I said.

Andropov's eyes narrowed even more tightly and his lips formed into an outright sneer. 'Are you acquainted with ancient Egyptian epigraphic literature, Lieutenant?' he enquired languidly.

'Try me.'

'Ever heard of a piece called *The Admonitions of Ipuwer*?'

'Sure, it's famous.'

He paused, trying to weigh up whether I was serious. 'Then since you're such an expert,' he said, 'you will know the text is thought to have been written during the reign of the Pharaoh Sesostris I, in the second millennium BC. The author was Ipuwer – a priest of the Ra Brotherhood at Heliopolis – and it indicates that there was total chaos in Egypt about that time. "The districts of Egypt are devastated," it runs, "every man says, we do not know what has happened to the land." The evidence seems clear that it was some natural cataclysm that brought about the devastation, which ended in social upheaval. Up till about 2500 BC, pharaonic tombs show the desert as being full of trees and animals. After that date, such images disappear.'

'Are *you* familiar with the ice-core samples taken by Blij and Neuven in Greenland in the nineteen-seventies?' I asked, remembering the report we'd found in Ibram's case.

He glanced at me and smiled condescendingly. 'So we've

been doing our homework, have we Lieutenant? Actually, the Blij and Neuven findings confirm that there was some kind of environmental crisis around 2500 BC. If you must know, I never disputed any of Adam's conclusions on this point – where we diverged was over the question of how and why this crisis had come about. The problem was that Adam felt the environmental change was made by interference in the biosphere. I couldn't go along with that. I agreed that human activities might affect the environment on a micro-level, but a few nomads with their goats, for instance, couldn't possibly have created the Sahara Desert. Adam was absolutely convinced. ''Look at Chernobyl,'' he would say, ''Look at the hole in the ozone layer. Human activities *can* bring about massive environmental change.'' I would protest that we were talking four thousand years ago. What could have had the power to change the environment on such a massive scale in that era? Volcanic activity, perhaps. An asteroid collision. But there weren't any nuclear reactors or CFC gases in those days. ''Oh,'' he used to say, ''How come you're so sure.'' That's when I decided to part company. I concentrated on water harvesting and irrigation and left him to theorize on his own. We still spoke from time to time and were superficially friendly, but I couldn't help noticing that over the last few years he'd got more and more political, more and more tied up with his influential friends. He became advisor to the US president on environmental matters and was very friendly with the president of Egypt. Understandably so, of course. Only eleven per cent of Egypt is cultivable land, and every president since Nasser has been presented with the problem of a burgeoning population increasingly unable to feed itself. The only answer to that is to increase cultivation. Adam became an environmental guru – his ideas of turning the desert green again, however impractical, had huge political appeal.'

I sat down and looked out of the window into the quadrangle where a moisture haze rose from the mass of irrigated plants. I could feel the greatness of Ibram's dream. No wonder he had been obsessed by it.

'Would you say Ibram was an ambitious man?' Daisy asked.

Andropov frowned as if it was a difficult question. 'If you mean, was he ambitious for power and material wealth,' he said, 'I'd say no. Oh, he wanted the things his parents had been deprived of in Egypt, of course – a comfortable house, a car, enough to eat. He was happy with his American wife and two children and never played around. But that was as far as it went. I think he had a real social conscience. He won the NASA Medal for distinguished public service, did you know that? He was just so taken with his dream of greening the desert that he lost touch with reality – that's my view.'

'Do you happen to know what Doctor Ibram was working on just before he died?' I asked.

He shrugged again as if it was a stupid question. 'He always had a lot of irons in the fire,' he said, 'but I think his main interest recently was the Millennium Committee.'

'Did that surprise you?'

'In one way, yes. It didn't fit in with his obsession with the desert. But in another way it wasn't entirely new, because for a couple of years he'd been passionately interested in the Giza plateau. Passion was part of him, naturally, I mean no one could have mastered all the subjects he did without it. Whenever he got interested in anything he rushed in full tilt – never rested until he knew it inside out. Anyway, about eighteen months ago I heard he'd managed to get funding for a project inside the Great Pyramid looking for some hidden chamber or other. If I remember rightly it was called the Chamber of Thoth. The pyramid was even shut down for a while. Personally I thought the whole idea was crazy – it was a measure of how far Adam had strayed from the orthodox scientific community. Of course he wasn't known for his work in that field and he had the sense to keep his name out of the press. A guy called Monod – Christian Monod – ran the programme. He's a talented Swiss engineer who's been working on pyramid projects for years, and has written God knows how many papers on it. He was meant to be on the Millennium Committee too, but then, a couple of months ago he suddenly disappeared. One potential member vanished and another murdered – that was enough for me. I quit. That's why I'm here.'

He sat back and folded his hands as if the interview was concluded. There was a look in his eyes that I couldn't quite pinpoint, and I realized that I wasn't satisfied. Everything he'd said seemed to make sense, but it was all too glib somehow. It was as if he'd prepared a statement and learned it parrot-fashion. He seemed too distant, his manner too cold and clinical for someone whose old postgrad buddy had been mown down in cold blood. Academics can be the worst backstabbers alive, I knew, but I doubted if his lack of concern was motivated simply by a difference of opinion. What then, I wondered? Jealousy? Had Andropov resented his old colleague's success? I pondered for a moment and suddenly remembered the graveyard outside.

'Water harvesting isn't the only thing you practise here is it, Professor?' I said. 'You also do medical work.'

If I'd hoped to faze him the strategy died a death. He turned a vulturine gaze on me and smiled. 'I trained as a medical doctor before I took up Earth Sciences,' he said, 'and I've had some experience. They're never been able to afford a doctor here at St Samuel's, so whenever I'm here I help out.'

'And you were here four years ago, when a young Bedouin boy had an accident in the desert?'

He was about to answer when there was a buzz from Daisy's mobile. She took it out and pressed the little green telephone signal that I now knew meant 'answer'. A voice grated and crackled for a moment and she lifted it to her ear, stood up and walked around the room looking annoyed. 'You're very weak,' she said, 'the signal's poor.' Finally she pressed the little red telephone button which meant 'stop' and put the mobile back into her handbag, looking worried. 'Come outside,' she said.

I excused myself and followed her through the heavy door into the passage. 'That was Hammoudi,' she said. 'He was speaking from the medical facility in Garden City. Seems Fawzi was taken very ill early this morning, and had a coronary. Our only witness to the Ibram killing just pegged out.'

17

HAMMOUDI WAS WAITING FOR US in the reception area of the medical facility, poised with an unlit Cleopatra between his fingers under a vast 'No Smoking' sign. Two big marines stood over him as if daring him to light the cigarette. They were wearing white helmets, I noticed, and carried spotless M16 rifles, looking as though they were ready for action. On the way from the landing-strip I'd spotted the *Mukhabaraat* Special Ops Squad under Major Rufi on standby only a block away, so perhaps US intelligence was better than I thought.

'Where's Marvin?' Daisy demanded. 'He should be here.'

'He was,' Hammoudi said, 'but he had to go and brief your ambassador.'

As soon as we had shown our IDs and signed on, Hammoudi rushed Daisy and me through the connecting door and up the corridor towards Fawzi's room with the two marines following. The closed-circuit TV cameras seemed to nod at us in recognition as we moved.

'How'd it happen?' I asked. 'I mean when we spoke to Fawzi he seemed fine. He was off the critical list, talking – joking even. Once the bleeding's stopped gunshot wounds in the thighs aren't supposed to be a big deal.'

'He was all right till this morning,' Hammoudi growled, 'he started puking a lot, then went into a coma and just croaked.'

Another marine guard in a white helmet was on sentry duty outside Fawzi's room, and the male nurse we'd met before was sitting in the observation area. Through the window I could see that the monitors and life support systems were switched off. There was a mausoleum air to the place. Fawzi's body lay under a starched white sheet that now covered him from head to foot, and the area around his plump midriff was raised like a tent.

'Marvin wanted to put him in a body bag,' Hammoudi said, 'but I insisted they left him there till you both arrived. Not that you can tell much by looking.'

I said hello to the male nurse who stood up and scowled at me as though he had something to get off his chest. Hammoudi must have guessed what it was because he cut him off abruptly, and pushed open the swing door in front of us. It was Daisy who lifted the sheet. Fawzi's face had looked bad enough last time I'd seen it, but in death it was horrific – a balloon of purplish-white flesh with bloodless lips curled back in agony, and the pupils under the acres of bruise-tissue contracted to black spots.

Daisy pulled the sheet back hastily. 'One day the guy's sitting up and talking,' she said, 'the next he's out like a light. It doesn't make sense.'

'It makes perfect sense,' a voice rasped, and we all looked up to see a figure shambling through the swing door – a man in a dark suit with a tadpole head and arms too long for his body. It was Jan Van Helsing.

'What the hell's he doing here?' I asked Hammoudi. 'Fawzi wasn't an American citizen. This case isn't within his jurisdiction.'

Van Helsing halted in front of us, and fixed me with his deep, narrow eyes. I felt my hackles rise instinctively. I couldn't explain it. Van Helsing didn't have to do anything or say anything to get me angry. His mere presence was enough to spark off my aggression. I wanted to let him have it with a baseball bat right between those narrow eyes, and rip that bird-like fringe out with my bare hands. I stepped back a pace, bristling, taking deep breaths to control my racing pulse, but Van Helsing seemed to engulf me with his long limbs like a spider so that everywhere I turned he was there. 'First mistake,' he said, with the oddly cadenced tone I remembered, 'is that you are on foreign soil. This facility is holy ground – a little bit of the USA – and the diplomatic shield covers it. That makes me the boss here, Lieutenant.'

I stared at him, wanting to ram the barrel of my Beretta down his throat. 'This is supposed to be a FBI case,' Hammoudi cut in suddenly, 'I've had no brief from the US Ambassador about the CIA. You already broke protocol by sequestering police evidence. This facility might be a diplomatic area, but who gave the US embassy the right to bring Fawzi here in the first place? I signed nothing, neither did my minister. What's happened is that you've illegally abducted an Egyptian citizen – and you must answer for his death.'

Van Helsing turned his gaze to Hammoudi and for a second I was certain he would lash out with those whipcord arms. His eyes were poison. 'Back off, Hammoudi,' he said, 'I know all about you and your reputation doesn't impress me.'

Whereas my instinct was always to move back, Hammoudi's was to move forward slightly, as if to get in range for one of his gunshot punches. He seemed unfazed, but there was a telltale pinkness about his ears, and a silence about him that was both familiar and ominous. For a split second they stared at one another, then Van Helsing looked away, and pointed a long bony finger at me.

'Here's the one responsible for Fawzi's death,' he spat, 'Mister Big-Detective Rashid of the SID.'

'What are you talking about?' I demanded.

Van Helsing suddenly reached out his uncannily long arm and jerked the sheet off Fawzi's face. 'Look at him!' he rasped. 'And remember. You did this. You killed him.'

'Like hell.'

'Ask the nurse. Wheel him in here. He'll tell you.' He beckoned to the nurse through the observation window, and a moment later the man in the white lab-coat presented himself in front of us. He had that same accusing look in his eye, and I realized my earlier intuition had been right. He had something to say to me and it wasn't congratulations on my haircut. 'OK,' Van Helsing said, 'tell him what you told me.'

The male nurse looked me coldly in the eyes. 'Fawzi was doing fine,' he said. 'We were about to move him out of intensive care. Then, about eight-fifteen this morning – I'd just come on duty and was dressing – the security man sounded the alarm. I ran up here but the patient was already vomiting severely. Appeared to be suffering from some kind of food poisoning. I got the stomach pump on the double, but it was too late. The stuff was already in his system.'

'What stuff?' Daisy enquired.

'I'll come to that. As I said, it was too late. He died shortly afterwards from a massive coronary infarction. I rang the security-room and asked the duty officer why he'd sounded the alarm. He said that he'd seen Fawzi eating something on the TV monitor. Close up, he said, it looked like cubes of hash. I remembered the five deals we found on him when he was admitted. I showed them to Agent Brooke, but last time I saw them they were in the possession of the Lieutenant here.' His eyes were glaring at me angrily now. 'You must have given them back to him. That was a negligent act. I never had a patient die before – not on my watch.'

I felt myself flushing. Daisy and Hammoudi were both staring at me. 'I don't believe it,' I stammered. 'Why would Fawzi eat dope?'

The nurse shrugged. 'I don't know,' he said, 'but that's not the point. The point is that they cut Red Lebanese with things like strychnine and arsenic. It can be lethal.'

Van Helsing looked satisfied now. 'Nice going, Rashid,' he said, 'real nice. You signed the death warrant of your only witness in the Ibram case, and I'll tell you – you're lucky Fawzi was an Egyptian. If he'd been a US citizen I'd have had you run in for manslaughter.'

I swallowed hard. Giving Fawzi back the deals had seemed a decent gesture at the time. How did I know the guy would be stupid enough to eat it? People eat grass all the time, of course, but mostly cooked. Fawzi had just been incredibly unlucky, that's all. Still, I knew I'd been a fool – there'd been no real reason to give him the stuff back – and Van Helsing was right. Fawzi's death was my fault and there was no getting away from it. I looked at Hammoudi. He had remained impassive, weighing up the pros and cons. It was at times like this that I appreciated his professionalism.

'Did Fawzi have any visitors this morning?' he asked the nurse. 'Anyone at all.'

'Not that I know of,' the nurse said, 'but the wards are monitored constantly and any visitor would show up on the screen.'

'The security staff reported no visitors,' Van Helsing cut in.

'Are the TV monitors taped?' Hammoudi enquired.

'Sure they are,' Van Helsing said, 'no point if they weren't. But the video tapes are US property and they're classified.'

'Convenient,' Hammoudi said. 'So apart from the nurse's testimony there's no proof of your accusation, Mr Van Helsing.'

The CIA man grinned, showing sharply chiselled teeth. 'There can't be any doubt. The security supervisor swears he saw Fawzi eating the dope.'

'OK,' Hammoudi said, 'but even if Fawzi did eat the stuff, the security man can't swear that was the cause of death. I mean he's not a pathologist. It could have been something else.'

'Our pathologist is already standing by,' Van Helsing said.

Hammoudi allowed himself a flicker of a smile. 'I don't think this is the proper place for the autopsy. Fawzi should never have been brought here at all, but I accepted it as it had already been done. Technically Fawzi was abducted by foreign agents. An Egyptian police pathologist on Egyptian territory will carry out the autopsy. If the result shows that his death was linked with culpable negligence on the part of Lieutenant Rashid, then disciplinary action will be taken. By me, that is, not by the CIA.'

Van Helsing had been listening with mounting amusement

obvious on his face. He nodded towards the three big marines who were now on guard in the observation area. 'What I see,' he said, 'is that the stiff's here. It'd be quite a headache getting it past all the cameras and those boys.'

Hammoudi shrugged, brought a cellphone from his pocket and punched in a number. After a second or two there came an answering voice. 'Captain Rufi?' Hammoudi said. 'Cordon off the entrance to the facility, and bring the ambulance. If I'm not out in exactly five minutes, you have my permission to move in with force if necessary.' He put the phone away. 'I took the liberty of having our Special Ops Squad put on standby,' he told Van Helsing. 'They are two hundred strong and at this moment they're only a block away. You stand in my way, and they'll be in here like jackals.'

Van Helsing scoffed. 'Jackals,' he spat, 'I've seen those boys. A bunch of nancies.'

'They may not be as well trained as your marines,' Hammoudi said, 'but believe me, they can make one hell of a mess.'

Van Helsing leered again. 'You'll cause an international incident,' he said.

Hammoudi remained completely unruffled. 'No, you will,' he said. 'You're not getting away with abducting an Egyptian, not even a dead one.'

Van Helsing smiled suddenly, a smile so suggestive it was infinitely worse than his scowl. 'OK,' he said, 'take the stiff. But it won't do you any good.'

As we pushed Fawzi's body down the corridor on the trolley I couldn't look Daisy in the eye. OK, Hammoudi had got me off the hook for now, but whatever the autopsy proved, I knew I'd screwed up.

18

After Hammoudi had left in the ambulance I walked down the Corniche and across the Manial Bridge to Roda Island, into the honeycomb of streets behind my apartment-block. It was after sundown and the last spurt of crimson lit up the eastern sky, throwing blood-coloured slashes high up on the faceless walls of the buildings. Sidewalks were deserted and traffic had vanished. It was the third day of Ramadan – the holy fasting month – and the population had beaten a hasty retreat from shops and offices to enjoy a meal after twelve hours without eating or drinking. Muezzins were chiming in from the minarets of mosques all over Cairo, each call out of kilter, so that the city seemed dominated by a strange communion of dissonant voices echoing and re-echoing across the night. I knew these backstreets like the palm of my hand, yet tonight they seemed distorted and so unfamiliar that I scarcely recognized them. Pillars of blackness seemed to fall across my path at surreal angles, and the very shape and texture of the place seemed somehow wrong. Knots of light lingered in odd corners and there were occasional islands of brilliance where streetlamps had been installed. As I passed them my shadow flopped out in front of me like an elongated squeeze of darkness.

The muezzins' calls died out, leaving an eerie vacuum. I shivered. The night chill had already seeped into the alleys, and I zipped up my jacket and rubbed my hands, straining my ears instinctively for sounds, hearing only the soft fall of my trainers on the flagstones. I'd been brought up in backstreets like this and the dark didn't usually worry me. Tonight, though, there was a feeling in the air – a kind of heaviness – that set my teeth on edge. It had been on a night like this – only two weeks ago – that I'd found the tailor's boy dead in Khan al-Khalili, his body ripped and torn to bloody slivers. I'd glimpsed the creature then – the ghoul or whatever you wanted to call it – a slinking, evil presence, side-winding down the alley like the shadow of some enormous human crab. One thing was certain – the beast's attacks were becoming more frequent. It occurred to me suddenly how precisely the ghoul's presence seemed to counterpoint the Ibram investigation. Ibram himself had been interested in ghouls; Fawzi had mentioned them; Sanusi was a full-blown expert.

Then there was Andropov, who'd retreated to the Fayoum, where the first reports of the ghoul had come from four years ago. I thought of the old Bedouin at St Samuel's graveyard only that morning: '*The boy was killed by a ghoul. Everybody knows it . . . Found him still alive, half torn to shreds – and one of them saw a creature running off in the distance.*' I thought of the beast I'd seen in the vision when I'd touched Ibram's dead hand, then of the Great Sphinx and its shapeshifter's features, then of the spiderish Van Helsing and the unaccountable fear and loathing I felt in his presence. Somehow there was a whole monstrous design there, half-seen, half-guessed in the gloom. I turned a sharp corner and looked suddenly into deep yellow eyes, then something screeched and leapt away from me. I ducked instantly and went for my Beretta and my torch at the same time, my pulse thumping drumbeats in my ears. In the torch-beam a big black cat yowled as it skipped and bounced frantically away from me along a high wall. I stood up, chuckling, sheathed my pistol and moved cautiously forward down the alley, letting my beam play across weathered sandstone.

At the end the alley forked, and I hesitated there for a second, seeing only darkness in both directions. At that moment there was a terrible scream from somewhere close by – a scream of such wild horror and agony that my blood turned to ice-water. For a moment my muscles seized up and I stopped breathing. Shakily, I slipped my weapon back into my hand. The cry came again, louder, nearer and more anguished than before, but this time there was another sound mingling with it – a threatening bass rumble like the hunting-pant of a hyena. I heard a noise like tough cardboard being wrenched apart, and another paroxysm of shrieks that was drowned by a frenzy of deep-throated roars. I took a deep breath, cocked my weapon and rushed blindly down the alley, whipping my flashlight beam from side to side. My trainer connected with something rough and hard and I fell cleanly, dropping the torch and rolling instinctively into a somersault. The torch bounced across the hard stones for a second, and in its last pulse of light I glimpsed the form of a squatting animal – all limbs and angles like a immense mosquito – that seemed to be dragging some dark burden down the alley. My torch hit a wall and the bulb went out, but almost at the same instant I squeezed the trigger of my Beretta.

The report shattered the silence, reverberating from the walls, and I held my breath and pumped the trigger convulsively again and again, scourging the alley with fire. Suddenly the hammer snapped down on an empty chamber, and I rolled to my feet, my ears straining in the darkness. There was a dark bundle on the flagstones in front of me and I ran to it. It was a body – probably the body of a youth – and as I crouched down to touch it my hand came into contact with stickiness. I smelled vomit and blood and retched. There was a flutter of movement further down the alley and I froze for a second, then slammed another mag into my Beretta. In the dim light of the moon and stars I could just make out a spidery shadow floating away like a ghost. I shouted, fired twice, then ran after the shadow, bellowing wildly to encourage myself. Whatever was there terrified me, but this time I knew that no matter what happened I couldn't let it escape. I'd been hunting that thing night after night for almost four years. Two weeks ago I'd seen it and it had slipped through my fingers, but that wasn't going to happen again. Sanusi had claimed the man who took the amulet had been the ghoul in disguise. Maybe that was garbage, or maybe it provided the most crucial link of the whole investigation.

As I sprinted down the alley I knew I had to get it this time. I needed to know why it had come back and what its purpose was, before other victims died: before it was too late. The shadow seemed to flit with incredible speed and I had nothing more to home in on than the faintest impression of motion. The walls passed me in a blur and I ran on panting, faster and faster until I came to a place where the street split four ways. Dim lights dickered along three of the streets but the other was in pitch darkness. I cocked my ear and heard a scuff of movement from the dark alley and plunged into it, sensing rather than seeing the creature drifting effortlessly in front of me. The alley turned abruptly into another street lit by a blinking lamp at the far end. As far as I could tell, the alley was completely deserted. I wondered suddenly if I'd simply imagined the ghoul in front of me. Maybe I'd imagined the whole thing.

I slowed to a walk and moved warily along the alley with my weapon at the ready, hardly daring to breathe, my head turning left and right. The walls were sheer, weathered sandstone maybe four hundred years old, broken only by the occasional slit window, but halfway down the alley was an arched doorway set into the stone down a couple of steps. The door was wide open and I glimpsed stone stairs beyond it, descending into inky blackness. I stood at the door and listened, and for a second I thought I made out a sibilation of air – a ghost-whisper like the sea-sound in shells. I glanced around. Either the thing was in here, or it was long gone, I thought. I gulped, extended my Beretta in both hands and began to descend the steps, feeling my way shakily. A fusty smell – dust, mould and rat urine – made my nostrils twitch. I reached the bottom of the steps and stood for a moment, helpless in the dark, listening for breathing, movement – anything that would tell me I was not alone.

Suddenly I remembered the box of matches I was carrying in

my jacket, and I put my handgun away, brought out the matches and struck one. It didn't ignite, so I dropped it, swearing to myself, and struck another. There was a momentary flare of sulphurous light in which I saw another door in the wall nearby – a door scrawled with what looked like a crude graffito of the ibis-headed god Thoth, entwined with an enormous serpent as large as a boa-constrictor. That was all I had time to take in before the match burned my finger and went out, and something invisible swung out of the darkness, striking me a glancing blow across the forehead. I staggered and fell across the lower stairs, and as I struggled to remain conscious I had the sensation of some dark body stepping across me and susurrating up the stairs. I might have blacked out for a minute or two, but certainly no more. I dragged myself, half-crawling, up the steps, but in the alley outside there was no one and nothing. I felt my head and found a lump there and a trickle of blood. I filled my lungs with air and moved haltingly along the alley, hugging the deepest shadow.

Slowly, I retraced my way to the street where I'd first seen the ghoul, covering each successive turn carefully with my weapon. There was still no one about – no movement of any kind – and I was astonished that my salvo of shots hadn't brought people running. It was as if it had all happened in a dream, and when I reached the alley where I'd first spotted the ghoul it became even more dream-like. I found my broken torch lying against the wall, but the victim himself had vanished into thin air.

19

IT WAS ONLY A FEW minutes back to my apartment-block on the waterfront, but I was still wired up and every shadow had me jumping for cover. I cased the alley behind the block steadily, then worked my way to the basement door. My flat was on the top floor and I'd chosen it because it had two entrances, one approached by the lift from the front and the other by the firestairs to the back. Like I'd told Daisy, it always helped to have a back-up, and I used the front entrance so rarely that I'd have sworn the *ghaffir* hardly knew me. I closed the outer door, locked it, and let out a sigh of relief. It was good to be out of the cold and in the safety of the familiar. I lurched down the dank corridor to the steel firedoor, which for security reasons could only be opened from the inside. Whenever I went out this way I left it jammed open with a wooden wedge, knowing by experience that none of the residents used this exit but me. As I bent to remove the wedge, though, a warning bell jangled in my head. The wedge was still there, but it wasn't in the exact same place I'd left it, I was certain. Someone – or something – had come in, removed the wedge to close the door, then thought better of it and put it back. A new burst of adrenalin washed through my blood and I grasped my Beretta. I thought of the ghoul, and for a moment I considered bugging out. Then I set my teeth and climbed the stairs unsteadily until I came to my back door. I put my ear to the wood. I heard nothing so I drew my keys, unlocked it and pushed it open.

There wasn't much to see in the kitchen – the contents of a couple of packets of cereal tipped out over the table, cutlery drawers open, the fridge door ajar – but enough to tell me that the place had been breached. In the living room, though, it was mayhem, as if it had been searched with increasing rage and frustration. My computer had been booted but was thankfully intact: the speakers of my stereo had been ripped open, pictures had been torn off the walls, chairs and cushions slashed open with a blade, books pulled out of shelves, ripped and scattered in pieces across the rug. I didn't go in much for personal knick-knacks, and Hammoudi always said my place was so impersonal that it was like someone was camping out rather than living there permanently. It wasn't that I felt any attachment to the pad, but the idea that I'd been compromised made me livid. I heard a scuffle coming from the bedroom. For a moment I stood listening, then I moved forward silently, nudged the door open with a trainer and eased myself into the room.

The mattress on my bed had been pulled up and cut open, and stuffing was strewn across the floor. There were only two possible hiding places – either the walk-in cupboard or the full-length curtains I'd left closed that morning. I went for the cupboard, and I lucked out. As soon as I turned, a dark figure exploded from behind the curtains, a black vortex of movement. For a split second I was certain it was the ghoul, but then I saw the long knife that flashed down on my gun hand. The blade clanked against gunmetal and I dropped the weapon, seizing the black-draped wrist that grasped the knife and yanking it down so that there was a shriek of pain. The knife fell, and turning I saw that I was wrestling with a hooded figure – the same veiled Bedouin woman who'd laid me out in the Khan the previous night. She was big – bigger even than I remembered – and I could feel the powerful muscles moving under the robe. I dodged a roundhouse punch that might have knocked me down, let go of the wrist and delivered five or six Hammoudi-style smashes to the jaw, one after the other. There was a lot of pent-up anger behind those punches. The woman staggered back drunkenly, and I did something I'd been itching to do for a long time – I tore off the veil.

I suppose I'd known all along what I would find. Not many women have a punch that powerful, and few Bedouin women are that tall. If this was a woman, she was one hell of a dyke, with a two-day shadow on a square chin, now bloody from my punches, to go with iron pectorals and biceps, and size eleven hands and feet. The guy was still staggering when I picked up my Beretta. I levelled it right between his legs and smiled. 'Stop it right there,' I said, 'or you really will find out what it's like to be a woman.' Without taking my eyes off him, I tipped a wooden-framed camp-chair upright. 'Sit down,' I said.

The man looked at the gun sullenly as if trying to gauge the distance between us. He didn't sit down. Blood dripped out of his nose and he put up a hand to touch it, then looked at the blood on his fingers. 'I ought to rip you apart,' he said, the voice coming out bass and slightly hoarse. He made a sudden move towards me and I raised the gun a little and squeezed the trigger. There was a deafening thunk, and the guy ducked. The round whanged into the wall behind him – it must have missed his ear by about a millimetre. He put a shaky hand up to feel if his head was still in one piece, and then abruptly sat down on the chair.

'That's better,' I said. 'Believe me, the next one really will be in your *cojones*.'

'I know what you did to Ibram,' he said coolly, wiping blood off his chin, 'and sooner or later you're going to pay.'

He was scared but in control, I realized. He had the same sort of quiet power Hammoudi had – a power that came from physical strength and the ability to handle oneself. He wasn't in much of a position to rip me apart right now, but I'd actually felt the power of those ham-like fists, and I didn't underestimate his ability to do it if given the ghost of a chance. He looked fit and alert, his blue eyes clear, watchful and full of hate. He spoke

Arabic almost perfectly, but he certainly wasn't a Bedouin – not even an Arab, I thought.

'I think we've got our wires crossed,' I said. 'Last I heard I was the one investigating Ibram's death.'

'You cops are mixed up in this – right up to the elbows.'

I wondered how much he knew, and looked him up and down. Beneath the woman's robe he was wearing rubber sandals made out of the inner tubes of motorcar tyres – the Arabs called them *tamut takhalli* – 'die and leave them' – because of their legendary inability to wear out. I distinctly remembered their eerie slapping on the flagstones of Khan al-Khalili.

'You've been following me, I said. 'You followed me to the US medical facility. You were there at the Mena Palace and in the alley last night coming back from Sanusi's. You must have followed me here, too, and found your way in. I want to know why.'

He folded his big hands in his lap with a show of complacency. 'Because Ibram's dead.'

'And you think I did it?'

'Maybe you didn't gun him down yourself, but you and that big detective and the girl – you're in it up to the eyes. You SID are just another death squad when it comes down to it, there to protect the establishment.'

'Turn out your pockets,' I snapped. He literally turned them inside out, but there was only a wedge of Egyptian money and some keys – no credit cards or ID.

'Why are you wearing drag?' I asked.

'I had to stay alive long enough to get even with those who did it. I know I'm on the hit-list and it seemed a good disguise.'

'Hit-list,' I said, turning his words over in my head. 'I talked to someone else today who claimed to be on the hit-list, only this guy was convinced it was drawn up by the Militants.' His eyes were full of interest now I noted. 'Guy called Andropov – a former member of the Millennium Committee – like Ibram. He told me a great deal. Said there was another potential member of the committee who vanished. Maybe he didn't vanish. Maybe he was just going round in drag.' He opened his eyes wide, knowing I'd got him, and that slight flicker told me all. 'Christian Monod,' I said.

He winced. 'All right,' he said, 'you're probably going to kill me anyway, so what the hell.'

'Doctor Ibram called you on the phone just before he was shot,' I said. 'I hope it was worth it, because it cost him his life.'

'You should know.'

'Look, why would I or my people want to take out Ibram?'

'Because he was on to it. He was on to the whole thing.'

The whole thing? I decided to risk it. Maybe Daisy's shock-tactics were best after all. 'You mean Firebird?' I said. The word dropped into the room like a mortar bomb and his face crashed shut.

'You tell me,' he said, 'the only Firebird I know is an American car.'

I laughed. I couldn't help it. Monod stared back at me uneasily. 'You're in a great deal of trouble,' I said. 'Assault on a police officer – twice – once with a deadly weapon. Attempted murder. Aggravated burglary. You could be inside for a long time. Ever been in an Egyptian jail?'

'It won't come to that, will it? A bullet in the skull down a dark alley is more like it.'

'Why were you following me?'

He went silent, but he'd already revealed too much. 'All right,' I said, 'Let me tell you why. Since you took the trouble to trash my place, you must have been searching for something. What was it? Not my silverware or my set of rare postage stamps, I'll bet. No, you think I have something that belonged to Ibram. A map, perhaps? Or should we say, half a map?'

I knew by the slightest flutter of his eyelids that I'd been right.

'Where is it?' he said.

'It's in a place you'll never find it, not unless I want you to that is.'

'You bastard!'

 154

'Why are you looking for the map?'

'Forget it,' he said, 'I'm not talking.'

For an instant I saw red. I squeezed the trigger and a round banjoed between Monod's legs, only just missing the groin. The big man flinched and half-stood, and in that second I switched the pistol to my left hand, whipped out my stiletto and took two paces over to him. Before he could stop me I slashed his bunched right fist across the knuckles with my blade and pistol-whipped him across the jowls with the butt of the Beretta. He screamed and sat down heavily, clutching his injured hand. I poked the muzzle of my pistol right into his ear and held my blade across his Adam's apple. 'The next one is your throat,' I said. 'Now who are you, Monod?'

'All right! OK!' he stammered. 'I'm an engineer, that's all. I worked on a project in the Great Pyramid with Ibram. Then I got warned off by some shits who told me they were police officers. Said they'd kill my wife and kids, so I disappeared and disguised myself as a woman.'

'You sure these guys were police?'

'They had official ID, but they could have been anything. They were done up in these long black raincoats with black hats, like characters out of a ''B'' horror movie.'

I let the blade drop and shifted the the muzzle of my handgun out of his ear. I took a step back. 'Whoever those guys were,' I said, 'I'm not one of them.'

Monod wiped blood off his knuckles. 'You do a damn good impersonation,' he said.

I picked up a clean handkerchief from the laundry he'd scattered over the floor. 'Just hold this over it.'

He covered the wound carefully, his eyes never leaving my face. 'You're a cop,' he said, 'and the cops are mixed up in this. You're all in on it – the SID, the uniforms, the FBI – even the CIA.'

I sighed. We were at an impasse, I could see that. Monod could have been involved in Ibram's murder, but my instinct told me otherwise. I could have forced the information out of him, but that might have ended up being very messy and even counterproductive. He thought I was lying, and to get him to tell me of his own volition I'd have to prove I wasn't.

'I'll tell you what, Monod,' I said, slowly, 'I think we have a bunch of things to talk about, things that would be of mutual benefit. I need to know about the map and Firebird.'

He watched me silently, biding his time. 'I'm not going to make you talk,' I said, 'I want you to talk to me of your own free will. I'm ready to stick my neck out to show you I'm on the level. I'm letting you go.'

His eyes were heavy with disbelief, and I knew he scented a trap. 'What for?' he asked.

'To show you I'm telling the truth. Think it over and we'll meet up in a couple of days. Whatever you think, I'm not one of them.'

'It's a set-up.'

'Consider it,' I said, 'it'll take you about three minutes to get into the street from here, and not even Clark Kent could get a hit-team together that fast. It's night and the moment you get out there, I've lost you. Like I say, I know I'm sticking my neck out and I might never see you again. But if I'm really a state assassin like you're suggesting, I could easily pop you right here and no one'd say a dicky-bird.'

'You want information.'

'Sure I do. I want to know what the map is, and what Firebird is, but if I was what you say I am I'd know already. And believe me, if it was something else I wanted I could call the persuaders in and have your balls grilled right now. Why would I take the trouble of letting you go just to set you up?'

I could see from his eyes that he was wavering. It might be a trick, he was thinking, but even if it was, what did he have to lose? If he stayed here there was a good chance I'd rub him out anyway. And there might be the ghost of a chance I was telling the truth. I let the Beretta drop all the way to my side and Monod watched it. He wanted to believe me, but like all the hardest things in life it required a leap of faith. As Sanusi said, faith is what counts. The difficult part would be getting from the chair to the door. At last he stood up shakily, never taking his eyes off the Beretta. I handed him a blank card with Hammoudi's number on it.

'I'm Sammy Rashid,' I said. 'When you're ready, ring this number and give your instructions to whoever answers. Whatever you think, this is not a set-up.' I picked up his veil. 'Oh,' I said, 'and you're going to need this.'

He took the veil and grinned weakly, then turned and marched to the door. He closed it behind him gently, and the last thing I heard was the slap of his *tamut takhalli* on the stairs.

20

I T WAS ONLY AFTER MONOD had left that I remembered Anton Halaby. I had an appointment to meet him tonight at the Scorpion Club, and I knew he would be there. Halaby was the best police informant in the business – not a ten-dollar snitch but a retired intelligence agent who had been around state secrets most of his life. If he hadn't been caught with his hand in the till a few years back, he might still have been a highly paid consultant rather than being obliged to do spadework for the likes of Hammoudi and me. He'd only let me down once – when I'd asked him to put a trace on my father, Desmond Redfield. He'd told me what I already knew – that he'd disappeared without trace. 'Which is passing strange,' he'd commented ominously, 'feels like someone wanted to obliterate his name from the face of the earth.'

I was dog-tired. The encounters with the ghoul and Monod had drained me of energy and the last thing I wanted was to go out. But Hammoudi had set Halaby a couple of questions and I knew he'd have the answers. I looked at my bed, now lying scattered in bits all over the bedroom floor. It didn't look inviting. Damn bloody Monod, I thought. I mean, I'd have expected a guy like him to have been more methodical. I walked round the flat picking up books and pictures, righting furniture, then I gave up. It was an exercise in futility. Instead I dragged myself to the shower, bathed the bump on my head and lathered myself, letting the hot water relax my muscles. Then I went out on to my balcony, breathed in the coolness of the air and listened to the sounds of the night. My apartment was on the top storey of a waterfront block, an end flat so that my balcony curved round art-deco style to give an interesting field of view. The Nile here was only about thirty metres wide so you could clearly see and hear the constant stream of motor vehicles grinding and roaring along the Corniche. Almost directly opposite my flat was the great buttress wall of the Roman viaduct, but that was invisible tonight. To my right, though, I could make out necklaces of light around the Coptic churches of Old Cairo – St Sergius, the Hanging Church, St Barbasa – and the mosque of 'Amr Ibn al-Aas – probably the oldest mosque in Africa. These sites were actually built on top of the ruins of an ancient fortress called Babylon, which was probably constructed in pharaonic times by Babylonian prisoners of war.

The story went that Babylon was the entrance to a vast network of subterranean tunnels and catacombs which spanned the whole city, from Old Cairo to Heliopolis and Giza. It was a labyrinth whose origin was supposed to go back to the time of the Ra Brotherhood, and whose secret entrances were guarded by giant serpents. I thought about the ghoul, and the door, only blocks from here, that opened into a staircase down which he'd disappeared. I fingered the bruise on my forehead. Right before someone or something had clubbed me, I'd thought I'd spotted a crude graffito of the ibis-headed god Thoth down there – a figure folded in the coils of a giant snake. Thoth was the ancient Egyptian god of magic, who was supposed to have come from afar and introduced mathematics, science, writing, astrology, medicine, music and engineering to the Nile Valley. He was credited with having created the ancient Egyptian priesthood, or its forerunner, the mysterious organization known as the Shemsu-Hor. Throughout history there had been legends about the Books of Thoth, which were a repository of all the secret wisdom accumulated by the Brotherhood over the millennia. Eighteen

159

months ago, Ibram had been searching for an undiscovered chamber inside the Great Pyramid. '*If I remember rightly,*' Andropov had said, '*it was called the Chamber of Thoth.*' Maybe Ibram had been looking for the Books of Thoth – the greatest prize in the history of Egyptology. Maybe that's what the map was about.

'Shit!' I shouted to the walls, bringing my fist down hard on the table, 'Monod knew all the answers and I fucking let him go!'

21

THE RAMADAN CROWDS WERE OUT when I emerged from my block and I could hardly believe these were the same streets where I'd chased the creature only hours before. Still, I felt somehow conspicuous and vulnerable and I dodged through the shadows along the riverbank as niftily as my exhausted state would allow. Standing under a streetlamp at the corner of my block were two men in ankle-length black Barbour coats with flaps at the shoulders. They wore dark hats tilted over eyes that were swathed in shadow, the lower parts of their faces showing vampire-pale like slices of the waning moon. I put some distance between myself and them and hailed a black and white taxi. The driver was a morose man whose shifty eyes flickered over me constantly in the mirror as if he suspected I might run off without paying.

The area around the Scorpion was semi-derelict – frontier territory, with fires in steel braziers and hunched figures with hostile eyes. The cheery crowd of revellers at the door came like an oasis in the desert. I pushed my way through them and nodded to Bakhit, the doorman. The big Turk laid a pudgy hand on my arm and led me aside into an alcove.

'Had some guys here tonight asking for you,' he said. 'Pale guys – skin like feta cheese – wearing long black trenchcoats and black hats. Looked like refugees from an undertaker's parlour.'

'Who were they?' I asked.

'Said they were cops,' he said, 'but they didn't look like any cops I've ever seen.'

'Funny,' I said, 'that's just what they say about me.'

Bakhit gave me a sliver of a grin. 'Watch your step, they could still be around.'

I thanked him and shuffled painfully down the steps. The place was more crowded than it had been the night before, or maybe I just arrived later. There was no snake-charmer tonight, and I searched in vain for escaped cobras under the tables. I bought a bottle of Stella beer from one of the animated shirts behind the bar, and stalked off in search of Halaby. The club was full of deafening music – there was a pop singer on stage, a foreign woman with Mohican hair dyed blue, paperclips in her ears, safety-pins in her nose, studs in her lips, and a tiny gold chain strung from earlobe to nostril. She was stubby and muscular with leather trousers, a fishnet blouse, ghastly red lipstick and cowboy boots that gave her the look of a streetwalker moonlighting. She sang with a rock band – long-haired, emaciated men with vacant faces – and her voice was like a mangle. I grimaced, longing for Nadia, but the clientele seemed to be enjoying it, whooping up on the dance-floor, so that I had to push through them. A cute-looking woman with a blonde fringe and a sequinned dress, smoking a cigarette, looked me up and down – not without interest, I thought. I made a mental note, and moved on, scrunching up my face against the decibels. I was relieved to find Halaby sitting at a table in the darkest of the alcoves, near the bathroom, and as far as it was physically possible to get from the raucous performer.

In spite of his Western dress, Halaby looked like some ancient tribal chief, a heavy man with a broad inscrutable face, his eye sockets so sandbagged with drinking that he could almost have been an Eskimo. His hair was all there but it was white and bristly and he wore an expensive well-cut suit, twenty years old, which hadn't been to the menders or the cleaners in many a moon. He didn't get up as I approached, in fact he showed no sign of having recognized me at all until I sat down in front of him with my beer, and then he glanced at me as if I'd been sitting there all along. He poured himself an araq from a bottle on the table.

'Have a real drink,' he said. He spoke Arabic like an aristocrat, with almost no Cairene accent, and his voice sounded as though he had a mouthful of treacle. Ironically, he always said that he came from a long line of gypsies – folk who wandered up and down the Nile telling fortunes, grinding knives and mending pans.

I sniffed the araq and was nauseated by the smell of aniseed. 'No thanks,' I said, 'I'm sticking to beer.'

Halaby gulped down araq. 'I suppose you're right,' he said. 'After all, Egypt has always been a beer-swilling culture. Beer has been brewed in this country for thousands of years. Think of that! There was no wine here till Akhnaton planted grapes and that's when everything started to go bad. If we'd stuck to beer, we'd probably still have been top dogs, but once wine appeared everything started to get soft and nancified!'

I chuckled, and Halaby leaned over towards me confidentially. 'I don't like it,' he whispered. 'There are goons following me.'

'Who?' I asked.

'I don't know. Not the usual watchers. Creeps in black coats and hats – like a uniform. Like they want you to know they're there.'

'Tell me about it,' I said, 'I've got the same problem.'

I drank some beer, and watched the couples on the dance-floor. The tempo of the music had changed abruptly – now it was soft and smoochy and the dancers were moving sensuously, coiling around each other's bodies. A glittering light turned circles above the dance-floor like an immense revolving eye. There were smells of tobacco-smoke and incense, and the atmosphere had started to become seductive. I saw the attractive sequinned woman dancing with a man and felt a pang of regret for missed opportunities. I tried to picture Daisy but the image was crushed by an overwhelming sense of guilt over Fawzi's death. As if reading my thoughts, Halaby said: 'Fawzi's dead then?'

'My God. The news travels quick,' I said.

'The dead travel quick, as they say,' he said, 'or something like that. Isn't it Goethe? That bloody medical facility the Yanks have is lethal. A place where many go in but few come out except in body bags. They missed Fawzi the first time round but I knew they'd get him in the end.'

I dragged my gaze away from the smooching dancers and peered at him candidly. 'They said it was food poisoning,' I said. 'Do you know something I don't?'

'I know plenty you don't. That's why you pay me. I remember Fawzi when he was a snotty-nosed street urchin begging for scraps. Food poisoning? I doubt it.' He tapped his nose with his finger and took a gulp of araq. He drank it neat, I noticed. 'I've been in this game a long time,' he said, 'ever since the British were here. Learned the spook trade from the Brits – they were the masters long before the CIA was ever heard of.'

'So?' I said, not seeing where this was leading.

'So, I've seen plenty of hit-jobs in my time. The Ibram hit looked like a professional operation, but then they screwed up by leaving Fawzi alive. They had to redress that somehow.'

'You mean Fawzi was got at? In a US medical facility guarded by marines and TV cameras?' I stared at him, and he gulped again. The action reminded me of a very large fish.

'Halaby knows,' he said, almost gloating.

'It'll all come out at the autopsy anyway,' I said.

'Maybe. Maybe not. Remember the Cranwell case a few years back? Body identified and sent off in an ambulance, but never reached the morgue?'

I shifted uncomfortably and tried to keep my face deadpan. 'You think this is connected?'

Halaby scratched his chin and narrowed the puffy eyes. 'I didn't say that,' he said, 'but when you've been in the business as long as me, you can feel when something big's going down. It's like a sixth sense. Faces shut up, telephones engaged, hushed voices, people acting out of character – small things like that.'

'And now the men in black.'

'Yes, the watchers. I don't like it, Sammy. I don't like it at all.'

He took a giant cigar out of his inside pocket and bit the end off. It looked like a real Havana, I thought. I watched as he lit it with a well-worn silver lighter. No matter how down-at-heel, guys like Halaby always had money for smokes and drink. He puffed out a circlet of cigar-smoke and watched me pensively, like a ruminating toad. 'I mean, why would the Militants take out a guy like Ibram?' he said. 'He wasn't even a Yank – not really. If you want to make a statement, plant a bloody bomb in a US embassy like they did in Nairobi in 'ninety-eight. And then why Fawzi? No, there's got to be something more to it than that.'

I deliberately changed the subject. 'You get any of the stuff Hammoudi asked for?'

He drew himself up slightly and puffed on the cigar, sucking in his cheeks. Then he blew out a series of rings, ignoring my question and regarding me with faint disdain, as though it had been vulgar of me to remind him of work. I knew he was stalling, spinning it out as long as possible. He might have been laying on the gravity just to up the fee, but I suspected that it was really because he had something interesting to tell me and wanted to make it as dramatic as possible. Halaby had a prodigious memory for detail, and he probably knew more political secrets than any other Egyptian alive. If he hadn't got himself mixed up with the Shadowmen and started taking rake-offs to keep his trap shut he'd have retired a national hero.

At first Hammoudi had suspected Halaby was the stoolie who'd tipped the Shadowmen off the day we'd staked out the Gallery – the day I'd ended up as a human shield for Hammoudi and got a round in my lung for it. But Hammoudi had interrogated him personally and had been satisfied it was someone else. We knew about Halaby's involvement of course, and he'd been lucky to escape prison, but I suppose in the end he knew too much about too many people, and the top brass wouldn't go for it. His silence was his ticket to staying out of jail, but who knew when someone might decide he had to be silenced for all time. No wonder he drank, I thought. I wouldn't have wanted to be in his position for a million pounds. But then I don't suppose he'd have wanted to be in mine.

He looked at me with his big toad eyes and assumed a dignified expression. 'Let's get something straight,' he said, 'I don't do it for the money, you know. I do it because it interests me.'

I knew I'd been too peremptory. With people like Halaby you had to work your way round to things slowly in old Arab style, otherwise the prickles came up. I guess I was just too tired to play the game. 'Of course, Anton,' I said, soothingly, 'I know that. Everybody does. You've got enough stashed away from your . . . well, your arrangements, to last you for good. And I know, you only dabbled a bit because they didn't pay you enough. They never paid you anything like what you were worth.'

He nodded happily. We both knew it was a lie, but a necessary fiction I indulged in to allow him to keep his face. I was still anxious to get to the nitty-gritty, though. He took a great drag of smoke from his cigar and let it out. 'First, Monod,' he said.

I nodded. I wasn't going to let on that I'd actually met Monod. Halaby didn't need to know, and if he knew it would have spoiled his performance anyway.

'The guy's Swiss,' Halaby said, 'but spent years in Egypt. He's an engineer by training and has worked on dams and irrigation projects all over Africa and the Middle East. Married to an Egyptian woman of an old family, and his wife and kids live in Geneva. Speaks Arabic like a native. Seems he's most well known in Egypt for his theory about the pyramids, though. He's written a lot of stuff about it.'

'What is his theory?'

Halaby grunted, as if annoyed that I'd cut off his flow. 'It's all mathematics,' he said. 'Very involved. You know I don't have a head for all that stuff, but basically he reckons he's discovered that the Great Pyramid was built in alignment with various constellations. It's kind of complicated.'

I scratched my head. 'Seems to me I've heard this stuff before, but the name Monod means nothing to me and records came up with zero.'

Halaby looked pleased, as if he'd been waiting for this one. 'Ah,' he said, 'that's because he writes under a pseudonym. Calls himself Max Heinberg – ever heard the name.'

'Sure – books are on every news stand. That explains a lot.'

'Yeah, like I told you, I know lots of things you don't. Anyway, this Monod-Heinberg was listed for appointment to the Millennium Committee, but about two months ago he just vanished. At first I thought he might be dead, but a little bird told me he's alive, and hiding out in Khan al-Khalili. From what I don't know – maybe his wife!'

I weighed up his words, or at least I made a show of appearing to. 'Andropov said he'd been getting threats from the Militants,' I said. 'Reckoned that Monod had dipped out for the same reason. If you look at it we've got three prominent men, either potential members or actual members of the Millennium Committee. Monod vanishes, Ibram gets himself whacked out, and Andropov gets cold feet and resigns. We know the Militants have threatened the millennium celebrations. What makes you so sure it's something else?'

Halaby gulped and blew out his cheeks. 'I told you,' he said, 'it's just my nose. Militant terrorism is a war fought in the media – it's about publicity, about getting your name on TV. Why no claims in the press about the Ibram killing, then? Somehow it's not right. And anyway, what makes you so damn sure Andropov is telling the truth?'

'OK,' I said. My head was throbbing and I wished to hell I hadn't let Monod escape. 'What about Sanusi? Anything on him?'

He sipped araq and wrinkled his face up into a good imitation of a giant prune. I looked at him, seeing what might have been veiled excitement in his eyes. Halaby had seen everything in his time, so anything that excited him had to be worth knowing. 'Now, this is quite interesting,' he said. That meant it was very interesting. 'You wanted to know if Sanusi is bona fide – he is. He is the son of King Idris – last king of Libya – and would have been in line for the throne if Gaddaffi hadn't kicked the monarchy out. It's also true he's a distinguished Egyptologist. He's done quite a few excavations in his time – notably at Amarna where he unearthed a famous bust of Nefertiti. My sources reckon he's actually a first-class field archaeologist but he's said to be more than the usual eccentric – definitely not playing with a full deck of cards.'

He sat back and sipped araq as if he'd said it all. I knew there was more to come, but I played along and pretended to be aghast. 'Is that it?' I said. 'Is that what you call interesting? There's nothing there I didn't know or couldn't have found out myself.'

Halaby examined his cigar and smiled with satisfaction. He loved to be badgered – made him feel wanted, I suppose. 'You people,' he said. 'Too hasty. Too hasty by half. In the old days an agent would sit patiently for hours to get to the end of the story. Now you're giving up before we've even started.' He exhaled smoke in my direction, and I looked at him expectantly. The girl singer was growling out a throaty tune which bordered on a decent melody. 'Let's say our Doctor Sanusi is who he reckons he is,' Halaby said, 'but that he only told you half the story. Let's say he failed to give you certain information you might have found relevant to the case.'

I finished my beer, and he pushed over the bottle of araq. I shook my head. 'Like what?' I said.

'Let's start with history – Sanusi's favourite subject. When the Brits whupped the Sanusiya in 1916, they pushed them out of Siwa Oasis and captured a whole bunch of fully fledged, card-carrying Brothers. These weren't the rank and file Bedouin fighters who wore amulets like the ones you found, but big honchos of the Brotherhood, all trained in the Sanusi University at Jaghbub, all initiates into the inner workings of the organiz-ation. The British GHQ in Cairo sent one of their top Intelligence boys down to Siwa to interrogate them, and the results were collected in a fat file. All this was long before my time, of course, but as they say, "He who lives long will see the camel slaughtered". Well, the file passed through my hands once. I was only meant to consign it to someone else, and I never read the whole thing. But I do remember that this blue-eyed boy was from the Cairo Intelligence Section – which used to be in the old Savoy Hotel in what's now Medan Talat Harb. His name was Captain Thomas Lawrence.'

I looked at him, startled, but Halaby's gaze was distracted by something, and I gazed over my shoulder to see Bakhit, the doorman, easing his bulk through the crowds on the dance-floor. He looked unhurried, imperturbable, yet there was still something about his demeanour that disturbed me. 'He never comes down here,' Halaby whispered. 'There's trouble.'

I tore my gaze away from the bouncer. 'OK,' I said, 'but I want to hear the end of it. You mean the guy investigating the Sanusiya was Lawrence of Arabia?'

Halaby narrowed his eyes, keeping them half on Bakhit's advancing figure. 'I don't know,' he said, 'I mean, the name isn't that rare among the Brits, so it could have been someone else. But T. E. Lawrence *was* working in GHQ Cairo then – it was before he was officially transferred to the Arab Bureau – and according to his own writings he did do some kind of hush-hush trip to the Sanusiya in 1916, though he never let on any details about the mission.'

'What was the mission?' I asked, feeling the excitement mounting now. Halaby had been deliberately leading up to this all evening, I realized.

Suddenly Bakhit was looming over us, his scarred face a map of darkness in the ultra-violet light. 'Your friends came back,' he breathed. 'You know – the Undertakers.'

'You find out who they are?'

'They got ID cards issued by the police department here. I said I hadn't had a sniff of you tonight and threw them out, but you could tell they didn't buy it.'

'Thanks friend,' I said, 'I owe you.'

Bakhit fingered the scar on his face, 'Nah,' he said, 'you covered my ass when I needed it.'

I thanked him again and watched him oozing off into the crowd.

'Sound guy, Bakhit,' Halaby said, 'for a Turk.'

I cast a discreet glance at Halaby. 'Who are these assholes?' I said.

He flicked cigar-ash into the ashtray, blinked his eyelids mechanically, and brought out a Luger pistol that looked like it had come out of the Ark. He laid it on the table in front of him.

'That thing belongs in a museum,' I said.

'Don't you believe it,' he said, 'best handgun ever made.'

'We ought to bug out of it.'

'Yes,' he said, but he didn't make a move. 'Let them stew a bit first.'

I looked back at the stairs, through the pulsating dancers. Then I fixed on Halaby. 'Right,' I said, 'what about this file?'

'As I said, I didn't really read it,' he said distantly. 'It seemed like old hat when I was a young sprog in the 1940s. There was a war on, Rommel was advancing on Cairo, and the Brits were more concerned about an uprising among the Egyptians and the Rebecca spy-ring than digging up ancient files. But I do know that it was this Lawrence's job to talk to the Sanusiya Brothers who'd been captured. The interrogations were very specific. They were concerned with an archaeological project – a project that the Brothers had organized in the Western Desert.'

'Wasn't Lawrence an archaeologist by profession?'

'Before the war he'd spent years digging up Hittite cities in Syria, and he'd even worked in Egypt with Flinders Petrie. So he certainly would have been the right man for the job. Now, all I remember from my quick scan of the file was that this dig was being carried out by Sanusi labourers under the supervision of German and Austrian archaeologists. That's why the Brits were so interested of course – they probably thought it was a front for something else. The really odd thing is that the dig was taking place right smack in the middle of the Western Desert – the place they call the "Sea Without Water", the *Bahr Bela Ma*.'

'That's the most God-forsaken place in the Sahara,' I said. 'Why would anyone be digging out there?'

Halaby pouted and laid his cigar in the ashtray. 'I can't answer that,' he said, 'but I'll tell you something surprising. About half a year back, our Doctor Sanusi also worked on a dig out in the Western Desert. It was kept very secret. No one I've talked to knows exactly what they were digging up, but there are two very intriguing coincidences . . .' His eyes focused over my shoulder again, and he placed his big calloused hand on the Luger as if gaining comfort from its presence. 'First, the director of the project was none other than your murdered man, Adam Ibram, and second, the excavation took place in the Sea Without Water – exactly where Sanusi's ancestors were digging with the Krauts in 1916.'

'You're joking!'

'One hundred per cent gilt-edged source.'

'That lying bastard told me he didn't know Ibram.'

Halaby smirked. 'Saw you coming,' he said.

'Anton,' I said, 'where would that file be now? Shredded?'

'Guys like the Brits don't shred files. If it's anywhere it'll be the basement archives of the old British embassy in Garden City. Now let's get the hell out before we get shredded ourselves!'

22

WE PAUSED FOR A MOMENT at the top of the outside stairs, and I spotted a huddle of dark-cloaked figures lurking in a den of shadows farther down the street. 'It's them,' I told Halaby. 'Let's go the other way.'

The old man creased a smile at me and tapped the Luger in his pocket. 'I'm too old for cloak and dagger,' he said.

We shook hands, and while Halaby trolled off defiantly in their direction, I slipped quickly into the combat-zone – the wedge of ruined streets that lay between here and the smart island suburb of Zamalek. It was a dark underside of Cairo – a place where illicit araq stills lay hidden among disused brick-kilns and dyers' yards. There were basements that housed hashish- and opium-dens, and filthy garrets that served as brothels. The place reeked of vice, I thought. You could get almost anything illegal or salacious here from a shot of heroin to a blow-job from a child. The unlit alleys were full of cameo figures smoking at corners with only the glowing butts of their Cleopatras visible in the darkness. Cairene voices muttered and grated. The air was full of the smells of cooking oil, gasoline fumes, urine and honey-tobacco, with the occasional distinct whiff of strong hashish. This wasn't a place for cops to go wandering in alone at night, but that suited me fine. I glanced around cautiously and zipped up my jacket. I pushed my hands into my pockets and hunched up defensively as I turned along the street. A girl – a ghost figure in an ankle-length dress – suddenly put her arms round me in the darkness. For a second I felt frantically for my stiletto. 'You want to fuck me, friend?' she said. Her body was thin but hard under the cloth, and I could smell the cheap alcohol on her breath like a trademark. Almost at once I caught the hand that streaked towards the back pocket of my jeans, and wrenched it savagely, bending the wrist back with both hands until the girl screamed in pain. 'Son-of-a-bitch!' she gasped.

'You'll have to do better than that, sister,' I told her, 'I grew up in a place like this. Let me show you how it's done some time.' I let her go and as she melted into the night, I glanced back into the shadows. Dark figures were moving there, but whether they were my watchers I couldn't be certain, and I wasn't going to wait to find out. I cut down an alley between big warehouse-type buildings, so narrow that I almost had to turn sideways. It came out into a welcome splash of light along Aziz Abaza Street by the river, from where I could see the Nile glinting – a stream of diamonds on black velvet – and the security lights in the twin pagodas of Cairo Plaza across the river. Cars and pedestrians passed busily up and down the street, and I came to a black and white taxi rank and climbed in the first car. The driver started without even asking me where I was going, and it was only when he pulled out into the traffic that he turned around slightly and I recognized the same morose, shifty guy who'd brought me from Roda earlier in the evening.

'I've been waiting for you,' he said.

'Thanks,' I said, uneasily. A warning light was blinking behind my eyes. I hadn't asked him to wait, and how could he possibly have known I'd head for this particular rank? It could have been pure coincidence, but how often do you hail the same cab twice anywhere, let alone in Cairo?

His eyes focused on me in the mirror. 'Back to Roda?' he enquired.

'No,' I said, 'I changed my mind. Stop right here.'

'Anything you say, Lieutenant Rashid,' he said, jerking his foot down on the brake so hard I was hurled forward against the back of his seat. Next thing I knew there was a gun in his right hand and a walkie-talkie in his left, and he was out of the open door with the hardware levelled at me. 'Get out!' he growled, 'Get out now!'

I pulled on the handle with my right foot braced against the door and kicked it open as hard as I could, catching him right in the midriff. He took a step back and doubled over gasping for breath, and in that second I leapt out and kicked him in the head. As he buckled I wrenched the pistol out of his hand, grabbed the walkie-talkie and tossed it into the river below us. It plummeted thirty feet down and landed with a splash. Passing cars were starting to hoot and flash headlights at us and there was a screech of brakes as a police squad car arrived. Four blackjackets armed with kalashnikovs jumped out and sur-rounded me. The taxi driver cowered against the wall rubbing his head, as I slipped out my ID card. 'Lieutenant Rashid, SID,' I said, 'I'm arresting this man for assault on a police officer.'

The senior blackjacket was a rotund man with a piggy face and great dewlaps of fat round his chin. His uniform was stained and ragged and his boots unlaced. He smiled crookedly at me. 'It's you who's under arrest, Lieutenant,' he said. 'There's a general alert out for you!'

For a moment I didn't know whether to run or fight. 'What the shit are you talking about?' I said. 'On whose orders?'

'Mahmud Siyudi – the Commissioner of Police.'

'You lying sleaze-wad!' I said. Piggy-face scowled and went for his night-stick. I bunnied out of range and grabbed the taxi driver by the throat, wheeling him around and digging the tip of my stiletto into his back. 'One step closer and this guy will be stewing-steak,' I said. For a moment the other blackjackets looked at Piggy-face, uncertain what to do. In that instant I kicked the driver towards them, jumped on to the wall, and leapt clean through the night air, thirty feet down into the indigo waters of the Nile.

23

I PULLED MYSELF OUT OF the Nile dripping and quaking with cold further down the bank. The cops hadn't been brave enough to jump in after me, and evidently they'd been given orders not to open fire. No one came for me, and there was no one much about to see the trail of dirty water I left all the way along the sidewalk. I decided not to go home. Tonight I was number one on the wanted list, and I had to lay low, so I made for a doss-house I knew near the Marriott Hotel where they didn't ask questions. I slept naked with my clothes on the radiator and in the morning they'd dried out. The first thing I did after I left the place was ring Hammoudi, praying that his phone wasn't tapped. 'What the hell's this about a general alert?' I demanded as soon as he answered.

'It's Fawzi,' he said, 'Van Helsing made a big brouhaha about his death and your negligence. I tried to stop it but he went over my head – to the police commissioner himself. The Big Man wants you picked up just to keep the Yanks quiet. That's pending the outcome of the autopsy, which will be done today. At least, that's the story.'

'What do you mean?'

'There's always a story within a story, Sammy, wheels within wheels.'

'You mean maybe Fawzi's only an excuse, and Van Helsing wants me out of the way?'

'Could be. Whatever you do, don't come in. I just had a call from Little Miss Muffet, and she knows the heat is on you. Says to meet her at the mummies room in the Egyptian museum as soon as it opens.'

'Can we trust her?'

'God only knows.'

There were Tourism and Antiquities policemen on duty at the museum, so instead of showing my ID, I bundled my handgun and my blade up in a plastic bag and handed it in at the cloakroom. Then I bought a ticket and went through the metal-detector as a tourist. When I arrived at the mummies room, Daisy was already there, staring intently at the egg-shell fragile skull of Ramses II in his glass case. 'Sammy!' she said, as I kissed her on both cheeks, Italian style. 'What the hell is happening?'

'I don't know,' I said, 'I talked to an informant last night. He says Sanusi was lying. He and Ibram knew each other well. They worked on a project together in the *Bahr Bela Ma* – that's in the Western Desert – only a matter of months ago.'

'Son-of-a-bitch!' Daisy said. 'He said he'd never heard of Ibram until he died. I'll lay fifty bucks all that crap about *Jinns* and Mamluks was thrown in to put us off the scent, too.'

'Sssh!' the security guard said suddenly, and for a moment we pretended to be absorbed by the bodies of half a dozen of the greatest kings and queens in history laid out for public view. What struck me was how incredibly feeble they looked. Ramses II of the Nineteenth Dynasty was supposed to have been one of the richest of the pharaohs. He'd had vast temple complexes built, like Abu Simbel, with its immense statues. Yet his cadaver looked so rat-like, with its protruding teeth and emaciated limbs that you couldn't suppress the feeling that it had all been megalomania – dwarves making themselves into giants for posterity. I couldn't help thinking of the wizard in *The Wizard of Oz* – the poor old man who used a projector to make himself look frightening on a cinema screen. No matter how great and noble you believed yourself to be in life, you ended up like this – a shrivelled bag of bones lying in a box – in this case a glass box, for every Tom, Dick and Harry in the world to gawk at.

Daisy looked up and touched my hand. 'By rights I should turn you in,' she whispered, 'this is my case too, remember. Right now you're officially renegade.'

'The whole thing stinks. Why didn't they wait for the autopsy on Fawzi?'

'Ssh!' the guard insisted. 'Silence please. If you go on disturbing everyone I shall have to ask you to leave.'

Daisy giggled and looked around. Apart from the dead bodies there was no one but ourselves in the chamber. 'But who are we disturbing?' she asked.

'Madam,' the guard said, 'you are disturbing the dead.'

We were still chuckling when we came down the steps to the main concourse. Daisy halted to examine some models in glass cases – squads of black Nubian soldiers carrying bows and arrows, and Egyptian spearmen which had been found buried with a mummified ruler of Asyut, and dated from the First Intermediate Period. 'That was the time Andropov was talking about,' I told Daisy. 'The First Intermediate Period came after the collapse of the Old Kingdom – the so-called "Golden Age".'

'What was your feeling about Andropov, anyway?'

'Kind of glib and egocentric. Reeled off his story like he'd learned it by heart. No emotion about Ibram's death, and did you notice – the monks seemed scared shitless about something.'

'Yeah, Grigori couldn't keep his hand still enough to light a cigarette.' She read the caption with interest. 'The First Intermediate Period,' she said. 'Isn't that when Ibram reckoned the Sahara turned to desert?'

'Yes. There's no doubt there was a lot of turmoil in the Nile Valley at that time. Monuments from the period are very few – just pathetic copies of older ones, and fine carving disappears. Every local ruler was at war with his neighbour – that's why they had themselves buried with squads of model soldiers – they believed the same petty wars would continue in the afterlife.'

Daisy moved on and examined a lion-sphinx of the Nubian period, small but powerful-looking with an almost human face. 'So we've now got three guys Ibram worked with in the past,' she said. 'First he works on desertification theory with Andropov, then, a year ago with this Monod in the Great Pyramid at Giza, and more recently, six months ago, with Sanusi in the what was it . . . the *Bahr* . . .'

'*Bahr Bela Ma.*'

I ran my hand over the sphinx's fine carving, knowing it was not allowed, but wanting to do it all the same. Another security guard started looking at me hard, so I took Daisy by the elbow, moving her through distorted oblongs of light thrown across the floor from the high windows. We ducked into a side room where there were more reliefs from the First Intermediate Period, very crudely done compared with those of an earlier age.

'Man, they really lost it,' Daisy said.

'There were a lot of invasions from nomads – Semites from the east and Libyans from the west, taking advantage of the disorder – and look at this.' I pointed to some models of funerary boats, roughly carved, their cabin roofs protected by cowhide shields. 'You won't see shields on the funerary boats of any other period,' I said. 'That gives you an idea of the defensive mentality they must have had.'

Daisy looked up suddenly. 'What do you know about this *Bahr Bela Ma*?' she asked. I noticed she was pronouncing it perfectly now.

'It's one of the most arid regions of the Western Desert,' I said. 'Just sand-dunes rolling on and on for ever. Nothing lives out there – it's as sterile as the icecaps, but there are legends that there was an inland sea there in ancient times.'

'Why would anyone be doing archaeology out there?'

'Search me. The ancient Egyptians were shit-scared of the wilderness outside the banks of the Nile and never built out there. The only possibility I can think of is some neolithic find like Nabta Playa – a prehistoric water-hole with traces of generations of human settlement.'

'But Sanusi's an Egyptologist, not a prehistorian, and he was along for a reason.'

'Sure, because Ibram was digging in the same place Sanusi's ancestors were digging when they were defeated by the British in 1916. Whatever it was the Sanusiya and the Germans were looking for then, Ibram must have been looking for too.'

'Let's get into the light,' she said, 'it's too gloomy in here.' We hurried down the long colonnaded stairs, though knots of sightseers, past the gift shop and out into the blazing light of the museum garden. It was packed with tourists queuing to go in and others picknicking or just sitting on the lawns. A brass band in Ruritanian uniforms of purple with gold braid was about to strike up, and bootblacks and ice-cream sellers prowled through the crowds. We blinked in the light and sat on the grass by the ornamental fountain, from where I was able to keep a careful eye on the guards at the gate. I felt naked without my Beretta.

Daisy was wearing grey slacks cut off at the knees and a close-fitting blue blouse, and she sat with her legs folded enticingly sideways, with all the elegance of a ballet-dancer. She tossed her long plait and pinned me down with her soft blue eyes. 'Your stoolie told you he saw Lawrence's report, right?' she asked.

'He said it was a fat file, and he reckons it's probably still in the archives of the old British embassy.'

Daisy's eyes came alive again and for an optimistic moment I thought it might be because she'd suddenly developed the hots for me. 'I read about that recently in an Int. Brief,' she said. 'The Brits moved their embassy out of the city centre, but they left some of the old Arab Bureau files from World War One in there, pending transfer to the UK.' Her eyes sparkled. 'You know,' she said, 'it would be a pretty easy job to get into that old place, wouldn't it?'

I gaped at her, remembering that I was being hunted by my own side. 'Are you crazy?' I said. 'That's all I need.'

She smiled again and tipped her head to one side mockingly. She looked incredibly alluring and it was all I could do to stop myself throwing my arms round her there and then. 'OK,' she said, 'but how else are we going to find out?'

'It'd be a whole lot easier just to ask the Brits.'

'We have to keep this in the family. We don't know what's really behind it.'

'Why not lean on Sanusi?'

'The file would give us a lever. Anyhow, forget it – I wouldn't expect a dedicated SID man like you to do anything illegal.'

I almost choked. 'You conniving little –' She stopped me in mid-sentence, grinning beautifully, displaying even white teeth and wriggling slightly as if angling her body into seduction mode. I knew I was being manipulated by the oldest trick in the book, but I couldn't resist it anyhow.

24

THE OLD BRITISH EMBASSY WAS built in 1893 by a guy called Sir Evelyn Baring, who was known as British Agent, to disguise the fact that in those days it was the Brits, not the Khedive, who really called the shots. Officially Egypt was part of the Turkish Empire up till the Brits creamed the Turks in 1918. Then the Agent was renamed High Commissioner, but his power stayed the same right up till 1920, when the country got its nominal independence. Throughout the colonial period this house had been the centre of power, but like the Sanusiya it was only history now. Through the window of Daisy's Fiat it looked deserted – there were no TV cameras or para-military guards on the gate.

'Why don't we just steam in from the front?' I suggested.

Daisy made a face. 'It might look decrepit,' she said, 'but the archives are well guarded.'

I glanced at her quizzically. 'How the hell can you be so sure?' I said.

'US Mark One Eyeball,' she said. 'One of our guys got in there under some pretext a while ago and wrote a brief just in case anyone might need it. Said there are guards with dogs outside.'

'So how do you propose to get in, if it's not through the front door.'

She grinned, enjoying this. 'There's more than one way to skin a cat.'

She halted the car under a convenient gamez tree on the Corniche and flipped a folded document from the back seat on to my knee. It was a map, but one you certainly couldn't buy at a corner stationer's – a Cairo street-plan dating back to colonial times, almost yellow with age. 'God bless the US embassy resources section,' she said.

I looked at her in surprise. 'You didn't register it, did you?' I asked. 'We'll be up shit creek if anyone gets even a whisper of this.'

She shot me an irritated glance. 'This is not my first time on covert,' she snapped. 'Of course I didn't register. I just borrowed it.'

'Hey, don't take that tone with me, miss. You guys aren't famous for discretion.'

She pouted at me, and pointed a finger at the map. 'Here's the old embassy complex,' she said. 'The basement where the Arab Bureau files are kept is directly under the old chancellery building – here.' As she leaned over to look I smelled her hair, like wild grass, and a hint of perfume that was almost intoxicating. I blinked deliberately to remind myself to concentrate. 'Now look at this,' she said. 'There's a drain connecting the complex to the Nile – a big one – and it passes right under the chancellery. If we could get up that drain, I'll bet we could enter the basement.'

I raised my eyebrows. 'It's a big if,' I said. 'In case you hadn't noticed, the Nile's quite high these days. That drain is going to be flooded, and anyway who says the drain connects with the archives?'

'Our scout does. He reported that there is an iron grille set in the floor of a passage which leads to the archives' main door – a steel door with a padlock.'

I scratched the stubble on my chin. 'So even if we got through the grille, we'd have the door to deal with.'

'Yeah, but the good news is that the guards are outside the building.'

'OK, but you still have to get up a flooded drain.'

Daisy ran a hand through her silky blonde hair, just above the ear. 'No problem to me,' she said, 'I'm from California. I could snorkel when I was five and use scuba gear at ten. I've done the sub-aqua course with the Navy Seals, which included underwater demolitions.'

I let out a long gasp. 'You mean the plan is to blast your way in with explosives?'

She chuckled. 'No way,' she said, shaking her head, 'we'll use oxyacetylene torches. Almost the first thing you learn with the Seals. Go through the grille like a knife through butter.'

'What do you mean we?' I said. 'I never agreed to any of this.'

She flashed me a pitying look, 'Oh dear,' she said. 'Whatsamatter? Can't you swim or what?'

'I'm a land person, I've always had a deep distrust for water.'

This time her surprise was genuine. 'You're kidding,' she said. 'I thought you grew up on the banks of the world's longest river!'

I laughed. 'Had you going though,' I said. 'We've got some of the best sub-aqua sites in the world here on the Red Sea coast. I know how to put an aqualung on anyway – the oxyacetylene business is your baby, but I'm mustard on doors and locks.'

She looked at me with real pleasure. 'So you're in then?' she said.

I sighed. 'For you, Special Agent, anything.'

25

IT WAS JUST SUNSET WHEN I nursed the launch out of the docks at Bulaq, and the Nile was a river of fire, painted crimson by a sun melting into soft golden wreaths. We'd worked like skivvies to get everything assembled in a day. Daisy had hired the scuba gear from an American company that specialized in supplying Egypt's off-shore oil-rigs in the Red Sea, while it had been my job to hire the boat. All I could get at such short notice was a Nile longboat with an awning and an outboard motor. I had to pay a lot of bakshish to my old buddy Gasim Abd al-Majid at the docks, to take the boat out myself and to keep his mouth shut. The launch was called *Princess Maria* and though she wasn't fast she was solid and comfortable, with plenty of room for our tanks. As we headed downstream towards Garden City the colours slowly burned out of the river, reducing it to a slick blackness, and the boat seemed to merge into the waters, a diaphanous dark ghost. Daisy sat in the bows in her wet-suit, looking at the great buildings that reared up on both sides of us like colossal networks of coloured lights – gold, emerald green, sodium orange, scarlet and methylene blue. It was like running in a deep ravine between chasms hung with billions of pulsating jewels. For a moment the noises of the city faded and the lights went out of focus, blending with the stars into an infinite galaxy of sparkling points. For a moment I was absorbed into the waters:

the Horus-King drifting in his Royal Bark through the Great River in the Sky.

For this crossing I had adopted yet another persona – I stood at the tiller like a real Nile boatman, wearing a loosely bound turban and a flowing *gallabiyya* with my wet-suit underneath. I guided the boat past the great floating restaurants north of Tahrir Bridge, galaxies of light-bulbs scintillating in the darkness, and chugged on under the bridge itself, veering to the eastern bank. I was born almost in sight of the Nile, and despite years away I have never lost my awe of the river. Its perennial waters flow out of Lake Victoria, four thousand miles south of here, and take three months to reach the Mediterranean Sea. The annual spate on which the entire edifice of ancient Egyptian civilization rested, though, was due mainly to the rain that fell on the mountains of Ethiopia and rushed down the Blue Nile, meeting the White Nile at Khartoum, then surging north into Egypt itself. The ancient Egyptians never discovered the source of the Nile. They believed that the stream issued from a cave under Elephantine Island at Aswan, presided over by the ram-headed deity, Khnum. The pharaoh was regarded as no less than the creator of the Nile flood, and one of his main duties was to perform magical rites to ensure that it would be bountiful – rites which probably included the drowning of a sacrificial victim. At times like the First Intermediate Period, when the flood failed, though, it was the pharaoh himself who became the scapegoat.

At the northern end of Roda Island the river narrowed, and we passed under a bridge lined with yellow globes which threw streaks of flame on the velveteen waters. Near Garden City I drew in closer to the bank and throttled down. Daisy shifted place, careful to maintain balance, creeping up beside me. She opened a rucksack and brought out our old city map covered in polythene, a sub-aqua spotlight, and a handheld GPS. It took her only a minute to punch in the coordinates. 'Here it is!' she said, flashing her spotlight at the bank, which was lined with masonry blocks. I slowed down and let the craft glide in along the masonry, where the mouth of a giant drain suddenly yawned at us in the torchlight. The details of the masonry and the chance play of light and shade made it look momentarily like the open jaws of Apop – the Eternal Snake. Closer up, we could both see that the drain was covered by a deeply rusted iron grille that looked at least a hundred years old. Daisy switched the torch off and I cut the engine and dropped anchor. Higher up the bank the Corniche was lined with ornamental trees, and from behind them came the unceasing growl of the traffic. I knew now we'd been right to launch the op in the early hours of the evening rather than the dead of night. At three in the morning we'd have stuck out like sore thumbs. We sat in the shadow of the awning while Daisy made last adjustments to the tanks.

'That grille's wrought iron,' I said. 'It's going to be a bunch of laughs cutting your way through it in muddy water at night.'

Daisy was faceless in the shadows, with only highlights picked out on her wet-suit zips, and hair. 'I'll do a recce,' she said. 'At least we don't have to worry about sharks.'

'No,' I said, 'but watch out. A hundred-pound Nile perch can give you a nasty suck.'

She giggled as she pulled on her flippers, and I helped her to check and fit the double tanks. Finally she fitted a hood and mask, and I opened the oxygen for her. She took a long breath from the mouthpiece and gave me the thumbs-up. I helped her to the bows, where she squatted down awkwardly then rolled backwards into the water with a splash, instantly disappearing into the darkness. The boat rocked slightly, and I moved back amidships where the rest of our gear was stowed under a dark oilcloth. I was about to strip off my *gallabiyya*, when I noticed the beam of a searchlight playing along the river from the south. I stopped and peered into the night. The searchlight was powerful and it was attached to a launch, invisible behind the glare, but moving up towards me fast. A moment later the beam hit me full in the face and stayed there. I blinked in the light. The launch swept closer and the *Princess Maria* wobbled in its wash. I peered at it, certain now that it was a police patrol vessel. Nothing else would carry such a powerful light, or have the effrontery to use it on the river at night. I heard the launch's engine change to idle, and made out the movement of crouching figures on deck. I knew that police launches carried machine-guns, and became horribly aware that right now I was a sitting duck.

'Hey!' I shouted, trying to shade my eyes and putting on my broadest, most indignant Cairene accent. 'What's the big idea?'

'Police!' a gravel voice called through a megaphone. 'Everything all right, *Princess Maria*?'

'It was till you come alongside blinding me – Your Presence.'

'What are you doing at anchor off Garden City?'

I paused and brought out a fishing line I'd found in the stern, wound around two pegs of wood. I held it up and grinned broadly in the searchlight beam. 'Supper!' I said.

There was a moment's silence from the launch and in that moment I heard a faint splash behind me. It could only be Daisy surfacing, I thought, and in a second she would probably throw herself across the bow with some exclamation, right into the searchlight. I waited, frozen with fear, the grin etched painfully on my face. The seconds passed with excruciating slowness. 'Watch out for anything unusual,' the voice from the launch came back suddenly, 'and report it immediately to the river police. There are a lot of drug smugglers about.' I nodded and forced myself to smile. Then mercifully the beam flashed on some other vessel downstream and the launch's engine was engaged. The vessel grumbled past, sending *Princess Maria* rocking in its wake. '*Tisbah 'ala khayr!*' I shouted as it went, 'Wake up with the goodness!' I watched it melt into the night, adding 'and drown yourselves you bastards!' under my breath. Only when the throb of its engine had faded completely did I heave a sigh of relief and shift to the bows.

Daisy was patiently treading water and I hauled her out, holding her tighter than politeness permitted. If she minded she didn't say anything, and her body felt taut and hard under the wet-suit. 'Jesus Christ!' she panted as she pulled the mask off. 'You try treading water with two full tanks and a weighted belt. What the hell was that about, anyway?'

'Police,' I said, 'on the lookout for drug smugglers. At least, that was what they said.'

She slipped off her hood and shook out her wet hair, which caught the light and sparkled exotically. She sat down on one of the plank seats. 'You think they were on to you?' she enquired.

'Who knows?' I said. 'Bit of a coincidence picking on us like that. For a moment I knew how a hare feels when you get it in your headlights. Anyway, if they come back, I'm prepared.' I showed her the oilskin bag in which I'd sealed my Beretta.

She felt the metal through the waxy material. 'You mean you're ready to take on your own people?' she asked. There was wonder in her voice.

'I didn't say that,' I said, 'but there's a general alert out for your favourite SID lieutenant, and tonight we're on the wrong side of the law. Let's say if the moment comes I'm going to have to think very carefully about whether I want to be taken in.'

There were a few seconds of silence, and I could feel rather than see Daisy's eyes boring into me. She was wondering if it was bravado, and if not what kind of cop it was who was ready to shoot it out with his own team. She was concluding that it could either be a cop who was secretly on the make, or one who was working to some higher agenda. Which of those was Sammy Rashid, she must have thought.

'I'm a bit awed that you're willing to go to such extremes for me,' she said. 'I mean, I know I'm charming and all, but I didn't realize it was as powerful as that!'

I smirked, catching the irony in her tone. 'OK,' I said, 'let's drop the mutual admiration society meeting, shall we? What did you find down there?'

She must have grinned, but I only got a flash of silver-white teeth. 'That's the good news,' she said. 'The masonry's sandstone, and it's been eaten away by the water. The grille's come loose at the bottom and I pulled it almost all the way out, so we can go through the drain like a dose of salts.'

26

T HE WATER WAS COLD EVEN in the wet-suit. I carried my
oilskin bag slung from a weighted belt, and drew in lungfuls
of canned air in great huffs. I towed the oxyacetylene gear behind
me, not out of chivalry, but so Daisy could light the way in front
with her sub-aqua torch. In its powerful beam I saw things I'd
rather not have seen, dead rats, birds, human faeces – and, just
in front of the grating the torch picked out the bloated cadaver
of a huge black dog, staring right at us with its diseased yellow
eyes. I shivered, thinking of the dog-headed god Anubis, protec-
tor of the secret passages.

We passed under the grille and into the pitch darkness beyond
where there was no sound but the slop of water on old masonry
and the constant eruption of bubbles from our mouthpieces. The
only light was the starburst around Daisy's head, from which I
could see her body in silhouette, sleek and undulating, as stream-
lined as a seal. In the spotlight the water looked smooth and
creamy, but the drain zigzagged left and right, occasionally leaving me in total oblivion. It was frighteningly claustrophobic, and
I wondered whether it would be like this at the bottom of the
deepest ocean. In those dark moments I thought I saw shadows
flitting by, floating beings with hieroglyph faces – falcon-headed
men, lion-headed women, creatures with the heads of men and
the bodies of dogs or lions, many-headed hydras, sharp-taloned

ghouls. I thought of Ra's battle with demons in the waterways of the night, and then I realized that these images were products of my own imagination – projections of my unconscious mind on the emptiness.

Suddenly Daisy stopped. The drain seemed lower and narrower here, and she was standing, crouching with her flippers on the bottom, shining the spotlight upwards and pointing emphatically. She cut the light and immediately there was a faint, greenish answering glow from the surface. I touched bottom with my feet, feeling the slime under my flippers. I stood upright and found my head in an airpocket between the arch of the tunnel roof and the water surface. The water was up to my shoulders, and immediately above my head, almost touching it, was a grille about half a metre square, riveted into the masonry by four brackets, its iron bars covered in some kind of steel gauze. I switched off my oxygen, and pulled away my mouthpiece, sucking in dank air. A moment later Daisy surfaced, pushed her mask up and her mouthpiece down, and coughed. The water was almost up to her chin when she stood upright.

'Jesus,' she said, 'it's going to be tricky cutting iron in this depth of water.'

I handed her the cutting-rig and grasped the iron bars, pulling down with all my weight. 'No way,' I said. 'It's firm.'

The greenish glow from behind the grating was obviously a security light left on in the corridor. It was dim, but enough to work in. 'Better get started,' Daisy said. She had just handed the cylinder back to me and pulled her mask down ready to submerge again, when I heard the distinct sound of a key snicking in a lock and a door creaking open. I made a frantic gesture and we stood stock-still, hearing footfalls above, muffled but distinct on the heavy stonework. A moment later a shadow passed over us, and then a second, smaller one. The footfalls grew softer and disappeared, and Daisy was about to duck under water when I grabbed her shoulder urgently. The footsteps were coming back towards us again and a moment later the large shadow tramped across the grille quickly. The smaller one lingered, though, and suddenly I became aware of a snuffling noise, followed by a deep-throated growl. An elongated snout pressed itself against the gauze, foreshortened by my peculiar angle of view. '*Allah*,' a man's voice said, 'it's only rats. Come on, boy!' Suddenly the dog barked, and the sound made my skin prickle. I realized that there were glaring red eyes behind the snout, and that they were looking straight into mine. I made a hand-signal to Daisy and we both took a breath and slid silently under the water. When we emerged cautiously a couple of minutes later the shadows had gone.

'That's the extent of the interior patrol,' Daisy said, 'but how do we know how often they look in? Maybe once a night, maybe once an hour, maybe completely random.'

'We can't wait all night to find out,' I said. 'We either bug out now or we go in and take the chance.'

Daisy nodded. One after the other we stripped off our tanks and laid them gently on the slimy floor of the drain beneath us. Then Daisy dipped under again with the oxyacetylene torch and there was a fizz of chemicals as she fired it. A moment later she emerged with what looked like a giant sparkler on a stick, grasping the handle with both hands as if scared it might get away from her. The roar of the fire was sickening and the blue-orange flame was so hot I had to back away. I hoped to hell Daisy knew what she was doing – one slip of the feet and either of us could have been fried. She wielded the sizzling thing like a sword, shakily applying the nozzle to the first bracket on the grille. In minutes the old pig-iron had turned brilliant lava-red, and the burner began to slice through it like cheese. It was nauseating work though, cradling the heavy cylinder, gasping, sweating and spluttering in the fumes and the heat, and wondering any minute whether the door would open and the guard come in. By the time the first bracket was severed Daisy's arms were trembling with effort.

'Shit,' she said, 'I never thought I'd have to do it like this. When you're fully submerged the water does the work.'

'Yeah,' I said, 'we'd have been better off with a good

old-fashioned hacksaw.' She lowered the gear for a moment to rest. 'Let me have a turn,' I said, passing the cylinder to her, 'I'm taller than you.'

She nodded reluctantly and handed me the burner, showing me how to squeeze the trigger that released the gases. I turned the flame on the second bracket and clung to the trigger doggedly until sweat was dripping from my face into the water and my shoulders screamed with pain. One bracket at a time was all we could manage, and we took turns to cut the remaining two. 'It's about to go,' Daisy told me urgently, as I worked on the last one. 'Don't let it fall.' The thing was already buckling under its own weight, and I knew there was no way we could stop it crashing down on us. When the last fragment parted we both leapt aside frantically as the heavy mass of iron toppled and fell, hitting the water with a splash, missing us by inches. 'Cut the torch,' Daisy yelled.

I cut it, and laid the oxyacetylene cylinder down on the tunnel floor. We got rid of excess baggage, then I made my hands into a foothold and gave her a leg up through the opening into the green-lit tunnel above. I watched her for a moment as she poised there on one knee, then grasped the edge of the hole and levered myself up from a standing position by working my legs. Daisy helped me up the last couple of feet, and we both crouched in the half-light, breathing heavily, listening for movement. The corridor was built of solid limestone blocks, some of them stained with a patina of green lichen, and others damp and dripping with moisture. The atmosphere was clammy and the air thick and fetid – hardly the kind of place, I thought to put archives. I had a feeling that this basement complex was old – much older than the embassy buildings above: judging by the precision with which the blocks had been fitted it might have been here since ancient Egyptian times.

I unsealed my oilskin bag, brought out my Beretta and cocked it. The noise of the mechanism sliding back seemed to echo round the tunnel, and Daisy stared at me in irritation. The place was low and the ceiling seemed to bulge down at us as if it was slightly warped, curving away very gently out of sight. At one end there was a flight of stone steps leading up to an iron door – presumably the one the guard had come through. About ten metres in the other direction stood another metal door with a brass padlock, which had to be the entrance to the archives. What worried me was that if the guard came visiting while we were inside our escape route would be entirely cut off. That meant that strong-arm tactics would be necessary and despite packing my piece I didn't relish the idea of popping a security guard. For a moment I played with the idea of one of us standing watch, but rejected it. Just finding the file was going to need us both.

Daisy pointed down the tunnel silently. I stuffed the pistol into my bag and followed her to the archive door. 'A bloody whopper!' she whispered, eyeing the enormous padlock. 'The only way to get through that thing is to shoot it off or cut it with the oxyacetylene.'

'Nah!' I whispered back. 'Like you said, there's more ways than one of skinning a cat. The harder they come the harder they fall.'

I took my homemade wire burglar's tool from my bag, and inserted it in the eye of the lock, then held the heavy brass close to my ear, probing for the right pressure. It was a tricky job and it took time. Daisy shifted uncomfortably from foot to foot, glancing behind her occasionally. Five minutes passed then ten.

'That damn guard's going to be back in a minute,' she said. 'For God's sake let's blast it off!'

Just at that moment there was a satisfying click and the lock sprang open. Daisy let out a hiss of relief. 'About time,' she whispered.

'The skills of a mis-spent youth!' I said.

The door opened outwards, and as we entered the musty smell of old documents hit us full in the face. The room was big, lined with row upon row of steel shelves that stretched almost from floor to ceiling. Like the corridor, the archives were lit with green night-lights. Daisy tiptoed around with her torch, examining the index-lists on the end of each set of shelves, while I closed the door gently behind us, then had second thoughts and opened it again. 'Find anything?' I asked.

'The files are organized according to the old British system,' she whispered. 'That is, no one knows how they're organized but the archivist. It was a cunning tactic archivists developed to keep themselves in a job.'

I was impressed that she was cool enough to joke in a situation like this. 'Look under "S" for Sanusiya,' I told her.

We found the bay marked 'S' and worked our way down dozens and dozens of files, many so dusty that we had to smack the dust off to read them. The odd thing was that the files appeared to be in reverse alphabetical order, so that we had to work back from 'Sy' to 'Sa', which we found on the topmost shelf of the last section, far out of reach. 'How the hell did they get up there?' Daisy asked.

'Either they could fly, or they had a ladder,' I said. 'I'd put money on the ladder.' A few seconds later I found a wheeled ladder and pushed it along to the first section, its wheels squeaking excruciatingly as it moved. To our sensitized ears, the thing sounded as loud as a farm-cart. I held the ladder still while Daisy shimmied up with her spotlight. Now it was my turn to wait impatiently. The minutes seemed to pass by with grinding slowness. 'Anything?' I whispered urgently.

'Just a minute,' she answered.

Thirty seconds later she almost slid down the ladder, grasping a battered envelope-type file tied with ribbon, smiling with anticipation. The file was marked 'Sanusiya 1916'.

'Yes!' I said.

She untied the string with shaky fingers while I held the torch. Halaby had described it as a fat file, and it probably had been once, but now it contained only a slim sheaf of typed papers. Daisy laid the papers on a step of the ladder, picked up her utility bag and brought out a tiny document camera sealed in heavy-duty polythene. She unsealed the bag and clicked the camera's priming mechanism. 'Hold the flashlight!' she ordered. I shone it on the first page, and Daisy focused the camera. When she pressed the shutter, though, there was a dry click. She pressed again and again, producing nothing but more dry clicks, then threw the camera into her bag angrily. 'Damn water's got in!' she said. She picked up the file and motioned me to hold the spotlight close while she read, concentrating hard, moving her finger swiftly down the page. 'This is incredible!' she said suddenly

'What is it?'

'It's an essay on Cambyses' army by T. E. Lawrence.'

'What?'

'Cambyses' army.'

'That's ancient history – a Persian invasion force that attempted to attack Siwa Oasis in 525 BC and was lost in the desert. What's that got to do with the Sanusiya?'

She shook her head frantically, and I could tell the pressure was getting to her at last. 'It's not here,' she said, almost sobbing, 'looks like it's all been torn out. We stuck our heads in the fire for nothing!' She slapped the sheaf of papers closed and suddenly I noticed something that sent me almost rigid with anticipation. I drew in my breath sharply and Daisy stared at me.

'Look!' I said, pointing. The title on the outside of the file had been 'Sanusiya 1916', but the name on the title page clearly read *Operation Firebird*. Daisy gasped, and at that moment precisely there came heavy, rapid footsteps from the tunnel outside.

27

DAISY CUT THE LIGHT AND we stood like statues, squeezed up in the shadows of the great galleries of the shelves. An instant later a figure stood framed in the doorway carrying a security flashlight in one hand and a revolver in the other. Thankfully there was no sign of the dog. He paused there, probably unaware that his silhouette made a perfect target, traversing the avenues between the shelves methodically with his beam. He took a step forward into the room, and I eased my Beretta out silently. I turned to glance at Daisy, and I suddenly realized that she'd vanished – just disappeared into thin air. I cast about desperately, hardly believing my eyes, and at almost the same time the security guard advanced cautiously weaving the flashlight from side to side. I pressed further into the shadow and lifted the Beretta slowly. I didn't want to shoot, but it was starting to look as if I'd have no choice. The guard passed a gap in the rows of shelves and halted, shining his torch right into my face. 'OK,' he growled, 'I've got you cold. Drop that thing and put your hands where I can see them.'

For an instant mister-nice-guy got the better of me and I let the Beretta waver. Right then a hand flashed out of the shadows with the force of a sledgehammer, and smacked into the big guy's neck. He stiffened and collapsed, and both torch and revolver skittered across the stone floor. Daisy stepped out of the gap, kicked the fallen revolver under the shelves and skipped lightly over the inert body. For a second I stared in amazement. I realized she must have moved away from me and sneaked behind the shelves with the silence of a phantom,. She'd poleaxed a guard twice her weight with a blow so sure and powerful that most men couldn't have delivered it.

'Come on!' she whispered, and a moment later we were both dashing for the door. We got into the tunnel just in time to see a big Dobermann hurtling straight towards us from the direction of the outside entrance at the other end. Daisy paused to grope in her holdall, and I gripped my Beretta in both hands. I was about to squeeze the trigger when she yelled, 'Cover your ears!' from behind, and there was an ear-splitting boom as a great gash of orange flame shot out, almost touching the running dog. The shock of the noise was so shattering that I had to hold on to the wall with one hand, feeling nausea welling up in my guts.

The dog yelped once, rolled over and lay still, and I turned to see Daisy, wearing a pair of ear defenders, standing in firing position and holding something that looked like a cross between a flare-pistol and a hand-sized blunderbuss. Just then a klaxon sounded and another guard appeared at the open door on the flight of steps at the end of the tunnel, with a shotgun in his hands. For a fraction of a second he hesitated and there was another almighty whumf as a tongue of flame licked towards him from Daisy's weapon, bowling him against the doorframe in a soggy heap. This time I'd managed to cover my ears, but the shock of the blast almost knocked me down. I doubled over, retching, for a moment, and Daisy ran past me, reached our hole, and was about to drop into the dark water beneath, when a third guard appeared at the outisde door, carrying what looked like a Sterling submachine-gun. I raised my Beretta and fired two quick snap-shots that clanked into the iron door-bracket. The guard ducked and vanished. Daisy eased herself through the hole, and a second later I followed. We both had our masks and snorkels round our necks and our sub-aqua holdalls tied to our waists. We fitted masks and snorkels but there was no time for the tanks

198

or even our flippers. Daisy held the sub-aqua flashlight before her and we swam down the drain as fast as dolphins, keeping the tips of our snorkels in the air-pocket between the surface and the ceiling. It seemed to take hours to get to the outer grille, where we dived down and came up to find *Princess Maria* still at anchor just where we'd left her. No sight could have been more welcoming.

I surfaced, pulled off my snorkel and took a deep lungful of chocolatey Cairene night-air. I pulled myself aboard the boat, working my legs to give me thrust. Everything seemed quiet, so I turned, took Daisy's flashlight, and pulled her over the bows. 'Let's get the hell out of here!' I whispered. I jerked the starter-handle and mumbled a silent prayer as the outboard fired first time. I lowered the propeller while Daisy heaved the anchor on board, then I opened the throttle and went straight into a hundred-and-eighty-degree turn heading the bows back towards Bulaq. The lights of the city were blinding meteors now and I narrowed my eyes at them. Daisy sat down next to me on the plank-seat, so close I could feel her thigh against mine. Her breaths came in heaving gasps, and her wet hair caught the breeze, wafting in my face. I still felt sick and my head was spinning wildly from the noise of her blunderbuss. 'What was that thing?' I demanded. My voice sounded breathless and far away, I thought.

Daisy put a hand on my leg as if to steady herself. 'Stun grenade launcher,' she croaked, 'state-of-the-art baton-rounds, designed for crowd-control. You have to wear ear-defenders, though.'

'Thanks for telling me,' I said. 'Where the hell did you get it? I've never seen anything like it.' She forced a smile, her teeth glinting in the light from the buildings along the Corniche. She didn't take her hand away, and her body leaned on mine heavily. When I put my arm round her shoulders she didn't shrug it off. 'I thought you'd vanished,' I told her, 'I've never seen anyone move so quickly and quietly – and where did you learn to punch like that?'

'Amazing what they teach you at Quantico.'

We had just passed under Roda Bridge, with the vast ethereal monolith of the Cairo Meridian, into the main sweep of the Nile, when a powerful spotlight beam sprang on us suddenly out of the darkness. I blinked, searching desperately for a way out of it, when a megaphone-enhanced voice bawled, 'Ahoy, *Princess Maria*. This is the police. Pull over or we'll fire!'

I hauled the tiller round another half-circle, and the craft banked so abruptly that Daisy had to catch hold of the gunwale. I headed our bow back down into the darkness beyond Roda Bridge, heading instinctively, I suppose, towards my apartment. The *Princess Maria* handled brilliantly, turning on a sixpence, but as soon as we completed the turn there came the sobering rattle of machine-gun fire. I glanced back to see phosphorus tracer streaming out of the night.

28

DAISY CROUCHED IN THE BOTTOM of the boat as bullets kicked up the dark river around us and punctured the wooden sides, splintering the gunwales to chips. I gripped the tiller, trying to zigzag out of the spotlight. But I knew it was hopeless, and that the next clip would ignite the engine's fuel-cell and rip *Princess Maria* apart. We still had our masks and snorkels round our necks and the distance to the bank on Roda Island couldn't have been more than twenty-five metres. I squeezed Daisy's shoulder through the rubber and yelled, 'Jump!' in her ear. She looked at me dazed for a split second, then grabbed her rucksack and rolled over the side into the water. I followed her, and just as I hit the surface there was a shattering explosion as the outboard tore itself to bits.

I dived into the blackness and silence closed in around me, as pristine as the silence of the deepest desert. For a moment it was as if I was hanging there in a weightless limbo between time and space. Then Daisy's hand groped for mine and I pulled her to me, and swam on powerfully underwater until my lungs were bursting. When we came up for air we were already in the shadow of the apartment-blocks on Roda. Incandescent spangles of orange and yellow from the streetlights were shimmering on the oily surface. The last timbers of *Princess Maria* were fizzling by the bridge, and the police searchlight was scanning left and right across the river – no doubt looking for us. A flotilla of little Nile boats had gathered, and an excited babble of voices drifted over to us, but attention was on the burning hulk, not the shore of Roda. The bank was a matrix of light and shade and we floated to shore gently, lost in the play of shadows.

We dragged ourselves ashore almost under the Manial Bridge, and I helped Daisy to slither up the sloping river wall and into the shelter belt of palm and tamarix trees that lined the bank here. We slumped down on a patch of grass, and gaped apathetically at the streams of headlights passing only metres away, grateful for their anonymity. For a moment we stared at each other, and Daisy's eyes strobed from light to dark in the passing headlight-beams. There was an icy desert wind blowing, and her teeth began to chatter. 'Were those the cops?' she gasped.

'Yeah. Looks like they were tipped off after all.'

'Why didn't they pick you up the first time then?'

'How the hell would I know?'

Daisy looked at me questioningly, but I was too sick and out of breath to say any more. The rush of adrenaline had cured my nausea for a while, but my head still felt like it'd been whomped by a pair of giant cymbals. We both had rubber flip-flops in our gear and we put them on. They wouldn't be much good if we had to run for it, but they were better than going barefoot in the street. I stood up and took Daisy by the hand.

'Where are we going?' she asked distractedly.

'To my place,' I said.

It took us almost half an hour to get to my building, dodging across main roads, and by the time we got there our hands and feet had almost turned blue from the cold. There were little squads of blackjackets on the streets and we avoided them like the plague. Well-dressed groups and couples in cloaks and overcoats sauntered down the sidewalks, but they were too self-absorbed to give us a second glance in our rubber suits. The alley behind the block was quiet and criss-crossed by alternating pillars of light and darkness. Few people were out on their balconies – the night was too cold for that. I fumbled for my key, let us in, and led Daisy down the corridor to the iron firedoor, this time checking carefully that my wedge was in place. Getting up the stairs was much more effort than I'd anticipated – the adrenaline rush had passed and my muscles felt like jelly, as if I'd just run a marathon in three and a half. I clicked the locks behind us, and led Daisy into the sitting room, which still bore the signs of Monod's trashing.

'Man,' Daisy said, throwing herself down into a ripped-up armchair. 'Have *you* been having a party!'

'I had a visitor,' I said, flopping down beside her. 'Guy named Monod. He was waiting for me when I got back from the medical facility the day before yesterday – the day Fawzi died. The guy had turned over my apartment looking for something.'

Daisy regarded me with eyes that were alert despite our exertion. 'You mean *Christian* Monod? The guy Andropov said worked with Ibram on the Great Pyramid? The guy Fawzi said Ibram was calling when he was popped?'

'Yeah, that Monod. He was dressed up as a Bedouin woman – the same one I spotted at the Mena Palace and the medical facility – the same one who was stalking us in Khan al-Khalili the other night. He tried to kill me. I had him but I let him go.'

'You're kidding! Why the hell? He could have been a suspect.'

'My intuition told me he was on the up and up.'

'You mean after he stalked us, walloped you in the street and trashed your pad? Some intuition.'

I caught my breath. Daisy didn't need to know the real reason I'd let Monod go, and I decided to keep it to myself for the time being.

She puzzled over it for a moment, blinking water-swollen eyes. 'Why did he trash your place?' she asked. 'I mean what the hell was he looking for?'

'I'd guess it was Ibram's map. Said a lot of other people are mixed up in this business too – you guys, the CIA – even the Egyptian police.'

'That's bullshit.'

'Is it? Then how do you explain the fact that the cops are there waiting for us tonight? How do you explain the fact I've been stalked leaving my apartment? Why is there an alert out for me, when it hasn't even been proved I'm responsible for Fawzi's death? Why has Marvin been so quiet in this case, when Van Helsing's breathing down his neck, and why did the CIA take Ibram's suitcase instead of following protocol?'

'Come on, Sammy! You really believe there's a vast international conspiracy just to get hold of a map? And not even a whole map – it's only half of one!'

I stopped suddenly, and we stared into each other's eyes for a moment. 'You're right! I keep on thinking of it as a whole map. But it's not. There's two halves to it. What if Ibram passed Monod half of it, and we've got the other half? He was searching my place to find the missing portion.'

Daisy stared at me again and I could almost follow her train of thought from the twitch of her facial muscles. 'So you're saying Ibram keeps half the map and gives the other half to Monod,' she said. 'Ibram leaves his half in his hotel room and after he gets rubbed out, somebody goes there looking for it.'

'Yeah,' I said, 'Mr Dracula Van Helsing and his thugs. That must have been what they wanted. That's why Van Helsing was so ready to break protocol by taking the suitcase. They thought the map was inside, but they lucked out. By chance it was in another case, and just out of sheer ornery cussedness, the front desk man passes it to us instead.'

'How did Monod know we'd got it?'

'He was at the Mena that night, disguised as a woman. I saw him, remember? He must have been watching and spotted Abd al-Ali handing over the attaché case. Monod's right – the CIA's in on this, maybe your own boss, Marvin, too, and certainly the Egyptian police.'

'What about Hammoudi?'

'What about you? What about me? We've got to trust somebody, and I'd stake my life Hammoudi's not in on it. Right now he's the only guy knows where our half of the map is, and if he's in on it why not just give it to Van Helsing?'

'Why would the CIA want it?'

'Cambyses' army. Maybe that's what the Operation Firebird file was about.'

'What *is* Cambyses' army?'

'Cambyses II was a king of Persia, who successfully invaded Egypt in 525 BC. After he'd taken the capital, Babylon – which was just across the river from here – he sent a force of fifty thousand men across the desert to bump Siwa Oasis. Actually they started from Thebes – the modern Luxor – and marched through a place called "Oasis", which was almost certainly Kharja. They got about halfway to Siwa – in the *Bahr Bela Ma* – when a sandstorm blew up and buried the whole column.'

'I never heard of a sandstorm that could bury an army.'

'Neither have I. It's just a legend, of course, and Herodotus is the only source. Fifty thousand men in armour with all their chariots and camels would be a pretty big show to hide, even in the Western Desert, and the remains of the column's never turned up. If it did it would be one of the most sensational archaeological discoveries of all time.'

'Why did they want to attack Siwa?'

'That's the big mystery. It wasn't much more than a village, and it was only famous because it was the home of a well-known oracle. It posed no conceivable military threat to Cambyses.'

Daisy eyed me dubiously, and I realized suddenly that my body was still wet under the rubber suit. I opened the French windows on to the balcony to let in the chill night air, and gazed out at the Nile. The never-ending carousel of headlights was still flowing down the Corniche opposite, but I could see no sign of the burning *Princess Maria*, or the police launch downstream. I stripped off my wet-suit jacket and felt the icy breeze on my skin. I shivered.

'Got to get out of this thing,' Daisy said, standing up. I watched from the balcony as she unzipped the rubber jacket carefully, letting her firm, tanned breasts emerge, wriggling slightly, giving a glimpse of trim shoulders. For me, shoulders are the most arousing features of a woman's figure, and hers were perfect, as brown as the rest of her body and covered in little clusters of freckles. She sat down and pulled the rubber trousers off. Her legs were smooth, almost hairless, and under the wet-suit she was wearing only a tiny white bikini that showed off the full curves of her body, the flat brown stomach, the slight, athletic flare of the hips. It hit me suddenly that I'd guessed right about her figure at first glance – her loose-fitting mannish clothes had never done it justice. She was sleek and spare, like a long-distance runner, but with all the right curves in all the right places. I stepped closer to her and touched the damp blonde hair that fell in two tresses either side of her face, then I bent and kissed one of the clusters of freckles on her right shoulder. I kissed the base of her neck and she raised her head slightly, then gasped. I realized that I felt incredibly turned on. I'd read that closeness to death could make you horny, but this was the first time I'd encountered it first-hand. I was burning to hold her, and I groaned as I fought to suppress it, but lost. I took her smooth body in my arms and ran my hands down the cleft in her back and across the flat of her stomach. She held me and gasped again through her slightly parted lips, her fingertips stroking my neck. I shivered and kissed her shoulder once more, feeling the muscles quiver. She touched the barely healed bullet wound on my chest where the Shadowmen had zapped me, and ran her fingers down my back, tensing suddenly as she felt the long scars there. She turned me round gently and examined them – whip scars running diagonally across my back from the base of my neck to the cleft in my buttocks.

'Holy shit!' she whispered. 'Where did you get those?'

'It's a long story,' I said. I took her head softly in both hands and kissed the brooding, trembling lips, pressing them hard and desperately, exploring her mouth with my tongue. It was a long kiss. Her rich lips seemed to envelop mine, sending eddies of pleasure through me – a vortex of patterns inside patterns, variations inside variations. After what seemed a while, though, she pulled away and drew a finger gently across my mouth.

'Wait, Sammy,' she whispered. 'This is crazy. How do you know they won't find us here?'

'I don't, but *carpe diem*, as they say.'

She stepped back a little, dropped her arms and pulled her moist hair out of her eyes. I swallowed hard and forced a smile. 'There's a shower in there,' I said pointing to the bathroom. 'We're shattered. I'll fix up some coffee and eats.'

She was about to say something but I stopped her and moved aside.

A second later I heard the shower sizzling. I groaned again, and felt my head: my ears were still ringing from the blast of Daisy's baton-rounds. I went into the bedroom, stripped off my wet-suit trousers, dried myself with a towel from the airing cupboard. I put on a fresh pair of trainers, socks, a clean T-shirt and stretch jeans. By the time Daisy emerged from the bathroom dressed in the chinos and patch-pocket safari shirt she'd carried in her rucksack, I was pouring fresh coffee at the living room table. I'd set out a meal of Egyptian bread, hummus, cheese, pickles and black olives – all I could find in the kitchen that could be disposed of quickly. She came out still drying her hair, shaking her head slightly. I watched her entranced.

'That was good,' she said, standing by the French windows, taking in the rush of traffic, the lights, the caravans of barges passing by far below on the river. 'I feel better.' She sat down on my sea grass sofa, and I poured her coffee with more than a dash of cognac. She nodded at it approvingly. 'By God,' she said, 'I need that!'

I poured myself coffee and cognac and sat down next to her. For a moment we drank and ate. I poured more coffee and we lay back. The cognac had made me feel warm and more relaxed and I finished it and looked at Daisy. Her eyes glowed and her lips parted slightly giving me a glimpse of even teeth. 'Thanks, Sammy,' she said softly.

'For what?' I said.

'For being there,' she said, moving her lips so close I could feel her soft breath.

I closed my eyes and kissed her again. She responded, moaning slightly, and I held her tightly, feeling her body trembling under my touch. I ran my fingers down her throat and neck, and she sucked in her breath sharply. I felt her breasts pressing through the shirt and my hand began to caress the velvet skin underneath, stroking her pliant stomach, gently cupping each breast in turn. She groaned and squirmed slightly under my touch, grasping my face and biting my lips hard with passion. Just then the telephone rang in the kitchen and we both froze.

'Shit!' I said. 'Shit! Shit! Shit!'

Daisy pulled herself away and listened intently, as though she might be able to divine who was on the other end. 'Hammoudi?' she said.

I got up cursing, stepped into the kitchen and lifted the receiver. It wasn't Hammoudi. It was my *ghaffir* on the front entrance – the one I'd have sworn didn't know my name. Only he did know it. 'Mr Rashid,' he said tensely, 'I think you ought to know, Your Presence, that four men just asked the number of your apartment and are coming up in the lift now. And I can tell you, sir, I didn't like the look of them at all.'

I slammed the phone down. 'Daisy!' I bawled, grabbing my Beretta and its shoulder-rig from the back of a chair. Daisy ran into the kitchen looking shaken.

'They're on the way now!' I snapped. 'You got anything more kosher than that ear-blaster in your baggage?' We went back into the sitting room and she groped in her rucksack, coming out with her big SIG 9mm and several clips. I switched off the light. There was a whuff of percussion from outside and the door disintegrated, sending splinters of wood across the room. A dark figure in a black ankle-length Barbour coat, with dark glasses for eyes and his head bound in a tight *shamagh*, was lurking outside. He held two small submachine-pistols in his hands, and if he'd been quick enough he could have taken us both out there and then. But black smoke from the charge he'd put on the door was rolling into the room in wafts, and as he inched forward slightly to escape it there was a fraction of a second's hiatus. In that instant Daisy shot him in the guts.

We didn't wait to see the guy fall or to watch if more came in. We retreated into the kitchen, closed and locked the door and pulled a table and chairs across it. Not that I kidded myself this would stop anyone: I was just hoping it would slow them down for a few seconds. We rushed out through my rear exit, and I whispered a silent prayer of thanks that I'd had the gumption to choose an apartment with a bolthole. We dashed down the stairs to the cellar door, and this time I didn't bother with my wedge. My safe house had been blown. I knew I wouldn't be coming back, and I was glad I'd never got attached to the place. Something – an intuition – told me that I'd served my time, that one way or another the old double life was over.

We burst out through the street door almost colliding with two shadows in *shamaghs* and long black coats, armed with automatic rifles. We weren't expected, I could tell. One of them got a round off and Daisy grunted and fell, rolling over on the stone steps. I ducked as bullets blammed over my head and let the first guy have it in the groin at almost hard-contact range. He screeched as his balls blew apart and dropped his rifle. I lunged at the other guy, getting his neck in the crook of one elbow and strangling him with his own weapon. He was taller than me, but not much heavier, and I dragged his head down and kneed him in the face. He folded, gurgling, and I kicked him in the balls and rammed his head against the stonework. As he reeled I jerked the weapon from his grip. He stretched out a clawed hand and locked it round my neck, but I grabbed the wrist with my left and snapped backwards. There was a crunch as the bones parted company and the guy screamed and clutched at his wrist, not quite quick enough to cover up a small icon that was tattooed there. A beam of light from a window caught it, and I realized that it was a hieroglyph, punched into the skin like a brand – so hard that the flesh was raised. I only saw it for a moment but I would have sworn it was the hieroglyph for the goddess of devastation, Sekhmet – the incarnation of the Eye of Ra.

Suddenly the street door banged open and I glimpsed three or four more black-coated, muffled figures beyond. I was about to fire when rounds whizzed past my ear and the first guy flew back and slammed into the others. I jumped backwards to see Daisy already on her feet, blasting away with her SIG, clutching a bloody shoulder with her left hand. 'I'm OK,' she shouted in an unsteady voice, 'it's cool.'

'Come on!' I yelled, grabbing her hand.

We ran for the nearest intersecting alley that twisted and turned around a maze of blocks, curving back eventually to the perimeter road. Before we'd gone ten metres, though, there were bursts of submachine-gun fire and rounds whined around our feet and pitched over our heads. We sprinted away like greyhounds, weaving left and right, zigzagging, turning sharply, dipping along the walls, dodging behind clumps of trash cans and iron skips. Cats and dogs fled from us yelping, and women in long house-coats and head scarves peered at us over balconies, mystified, then squealed as bullets pinged off the walls in showers of brickdust. We took shelter in a deep doorway, and pressed ourselves against the uneven wall, panting. I probed Daisy's shoulder delicately with my fingers. She winced.

'Thank the Divine Spirit,' I said. 'Must have missed the bone by a quarter of an inch.' She gave me a hard glance, then forced a grin, took a deep breath, and slapped another mag into her SIG. 'Look,' I said, 'if we get separated – if anything happens – I'll be at the Badestan coffee-house in Khan al-Khalili at sunrise tomorrow.'

She nodded tensely and cocked her weapon. Booted feet pattered along the alley close by and we leaped out, fired a frenzied broadside at the dark-cowled figures racing towards us, and steamed off into the shadows. I had no plan, no idea where we should go or what we should do. I didn't know who these guys were: Militants, hired killers – even a death squad from my own government. My only ally was Hammoudi, and I hadn't a clue where he was right now. We headed for the main road, and just as we reached the junction a big black Mercedes came drifting straight towards us out of the night, transfixing us in its blinding headlights. I turned my pistol towards the car instinctively and was about to put a round through each of the lamps, when a door opened. 'Get in!' someone growled, and I thought I recognized Hammoudi's voice. I took a last look at the phalanx of shadows coming at us down the alley, still firing, and I pushed Daisy into the car, and jumped in myself. An invisible hand pulled the door closed, and the car went into a racing start with a screech of tyres. There was a last burst of gunshots over our heads, and then the alley was far behind us. There were four dark-suited men in the car, but it was only as the light from the streetlamps along the shore flashed in through the windows that I saw the one sitting next to us wasn't Hammoudi at all. It was Jan Van Helsing.

29

'DON'T TRY ANYTHING,' VAN HELSING said, holding up his SIG, 'just lay your hardware down nice and gentle.'

'This is kidnapping,' I said. I dropped my Beretta on the floor of the car.

'Shut up,' he snapped, 'I just saved your goddamned sorry hides. You should both be down on your knees kissing my ass.'

'Go fuck yourself, Mr Van Helsing,' Daisy said. She laid her SIG down on the floor, grimaced and held on to her shoulder where the bullet had grazed it. Van Helsing eyed her truculently as the streetlights pulsed across her body.

'God bless America,' he said, 'the super-brat speaks. I warned you what would happen if you got out of line, miss, and tonight you just took the booby prize.' He leaned over, grabbed the hand that covered the wound and squeezed until fresh blood welled between Daisy's fingers.

'Son-of-a-bitch!' she yelped. 'Fuck you!'

A bolt of blind rage surged through me and I lunged at Van Helsing, but before I got anywhere near him something very cold and very hard smashed down on my scalp and I found myself scrabbling through oblivion.

When I came round I was sitting on a chair in a cell-like office with a linoleum floor, a desk, two chairs, a coffee machine, and a signed photo of the US president on the wall. I sat there for a few minutes listening to my heart beat. I felt exhausted, shattered after the running gun battle, my head pounding from the blow Van Helsing's thug had given me, my eardrums throbbing. I was taking several deep breaths to calm myself, when the door banged open and Van Helsing stalked in on his spindly, bow-shaped shanks. He was dressed in a funereal suit with polished black shoes and a white silk handkerchief flowing from his top pocket. Despite the elegance he still did a fair impersonation of an overdressed baboon, I thought. He leered at me with his tadpole face, and I saw narrow eyes, pock-marks and sharp little teeth.

'Where's Daisy?' I said.

Van Helsing made a retching laugh. 'Oh how touching,' he said, 'how chivalrous! The bitch is in the medical facility. Where else do you suppose she'd be with a gunshot wound in the shoulder?'

'If you're lying –' I never finished the sentence because he took a bound over to me and slapped me hard round the face with an open hand, jerking my head back.

'Who do you think you're talking to, asshole,' he said. 'I'm the CIA Resident in Egypt, so just watch your lip.'

It was only when I tried to put my hand up to feel my face that I realized I was handcuffed to the chair. 'So,' I said, 'now you've kidnapped a foreign police officer in his own country, Mr Van Helsing. For a CIA man, you don't have much respect for the law.'

Another dry, retching laugh like crinkling paper came from Van Helsing's direction. 'The law stinks,' he said, 'we make up our own law. In case you hadn't noticed, buddy boy, there's a lot of animals out there on the streets. Guys who think nothing of whacking out women and children. The only way to fight them is to play it by their rules. I'm CIA Resident and I am the law here. If I was to have you thrown into the Nile in a concrete necklace right now, nobody'd shed a tear, not even Miss Dickless Tracy there whom you show so much concern about. She doesn't give two shakes of a monkey's ass about you, Rashid. She dumped on you real good tonight.'

The hairs on the back of my neck prickled. 'What are you talking about?' I said.

Van Helsing drew up a chair opposite me and leaned his elbows on the desk, sneering. 'The cops were waiting for you when you bugged out of the archives,' he said. 'Who do you think snitched, Santa Claus?'

'How do you know about that?'

'You've been out cold nearly half an hour. Time for me to have a little talk with the FBI bitch. She told me she snitched on you to the cops, which is how come they were ready for you.'

'Bullshit.'

Van Helsing laughed and stood up again. 'I feel sorry for you, Rashid,' he said, 'you really are a sucker. You don't know kids like Brooke, but I do. I've had my bellyful of super-brats brought up to believe they're princes or princesses and everyone else is there to wipe their butts. There's plenty like her in the States. Daddy's a big-noise politician with a big mouth and a fat bank roll, and she never had to fight or struggle for it – not like the rest of us. Just walked into everything – private school, Berkeley, the FBI – with a flick of the fingers. I hate those cruds. How do you think she felt about having a fourth-rate raghead cop like you steal her thunder? You don't give a bitch like that a hard time, you'll find her frying your sorry ass. I think she just fried yours.'

I angled my head away from him and stared at the floor. 'I don't believe it,' I said.

He snorted. 'Denial,' he said slowly, 'that's a predictable reaction. Now let's try a little rationality, shall we? Tell me, who else but you and Brooke knew about the break-in job tonight?'

I didn't answer. Only two people other than myself had known we planned to do a job on the old British embassy – Daisy and Hammoudi – and Hammoudi would have guarded the secret with his life.

'OK,' he said, 'plead the Fifth if you want, but you can't

plead it to yourself. Whose idea was the break-in job anyway, yours or hers?'

I stayed silent, but I felt a lump swelling in my throat. I remembered how Daisy had handled herself tonight and how she'd rallied despite taking a graze in the shoulder. I remembered the way she'd kissed me. I could still feel the taste of her in my mouth. 'Look,' I said at last, 'Daisy came as near to getting slotted tonight as I did. Why would anyone whack their own snitch?'

Van Helsing shrugged – a curious jelly-like movement of the shoulders. 'Accidents happen all the time,' he said, 'specially in Egypt. Maybe they wanted her for another reason – I hear tell there's elements in the police who are highly sympathetic to the Militants. Things aren't always what they seem.'

That was just what Sanusi had said, I thought. 'You saying those slimebags who hit my place tonight are my own people?' I demanded.

'Maybe,' Van Helsing said, 'maybe cops with Militant tendencies who don't like you investigating the Sanusiya Brotherhood.'

I opened my eyes wide and Van Helsing guffawed. It wasn't a pleasant sound. 'I know all about your trip to Sanusi,' he said, 'and he lied to you. The Brotherhood *has* been revived, and he damn well knew it. Word is a bunch of its new members are serving in the police and army. It was the Sanusiya who stiffed Ibram, and probably the same guys who came gunning for you and Little Miss Muffet tonight. We'd been tracking that active service unit for two days when they turned up on Roda, and I assume that was your place they bumped. It was lucky for you we were trailing them, or you'd both have been dogmeat by now.'

'Maybe. But if it was Militants who stiffed Ibram, why didn't they claim it as a victory? Terrorism's a publicity game.'

Van Helsing got up. He moved towards me menacingly and I wondered if he would hit me again. I'd have given a lot to have had my hands free. He put his face so near to mine that I could smell the edge of sourness on his breath. 'It wasn't a

215

political killing,' he said. 'The Militants wouldn't have gained jack from claiming it because Ibram was a national hero.'

'OK, then why murder him?'

'Because among other things he was supplying information to the US government about the activities of Militant groups.'

'You mean Ibram was spying for the US?'

Van Helsing smirked. 'I can't tell you the details,' he said, 'it's classified. Puts a different spin on it though, doesn't it? See, Rashid, you and Miss Dickless are completely out of your depth. Brooke is off the case officially as from now. She should never have been assigned to it from the start. It's a bureaucratic screw-up and Brooke's a smartass who doesn't know shit from shinola.'

'If it's spying we're talking about, I'll have to report it.'

Van Helsing let a smile play round his uneven lips. 'Hail the conquering hero!' he sneered. 'And who'll you report it to? That superannuated refugee from Rent-a-Thug, Colonel Hammoudi? I think not, old fellow. The Colonel got his marching orders tonight, and I don't see the top brass exactly doing a jig when they get a report from a dirty cop who was already on the run and to cap it all just broke into foreign archives.' He turned and stared me in the face, his eyes gloating. 'There's a general alert out for you,' he said. 'Seems to me you're in deep shit. You got yourself elected to the Militants' hit-list and you're wanted for questioning by your own team. One phone call from me, and you'll be in your own slammer before sunup. Not a nice prospect for you, eh Rashid? Not with all those Shadowmen guys you and Hammoudi put in there.'

I didn't say anything, but he must have read the surprise in my eyes. He lowered his face close to my ear and spoke almost tenderly. 'I hear they're pretty sore with you and Hammoudi,' he whispered. 'He's a mean customer when he gets going, right? I hear tales of cattle-prods and electrodes. You can say you were just following orders, but that won't mean jack to them when you're on the inside. There are things worse than being slotted, eh? I mean, they could force you to give them blow-jobs and take it up the ass for the rest of your time. A living death for a guy like you, Rashid.'

I felt anger and resentment rushing through me, but I quelled it quickly. Van Helsing was trying to confuse and disorient me. 'You're not going to do it, though, are you?' I said.

For a moment he looked crestfallen. Then his eyes narrowed like a predator's and I knew he was coming in for the kill. 'No, I'm not,' he said, 'I'm giving you a fighting chance. I'm letting you go.'

I almost smiled. It was the same deal I'd given Monod the other night. 'OK,' I said evenly, 'and how do you know I won't go straight to the Commissioner of Police? I broke into the archives in the process of busting the case. So it was illegal, so what? Spying is one hell of a lot more serious.'

Van Helsing smiled the crooked smile again. 'Try it,' he said. 'Who do you think put out the general alert for you? The Commissioner of Police, Mahmud Siyudi, happens to be a good friend of mine. Let's say he has fingers in a lot of pies, and let's say I keep my eyes and ears open. I know things he wouldn't like broadcast on Voice of America. Funny how you never found the big boys behind the Shadowmen, eh?'

I looked into his eyes and for a moment I really was disoriented. Van Helsing was a professional liar and as polished as they came, and I couldn't navigate my way through his pastiche of lies, truths and half-truths. Suddenly, though, I smelt the salt dust of the desert, and for a moment I shut my eyes. I was no longer in the room, but in a tiny cave in the middle of the emptiness they called al-Ghul. It was the Old Man who had brought me here – just the two of us, alone on camels. He hadn't told me the purpose of the trip, and I remembered how the desert had seemed full of foreboding, alive with malicious spirits. It was night and beyond the mouth of the cave stars winked across an endless expanse of sand and grit. We were sitting cross-legged next to a smoky fire of gorse we had brought with us, and the Old Man was mixing an orange-coloured liquid in a gourd. I watched, fascinated, with a heavy feeling of fear in my belly. 'You have the Shining power,' the Old Man was saying, 'but it is not strong in you. You will never be a great *amnir*, Sammy. That is not your destiny. But if the Divine Spirit wills, you will one day use what power you have for the good of the tribe.' He held up the gourd. 'Drink!' he said. 'This is the Divine Waters of the Shining. Let it teach you. Let it show you your strength.' This was my first experience of the Divine Waters, and I could still taste it – thick and sour like native beer. After I'd drunk he'd handed me a stick. 'Hold it,' he said, 'never let it go, no matter how it changes.'

I held on to that stick desperately for hours – at least it seemed that way – while it writhed and trembled and quivered in my hands. Once it was a giant green snake with red eyes that tried to coil itself round my neck and suffocate me, and another time it was a huge jade-coloured scorpion whose vicious darting sting I had to duck and dodge. I held on grimly, though, sweating and quaking, screaming inwardly, until my hands went numb and my muscles seized up. The stick was alive, twisting and jerking, going through transformation after transformation, each one of them more powerful, until I was on the verge of letting go. At the very moment I felt I couldn't stand it any more, though, the potion had burned itself out suddenly, and I was left grasping what was only a very ordinary stick. The Old Man looked at me and laughed. 'The Divine Spirit be praised,' he said, 'the stick is truth. No matter how it twists and turns, you must always hold on to it. Then nothing can harm you. Hold on to yourself and watch carefully. Observe. Always there will be a sign that will show you the way.'

I opened my eyes wide and smiled dreamily at Van Helsing, who was resting his bony elbows on the desk top with his fingers entwined. His eyes were focused intently on me. Too intently, I thought. His shirt cuffs had parted revealing the beginning of hairy forearms, and on the left arm, not far above the wrist, I could clearly make out a small icon tattooed or branded on so hard that the skin actually stood up. It was the twin of the one

I'd seen on the man I'd knocked down outside my apartment-block earlier in the evening – the hieroglyph of the lion-goddess Sekhmet, the Eye of Ra.

30

WHEN THEY LEFT ME STANDING in an alley with my finger-tips against the wall and a sack over my head, I almost thought I was a dead man. Almost, but not quite. My memory of the Old Man's test had restored my equilibrium, and I knew that whatever the reason Van Helsing had let me go, it wasn't out of compassion or concern for the state of my health. Van Helsing wanted something he thought I could supply, and I had a good idea what it was. They'd told me to count to fifty before I moved, but as soon as the car engine had droned away I pulled the hood off and looked around. It was still dark – my watch told me it was 3.20 a.m. – not the best time for positive action. I felt like Ra in the Underworld of the night, passing from Sacred Hour to Sacred Hour by means of spells and incantations, never knowing what enemies might wait for him in each. There were Twelve Hours of the night in the ancient Egyptian reckoning, and this was the Tenth. By this time Ra had already fought and overcome his arch-adversary Apop – the Eternal Serpent – and was looking forward to emerging once more victorious into the dawn. From where I stood, though, the dawn looked one hell of a long way off. I'd had no sleep and my nerves were shot, but I knew I had to keep going, because everything might depend on what I did now.

There was one pleasure in store for me. Van Helsing had left my Beretta and its shoulder-rig on the ground at my feet, with a full round of shells, unclipped in a little pile. Next to it was my stiletto in its sheath. I strapped on my blade, then filled the magazine and loaded my piece. Van Helsing was giving me full rein, I thought. Whatever it was he wanted, he was making sure I could zap anyone who tried to stop me getting it. He wanted it bad, and he was confident that he'd be able to take it from me when he decided it was hand-over time. That's when he would get the shock of his life. I buckled on the shoulder-rig and let the weapon ride, then I cased the alley. I was in a half-derelict back street, somewhere in Old Cairo, I guessed – a place full of rubble and dustbins. It was cold. I zipped up my jacket and turned in what I reckoned was the direction of the river. In Cairo, all roads lead to the Nile.

Before I'd gone ten metres, though, I heard a scuffling sound behind me, and I turned instinctively, unzipping my jacket ready to draw. Behind me the street basked in stillness, punctuated by bars of darkness and pockets of light. I drew in a breath and continued, but almost at once the scuffling sound came again. I stopped once more, and just as I turned to look I caught the faintest outline of a fleeting shadow in a square of light. It was only for the slightest fragment of a second, but the shadow stamped itself on my retina – strangely insectile: a head with a protruding jaw and a cranium that projected backwards too far. I had the urge to run, but I checked myself and turned back into the zebra pattern of light and shade. There was a broken doorway with no door in it, and I halted there and listened. It seemed to me I could hear laboured breathing from inside, and I held my own breath to make certain it wasn't me. When I stopped the breathing seemed to stop also, but when I started again I thought I could make out whispering – a raw, rough-cut voice speaking my name, '*Sammy . . . Sammy . . . Sammy*,' over and over again. The hair on the back of my scalp started to stand up and a thread of perspiration ran down my neck. The whispering came again, but so low and subliminal that I couldn't swear I heard it at all. A sensation of pure fear began to swell through me, starting somewhere in my belly and working outwards, and my heart began to pound. The urge to escape burst through me powerfully again, but I clenched my fists and held on to myself, torn between abject terror and fascination. Instead of pulling my Beretta I slipped my dagger into my hand. It was a far more primitive weapon and just having it there, clasped in my fingers, answered something wild and ancient in my psyche. The moonlight glinted suddenly on the blade – faintly, but enough to drive me forward quakily into the old house, which loomed over me dimensionless, like a vast cavern.

I halted again, and held my breath. This time I was certain I could hear whispering – no, not whispering but the slightest rumble of animal breath that sounded like it was being formed into vowels and consonants. I let my own breath out and stepped forward and something erupted out of the darkness at me with a banshee shriek so piercing that I actually dropped my blade and sank to the floor. It was like the cry of a swooping eagle magnified through a bank of speakers – a dinosaur scream that seemed to come right out of the bowels of time. Never in all my experience had I heard anything so utterly terrifying. I scrambled for my knife in the darkness and in that instant something seemed to pass over me – something huge and dark like a giant bat, and for an instant a gangling, spider silhouette showed clearly in the frame of the door. Then it was gone. My hand came into contact with warm, viscous liquid on the floor, then something solid, warm and tactile. I found my knife, replaced it in its sheath, and felt for my pocket-torch. In its thin beam I saw that the warm and sticky stuff was a pool of blood. In the centre of it, like an eldritch island, wide, terror-filled, dead eyes stared at me from the sockets of a severed human head.

31

I HUNG ON THE DOORFRAME and vomited in the street. It had
been the ghoul of course, and the skull belonged to a child –
a little girl, maybe no more than ten years old. It didn't belong
to the body I'd seen the previous night, which meant the ghoul
had killed twice in two days. If the frequency was shifting from
weeks to days, that was serious – it meant that time was running
out. I didn't have the nerve to go back into the derelict house –
I needed to see Hammoudi. I pushed on towards the Corniche,
gagging as I went.

There was a patrol of blackjackets by the butt-end of the
aqueduct, huddling together against the cold by a wall and smoking cigarettes. They looked as alert as glue-sniffers and I didn't
rate their chances of recognizing me off-hand. Still, they were
bored enough to stop any lone passer-by at this time of the
morning, so I avoided them and crossed the road in the shadow
of some pencil cedars. From the promenade the Nile was like
oil, and looking across it I could see my old apartment-block
rising out of the darkness. I felt no regrets about not being able
to go back, only a pang of unfulfilled desire when I thought of
what might have happened between Daisy and me. There was a
payphone a couple of hundred metres away, but I didn't go for
it. I wanted to see Hammoudi badly, but I didn't have to call.
I'd missed my nightly report, and if that happened we had a

fall-back plan. Hammoudi would wait for me as long as it took. Van Helsing's mob wouldn't know about that. All right, they would follow me, but friendless as I was I still had at least one favour up my sleeve.

The taxi was parked at the kerb and the driver jumped when I woke him up.

'Curse your father!' he said. 'For a minute I thought it was *Jinns*!'

'There's plenty about,' I commented.

There were a few cars out on the Corniche, and as we turned across Tahrir Bridge a pair of headlamps beamed after us. I watched them for a while, then gave up. Van Helsing would find me whatever happened, I thought. Still, I paid the driver off a couple of blocks from the Scorpion Club and made my way there by all the devious means I could, down alleys too narrow to take motor-vehicles, in and out of ruined buildings – at one stage I even crawled through a cellar. No point in making it too easy for them, and every second gained was a head-start.

The Scorpion was still open, but it was dead as a doornail. There was no one around but Bakhit, the Turkish bouncer, who was sitting on an stool inside, smoking a Cleopatra and reading a nudie magazine. He cocked his good eye at me and grunted when I appeared. 'Is he here?' I asked.

'Yeah,' he grinned, 'he's our only customer. Even the barmen have gone bye-byes. Things I do for you boys.'

'Hey,' I said, 'I need you to do something else.'

He put down the nudie magazine and started to look interested. 'Yeah?' he said. 'What you got?'

'Don't know,' I said, 'but maybe you'll be getting a visit from the same guys who came looking for me last night.'

'The Undertakers?'

'Maybe. Maybe not. But whoever they are, they might not take no for an answer this time. Just keep them off till Boutros and me've had a little talk.'

'My pleasure,' he said, beaming. He closed the outside door

with a clang and bolted it, then opened the padded seat of his stool. Inside was a silver Colt Cougar Magnum revolver with a bunch of rounds. He picked it up in his big mitt and spun the chamber with a whizzing sound, then snapped it open and began to fill it. He winked his good eye after me as I hurried down the stairs.

The club looked big and lonely without its clientele, and the ultra-violet lights were off. Hammoudi sat at a table at the far end, almost where Halaby and I had last talked. He was wearing a ragged old combat smock from his parachute days, and his .44 pistol lay on the table in front of him, next to a pack of Cleopatras, his lighter, and a pitcher of water. He looked worn in the light of the table-lamp – like an old soldier waiting to die. As I came up he laid two big blue pills on the table. 'You've had a long night, Sammy,' he said, 'you need these.'

I sat down and eyed them hesitantly. 'Bennies,' he said, 'we used to take them on night patrol behind enemy lines. When the chips are down they can mean life or death.' He gestured towards them, but I ignored him.

'The cops were waiting for us on the river,' I said. 'Then some hit-team bumped my apartment. Finally, I got picked up by Van Helsing, and he let me go.'

Hammoudi didn't look surprised. 'What does he want?'

'He didn't say, but I'd guess it's the map. That's what he was hoping to find in Ibram's suitcase, only it wasn't there. He reckons I'll lead him to it.'

'Problem is,' he said, 'it's only half a map.' He drew out a slim brown envelope from inside his jacket and held it out to me. 'You sure you want it, Sammy?' he asked.

I took the envelope and put it away inside my own jacket, then I snatched the bennies from the table and swallowed them with a gulp of water from the pitcher. For a moment I retched at their bitterness. 'Van Helsing's got a Sekhmet tattoo,' I said, 'more like a brand – on his left arm. I saw the same thing on one of the guys who bumped us tonight.'

Hammoudi stared at me and for a moment I thought I saw a pulse of fear in his eyes. Or maybe I'd imagined it. The bennies were already starting to sizzle through my system, raising my heart rate, rousing my exhausted muscles. My tongue had started to go numb and I had an irresistible impulse to suck my teeth.

'It looks like the rats are coming out of the woodwork,' Hammoudi said, 'and they aren't Militant rats.'

'Yeah. Van Helsing tried to tell me the Sanusiya's been revived and that it's got members in the army and the police. He hinted they did Ibram because he was supplying info on Militants to the US. Also hinted that Ibram was mixed up with US national security in other ways. It might be a crock of shit, but I think the map shows where Ibram and Sanusi were working in the desert, and it was the same place the Germans and the Sanusiya were working in 1916. Daisy and I found the British file on the project in the archives tonight. It's entitled *Operation Firebird*, but all the good stuff's been torn out.'

'Anything left?'

'Yeah, an essay on Cambyses' army by T.E. Lawrence.'

'What in the name of Holy Mary is that about?'

'I don't know.' There was hammering on the steel door upstairs followed by the clamour of excited voices. 'They're here,' I said, groping for my pistol. Hammoudi stopped me with a gesture. We listened for a few seconds and heard Bakhit mouthing a string of abuse.

Hammoudi didn't move, except to light another cigarette. 'We've got a couple of minutes,' he said. 'That door's solid steel, and Bakhit's a good man. The time for fighting'll come.'

'The game's over, Boutros,' I said.

'I know,' he said, calmly. 'It's over for both of us. I got removed from the case officially tonight, and a little bird tells me there's a demand for my resignation to follow. I can fight it, of course, but I'll only end up with a slug in my spine down some alley. The shit has finally hit the fan. They know who I am – that I'm protecting you – and they're going to get us both. What the hell? We always were on our own.' He sucked on his cigarette as if it was going to be his last. 'You're not the only ones who've been busy today,' he went on. 'Someone snuffed Halaby this morning. Found hanging from a ceiling-bracket in his flat. Neck broken and signs of torture – I mean, real bad torture. They lacerated his balls.'

'Shit. They must have picked him up outside the Scorpion last night.'

'Maybe. Halaby was bent as they come, but he was a smooth operator. Professional.'

'Sanusi's got a lot to answer for,' I said. 'Somehow I feel he was trying to get a message through to me but I didn't read him right.'

'Forget it,' Hammoudi said, 'Sanusi also went walkies today. I told you someone'd been busy. He was found floating in his own ornamental pool early this evening with a bullet smack in the forehead.'

'Bloody hell.'

'Yeah. That's the bad news – or most of it. The good news is that the results of Fawzi's autopsy came through. You didn't kill him, Sammy. The doc found traces of poison in his body, but it didn't come from any hash. They're not sure what it was yet, but it sounds like ivacaine – what they used to call soba.'

'The ancient Egyptian special!'

'That's it. The stuff's supposed to disappear without trace, but the dope Fawzi ate somehow inhibited the breakdown. Doc said the sauce had probably been introduced into his drip. Now, I got a little stoolie in the medical facility who tells me the last person to see Fawzi before he died was Van Helsing.'

The bennies had come fully on line now, and my body felt electric. I sucked at my teeth and fidgeted, hardly able to stay in my chair. Upstairs there was a boom of iron on iron as if they were trying to ram their way through the door. Bakhit's voice had reached a crescendo.

I made to stand up, but Hammoudi placed his massive hand gently on my arm. 'You haven't heard it all yet,' he said, 'I had a phone call from a guy called Monod today. Said you'd given him the number. Wants you to meet him at a place called the Austet Inn in Khan al-Khalili, tomorrow 8 a.m. You better be there, Sammy. When you've talked to Monod, get out of it. Just disappear.'

'I can't. I never found the ghoul. I saw it though – last night and tonight – with different victims. It's killed twice in two days. That never happened before, Boutros. It's building up its strength ready for something big.'

'You're right, Sammy. Whatever it's been planning is going to take off pretty soon. Time's running out, and we don't even know what the hell is going down. But it's too late now. We have to fall back on our emergency plan, or we're both going to wind up dead.'

'Is Van Helsing the ghoul, Boutros?'

'Sammy, it could be anybody.'

'What about Daisy? Van Helsing made out she'd snitched to the police about the archives job. That's how come they were waiting for us outside.'

Hammoudi looked worried. 'Yeah, Special Agent Brooke,' he said. 'I ran a check on our Barbie doll through various contacts in Interpol. There *is* a US senator called Brooke, an ex-army general who was decorated for his service in Korea and Vietnam. He does have a daughter named Daisy who read Middle Eastern Studies at Berkeley all right, and she did train with the FBI at Quantico. That's all straight – but there's a small hitch.' He brought out a brown paper bag from his pocket and tipped out a two-by-four-inch black and white snapshot. 'Take a look,' he said.

I took the photo and stared at it. It showed a plain-looking girl with a retroussé nose, glasses, brown eyes and thick brown hair. 'Who's this?' I said.

Hammoudi smiled grimly. 'That's Daisy Brooke aged eighteen,' he said. 'Now tastes differ, and people change as they get older. Hair can be dyed – there's even such a thing as plastic surgery. On the other hand she doesn't look much like any Barbie doll I've ever seen.'

From above came the sound of the door bursting open, and the blat of submachine-guns. There were yells, belching gunfire, and the answering deep boom of Bakhit's Cougar. Someone screamed in pain, and I winced. The thud of Bakhit's weapon ceased suddenly, and Hammoudi looked sharply towards the stairs. I put the photo away. Hammoudi stood up, picked up his .44 Magnum and cocked the mechanism.

'Boutros, you're crazy,' I said, 'there's no need to stay. You'll be killed.'

'Maybe,' he said, 'but I've got out of tighter spots than this. I been round a long time, boy. I promised your people I'd protect you with my life, and you ended up saving mine. You think there's ever a day gone past I haven't thought about that? Nah, I'm too old to run. At least I can buy you some time. You remember our emergency exit: through the Gents and up the stairs. Now get out of here!'

I threw my arms round him, hugging the huge weight-lifter's torso. There were tears in my eyes. 'May the Divine Spirit protect you,' I said.

'Yeah, yeah,' he said, shrugging me off and turning towards the entrance. The last I saw he was crouching behind a brick pillar drawing a bead on a squad of shadows swarming down the stairs.

32

B Y THE TIME I REACHED the Khan it was sunrise, and the muezzins were chanting out the call to prayers from the minarets through booming speakers. Like Ra, I'd come through the Twelve Hours of the night, descended into a watery Underworld, fought with demons, wrestled with the Great Serpent Apop, survived treachery, trickery and terror. Nothing ever seems so bad in the light of day, and as I watched the sun come up cold between the tortured buildings, its heat diluted by an icy wind and a furrow of ash-grey cloud, I rejoiced as the ancient Egyptians must have rejoiced. I suppose it could have been the bennies, but for a minute I almost got on my knees and bowed down in worship. Then I realized I was standing in front of the teashop where they'd slotted Ibram, and I pulled myself together. Sayyidna Hussayn square was already full of early-morning crowds and an antique steam-roller was grinding through a pall of leaden smoke, followed by a gang of labourers in rotten shoes wielding forks and sweeping-brushes. There were plenty of cops about, but I knew the crowds were my best hiding place, and I melted into the stream of unwashed humanity, another unshaven, unkempt nobody in down-at-heel togs. None of them gave me a second glance. All along the Muski there were *shawarma* stalls, juice-sellers with glass globes of tamarind and hibiscus juice like space-helmets, and *fuul*-sellers with their big burnished pots on braziers, mounted on gypsy-carts painted garish colours. An untimely ice-cream man had moored his float in the middle of the street, and was leaning morosely through his hatch in an overcoat and listening to readings from the Quran that blasted from a battered transistor. It was an incongruous combination, I thought – ice-cream and Islam. The air was a compound of delicious smells – grilled meat, fresh bread, spices, but the bennies had taken the edge off my hunger, and I pressed on through the crowds and turned down into the Badestan Gate, a sixteenth-century passageway that led straight as a die into the heart of the bazaar.

The Badestan coffee-shop lay at the corner of the street, almost under the eaves of the Badestan Gate. As I turned the corner I suddenly remembered that this was where Sanusi claimed to have seen the ghoul chewing bones. I had laughed at him for Daisy's sake, but I had grown up in a society where such visions were taken for granted. We're conditioned what to believe in from birth, and if you happen to be brought up in a society that believes in ghosts and ghouls and things that go bump in the night, they're as real as apple pie.

I stood on the corner for a moment, surveying the street. The old gate was one of the early entrances to the bazaar, and the street beyond passed what had been the façade of the original caravanserai. The word 'Badestan' derived from the Turkish word 'Bazzestan', meaning a market for silk, cotton, linen and precious objects. The gate itself was a saracenic arch made up of fitted blocks, surmounted by a band of dense fractal Islamic calligraphy, but there was no ghoul sitting on it this morning. The coffee-shop was sited almost beneath the archway – a place of peeling green paint where men in trench-coats, shawls and turbans sat warming themselves with tea and *shishas*. All the way from the Gezira I'd wondered if Daisy would make the rendezvous. I knew that she could have set me up last night, but it hardly mattered. I knew she could be setting me up now and I might be walking into a spider's web, but I also knew they wouldn't kill me until I'd got what they wanted, and at present I only had half of it. I wondered if Daisy and Van Helsing had been working together from the beginning, and if those little scenes at the Mena and in the car last night had been manufactured for my benefit. By the time I'd reached the coffee-shop, though, I'd decided she would show whatever happened. Van Helsing had said Daisy was off the case, but whoever and whatever she was, Daisy was a player and I had the feeling she'd see the game out to the bitter end.

Standing on the corner I saw that my hunch had been right. She was sitting at one of the small tables in the street, sipping tea, wearing a heavy dress, a shawl and a weighted headcloth of black muslin that concealed her blonde hair. Nobody was bothering her – at last she'd got the message about keeping a low profile, I thought. Or maybe she'd got it from the beginning and that whole feminist thing was part of the role-playing. I did a quick check for hidden eyes and moved in silently, sitting down in the chair next to her before she even looked up.

'I thought you were off the case,' I said.

She lifted her eyes to me and I saw a flash of tenderness there. If she wasn't pleased to see me, she did a damned good act. But then Daisy had always done a good act, I thought. Her eyes were red-rimmed and puffy as if she'd been crying and her skin was drawn and pale from lack of sleep. A wan smile flickered around the generous mouth. 'Van Helsing gave it his best shot,' she said, 'but I got the ambassador up in the middle of the night. He wasn't amused, I can tell you. I pointed out that I was assigned to this case by FBI HQ in the States, and it wasn't Van Helsing's right to have me removed. Van Helsing muttered about "renegade agents" but I pled the Fifth about the archives job, and Dracula had no proof.'

I thought about it. It seemed to me that the ambassador had been very easily swayed. 'So,' I said, 'you blamed it all on me?'

She looked hurt. 'Are you kidding?' she said. 'That would have been like hara-kiri. I denied all knowledge, full stop. All Van Helsing saw was a bunch of thugs chasing us down the street on Roda. He reckoned they were Militants himself, so they can't book me for that.'

A waiter in a faded *gallabiyya*, a ragged tweed jacket and a woolly hat shuffled up and I ordered strong black coffee. The bennies were still working my corpuscles over – they'd be on line for a full twelve hours at least, I reckoned, but I couldn't stop the urge to suck my teeth. It was an effort to keep still, too.

'Whatsamatter?' Daisy asked. 'You look agitated.'

'Yeah, well that's the effect Van Helsing has on me.'

The waiter brought lukewarm black coffee in a glass with a tiny dish of sugar on a battered brass tray. It wasn't exactly what I'd had in mind, but I spooned sugar in and drank it down in gulps. Daisy toyed with her tea and watched me through narrowed eyes. Suddenly she laid a warm hand on mine and fixed me with her hard, ice-coloured eyes. 'We're in this together,' she said, 'and like Hammoudi said, we're on the same side.'

'And what side is that?' I said.

'The side of the angels,' she said. The way she said it gave me an eerie jolt, and I withdrew my hand abruptly. As far as Daisy went, the jury was still out, I thought.

'Sanusi's dead,' I said, 'my informant too. Fawzi was found to have poison in his system that was introduced from his drip. One of the guys who bushwhacked us last night had a Sekhmet tattoo on his arm, and guess what? Van Helsing has the same thing. Now, do you know any other CIA officer who has the goddess of devastation tattooed on his wrist?'

For a moment Daisy looked confused. 'What's this about, Sammy?' she asked with a sudden swell of emotion.

I felt like telling her to drop the little-girl-lost act, but I just stared at her coolly. 'Ibram was mixed up with US national security,' I said. 'Dracula told me the Sanusiya's been revived and there are Militant sympathizers in the police and army. Ibram was taken out because he was supplying information on Militant activities to the US government. Van Helsing reckoned it was the same mob who came after us last night.'

'What about Cambyses' army?'

'It doesn't make sense. OK, finding an ancient Persian army lost for two and a half millennia might make *National Geographic*, but it wouldn't explain the national security angle or all the killing – Ibram, Fawzi, now Sanusi and my informant – not to mention the hit on us last night. Think of what we found in the archives – the Operation Firebird file. Why would they leave the Cambyses material in the file when the rest was ripped out? The only explanation is that whoever removed it thought the Cambyses story wasn't directly relevant.'

'Then why was it there in the first place?'

'I said not directly relevant. But maybe it *was* relevant incidentally. Cambyses' troops were meant to have been marching on Siwa, but why? It was no military threat. Maybe Herodotus got it wrong. Maybe the Persians weren't going for Siwa at all. Maybe they were looking for something else. What if Cambyses in 525 BC, the Germans in 1916, and the Ibram-Sanusi team this year were all looking for the same thing?'

She dropped her eyes for a moment and when she lifted them again, they were liquid pools. 'The only guy who could have told us was Sanusi,' she said, 'and he's dead.'

'No,' I said, 'there is someone else. Christian Monod, and *he's* here in the Khan right now.'

33

Nobody seemed to know where the Austet Inn was. We asked shopkeepers and pedestrians who looked like they belonged here, and no one seemed to have heard of it. Finally, we found an old man with a terracotta face sitting idly on the bed of a cart, smoking a *shisha* made out of an oil can. He told us that it was a derelict place that hadn't been used in years, sited near the Ashrafiyya complex – one of the oldest parts of the bazaar. We found it at the end of a long desolate alley, well outside the populated area, a place strewn with tin cans, bits of rusty engines, derelict cars, horse-dung, and piles of old rubble. A sign reading Austet Inn in Arabic still stood over the door, but the place was a shell – the carcass of a building that looked as though it had been worked on by giant vultures. All its orifices had been enlarged by attrition or vandalism, and half its walls had caved in and tumbled into the street outside. The place smelt of goats and human excrement, and the floor was covered in little black balls of goat-shit. There were some stairs at the back of the front room leading down into a dark cellar, and I groped for my pocket torch. I flashed the beam down there, and Daisy drew her SIG.

The cellar was obviously inhabited. The floor had been swept clean and there was a mattress losing stuffing, a sleeping bag and a couple of cowhide-covered stools pushed into a corner. A cardboard carton held tinned meat, soup and vegetables, and next to it there was a butane gas cooker, a twenty-litre jerrycan of water, a couple of oil-lamps and some pots and pans. I knelt down to touch the cooker and found it was still warm. 'Someone's been here until a few minutes ago!' I told Daisy. Just then there was a scuffle of heavy feet and a play of shadows as a dark-robed woman hurtled out of an invisible alcove. This time it wasn't a knife but a pick-helve she was waving. Daisy stepped in her way, cocked the SIG and thrust it into the veiled face in a single expert movement.

'Stop right there!' she snapped.

Monod stopped in mid-flight, dropped the pick-helve and pulled off his face-veil. 'What the hell is she doing here?' he asked me accusingly. 'You were supposed to come alone.'

'She's my partner,' I said, 'she can be trusted.'

He glanced at her dubiously, angles of his face highlighted in my torch-beam.

'After all, she could have shot you,' I said. 'You might have taken our heads off with that thing.'

Monod eyed me sullenly and I noticed his hand was seriously bandaged where I'd slashed him across the knuckles. 'You were supposed to come alone,' he said. 'The deal's off.'

'Listen, Monod. Ibram's dead, like you told me, and now Sanusi's dead, along with several other people involved. Last night they tried to kill me and Daisy here. Hammoudi – the big detective – might well be dead too. If you don't come clean now, then a lot more people are going to be rubbed out, including myself and you as well. I'd rather avoid that if possible.'

Monod stood defiantly, feet apart, weighing up the possibilities. 'How do I know you weren't followed?' he asked.

'Even I don't know that,' I said. 'You have to make a leap of faith. You can't fight this battle alone.'

He looked at his bandaged hand. 'Seems I'm required to take a lot on faith,' he said.

'Look. We're on your side.'

'And what side is that?'

'The side of the angels.'

Daisy grinned and Monod relaxed. 'I was never much for angels,' he said. He searched my face keenly, then knelt down and pulled a box of matches from his pocket. 'Point your torch on this will you?' he asked, gesturing to one of the oil-lamps. In my torch-beam I watched him flick up the mantle and light the wick with a single match. He turned the wick up slightly and eased the mantle down, then lit the second lamp. A warm earthenware glow spread through the cellar. He pulled out the mattress and pointed to the skin-covered stools. 'That's all I can offer,' he said, 'but it's better than the floor.' He sat down heavily on the mattress and Daisy and I arranged ourselves on the stools. I saw that she made sure she was well in sight of the entrance, just in case anyone might sneak up on us. Professional till the end, I thought. She laid the SIG, still cocked, on her knees. Monod sat in a lotus position and blinked at us expectantly. 'So,' he said, 'confession time. What do you want to know?'

'Everything,' I said. 'What is the map about?'

Monod hesitated and eyed Daisy's piece. 'Would you mind,' he said, 'it's like having the Sword of Damocles hanging over you.' Daisy removed the magazine expertly and ejected the round from the chamber right into her hand. She fed the round into the mag, slipped it back into the butt and put the SIG away. Monod watched her, then let out a long sigh. 'All right,' he said, 'The map shows the location of Firebird.'

'What is Firebird?' I asked.

Monod paused as if debating how to start. 'Have you ever heard of the secret Books of Thoth?' he asked.

'Sure,' I said, 'they were thought to contain all the wisdom the Egyptian priesthood had accumulated over the millennia. But they're only a legend, aren't they?'

'They *were* a legend. But a few years back, fragments of a manuscript were discovered in the library of a monastery in Cairo, by a British Egyptologist. It was written in Coptic, and was probably a copy of a copy of a copy and so on. The professor who found the text was certain it formed part of the missing

Books of Thoth, but before he could publicize the find, he died in a motor accident. The manuscript vanished from the public domain but turned up in the collection of an American, who allowed it to be studied in great secrecy by a select few. Doctor Adam Ibram was one of the few. The text was by no means complete, of course, but Adam pieced things together and realized that the Books of Thoth weren't an accumulation of wisdom or a record. They were a blueprint – a detailed plan made by the initiates called the Shemsu-Hor – probably the forerunners of the Ra Brotherhood – for a project they had put into effect over eight thousand years – the Rostau or Firebird project.'

'Eight thousand years!' Daisy said. 'How could anyone put a plan into effect over such a long time?'

'These guys thought big, and they had patience. They were working on the scale of the cosmos, not on the scale of our petty, materialist lives. By studying the astronomical material in the text, Adam came to the conclusion that the project had been initiated in the Age of Leo, around the time when the constellation Orion reached its nadir – that is about 10,500 BC. This, he realized, was the period the ancient Egyptians referred to as Zep-Tepi – the First Time. There were references in the text to the Great Sphinx at Rostau, which we now know as the Giza plateau.'

'You mean the Sphinx goes back to 10,500 BC?'

'Yes, in fact there's now scientific evidence to support the idea. The Great Sphinx has signs of water-erosion that could only have been made during a pluvial period that started in about 8000 BC, meaning that it's at least as old as that, and probably older. The fact that it was built in the form of a lion suggests that it may have been carved during the Age of Leo, which would put it at about 10,500 BC. The head it has now – which may or may not be Khafre – was probably carved later.'

'I always thought the head was too small for the body!'

'Exactly, and you're not the only one to have made that observation. Now, if the Sphinx was carved in the Age of Leo, then Giza had been chosen as a sacred site long before Old Kingdom times. But Adam went further. He said the manuscript proved that the whole complex – pyramids and all – had been planned in minute detail back in the Age of Leo and not completed until eight thousand years later.'

'Seems a heck of a long time to wait.'

'Yes, but the programme was directed by astronomical data. The Shemsu-Hor were waiting for a certain alignment of stars that would only occur around 2500 BC. The Books of Thoth were handed down from high priest to high priest over the ages to make certain the plan was never lost. The Shemsu-Hor and their successors, the Ra Brotherhood, were wheeling and dealing everything behind the scenes.'

'But what purpose could have been worth waiting for all those millennia?'

'Unfortunately the text didn't reveal that, but obviously it had to have been some very big deal, to say the least. What Adam did discover was that the central object of the whole show wasn't the Sphinx or the Great Pyramid – they were just accessories. The centrepiece was the Benben Stone, which was supposed to have fallen to earth from the stars, and was kept in the sacred Firebird Temple at Heliopolis for millennia, right up to about 2500 BC, when it was moved to Giza and set up as the capstone of the Great Pyramid.'

'So the Benben Stone was the original capstone?'

'Yes, and it was probably placed on top of the pyramid for some fantastic ritual that they'd all waited for for eight thousand years. Some kind of connection between the earth and the cosmos. Adam thought that if he could find the Benben Stone he could solve the mystery of the Firebird Project. There were references in the text to a hidden chamber under the Great Pyramid where the Benben Stone was kept after the great ceremony, and that's the point where I enter the story. Adam asked me to look for the chamber.'

'This was the "Thoth's Chamber" project.'

'You read about it, right?'

'Yeah, but according to what I read you only found the door, and the Antiquities Organization put the kibosh on any further exploration.'

'That was the official version. Actually we did unseal the door but it turned out to be a disappointment – the Benben Stone wasn't there. There were marks to suggest it had been there originally, but it had been moved out.'

'But that's not the end of the story.'

'It was the end of my direct involvement until two months ago, when Adam rang me up from the States. He seemed very agitated, and poured out the whole account of what had happened after we'd aborted Thoth's Chamber. First of all, he'd come across a reference in ancient Egyptian literature from the First Intermediate Period – the *Admonitions of Ipuwer*. Ever heard of it?'

'You're the second guy who's asked me that in three days. Yes, I have heard of it.'

'Well the quote ran something like, "that which the pyramid concealed is no longer there". Adam was certain this was a reference to the Benben Stone vanishing. He reckoned that after the big ritual in 2500 BC, it had been hidden inside the pyramid until about 2000 BC, then for some reason it was moved somewhere else. He started to do more research and came across ancient Persian legends referring to a stone hidden out in the *Bahr Bela Ma*. Somehow he came into contact with Sanusi, who told him his ancestors had found something out there in 1916 – something the Germans had been very interested in. Sanusi reckoned that it was the Persian legends that had led to Cambyses' invasion of Egypt in 525 BC, and to the expedition of a Persian army into the *Bahr Bela Ma*.'

Daisy was staring at him in fascination, her features blunted in the flickering lamplight. 'So you were right about that, Sammy,' she said.

For a moment Monod looked at her in surprise, then he went on. 'Naturally I enquired if he'd found the Stone,' he said, 'but he only told me the project was off and advised me to lay low for a while. I'd always known there was something not quite above board about the deal – the fact that the manuscript had been kept from the public and the disinformation about Thoth's Chamber, for instance – but I'd turned a blind eye because I was certain the Antiquities Organization knew about it. After all, they'd closed down the Great Pyramid for us and allowed us to open the chamber, even though it was officially given out that they hadn't. I thought he was exaggerating and fobbed him off, but the very next day I got a visit from some very unpleasant characters. They said they were police, but like I told you before, I'm not sure. They said if I breathed a word about any of it, they'd slit the throats of my wife and kids. I got them out of the country and vanished into the bazaar, rented a room with a bed and a phone, and went out dressed as a woman. Next thing I heard Adam was over here on a visit, and we arranged a meeting at my digs in the Khan. He turned up looking dreadful, saying they were after him. That was the last time I saw him alive. About nine o'clock the next morning I got a call, but all I heard was ''Monod, is that you?'' and the sound of shooting and screaming. I was scared stiff, but determined to find out what was happening. There was a commotion in Sayyidha Hussayn Square and I soon found out that Adam had been murdered. I saw them bring out the fat man, and heard them saying he was to be taken to the US medical facility. Then I saw you two and the big detective milling around, and I followed you. The rest I think you can work out yourselves.'

'Yes,' I said, 'you followed us, saw that guy at the Mena Palace give us Ibram's briefcase. You guessed what was in it.'

'That's right, but –'

'Get down!' Daisy screamed, and I realized with a shock that she'd sprung into a firing position so fast and silently that I hadn't even seen her move. A submachine-gun spattered drumfire from the steps, and I ducked and jumped on Monod, shielding him. Rounds whiplashed around us, clipping fragments out of the stonework that whizzed around our heads. A sliver hit one of the oil lamps, which toppled over spreading a slick of burning oil across the floor. In its sudden flare I saw dark, hooded figures in the doorway, and I drew my Beretta. Daisy whipped off a whole clip in double-taps, a solid wall of fire that filled the cellar with ear-splitting noise and poisoned fumes. 'This way!' Monod yelled, pointing to the dark alcove above. 'My escape hatch!' He had half-turned towards it when a bullet took him in the chest.

34

MONOD BUCKLED AND CHOKED BLOOD over my jacket. I stepped into the alcove and found a narrow, crumbling staircase spiralling up out of sight. I pulled Monod after me, and a moment later Daisy backed in, still firing. I holstered my pistol and Daisy and I grabbed an arm each and half-dragged, half-carried the body up the dark stairs and out into the blinding sunlight of another rank alley. It was full of the hulks of rusting cars, and we dodged behind them into another derelict, roofless house, where we laid Monod down gently in the goat-dung and refuse. We peered through the broken window. Figures in long, black Barbour coats – six or seven of them – were pouring out of the cellar exit and skirmishing towards us between the car wrecks. They worked in pairs, moving with the concentration of spiders, covering each other with fire.

'The same guys who bumped us last night!' Daisy said. 'The guys Van Helsing claimed were Militants!' She inserted a fresh mag into her SIG and began firing aimed shots through the window. After each shot she rolled back out of sight, just in time to duck the submachine-gun rounds that spattered the brickwork and reduced the window-frame to matchwood. Monod groaned and fought for breath. I ripped away the robe to see if I could stanch the bleeding, but I already knew what I'd find. Our clothes had sopped up litres of his blood like blotting paper, and most of the rest lay spilt in a trail along the derelict street. There was an entry-wound on his right pectoral, through which air wheezed nauseatingly in and out, and I cut a section out of my T-shirt with my blade and covered it. I couldn't reach the exit wound in the back, but I knew it must be huge, because most of the blood was coming from there. Monod gurgled and coughed.

'Can't breathe!' he whispered.

'Don't try,' I said, 'lie still. We'll get you out.'

A couple of bullets whazzed off the walls, fragmenting into bits of shrapnel. I bellowed as a piece took out a tiny bit of my right earlobe and blood streamed down my neck. Daisy popped up and fired a double-tap. 'Got the bastard!' she said, throwing herself back into cover. Monod's eye-lids fluttered, and he found my wrist, curling his fingers around it like tentacles.

'Inside my robe . . .' he said, then he coughed and a dribble of blood ran out of the side of his mouth. 'Ibram warned me . . .'

A hail of slugs hissed past my bleeding ear and I dipped down. I felt Monod's grip go limp and I realized suddenly that he wasn't breathing. My mind raced through possibilities of resuscitation – mouth to mouth, heart massage – but deep down I knew it was useless. I fumbled inside his robe. Stitched into the lining was a flat package, and I ripped it out with the help of my knife. It was already badly blood-stained and my ear bled on it even more copiously before I got it inside my jacket.

Daisy fired another double-tap and rolled. 'Look out!' she screamed. 'They're here.'

A face in shades and *shamagh* appeared at the window and Daisy popped up and shot it from a range of a couple of feet. The head seemed to detonate into a bloody mash of dark shards and bits of *shamagh*. Another face replaced it instantly, like a hydra's head, and almost simultaneously a third face and a body materialized at the door. The guy wore a flapping black trenchcoat and held a big handgun, but he opened his mouth to say something and in that moment I skewered him with my blade. It'd been a long time since I'd thrown it in anger, but I hadn't lost my touch. The stiletto took him bang in the abdomen, and he doubled over letting the handgun slip from his grasp. I kicked him in the face, put a stranglehold on his neck, retrieved my blade in a shower of fresh blood, and slashed off his *shamagh*. I don't know quite what I'd been expecting, but this guy was no Militant – not unless they'd started recruiting them from blond Nordic types. He looked more like a grizzled version of one of the US marine corporals at the medical facility.

'Sammy!' Daisy yelled, and I glanced up to see her struggling with another foot-soldier who'd launched himself through the window. The cry only distracted me for an instant, but it was long enough for my grizzled veteran to flex himself up, shrug off my stranglehold and grab his weapon. He pointed it at me shakily, holding his guts together with his left hand as blood pulsed through his fingers.

'Son-of-a-bitch!' he grunted in English, 'you're gonna die real slow for this.' He choked and blood dripped from his nose. 'You got something we want, *asshole*, and guess what? It's hand-over time. Dead or alive, it's all the same to me.' He'd lowered the weapon slightly for a nasty shot in my balls, when there was a crack as a brilliant red aureole developed in the side of his head. Half his grey matter splattered over the wall.

A second later Hammoudi torpedoed himself across in front of me and grabbed the guy Daisy was wrestling with round the throat. He dug the .44 into the guy's back and pulled the trigger, breaking his spine instantly. The foot-soldier slumped like a broken doll and Hammoudi pulled Daisy out of the way and ducked as another hail of bullets chopped up the window-frame.

I threw myself down next to them. 'I thought you were dead,' I said.

Hammoudi tried to wink, but his chest was heaving and his breaths came in sobs. 'Told you, boy,' he panted, 'I've been round a long time. You got what you came for?' I nodded. 'Then get out. You and the girl. Now!' He slapped a set of car-keys into my hand. 'There's a four-wheel-drive Daihatsu at the end of the street – the escape car – and it's kitted out. Take it. You know where to go.' He gestured to the hole he'd come in by, then spun round and fired at another face that had popped up behind the window. 'Jesus and Mary!' he said. 'How many of these creeps are there?'

He braced himself against the door-jamb and punched another clip into the .44. 'Go!' he bawled, but this time I didn't know whether he was speaking to us or himself, because the next I knew he'd dashed out in the street into a hail of gunfire. I grabbed Daisy by the hand and we belted out through the back of the ruined house and down a parallel street. I was ready for sentries, but these guys had evidently been so sure of themselves they hadn't bothered to post them. That was their mistake. It took us only seconds to reach the compact little silver-grey car and within a minute Daisy had the key in the ignition and the turbo roared into life. A second later we were racing through the tight alleys towards Shari' al-Azhar and my seat was already slippery with blood – most of it someone else's. Peasant faces in turbans and skullcaps glared at us. Some shouted curses and waved their fists. Daisy swerved around a narrow corner, almost colliding with a hand-cart full of fruit, and its owner jumped out of the way, screaming abuse. Dogs barked at us, and someone threw a stone that bounced feebly off the bonnet.

These streets had been built for a less frenetic world than the one we lived in – for camel-caravans and donkeys, not motorcars moving at sixty kilometres an hour. One alley was full of hundreds of porcelain baths and toilets, and Daisy ploughed through several ambitious displays, the bull-bars on the front of the car smashing or shunting them aside. There were more strings of curses, and men in *gallabiyyas* and vests shambled after us, gesticulating. Daisy steered us down an alley of one-room workshops caked in grease, where men waved welding torches at us threateningly. At last we shot out of the bazaar into the main road by the Azhar – a university that had stood here since before the American continent was even discovered. There were crowds on the streets and the skyway was full of traffic. Daisy ran serenely down the gears as if she was driving in a funeral cortège, and worked her way into the slow-moving stream of cars. She looked at me and giggled, showing off her white teeth.

'You look like an extra from *Nightmare on Elm Street*,' she laughed, 'your shirt is cut to pieces and you're soaked in blood.'

'I hope Hammoudi left me a change of clothes.'

The traffic speeded up as we drove through Opera Square and into the heart of modern Cairo. There were cops on traffic duty, and I sank down in my seat to keep my bloody face out of view. The only real wound I had was a nick on the ear, but that had bled profusely.

'What did you take from Monod?' Daisy asked.

I felt inside my jacket and came out with the package I'd found stitched inside his robe. The wrapping paper was soggy with blood – mine and other people's – but inside was a sheet of crumpled parchment that seemed relatively untouched. I opened it out and studied at carefully, then I opened the packet Hammoudi had given me. They were two halves of the same map, and they fitted together with perfect precision.

'What is it?' Daisy asked, trying to squint sideways and cope with the traffic at the same time.

'It's the other half of Ibram's map,' I told her, 'only this one's got the scale and coordinates on it.'

'And you recognize the place?'

'No, but I'd bet money it's the Sea Without Water, the *Bahr Bela Ma*. You remember that circle-thing you spotted on the torn edge of Ibram's map? Well Monod's bit has the rest of it, and it contains the ancient Egyptian hieroglyph for the Firebird. Ten to one poor old Monod just handed us the location of the Benben Stone.'

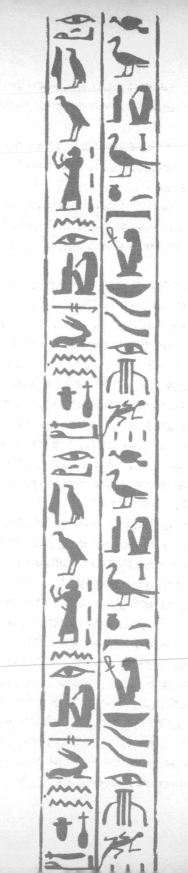

PART II

WESTERN DESERT OF EGYPT, DECEMBER 1999

35

THE STORY GOES THAT WHEN the god Ra became senile a group of human beings plotted to overthrow him, but someone snitched and he decided to rub out the whole race. At a celestial council, though, the elder god, Nou, advised him to convene a proper court, so that the conspirators could be proved guilty. Ra ignored this advice, because he guessed that if summoned to the court, the rebels would abscond into the Red Land – the desert – which was beyond the reach of the guardian gods of Egypt. Instead he sent his Eye – the wild beast Sekhmet – on a rampage, and she didn't stop tearing people apart until the land was red with blood. In fact, Ra – who'd regretted his decision – had to trick her into swallowing thousands of barrels of beer to get her canned enough to lay off. For me, the moral of that story had always been that if human beings had reached the desert they would have found the ultimate sanctuary from Sekhmet. There in the wilderness they would lie beyond even the power of Ra.

We mingled with the traffic in the city centre, and crossed the Nile by Tahrir Bridge, heading for Giza. 'Where the hell are we going?' Daisy asked.

'Don't ask,' I said, 'trust me.'

As she diced with the jams on Sudan Street, I searched the

glove compartment and found the spare shirt and the false ID card and driving licence Hammoudi had left for me. This was my escape kit. It wasn't much, but it would get me where I wanted to go. I wriggled into the new shirt, put on my shoulder-rig and jacket, and dropped my bloody T-shirt out of the window, then sealed my ear with a Band-aid and used some tissues to get the rest of the stuff off my hands and face. Daisy drove along Shari' Al-Ahram, past the pyramids at Giza and out along the road to the oases, where the black land gave away abruptly to the desert. The pyramids loomed over us like vast direction-pointers, and ahead of us the traffic slowed down for a military police road-block.

'Shit!' Daisy said. 'They're on to us.'

'No,' I said, 'it's just routine. Let me take the wheel. You get in the back. Cover your face with the veil and pretend to be asleep.'

There was a heavy-duty red-and-white striped barrier across the road, in front of a concrete blockhouse with a radio aerial sticking out of the roof. A robust corporal with a red armband and a scarlet beret, almost bursting out of his khaki, was checking the outgoing cars, while another MP raised and lowered the barrier. On both sides there were sand-bag emplacements protecting sentries in flak-jackets and steel-helmets, and a Russian-made jeep and two Suzuki motorcycles were pulled up near the block-house. When our turn came at the barrier I had my false papers ready for the corporal. He glanced into the back windows. 'Who's that?' he demanded.

'Just my wife,' I said, 'she's tired.' I rounded my hands across my stomach. 'You know.'

The corporal studied the picture on my ID card and glanced back at me with flinty eyes. He walked round to the front of the car and read the number plate.

'Where are you going?' he asked, still holding my documents.

'To Kharja,' I said, 'to see my relatives.'

The corporal handed the papers back to me reluctantly, and kept his eyes fixed on my face. He gave the signal to lift the barrier, and I put the car in gear. Just then another MP came trotting out of the sentry-post waving a clipboard. He shouted something to the corporal, who held up his hand to stop me, but the car was already moving and I was through the barrier. I rammed the accelerator as far down as it would go and the Daihatsu's turbo roared as the car exploded forwards. There were staccato shouts of '*Gif! Gif!*' and in the mirror I saw that the corporal had drawn his revolver. We rushed past the sentry in the sand-bag emplacement, and there was a volley of cracks as he opened up with a kalashnikov.

The rear windscreen shattered, sending a spray of glass over Daisy, but in a trice she was up with her SIG in her hand. 'There's two guys on motorcycles coming after us!' she shouted.

I was in third now, still with my foot jammed hard down, but I could see the MP motorcyclists in the mirror and they were gaining. I changed to fourth but they were almost up to us – within thirty metres, I reckoned – at any rate I could see their white helmets with 'MP' stencilled on them, and their dark glasses. I began to weave from side to side deliberately in case they started shooting, but Daisy squealed, 'No! Keep her still!' There were two pops from the SIG and I saw the leading motor-cyclist swerve to the right with the bike leaning dangerously on a flat tyre. Suddenly it slid over sideways right into the path of the other motorcyclist, who braked so suddenly that his bike turned somersault and hurled him into the road. The last thing I saw in the mirror was a miniature mushroom cloud as one of the tanks detonated.

'Bloody good shooting,' I told Daisy. 'That was really hot!'

I put the Daihatsu in top and we raced towards the vanishing point on the horizon, where the asphalt glittered like water in the high sun. To the west, the limestone desert undulated on to infinity, its shale and feldspar beaches lost in an iridescent sheen. Near the road the desert was made ugly by pylons and rubbish dumps, but beyond this flotsam of industrial society, I knew, it stretched on clean and unbroken for thousands of miles as far as the Atlantic coast. I put twenty kilometres between us and

253

the guard-post before I turned off the asphalt road and headed directly west into the desert.

'Where the hell are you going?' Daisy demanded again.

'Just relax,' I told her. 'If we stay on the road we're dead meat. There are other VCPs ahead and they're in radio contact.'

'But they can follow our tracks.'

'They won't know where we turned off the road. There are millions of car tracks here and it's going to take them hours to find good trackers. Even if they do find out, they'll think twice before they follow us into the desert. It's Cairene mentality. They're big-mouths on their home ground but you take them out into the Red Land and they're chicken-shit.'

'Sammy, they don't have to use trackers. There are such things as choppers and even landsat images now.'

'This is Egypt. You forgotten we had to use an FBI chopper just to get to the Fayoum? It will take them for ever to get it jacked up, and by then we'll be long gone.'

Daisy climbed back into the front seat and looked around in bewilderment. The road had already disappeared and the skyline was a uniform distance from us in each direction. The car was a silver insect lost in a landscape so vast it skewed the mind – an undulating plain of black limestone relieved only by a patina of white where mineral salts had been leached out of it, or by chains of amber-coloured barchans and strings of flat-topped hills far in the distance. The car crunched over sand-beaches littered with stones like the remnants of some ancient inferno – limestone blocks shaped like giant sponges, conch-shells, hollow rolls and petrified octopi. Here and there were grooves in the rock and angular groynes where a few salt bushes or desert succulents grew, and there would be tracks of spiders, beetles and snakes. Everywhere else, though, the desert seemed lifeless as far as the eye could see.

'Shit,' Daisy said, 'no wonder the ancient Gyps were scared of this place. I mean there's nothing to get a fix on. I wish I'd kept my GPS.'

'Nah,' I said, 'I don't need one. See the sun – old Father Ra up there? He's my GPS. I can drive in a straight line using the shadows on the stones.'

Daisy stared at me in open disbelief and gripped the side handle.

'At first this limestone desert appears all the same,' I said, 'but look harder. You'll see that it actually changes quite quickly, but the changes are small and you don't notice them unless you concentrate. I like to think of it as passing through a whole series of giant rooms. In one room there are marine fossils, in another nodules of chert and oxidized iron, in another small pebbles or silica balls. Real desert Bedouin can find their way blindfold simply by feeling the changing texture of the surface. What outsiders don't understand is that the desert has a kind of grammar – a geological syntax of its own.'

'Sammy. Where are we going? Do you know, or are we just heading off into the blue?

'You'll see.'

By three o'clock it was already cooler. The sun was listing to the west, still fiery but softening by the minute – the time when the furnace Ra of midday became the milder Atum of evening. The silica glittered like glass in places where the sun caught it, and there were sudden shimmers of intense light, opening and closing like winking eyes. In places tiny spools of dust unravelled, spinning across the stones like corkscrews. An hour later I spotted what I was looking for – a huge cairn of boulders which the Bedouin called Mahatt al-Mezraq – the Javelin Cast. I stopped the car by the mound and we got out and stretched. The silence was almost unearthly, broken only by the sudden rasp of sand on rock and the occasional high-pitched whistling the Hawazim called 'the Voices of the *Jinns*'. I sniffed the wind and took in the faint traces of flint and chalk. After four years of the sounds and smells of Cairo at last I felt at home. I showed Daisy the mass of graffiti carved on the cairn's larger boulders – mostly the camel-brands of passing tribes, some so old that the tribes themselves had long ago disappeared into history. I sought out the lizard brand of the Hawazim among them.

'This place has been a meeting point for the tribes for generations,' I told Daisy. 'It gets its name from an event that occurred
here hundreds of years ago. An old man and a girl of the Hawazim were travelling under the protection of two companions from
the Awlad 'Ali tribe. In Bedouin law, the office of *rafiq* or
"Way Companion" is sacred once you have eaten bread and
salt together. Well, when they got here, the two Awlad 'Ali tried
to rob them. That's a big no-no in Bedouin law. But they'd also
underestimated the Hawazim. The old guy was carrying two
javelins and he gave one to the girl. They skewered both the
double-crossers right here. Their bodies are buried under the
cairn and it exists as a reminder about the absolute sanctity of
the *rafiq*.'

Daisy was watching me carefully. 'OK,' she said, 'and is this
pile of rocks what we came for?'

'No,' I said, pointing to a huddle of stone buildings hidden
so cleverly in a dip behind us that she hadn't noticed them.
'That's our destination.'

Her mouth fell open in surprise. 'That?' she said incredulously.
'What is it?'

'It's called al-Manakh,' I said. 'That means the Kneeling Place
– or the place where camels kneel. A desert holy man or *faqi* –
one of Sanusi's relatives, probably – tried to set up a lodge
here, but it soon died out for lack of water. Only the buildings
remain.'

We got back into the car and a few minutes later we were
cruising slowly in amongst the stone huts. They were arranged
in a crude oblong around a yard, the gaps filled in with a dry
stone wall that had fallen down in many places. I stopped the
engine and we got out. Nothing moved in the place but the wind
sifting grains of dust, and bits of tumbleweed drifting through
the yard snagging on stones and boulders. I took in another
lungful of air, and felt a sudden sense of peace. I knew a long,
lonely phase of my life was over and whatever happened, I would
never go back to living in a city again. With the tranquillity,
though, came an intense weariness. The bennies had disguised

it, but now they'd worn off and my body suddenly realized it had gone a whole night without sleep. I yawned.

Daisy stared about her warily. The stone buildings were large – one or two of them as big as barns – and they looked as if no one had been near them for years. In the yard, though, there were signs of recent inhabitants – three-stone fireplaces with odd stubs of firewood and flattened tin cans, bits of leather from dried-out drippers, broken camel-hobbles, shards of old pots. In places there were shallow pits where camels had dug themselves in, surrounded by piles of their date-like droppings. I picked a piece of camel turd up and squeezed. It was brittle and bone-dry – months old – and it contained grains of undigested sorghum.

'The last visitors here came from the Sudan,' I said, 'probably in May or June.'

Daisy sniffed suspiciously. 'How do you know that?' she demanded.

'By the dryness of the dung, and by the sorghum in it. Only the Sudanese Bedouin feed their camels sorghum.'

There was a jerrycan of water in the car, and Daisy opened the back door, murmuring to herself as she examined the bullet-holes punched cleanly through the metal. She poured us both water in styrofoam cups, handed one to me and looked me in the eyes. 'So,' she said, 'what do we do now?'

'We wait.'

The sun was low on the western skyline, sinking into a wing of ashlar cloud and painting it molten gold and liquid orange. Daisy moved a step nearer, dropped her cup and put her hands on my shoulders. 'Wait for whom?' she asked softly. She opened her mouth and brushed my lips with hers, rounding them into a sensual pout. I kissed her lightly and was about to put my arms round her when her hand suddenly shot under my jacket and hooked out my Beretta. She leapt backwards and before I could react I was looking down the barrel of her SIG for the second time in a week.

'God dammit!' I said. 'I should have been wise to that move.'

'Don't try going for the stinger,' Daisy said, 'you know I'm fast, and I never miss. And like I told you, the cowboy won, so just ease it out carefully.'

I knew I wasn't going to try anything. She was about the fastest operator I'd ever seen, and she had too many questions to answer, anyway. I slipped out my stiletto and dropped it into the sand. Her blue eyes were cold and hard.

'Sanusi was right about you, Sammy,' she said, 'if that's really your name. You aren't a cop, I knew that from the beginning. You have a pierce-mark on your upper right ear, just where the Hawazim wear their famous *fidwa*, and you wear the Hawazim dagger – the notorious *khanjar*.'

She was going to find out soon enough, anyway, but I decided to play the innocent just to see how far she would go. 'I told you,' I said, keeping my hands raised, 'it was a street-gang.'

'I don't think so. Ever heard of a study called *Street Life of Aswan* by Howard Johnson? There was a copy in the US embassy resources section. It lists all the street gangs of Aswan over the past twenty years with their little eccentricities, and guess what? An earring in the upper right ear-fold, and a dagger on the wrist aren't featured at all. Sanusi put me on to you and I've done my homework, Sammy. You heard of a book called *Ghosts of the Desert – The Hawazim of Egypt*, by a Doctor Calvin Ross? It's all in there. You said yourself that the Nile Valley people are scared shitless of the desert, yet you seem to feel mighty comfortable here. You know your eyes were actually shining when you showed me that pile of rocks out there?'

'Yeah, well that's probably the bennies I dropped.'

'Bullshit! You know all about the law of companionship, sand-storms and camel-turds, don't you? Of course, you're a pretty smart guy – you might have learned it somehow, but you've got Hawazim whip scars all the way down your back, and that's not the kind of thing you get on a crash course in desert anthropology.'

'I had an accident,' I said.

'Yeah, you had an accident all right. When we were being chased down the alley on Roda, you used that phrase about the

''Divine Spirit''. Only the Hawazim use that term, and you don't pick that up from a weekend seminar either. You're Hawazim, Sammy, and the Hawazim are regarded as a bunch of cup-cakes by everyone, even the other Bedouin. They're despised but feared as a tribe of wizards with hocus-pocus powers. The question I've been asking myself is the same one Sanusi asked: how in the name of hell did a member of that tribe get into the SID? The Hawazim under Omar James Ross – the son of the guy who wrote the book, as I'm sure you know – virtually rose in rebellion against the government four years ago. Funny – that's about the same time you've been a cop.'

I looked at her and grinned, and it seemed to infuriate her. 'Start talking, Sammy,' she said, 'or God help me, I'll put you down.'

'OK,' I said. 'But first what about you, *Special Agent*? Sanusi was right about you, too, wasn't he? You're a faceless woman. Sure you're fast. You're faster than anyone I ever knew, and you can move more silently than a cat. You never miss a shot, never miss a trick, but last night I had a long and interesting talk with our Mr Van Helsing. He told me you ratted on me. Says you blew the whole thing to the cops, who conveniently happened to be there when we came out of the archives. Says you set me up deliberately because you couldn't stand a ''raghead'' stealing your thunder, and when I think about it only you and Hammoudi knew about the archives job, and I'd bet my life Hammoudi didn't snitch. Now, the question *I'm* asking myself is, are you really FBI, or a mole for someone else? Mossad? Even the Militants? Or maybe you've been in with Van Helsing since the beginning and those charming scenes at the Mena and in the car last night were an act. You do a very good act, miss . . . whatever your name is. It isn't Daisy Brooke, that's for sure.' I eased the black and white photo Hammoudi had given me out of my inside pocket and held it up between my forefinger and thumb. 'This is Daisy Brooke – a homely brunette . . .'

Daisy's eyes flickered slightly as she tried to focus on the photograph, and in that moment I threw it into her face and made a grab for the SIG, knocking the muzzle away and falling heavily on her. She landed under me with an 'Ooof!' and dropped the weapon, her nails raking viciously at my eyes as we rolled over in the sand. Just then there was a gunshot crack that sounded deafening in the silence, and a bullet thumped off the stones and ricocheted with a vibrating whizz. Daisy hesitated and I broke her hold, monkey-crawled away from her and turned to see a host of camel-riders loping in through the gaps in the wall – men in ochre-coloured *jibbas* with plumes of hair and gargoyle faces.

The first rider was mounted on a magnificent off-white she-camel. He wore a ragged *shamagh* across his face and carried a bolt-action sniper's rifle with telescopic sights – a rifle I recognized immediately. He made a *kkhyaakhyaaaa* sound and yanked his headrope, so that the camel raised her head disdainfully and settled into the sand with perfect grace. The rider slid out of the saddle and walked up to Daisy, slipping away his *shamagh* to reveal a lean, bearded, bespectacled face. He whipped off his glasses, wiped them ceremoniously on the sleeve of his *jibba*, then replaced them carefully.

'Allow me to introduce myself,' he said in English. 'My name is Omar James Ross.'

36

Daisy came up with her hard blue eyes flaming, and her full lips drawn back from bared teeth. Her headscarf had fallen off in the tussle and her blonde hair streaked out wildly in the desert breeze. To me she looked like a big, beautiful, dangerous pantheress about to spring. She was going for the SIG but Ross was quicker. He moved with the speed of a cobra, clawing it out of the sand and stuffing into his belt. Daisy panted and wiped dust off her lips with her cuff.

'Hey!' she said. 'That's mine!'

Ross peered at her over the top of his glasses. 'That depends on whether you're with us or against us,' he said. 'If you're against us, then by Hawazim custom this weapon is rightly mine. If you're with us, you can have it back. Now which is it?'

Daisy rocked back on the balls of her feet, still breathing heavily, and her full lips pouted first at Ross, then at me. There was a commotion as the rest of the tribesmen – twelve or thirteen of them – couched their camels amid a cacophony of snorts, bellows, grunts and shouts. They looked as if they had sprung out of the bowels of the earth, I thought, with their flint-coloured eyes and almond-shaped faces covered in thick beards, their bodies small, lean and robust. They wore their shocks of hair uncut and greased with fat or in plaits bleached with camel-urine. Their *jibbas* were stained russet red from the dye of the desert plant *abal*, though several of them were barechested, wearing only a loose pair of pantaloons and a coarse shawl passing round the back with the ends thrown over both shoulders. They wore cartridge-belts at their waists and carried their rifles as if they were extensions of their arms: each of them wore a tiny silver earring – the *fidwa* – in the upper fold of the right ear, and a stiletto blade strapped just above the left wrist. They were mostly barefooted, their feet wide-splayed and calloused from walking on sand and grit, and they moved with the precision and economy of trained acrobats. They gathered silently shoulder to shoulder, holding their rifles and swinging their slender camel-sticks, sensing the tension, watching keenly for their leader's next move.

Ross turned to me and slung the sniper's rifle. He clapped both hands on my shoulders, then clasped my right hand in both of his and looked me in the eyes, unblinking. 'Thank the Divine Spirit for your safe return, Nawayr,' he said. 'By God, you have left us in the wilderness. By the will of the Divine Spirit, no evil?'

'No evil, thank the Divine Spirit.'

'May the Divine Spirit grant you long life!'

'Praise be to God! The Divine Spirit grant long life to you and yours.'

'Welcome back.' He gave me the triple nose-kiss of the Hawazim, then suddenly threw his arms round me and embraced me hard. When he pulled away I saw there were tears in his eyes. 'We owe you, Sammy,' he said. 'No other Hazmi could have put in four years in the city.'

I knew this was literally true – to anyone brought up in the desert, four years in Cairo would have been a living death. Most Hawazim couldn't stand a single night under a solid roof. But then I had a natural advantage: unlike them I'd spent my first ten years in a town. I studied Ross and noted how his body had grown leaner and harder since I'd last seen him. He was a half-breed like me, but he looked more Arab than I did, with coffee-coloured skin, jet-black hair and the flint-coloured eyes of his mother's people. I was a Hazmi by adoption, but Ross had been reared in the desert and knew its ways from birth. It was only after his mother had died that his father had taken him away from the tribe and sent him to school in Britain, and as the Old Man used to say, 'a thing learned when young is a thing carven in rock'. Ross had returned to the tribe four years ago, bringing with him a beautiful half-Greek, half-Egyptian girl called Elena, who was now his wife and the mother of his son. They'd gone looking for the legendary lost oasis of Zerzura in the most desolate reaches of the Western Desert, and Ross had returned changed. I never knew what he'd found out there – I suspected Hammoudi did, but he'd kept his mouth shut. All I knew was that it had to have been something pretty important, because afterwards he and Elena had been picked up by the police.

I'd been among the team of Hawazim who'd disguised themselves as Camel Corps troopers to spring Ross and Elena, and I'd seen Ross put a bullet through a guy's head from a hundred metres with a snap-shot, while the guy had his handgun in Elena's ear. It was in the same battle that the Old Man had been snuffed, and Ross had taken his place as leader of the tribe. The Hawazim weren't led by a sheikh, but by a sort of shaman whom they called *amnir*, or 'One Who Lights The Way', and who had the intuitive sense they called 'the Shining power'. A lot of people had a touch of the power, just as I did, but Ross had it more strongly than any Hawazim *amnir* for several generations – stronger even than the Old Man himself.

Ross stooped and picked up my stiletto – the Hawazim *khanjar*. He passed it to me handle first. 'You've earned this forty times over,' he said, 'and this.' He brought a silver earring out of his pocket – my *fidwa* – engraved with my own personal brand. 'I kept it for you, like I promised,' he said. I hadn't worn it since I'd left the desert four years ago, and I took it and fitted it into the hole in my upper right ear. It was as if this was the signal the tribesmen had been waiting for. Suddenly they crowded round me, nose-kissing, clasping my hand, slapping me on the shoulders, shouting, 'Nawayr,' and 'Thank the Divine Spirit for your safe return!' I was moved by the warmth of their greeting. No matter where you went, I thought, you would never find any people so welcoming as the Hawazim. A small, squat man with a great shaggy beard and a chest as broad as a bull-camel's suddenly shot out of the crowd and charged at me with the force of a bullet.

'Nawayr!' he bawled, wrenching my hand as if he wanted to crush it. 'Good thing we came when we did! You're letting women down you now!' It was my blood-brother, Ahmad, who was nicknamed *Buraym* or 'Little Pot' – a miniature Samson, one of the strongest and bravest men in the tribe. 'By God!' he said, 'you've no more muscle on you than a camel-stick! You need a good dose of lizards' eggs and milk. And what do you look like in those rags! I hardly knew you, by God! Get some real clothes on and then we'll see the old Nawayr!'

A tall slender man heaved him out of the way and took my hand. He was thin and wiry, even for a Hazmi, his face long and narrow as a slice of melon, with a sharp goatee beard. It was my blood-brother, 'Ali – Ahmad's half-brother. 'Don't listen to the Little Pot,' he said, laughing, 'you haven't changed at all, brother. It's a miracle, thank the Divine Spirit. I don't know how you stood it in the city. All those fat and dishonest folk so stupid they don't even know their own ancestors – all that rottenness and perversion.'

'Ah,' I said, 'you know what Mukhtar used to say: *La yadhurr as-sihaab nabh al-kilaab*: The clouds are not harmed by the barking of dogs!' The tribesmen laughed and applauded. 'You knew I was coming?' I asked Ross.

'Of course,' he said, 'I saw it in the Shining – you, the girl, the exact place and time. I didn't see Hammoudi, though. Where is the old Night Butcher?'

'Last I saw he was drawing fire from a bunch of thugs who were trying to kill us. He's probably feeding the Nile perch now.'

Ross smirked. 'I doubt it. Hammoudi has a habit of getting himself resurrected. I killed him once myself, and it turned out he was wearing body armour!' He adjusted his glasses and handed the sniper's rifle back to 'Ali, its rightful owner. For years it had been his pride and joy.

'I knew that shot could only have come from the Hawk's Eye,' I said.

'True,' 'Ali said, caressing the weapon as if it was a child, 'but if it had been me I wouldn't have shot wide!' He glanced playfully at Daisy, who was cowering by the Daihatsu with the wild look still on her face. 'We'll have to take her with us,' he said.

Ross raised a quizzical eyebrow at me. Daisy stared at him. I picked up my Beretta and blew the sand off the working parts. 'She's put her ass on the line for me,' I told Ross. 'On the other hand she might have set me up, and I don't even know her real name.'

'She has a right to keep her name. But treachery against a *rafiq* is serious. Did she set you up?'

I put my pistol away and thought about it. The guards at the archives; the machine-gun tracer splintering the *Princess Maria*; the way she'd shot the guy who'd blasted open my front door, and another of the thugs in the street, the way she'd wrecked the two MP motorcyclists with brilliant shooting at their front tyres. I still didn't know who Daisy was, but like I'd told Monod, it was time for a leap of faith. OK, she might have a secret agenda of her own, but whatever Van Helsing had said she'd come too near to getting slotted too many times for it to have been an act.

I looked at Ross. 'I'll give her the benefit of the doubt,' I said, 'she saved my life.'

'Rolling in the sand is a funny way of saying thanks,' Ross said, grinning.

'It was a minor disagreement. Daisy wanted to know who I really was, and now she's got her answer.' I looked at her and the hard blue eyes met mine. 'You were right,' I told her, 'I'm not really a cop. Oh, I trained in the Police Academy all right, but they didn't know I'm really Nawayr, an adopted tribesman of the Hawazim – the Ghosts of the Desert. Sammy Rashid is my real name, and what I told you about my background was true. My father was a Yank and I did grow up on the streets of Aswan. One day I tried to rob an old man of the Hawazim, Mukhtar wald Salim – Ross's uncle. It turned out that he was the *amnir* of the tribe, and he recognized I had a touch of the Shining power. He adopted me, and after that I grew up in the desert. Ross is my cousin by adoption, and these two – 'Ali and Ahmad – are Mukhtar's sons, my blood-brothers.'

Daisy opened her mouth to ask a question, but 'Ali interrupted her. 'We have to get moving, *amnir*,' he told Ross, 'they'll be coming before long.'

Ross turned his attention back to Daisy. 'Will you ride with us as our companion?' he asked. Daisy nodded and he whipped out his stiletto so fast that its blade flashed in the lowering sun. 'Who's got salt?' he demanded. One of the tribesmen hurried forward with a decorated leather bag of salt crystals and Ross took a few and scattered them on the blade. He offered it to Daisy. 'Eat!' he said. 'This is the food-covenant of the tribe.'

Daisy blinked at me, then took a piece of salt from the blade with her teeth. Ross did the same, then shook hands with her and gave her back the SIG and its magazine. 'I don't know your real name,' he said, 'and you can keep it. Whoever you are, wherever you come from, whatever you've done in the past, doesn't matter. All that matters is what you do from now on. You've already put your life on the line for Sammy. We'll defend you with our lives and we expect no less from you.'

Daisy nodded solemnly. 'I won't let you down,' she said, 'but what's really going on here?'

Ross laughed. 'I'll tell you the whole thing in good time,' he said, 'but not now. Now we have to move. Come on. Let's ride!'

By the time we got the car under cover in one of the large buildings, Ahmad had brought up two spare camels, ready saddled and bridled. I saw to my delight that one of them was my own Umm ar-Rusasa – 'The Mother of the Bullet', a ten-year-old off-white racer belonging to *al-Bil* – the thoroughbred herd of the tribe. As a foal she'd been shot in a raid by the Fuqara and still carried the bullet in her body – hence her name. Actually the Old Man had given her to me as a three-year-old: she was bad-tempered and highly strung, and he'd said that he'd chosen her specially so I would be obliged to learn about camels the hard way. He said he wouldn't give me another till I'd mastered her, anyway, so if I lost or foundered her I'd have to walk. At first she'd tried to bite and kick me – twice she'd run away, and I'd had to track her down alone. But the Old Man had been right: I'd learned, and once we'd come to an uneasy truce, she'd turned out to be one of the fastest, most enduring camels in the herd.

'She's foaled twice since you were here,' Ahmad said, 'she's an old lady now. Still got fire in her belly, though. Are you sure you're still up to it, brother? You wouldn't like a docile old dowager instead?'

I sidled up to Umm ar-Rusasa and pulled at her flexible lower lip: she crooned and snuffled at me, but didn't snap. 'See!' 'Ali said. 'She knows you in your city clothes, even if the Little Pot doesn't!'

'Can you ride a camel?' Ahmad asked Daisy, pointing at the elderly she-camel he'd brought for her.

'It wasn't on my curriculum at Berkeley,' she said, 'but I'll give it a go.'

I helped her into the saddle and took the headrope. The she-camel stood up, groaning, letting her old joints unlimber. 'You don't have to do anything but sit,' I told Daisy, 'I'm hitching you behind me.'

'No!' she said. 'Give me the bridle. If I'm going to do this, I'm going to do it properly!'

I gave her the headrope and a camel-stick Ahmad had brought for her. 'This one's easy to manage,' Ahmad told Daisy. 'She's very even-tempered. Just yank the rope right or left depending on which way you want to turn, but only pull back when you want to stop. If you want to go faster, tap her on the flank lightly with the stick and wiggle your toes on her withers.'

'Wiggle my toes?'

'Yes. Wiggle your toes. And only tap *lightly* with the camel-stick or she'll be off like a gazelle. She's old but she's still got plenty of fight in her!'

Ross picked up his camel-stick and slipped on to the back of his she-camel – the signal to start. I vaulted into the saddle. Rusasa roared and lurched to her feet with the explosive power I remembered so well – she would have taken off, too, if I hadn't pulled back heavily on the rope. 'You're right,' I told Ahmad, 'she's still got the old fire.' He grinned and swung on to his own saddle. All around us camels snorted, spat and groaned as the troop mounted up. Then the *amnir* wheeled and led us at a fast trot out of the last vestige of the settled world and into the heart of the Red Land.

37

I WILL NEVER FORGET THAT night's march. It was a chance to reacquaint myself with the desert in a way that was impossible in a motorcar. The day's heat had dissipated by the time we left al-Manakh, and the sun was already hovering above the western horizon, fusing serenely into sheepskin cloud laced with long sets of matching colours – burgundy, quince, chrome yellow, magma orange – building up in stacks and galleries as the sunlight grew more diffuse. There was a stillness to the air that you only hear in the deepest desert, a silence so deep there was almost a music to it – a bass resonant harmonic that reverberated like percussion deep down in your psyche. We rode at a brisk walk as the Hawazim always did in the desert, and the camels' shadows were grasshopper creatures on the screen of the surface. As Rusasa swayed with her rollicking, easy gait, my eyes worked over the surface, picking out the signs of tiny dramas – the scuffle marks where a camel-spider had fought and killed a scorpion, the carcase of a quail which had fallen out of the sky exhausted on its migration south, the imprint of coils and foot-pads, where a snake had swallowed a lizard. I rode in silence reading these surface marks, lulled into a trance by the rocking motion of the camel, the crunch of camel-pads in the gravel, the familiar slosh of water in the drippers, until the cloud finally absorbed the sun's colours and the night unwrinkled like the folds of a great turtle-skin, enshrouding us in darkness. By then, though, the moon was up and the stars were out in their full imperial majesty, undimmed by the lights of the city. Daisy rode beside me silently, nursing her thoughts, staring at the great panoply of the sky or watching me and copying the way I handled the camel, mouthing the same glottal clicks to urge the beast forward. She learned fast, and she was a natural, I thought, not sitting stiffly in the saddle but letting her body roll and flop with the camel's jerky stride. We didn't speak much. The night was a blue dome weighed down with a billion-billion stars that sparkled like diamonds, rubies and sapphires – a glimpse of a cosmos so vast and unfathomable that Daisy gasped in awe and our camels pressed together shoulder to shoulder as if to remind themselves of their own existence.

It was midnight before we came to al-Bahrayn and by then it was all I could do to keep my eyes open. The place was an uninhabited oasis in the Western Desert containing two lakes and hundreds of acres of wild palm trees, that no one had tended for years. The main body of the Hawazim was encamped here, hidden under the palms, but all we could make out in the starlight was the glow of a few scattered cooking fires. As we came into the palm-groves someone shouted a challenge. 'Rein in!' Ahmad whispered urgently. 'We've posted a machine-gun on the approach.'

Ross shouted back and a moment later we were couching our camels among the palms and the familiar smells of woodsmoke and uncured leather that I always associated with desert life. Dozens of shadows darted silently out of the palms, helping us off the camels, slapping me on the back, shaking my hand and calling my name. There was no accompanying ululation from the women, though, and I realized that this was an all-male camp – a *qom* or raiding-party, without the black tents which were considered the property of the women. 'We left the rest back in the Jilf,' Ross told me, 'we had to move fast and light.'

'So you're here, you city slicker!' a voice cried in my ear, and I turned to see my third and eldest blood-brother, Mansur, grinning all over his face and letting his boss-eye roll maniacally. He shook my hand and hugged me, his one good eye blazing in the moonlight. 'Welcome back, Sammy!' he chanted. 'Thank God for your safe return! Upon you be no evil! May the Divine Spirit grant you long life!'

'No evil. May the Divine Spirit grant goodness to you and yours!'

He looked gaunt, I thought, but not as gaunt as his half-brother 'Ali who was built like a beanpole. Mansur had none of Ahmad's rope-like muscles, yet there was a sense of power about him, and he carried not a gram of spare fat. His body under the ragged *jibba* and *sirwal* looked all sharp angles, right up to his face, which was a nest of interlocking blades like a giant Swiss Army knife. His hair was a clotted mop of curls, thickly smeared with mutton fat. Ross was the *amnir* – the tribal leader, and held ultimate authority, but Mansur – 'The One-Eyed Warrior' – was the Water Master of the tribe.

'I've a new son, now, Nawayr,' Mansur said. 'He's called Mahdi. That's four I've got, thank the Divine Spirit. The wealth of the Hawazim is in their children, by God!'

'The Divine Spirit grant them all long life!'

'Amen. And who's this angel of delight you've brought with you?' he demanded, looking at Daisy. 'You married secretly, you devil, without telling the tribe!'

I laughed, and Daisy pouted. 'We're not married,' she said stiffly, shaking Mansur's hand.

'Not married!' he exclaimed in mock astonishment. 'What a fool you are, Sammy! You don't find such a beauty as this every day. She has eyes prettier than a gazelle!'

Daisy couldn't help grinning at the quaint compliment, and allowed Mansur to lead her to a roaring fire of dry bast the tribesmen were building up in a clearing between the palms. They laid out home-woven rugs and embroidered leather saddle-cushions for us to sit on. Daisy lowered herself down painfully. 'God almighty!' she said. 'I feel stiff!'

'Yeah, you get that the first time you ride a camel,' I told her, 'I did. You're using unaccustomed muscles, that's why. But it soon goes, and it never comes back.'

Ross sat down next to us and 'Ali and Ahmad settled cross-legged nearby. Mansur took up his place at the *amnir*'s right elbow, his blind eye glittering in the firelight. He opened an embroidered camel-skin saddlebag and took out two bundles of russet-coloured cloth, which he threw to me. 'Proper desert clothes for you both!' he said. 'Stained it myself when the *amnir* said you were coming. I wondered about the girl, but he said she was *Afrangi*, so I put her down as an honorary man!'

'You did right,' I said, looking at Daisy, 'she can move faster and shoot straighter than most men I know.' I examined one of the bundles and found a Hawazim *jibba* and *sirwal* – the baggy pantaloons the tribesmen wore – and even a new checked head-cloth and a pair of skin sandals. Daisy held her suit up to the firelight. 'Well,' she said, 'it's an improvement on this old widow's dress I'm wearing.'

We slipped off into the bushes for a moment to change and by the time we came back the camels had been expertly unloaded and turned into the shadows. Our double-horned saddles had been laid in a neat row behind the rugs, and from the horns of each one were slung two drippers – goatskin waterbags – bulging like giant slugs. The mass of tribesmen were gathering around the fire in a huge circle – there must have been fifty of them, the finest warriors of the tribe. The Hawazim were an open community and had no sense of privacy – every one of them considered himself entitled to hear what they called *saqanab* – 'the news'.

Daisy looked odd in her new desert-hued outfit, which hung loosely on her, disguising her feminine contours. It wasn't exactly a designer product – a poor match, I thought, for the Gucci handbag she carried her SIG in. But the value of Hawazim clothes lay in their comfort not their appearance, and they were far superior in the desert to anything outsiders had designed.

'Ah,' Ahmad commented as I took my place next to Ross,

fitting my shoulder-rig over the *jibba*. 'Now you look your old self!'

'I hope I never have to go back to wearing trousers,' I said, 'the Divine Spirit be praised!'

The One-Eyed Warrior grinned with pleasure, and I felt a flush of gratitude towards him when I remembered how he'd looked after me as a child. Ahmad had been devoted to Ross and had defended him against all comers, but he and 'Ali had resented my presence at first, and called me a 'town boy' and a 'fellah', until I'd lost my temper and gone for them with my fists. I'd always been fast, but even as a boy Ahmad had been built like Hercules, and I'd usually got the worst of it. The Old Man had seen what was going on, but in his wisdom he'd let it take its course, knowing that their mockery would oblige me to learn quickly. He'd been right about that, and eventually Ahmad, 'Ali and I had become close. But I'd never forgotten how Mansur – the eldest – had taken me under his wing, smoothed over the squabbles and made me feel part of the family. I'd had a special place in my heart for him ever since. It hadn't been easy becoming a Hazmi – their margin of survival was tight and they made no allowance for outsiders. Apart from my mother, though, they were the only real family I'd ever known.

Half a dozen of the men had begun to make coffee, toasting fresh beans on long spoons in the fire, then smashing them in brass mortars. Each mortar had a different tone, and each tribesman his own rhythm, so that the sound rang out like a peal of bells. Soon the delicious scent of fresh coffee filled the night and the coffee-servers were working their way through the tribesmen, each with a brass tray and a hornbill-spouted coffee-pot. The servers carried only one cup each – a dish a little bigger than the bowl of an egg-cup – and no more than a few drops of coffee were poured at a time. Each drinker was expected to drink three cups, and as new arrivals we were served first. The coffee was strong, spiced with ginger and cinnamon, and tasting nothing like the anaemic stuff I'd had in the city. By the time I'd drunk my third cup I'd begun to wake up, and I watched Daisy sipping hers experimentally. 'Drink it all in a swallow,' I told her, 'and take three cups. Any more is considered greedy, any less an insult.' When she'd finished I showed her how to waggle the cup from side to side in Hawazim fashion before replacing it on the tray. There was a bass murmur of voices from the assembled men, almost like a meditation, and the flames flickered in the hearth, playing patterns across the faces, illuminating some and obscuring others. They sat proudly upright, with their rifles nestling in the crooks of their elbows, each awaiting his turn at the coffee.

Ross put his cup back on the server's tray and removed his glasses, rubbing them on the sleeve of his *jibba*. He took five slow breaths and replaced them, then he turned to me. 'Elena told me to salute you from her,' he said, 'and from our son Risaala. He's four years old.'

'The Divine Spirit salute them,' I answered. Ross's son hadn't yet been born when I'd left the desert, and I was tickled to find out he had named him Risaala, 'The Message'.

'Now let's get down to business,' he said, '*saqanab*. What is the news?

Saqanab was a ritual acted out whenever two or more Hawazim encountered each other after an absence, and it had nothing to do with the townsman's concept of news – politics, disasters and international events. It was a sort of exchange of consciousness – a detailed description of everything the tribesman had seen, heard or experienced. Through *saqanab* the Hawazim built up a complete mental map of everything that had occurred or was occurring in the desert around them.

'*Amnir*,' I said to Ross, 'I never found the creature's hideout. I followed up every story, investigated every lead. It all came to nothing. Last night, and the night before I got near enough to touch it, but both times it gave me the slip. It has killed twice in two days –'

'Two days!' Ross cut in. 'It hasn't killed so frequently since it left the Fayoum. This means it's building up to something – getting ready for a big move.'

'Yeah,' I said, 'the problem is that it has to be well camouflaged now. It's inhabiting someone high up in society – could even be a face we know.'

Daisy listened with her mouth open. 'What are you talking about?' she demanded. 'Hell, we've been attacked by a hit-squad and fought a running battle with the police and God knows who else, and you're talking about some *creature*! I may be ignorant of your ways. I'm sure I'm behaving like an impatient asshole in your book. But I've been shot once and shot *at* a dozen times in the past twenty-four hours, and before it happens again perhaps some kind soul would tell me just what the hell is *going on*!'

38

Ross sat up straight and his eyes emerged from the darkness, his face reflecting the light in a warm, earth-coloured glow. There was a murmur of disapproval from the watching tribesmen. Daisy was right: to them she was an ignorant outsider and she'd broken protocol. The Old Man would have given her short shrift, I knew, but I wondered how Ross would react. He took a series of deep breaths and relaxed. 'OK,' he said, 'it's not our way, but you've risked your life for one of us, so maybe you have a right to know.' He paused and contemplated the situation for a moment. 'I'll make you a bargain,' he said, 'I'll tell you the whole story, as long as you level with us.'

'All right,' Daisy said, 'it's a deal.'

Ross pulled a skin bag from nearby and rummaged in it, bringing out two carved wooden pipes with brass stems, and a small pouch of tobacco. 'Smoke?' he asked Daisy. She wrinkled her nose and Ross passed one of the pipes to me. He took a handful of tobacco, then gave me the pouch, and we both filled our pipes. All around the fire the tribesmen were doing the same, I noticed, and the fragrance of tobacco was added to the coffee-scented air. I handed the pouch back to Ross and he took a long spill from the fire, lighting first my pipe, then his own. Bending over in the firelight, with his pipe, beard, and spectacles he looked like some time-ravaged but erudite college professor, I thought. Then he sank back, and only a net of dark, angular lines was left on his face. He took a deep toke on the pipe and let the smoke out slowly. I did the same, and coughed: it had been a long time.

Ross composed himself, blew out smoke, and glanced at Daisy. 'All right,' he said, 'what you're about to hear might sound crazy. You might think we're a pack of screwballs, but I can assure you it's all absolutely true, so please just hear me out.' He took a deep breath. 'It began four years ago,' he said, 'with a bad miscalculation on my part. In fact, it was almost my first act as *amnir* of the tribe, and I botched it. I had a very dangerous creature in the palm of my hand and I let it escape. This desert is the most arid tract of land in the world, and I thought the desert would do the dirty work. That was stupid. We had no knowledge at all of how this creature was made up, though we knew it was capable of changing form. I thought it would soon die of dehydration. I was wrong.'

Daisy stared at Ross, her eyes picked out in a ray of moonlight. 'What was this creature?' she asked in a small voice.

'A ghoul,' Ross said.

The matter-of-fact way he said it sent a shiver through me. Daisy looked shaken, and there was a mutter of 'The Divine Spirit protect us' from the ranks of tribesmen. I saw many of them making the sign for defence against the evil eye.

'Of course,' Ross went on, 'that's what we Hawazim call it. Actually it wasn't from this world at all. It probably came from somewhere in Canis Major – possibly from a planet that orbits the white dwarf Sirius B.'

'You mean an *alien*?'

'Sure, but the Hawazim don't know that term. The creature had been here for decades – perhaps centuries. It's a shapeshifter, able to ''cross over'' – to take on the appearance of human beings and assume their memories and personalities. It's not the first of its kind to visit our planet.'

'You mean it's still alive?'

'Unfortunately yes. Only a few months after I last saw it

running off into the desert, there were reports of attacks by a ghoul in the Fayoum Oasis. We were across the border in the Sudan at the time, but I sent 'Ali and Ahmad to find out what was going on –'

'The boy!' Daisy said, looking at me, 'the Muslim boy buried in a Christian graveyard at the Fayoum! The old Arab there said he'd been attacked by a ghoul!'

'Yes,' Ahmad said, 'one of the victims was taken to St Samuel's Monastery and died there. The *amnir* sent me to look into it because I'd been there with him when we let it go. I remember it well, because I had a slug in my thigh at the time, and but for Omar and Elena I might have bled to death. Well, it was winter, and by God it was cold! 'Ali and me left our camels with relatives at Sohaj and went to the Fayoum disguised as fellahs. We talked to the Bedouin there – the Harab – at least they call themselves Bedouin, but they aren't really. Most of them live in mud houses, and they have more cattle and water buffaloes than camels. We talked to folk who'd actually seen the ghoul. Said it was a hairy beast with a goat's head and bandy legs, exactly like the thing I'd seen running off into the desert that summer. And that was incredible, by God, because we'd last seen it somewhere near the Jilf, which meant it had made a distance of ten camel-days on foot and without water. No human being could have done that.'

He drew on his pipe again, and 'Ali interrupted him. 'You sound like you're in love with it!' he said, and the tribesmen chortled. 'Perhaps you should make it your second wife!'

'My wife would never stand it!' Ahmad rejoined instantly. 'She'd make its life a misery!'

There were more bursts of laughter from the tribesmen, but Ahmad blew out smoke and adopted a serious tone. 'The beast had struck at least four times in the Fayoum area,' he said, 'and the attacks had all happened in the space of a month. The victims were young Arab boys or girls out in lonely places herding camels or sheep, so there were no witnesses to the attacks, only people who arrived just afterwards and saw the creature disappearing into the distance. After that month, the attacks suddenly stopped. We even visited the Cave of the Owls where the Harab claimed the ghoul lived, but we found no sign of it. It was clear that it had moved on. Our visit to the Fayoum was worthwhile, though, because we found out something we didn't know – that the creature hunts human beings and drinks their blood.'

The tribesmen muttered darkly, holding up their fingers against the evil eye.

Daisy stared at him aghast. 'So Sanusi wasn't such a fruit-cake after all,' she said, 'there *was* a ghoul in Cairo.'

'Yeah,' I said, 'and I spent more than three years trying to track it down.'

'When the attacks stopped in the Fayoum, they started up in Khan al-Khalili,' Ross said, 'and we realized the ghoul had shifted to the city. I sent Sammy there to find it, posing as a cop. He was the only one apart from myself who could pass as a townsman, and Hammoudi helped manufacture a cover. Hammoudi hadn't seen the creature and was dubious, but he agreed to help. In fact Sammy's cover was Hammoudi's idea, and it was a good one, because as an SID man he would always have his ear to the ground. The problem is that the creature is tremendously powerful. It has some kind of hypnotic ability, and it's capable of getting people under its control. In its last life –'

'You mean it's happened before?'

'Yes, and last time it cost me the death of my best friend Julian Cranwell. My wife and I only escaped by the skin of our teeth, thanks to Hammoudi and some good friends here. That time it had spent years building up massive support – it'd resurrected a secret society called ''The Eye of Ra'' – the new incarnation of an ancient brotherhood going back to pharaonic times that was originally set up to make sure no ''uninvited guests'' got control of the planet.'

'Are you saying these creatures have been visiting earth for thousands of years?'

'Yes. I discovered that there's a whole secret history surrounding human civilization that you won't find in any history book. Over the centuries, the purpose of the brotherhood got perverted, and instead of defending earth against the aliens it started dealing with them to its own advantage. The alien's objective was to send some kind of message across 8.6 light-years of space to its home planet, and it had the patience to develop all the resources it needed to do that. The Eye of Ra organization was one of those resources, and in this century it has been responsible for the deaths of dozens of people who came near to finding out the truth. The creature had even created another organization in your country, composed of some of the top men.'

Daisy went very still suddenly, her eyes glued to Ross's face. 'What was the name of this organization?' she enquired.

'It was called MJ-12 – codenamed Majesty.'

For a moment Daisy looked completely disoriented. Her eyes started out of her head, and she seemed to be having trouble controlling her breath. Her eyes remained riveted on Ross, as though she'd seen something terrifying there. 'I don't believe this,' she stammered.

Ross smiled at her, the light of the flames glinting dimly on his teeth. 'I don't blame you,' he said, 'you'd be justified in thinking we're a bunch of looney-tunes.'

Daisy shook her head and shifted her gaze to the fire. 'I don't think you're a bunch of looney-tunes,' she said slowly, 'because I know all about MJ-12. It was supposed to have been formed in 1947 by President Truman in response to the Roswell Incident, when an alien spaceship crashed in New Mexico. Actually it existed long before that under the name of the ''Jason Scholars'', whose function was supposedly to assess any threat to earth from extraterrestrial life-forms. Most Americans believe it's a myth, but it's not – it has twelve members, and they include among others the chiefs of the FBI and the CIA.'

'So what don't you believe? That the creature exists?'

Daisy laughed tensely. 'I believe the creature exists,' she said, 'because one of my first jobs was to infiltrate a place called Area

51 in the Nevada desert. It's a test site for aircraft, and was within the same area as the Roswell Incident. I saw things there I didn't want to see. Bits of alien spacecraft, ancient teleportation devices – even the mummified bodies of the aliens themselves.'

Ross was gazing at her stiffly now. 'Who sent you to investigate Area 51?' he asked. 'The FBI?'

She raised her eyes and looked at him. 'My orders come directly from the White House. My assignment is to monitor the activities of MJ-12.'

There was a stunned silence, while we let the words sink in. Ross whipped off his glasses and glared at her. 'Ali and Ahmad put their pipes down and sat up.

'OK,' she said, 'the FBI role was my deep-cover, but I was recruited by the White House before I even went to Berkeley. A lot of people in the US government have been suspicious of MJ-12's activities for a long time, but they mostly keep quiet. Those who meddle have a habit of disappearing. They're convinced that Majesty has been dealing with aliens for years to get a handle on their technology. All that would be dandy if it wasn't that there are close links between MJ-12 and the military-industrial complex. What I can't believe is, you just confirmed that an alien is controlling MJ-12. Shit! I had to come all the way to the desert on a camel to find out.'

For a moment there was absolute silence, but for the crackle of the palm-bast in the fire. From somewhere behind us the camels spluttered and groaned ominously. Ross replaced his glasses. 'So who chose you for this . . . assignment?' he asked.

Daisy pursed her lips. 'That's the one thing I can't tell you. I was selected on the recommendation of backers who have to remain anonymous. But I swear I'm on the side of the angels. You have to believe me.'

'Someone once told me there are three kinds of creatures,' Ahmad commented, 'Human beings, *Jinns* and angels. The ghoul is a kind of *Jinn*, so being on the side of the angels can't be bad.'

'So how come you *are* here?' Ross asked.

Daisy grinned palely in the darkness. 'It was a spin-off from my operation inside Area 51. The place has become a sort of museum of weird material, and I discovered some ancient Egyptian artifacts – a thing called the Akhnaton Papyrus, and the original Piri Reis Portolan – a map of the world made on some stuff so light it can be carried in your top pocket. That's what put me on to Doctor Adam Ibram. He'd been at Area 51 researching the Egyptian material, and I found out he was a member of MJ-12.'

'God help us!' I said. 'Ibram was mixed up with Majesty?'

She smiled. 'Not mixed up,' she said, 'he was a fully fledged Klansman. It wasn't on his FBI security-file, though. I followed him here to Cairo and a week after I arrive the guy's been stiffed!'

'So Firebird's an MJ-12 project?'

'You can bet on it. All the stuff about Militants was dust in our eyes, Sammy. Whoever was behind the Ibram killing deliberately planted the Sanusi amulet to lead us up the garden path. Might have been Van Helsing – he's in this up to his eyeballs. Maybe he was the Sayf ad-Din character who stole it from Sanusi. He could even be your ghoul.'

'Shit!' I said. 'Why didn't you tell me all this before? It would have made things one hell of a lot simpler!'

'Trust works two ways, Sammy. I kept on dropping hints right from our first meeting but you didn't confide in me, you just retreated into your shell.'

Ross removed his glasses again, and wiped the lenses on his *jibba* carefully. He replaced them and the firelight caught them, turning his eyes behind them to flecks of orange flame. 'I've heard of Adam Ibram,' he said, 'but perhaps you ought to tell me about Firebird!'

'The Firebird Project was a plan originated by the Shemsu-Hor in about 10,500 BC,' I said, 'a plan that included the construction of the Great Sphinx and the Giza pyramids, and culminated in some kind of ritual about eight thousand years later. The central role in the ritual was played by the Benben Stone. It was the capstone of the Great Pyramid, but later vanished.'

Ross considered it silently. He didn't seem the least surprised at what I'd said, and I had the feeling he'd heard it before. 'OK,' he said, 'but what was Ibram's involvement?'

'Ibram was shot dead in a teashop in the Khan al-Khalili a week ago,' I told him, 'and I found out that six months back he and Sid'Ahmad as-Sanusi were searching for something in the *Bahr Bela Ma*. The project was called Operation Firebird: a guy called Monod told us they were looking for the Benben Stone.'

Ross gasped. 'The ghoul is behind this,' he said, 'it has to be. Within four years it's managed to get control of some of the most powerful people in society, and got them looking for something it needs for its own purposes, just like it did before. It needs the Benben Stone.'

'Yeah, that's right,' I said, 'several people have already been killed for the sake of that Stone, including Ibram and very nearly me and Daisy too. And that's not all, *amnir*. One of the thugs who tried to bump me and Daisy had a Sekhmet tattoo on his wrist and I saw another on the CIA man Jan Van Helsing. What's more, Ibram left a picture of Sekhmet in his effects, with the words of the hymn to Ra written under it:

'Let the Eye of Ra descend
That it may slay the evil conspirators.'

Ross swallowed hard. 'It's happening again,' he said. He removed his glasses once more and let his eyes go out of focus. I could see his shoulders rise and fall rhythmically in the firelight as he took in deep breaths. There was another long silence, then he opened his eyes wide and replaced his glasses.

'I think,' he said, 'our ghoul has reactivated the Eye of Ra society. It's regained control of MJ-12. The fact that it's fed twice in two days shows it's planning something very soon.'

'Yeah,' I said, 'and whatever it is depends on the thing that lies buried in the *Bahr Bela Ma*. We've got to find it before the Eye of Ra does.'

Ross looked troubled. 'I'm not sure, Sammy,' he said, 'I've had visions of the Sea Without Water in the Shining recently.

Visions warning me off. I've got a hunch something bad is waiting for us there.'

'*Amnir*, we *must* go,' I said, 'the key to Firebird lies out there.'

'But the Sea Without Water is a big place,' Mansur said. 'Where do we start looking?'

'I can answer that,' I said, bringing out the two halves of Ibram's map from my bundle of things. I held them up in the glow of the flames. The wavering light caught them and for a minute the hills and wadis almost seemed to crawl off the parchment. 'A lot of people have died for these bits of rag,' I said.

'What are they?' Ross asked.

'They're Doctor Adam Ibram's last will and testament,' I said, 'pieces of a map showing the exact position of the Benben Stone.'

39

I T WAS LONG AFTER DAWN when I awoke, and I probably would have slept on if the camels hadn't started grumbling and screeching in my ear. I blinked to remind myself where I was, and saw Daisy wrapped up in a thick Hawazim quilt on the other end of the rug, staring at me blearily. We were under a makeshift awning of goat's hair the tribesmen had slung between the palms. Outside, in ace-of-clubs-shaped dapples of light and shade where last night's fire had been, ten camels were being saddled and loaded amid roaring, spitting, and excited human shouts. The tribesmen were trim figures, barechested and barefooted, who moved around the herd like dancers and squabbled as they loaded. They seemed to take a pleasure in argument, and when two men disagreed, half a dozen others would sidle over and join in. They made 'Ow! Ow!' sounds to encourage the camels to sit still long enough to be saddled, but there was an occasional 'Curse your father, you son-of-a-bitch!' as one of the beasts rose up like a behemoth, throwing off his baggage and vomiting bile.

The camels were beautiful-looking creatures, I thought – sleek and lean with the off-white colour the Hawazim called *aghbash*, and with the wedge-shaped heads and small pricked-up ears the tribesmen prized. Each one bore the Hawazim lizard brand on its rear right rump, with modifications for each family or owner.

Among them I noticed my own she-camel Umm ar-Rusasa, and Daisy's old female of the previous night, waiting patiently for our attention. A moment later Ross came bustling towards us dangling two decorated headropes from his arm. 'Get up you city people!' he bawled. 'This is the desert not the town! We have to get moving if we're going to reach the *Bahr Bela Ma*!'

I rolled out of my quilt and shook hands with the *amnir*. 'Where're the rest?' I asked, gesturing to the camels.

'Fifty is too large a party to cross the open sands,' Ross said, 'too dangerous.' He frowned at me. 'A chopper came over just after first light, Sammy. Oh, they didn't see us. We were well hidden under the palms and anyway we had our camouflage nets up. But you can bet they'll be back, and I don't relish the idea of being shot up by a helicopter gunship in the middle of nowhere. Seven men will ride with us. The rest of the *qom* will remain here until we return.' He shook hands with Daisy and handed us each a headrope. 'You know Hawazim ways,' he told me, 'no passengers. If Daisy comes with us she'll have to learn to rope and saddle her own camel! Come on, it's already late!'

He was right. The chill of dawn had long gone and you could feel the heat in the air, and smell the scents of desert earth unscrambling as the sunlight warmed the surface. There was a slight blow from the south that carried spice with it, and made the palm fronds crackle. Al-Bahrayn was a forest of tangled palms darkening the desert in two directions, while to the north, behind the clumps of camels, I glimpsed the bluer-than-blue gleam of open water. To the south lay the vista of the desert, a sheet of amber sand and purple stone blazing in the morning sun. I led Daisy to where our camels were knee-hobbled close together, and showed her how to tie the loop of cord across the camel's head. The Ghosts of the Desert disdained the nose-rings, nose-pegs and chokers used by other tribes. Some Hawazim camels I'd seen were so well trained they'd respond simply to taps with a camel-stick, and could be ridden without a headrope at all. When we'd roped the animals we went to fetch our double-horned saddles – crude wooden frames padded with palm-fibre the Hawazim called *hawayyi*. Other tribes had more flashy saddles, but like everything the Hawazim had these were more practical, and far more comfortable for the camel.

I showed Daisy how to fit hers, tying the girth-rope under the animal's belly. 'The Hawazim rule is that every rider saddles his own camel,' I said, 'that way if anything goes wrong and the rider is thrown, he has no one to blame but himself.' When the saddles were in place we loaded the heavy drippers, one on each side, and slung the woven saddlebags and topped the saddle with quilts and blankets ready for riding. Not long after, 'Ali arrived with a huge bowl of frothing camel's milk.

'It's God's gift in the desert,' he told Daisy, 'it is our food and drink.'

By Hawazim custom only men could milk the camels, and it was strictly forbidden to drink the milk without first offering it to someone else. I knew tribesmen who'd been herding camels alone, and who'd had to go several days without drinking until someone else came along. I told Daisy to squat down as she drank: it was considered bad manners to drink camel's milk standing up. She drank deeply and when she passed the bowl to me she had an oval of froth around her mouth and nose.

'Mm,' she said, 'it tastes kind of savoury!'

'That's the desert sedges,' 'Ali said, 'they give it spice, you know – like pepper.'

I drank and handed the bowl back to 'Ali. The hubbub diminished and I looked up to see that Ross was making his way to the front of the kneeling column of camels. The tribesmen were silent now, standing up straight, cradling their rifles, looking at the *amnir* expectantly. He stood on a small hillock of sand and raised both hands in front of him, palms facing inwards. The tribesmen made the same gesture, and Daisy and I followed suit. '*Al-Fatih!*' Ross shouted, and we mumbled the first verse of the Quran. Suddenly the *amnir* vaulted into the saddle, and the tribesmen scrambled to do the same. The camels stood, their complex hinge-joints uncrimping as they bellowed and howled. I reached to hold Daisy's headrope but she snatched it away.

'No!' she said. 'The only way to learn is to do it myself!'

She stepped lightly on to the camel's back and had to cling on as the animal lurched jerkily to its feet. I laughed, then leapt on to Rusasa's back. By the time she came up on her feet, Ross had half-turned his mount towards the company. He raised his camel-stick. 'Let the Divine Spirit be your agent!' he cried, then he reined his mount towards the northwest.

For the first hour the oasis remained behind us, a dark blot of ink on the desert's page until it finally dissolved into the background, leaving us adrift in boundless space. In a motorcar the desert is always the Other – the great Out There, to be feared and subdued by technology. When you're on a camel or on foot though, you meet it on its own terms, you abandon yourself to it. That's why Islam – 'submission' – is the perfect desert religion. Like Daisy had said, there seemed nothing to get a fix on, but that didn't worry me. I saw a desert different from hers – not an empty wilderness but a map of places where events had happened in the past. Few of them were marked by cairns like the Javelin Cast, yet I knew them because they'd been inscribed on my memory as a youth. Unlike townsmen the desert nomads' thoughts were always connected with places, so that their desert was a vast mnemonic system that played a sort of silent music to them as the landscape unrolled.

There was an imperturbability about Ross that was reassuring. He led the column from the front, never looking at the map but simply following his instincts, occasionally extending his camel-stick left or right to indicate a slight shift in direction. We didn't move in a tight squad like military troopers, but loosely in knots and pairs, spread out but always within sight of the guide. The camels, well fed on the *agul* grass that grew at al-Bahrayn, stepped out valiantly, squaring their massive chests and raising their heads proudly. The crunch of their feet on the gravel made a stirring rhythm, and the tribesman sang along with it in their age-old *hida*, or camel marching-songs. The verse passed from one rider to another down the column, punctuated by the voices of the entire party roaring back the chorus. The chorus itself was a set piece, but the verses were made up spontaneously by the singers who vied with each other for the cleverest rhymes. If anyone botched the rhyme there were hoots of derision from the mounted men. Daisy and myself were each the subjects of different verses, I noticed, and they weren't entirely flattering.

Slowly the sun rose to its zenith, growing tighter and more hotheaded as it climbed, reducing our shadows to squiggles beneath the camels' bellies and making us wrap up in our head-cloths. The heat lifted back from the surface, basting our bodies from head to foot. That was where the Hawazim clothing came in – it was loose enough to allow a layer of cool air to circulate around the body, insulating it against the heat. As we had started late we didn't stop to drink until midday and then it was only one gourd of water each. Water discipline was tight on a march like this and a rider never touched his own water. At the halt only one dripper would be breached between five people and then, no matter how thirsty you might be, it was considered polite to refuse until the pourer insisted. After drinking we ate a handful of dates each and walked for a while to give the camels a rest, leading them by the headropes or merely driving them gently from behind. The ground was red-hot at this time of day and even the Hawazim, who'd been walking barefoot all their lives, had to put on their thick-soled sandals. The surface heat made no impression at all on the camels, though. I roped Daisy's camel to Rusasa and we walked behind them chewing dates, glad of the chance to stretch our legs. The motion of their great haunches was almost hypnotic from behind.

'So,' I said at last, 'what happened to the well-heeled father and the yachts?'

'That was all part of my cover,' she said. 'There *was* a girl called Daisy Brooke – the one in the photograph – but she was involved in a serious car crash not long after that photo was taken. She went into a coma with irreversible brain-damage, and they asked her father – who *is* a senator and an ex-general – to lend me her identity. David Brooke's a patriot just like I said –

he'd been through Korea and Nam, but when Daisy was kayoed it nearly killed him – I think he'd always had her earmarked her for some big role in the CIA or FBI. Senator Brooke is one of the good guys I told you about – concerned about the nexus between MJ-12 and the military-industrial complex. I mean, imagine getting superior weapons via alien technology and selling them to the highest bidder!'

'Not a happy thought when you see some of the people around these days.'

'Exactly. Area 51 was bad enough. I got in there posing as a technician, and believe me there's some folk there you wouldn't want to meet at night down a dark alley. They were getting on to me and I had to beat a very hasty retreat. The president's office had to give me a new identity, and when the docs told David that Daisy would be a vegetable on a drip for the rest of her life, he agreed to let me "become" her. I met him a few times – he's a real sweetie, and every bit as straight as I told you. He said the real Daisy would have been proud, and I guess he felt her life had served some patriotic purpose after all. It was almost like she'd been resurrected.'

'But surely there must have been people who knew the real Daisy Brooke? I mean, weren't you afraid you might run into them?'

'Yeah, but the real Daisy was kept on life support in a high-security hospital with my name on her records, and it was all kept hush-hush. There was the chance that MJ-12 might get their feelers in, but we had to risk it. If ever I met anyone who'd known Daisy I gave out that I'd suffered serious memory-loss as a result of the accident, and had had plastic surgery. I was also steered clear of relatives and people who'd been close to her.'

'So there were no horses, servants and parties?' I said.

Daisy laughed. 'You were cutting very close to the bone when you asked me about that,' she said. 'Actually, I'm an orphan like you. I never had a mother or a father. I was brought up in an institution by Catholic sisters, who are not my favourite people. They thought they were justified using any kind of pun-ishment. There was one of them – Sister Agnes – who got off thrashing little girls with a stick, stark naked. They used to lock us up alone in cupboards or dank cellars if we complained. When you get treated like that it either turns you scatty, or it makes you hard and determined to survive. I suppose you know all about that, Sammy?'

'Sure. Different details, same deal. But then I got my break aged ten. The Old Man took me under his wing. That's why my loyalty will always be to the tribe.'

'I had to wait longer, but I got my chance too. One day – I was sixteen – I was called into the principal's office to meet this woman. She said that she'd had good reports about my classwork, and noted that I was always took A's. This lady – she wasn't old, maybe middle-aged and kinda beautiful – took me out to lunch and told me she'd been looking for somebody like me. At first I thought it was a trick – you know, I'd heard stories about con artists and white slavers who sold girls into prostitution or got them hooked on drugs. I was very wary, but the woman – her name was Laura – came to see me almost every week and we got to know each other. She was always kind and generous, and she started taking me to Los Angeles for weekend trips. There was never any sign of funny business, so I gradually relaxed and got to trust her. She said she was sure I had the qualities she was looking for, but she never told me why or what qualities they were. Sometimes we went to a lab and she gave me tests.'

'What kind of tests?'

'You know – like personality tests, physiology, reaction-time, that kind of a deal. After a while I sort of clicked I'd somehow "passed" the tests, and they got me out of the orphanage and I moved in with Laura. It was like a five-star hotel after that place, and Laura became what she called my "mentor". I wanted to know what it was all about, of course, and she asked if I'd be willing to use my talents to serve the country. I said yes, as long as it was really serving the country and not some big honcho on the make. You know what she did?'

'What?'

291

'She took me to the White House and introduced me to the president! Can you imagine it? Me, a seventeen-year-old girl with a spotty face, only a few months out of an orphanage! The president said something like not only the USA but the entire future of Western society rested on my shoulders. It was just a pep-talk, of course, but I was sold on it after that. I soon realized that, apart from my talents, they needed someone who had no attachments, so if anything happened I could be written off. I didn't resent that, though: I'd been brought up close to the realities of life.'

'Are there any more like you?'

'If there are I don't know about them. I was trained specially in languages, sent on courses in Israel, taught modern combat techniques, underwater stuff, close-quarter battle – the full works. All that was while I was still a student at Berkeley. They pulled strings to get me into the FBI, but the training at Quantico was like eating candy after what I'd gone through. No wonder I finished top of my class. Poor bastards – I had the jump on all of them!'

We walked in silence for a few moments, listening to the click of the camels' feet on the pebbles, hearing the sough of the desert wind and taking in the scents of flint and chalk. 'So it was all an act then?' I said.

Daisy looked at me, pouting her full lips as if she was comforting a child. She knew what I was talking about. 'No,' she said, 'that thing in your flat . . . look Sammy, I was trained to stay aloof, to avoid getting mixed up with people, all right. Sometimes you just can't help it – things just sort of take over . . .'

The sentence petered out and I guessed she hadn't said exactly what she wanted to say. I knew how it was. Where emotions were concerned it was hard to string what your body was telling you into coherent sentences. I walked along quietly, watching my camel's undulating haunch.

'OK,' Daisy blurted out, 'I'm not a senator's daughter. I'm a penniless orphan from Monterey whose mother was probably a hooker and whose father was some foreign seaman or something. I'm sorry about that, Sammy, I'm sorry I'm not the real Daisy, all right!'

I grinned at her. 'Don't apologize,' I said, 'to tell the truth, I always found the real Daisy a bit over the top. Actually, I like you as you are.'

40

IN THE MORNING WE'D HAD freak heat, but in the afternoon a
cold wind washed off the horizon, obliging us to wrap up in
all our clothes. People talk about the cold on mountains and in
the Arctic, but no one who hasn't experienced it can imagine
how cold the desert can be. It's not the dull, wet cold of the
snow, but a raw, raging wind that chills you to the very bones.
The grey-purple plain was endless, shimmering like mercury in
places, with puff-devils spinning on the skyline. I had the familiar
feeling that we were actually going nowhere, just marking time
in the same spot. Only the sun changed, dropping slowly towards
the west in its giant parabola, its midday whiteness cooling and
mellowing as the day wore on. The Hawazim carried no watches
and had no concept of city time. They measured distance by a
camel's pace and could not tell you how many miles or kilometres
it was to a certain point. They had heard of the Sudan, Egypt
and Libya, but the idea of a nation was nebulous to them – they
never saw themselves as Egyptians, because their nation was the
tribe. To them, the Egyptians were the folk of the Nile Valley.
What's more, they believed the earth was flat and were convinced
that if you rode in a straight line long enough you would fall
off into what they called Al-Khuraab – the Great Desolation.

After we'd mounted up we rode alongside Mansur for a time.
'You never told me your *saqanab*,' I said.

His good eye ogled Daisy and his bad one lolled sideways, the dead pupil rising and falling to the camel's stride. 'That's because Gazelle Eyes broke custom,' he said, 'and demanded to know what was going on!'

Daisy looked at the ground as her camel undulated onwards. 'I'm sorry,' she said, 'but I had to know.'

Mansur sighed and took a deep breath. 'It's been a long time,' he said. 'You want to hear it all?'

'Of course. No less than everything.'

Mansur beamed. 'It's a pleasure,' he said, '*saqanab* for our newly returned brother!'

As the sun dimmed and the sky split into pads of altocumulus, like the gnarls on old elephant skin, and the camels trod on mesmerizingly into the afternoon, Mansur recounted how, after I'd left, the tribe had migrated through the desert of northern Sudan. He named all the places they had made camp, and described the pastures they had discovered, recounted how many camels had been born and how many died, how much rain had fallen, the state and depth of the wells they had found. He described meetings with Sudanese Bedouin and assessed the quality of their hospitality, went into the minute details of raids by the Gor'an nomads from Chad, listed the names of camels stolen and tribesmen injured, enumerating their wounds down to the last bloody finger. He told us of tribesmen lost on the salt-caravans who'd survived by drinking their camels' vomit, of great Shining ceremonies under the full moon, when the *amnir* had led the communal visions, of terrifying storms that had leached their drippers dry, of camels that had been lost and had found their way back to camp alone across hundreds of miles of wilderness, of small children left by accident in the desert who had tracked their way home on foot without water. He related how the tribe had wandered back over the frontier into Egypt, and how time and time again the government had sent patrols to capture the *amnir*, and how time and time again Ross had foreseen their coming and evaded them. Mansur talked and talked using the vividly poetic language of the Hawazim, and

295

Daisy and I listened spellbound. It was an epic to equal Homer – better than any tale from *The Arabian Nights* – and it evoked in me the same old excitement, the same old love for the life of the desert that I'd felt since I'd arrived here years ago.

We spurred our camels on and caught up with the *amnir* at the head of the caravan. Ross looked over his shoulder at us and smiled. 'How are you doing with the camel, Miss Brooke?' he enquired.

'OK,' she said, 'apart from a sore ass, that is.'

Ross laughed. 'I remember the first time Sammy rode a camel as a kid,' he said. 'My uncle Mukhtar gave him the wildest bull-camel in the herd, and it damn near ate him alive. Ahmad and 'Ali never let him forget it!'

I chuckled at the memory. The Old Man had believed in throwing people in at the deep end and seeing if they could swim. Actually, apart from Ross, I was about the only man in the tribe who *could* swim, but that wasn't a skill much respected in the desert.

'So,' I said, 'Mansur tells me they're still looking for you, *amnir*. They haven't let it go.'

Ross watched the spider shadows of our camels as they floated across the sand. 'No,' he said, 'I'm still a hunted man. Five times they came for me, and five times I predicted it and struck camp with the entire tribe. If I thought it would do the tribe any good, I'd give myself up. But I saw in the Shining that it's not my blood they want, but my . . . powers. That's why I can't let them capture me.' He rode in silence, brooding for a while. 'I hope this cool wind holds,' he said, 'it's uncomfortable, but it cuts down our moisture requirements. I reckon it'll take five days to get to the *Bahr* and even if it stays cool we'll be feeling the pinch of thirst by then.'

Daisy blanched, and I suspected she was already feeling it. The prospect of five days, even in the cool, on a couple of gourds of water evidently didn't thrill her. It didn't thrill me, either, and I secretly wondered how long we could survive.

Ross suddenly stiffened and cocked his ear towards the

east. 'Talk of the Devil!' he said. 'Listen! Can you hear it?'

I listened. It seemed to me I could make out a low throb, only a decibel or two louder than the moan of the wind. 'It's still way off,' Ross said, 'we've got time. 'Ali! Break out the cam-nets! Quick now! Everyone knows the drill.'

At once the camel riders formed two groups and couched their camels shoulder to shoulder. There was none of the squabbling or confusion that had marked our departure, I noticed. Two large packs were opened, each one containing a huge camouflage net, cleverly mottled to match the desert surface. Within a minute all the camels had been hobbled and the nets spread over them, and we were crouching together in the dark like hunted beasts. The throb of the chopper's engine came nearer and nearer. It seemed to hang above us endlessly and I imagined it circling around overhead. There was a moment of suspense, and the camels rumbled nervously. Then its engine dopplered past and I peered up from beneath a corner of the cam-net and realized it hadn't lost height at all.

'Never even guessed we were here!' 'Ali commented. 'With these things you're invisible, by God!'

Daisy stared after the aircraft with her eagle eyes. 'That's a Jetstream,' she said, 'I swear it's the FBI spotter – the one that took us to the Fayoum.'

It was sunset when Ross called a halt, in a field of low dunes surrounding a miniature oasis of sedges the Hawazim called a *hattia*. The sun was already lodged on the distant skyline in a miasma of cloud – a great glowing zeppelin five times larger than it had been at midday. The wind dropped abruptly and even before the camels had been unsaddled and hobbled amongst the sedge the shadows had gone. The night closed in, hiding the lonely reaches of the desert, but revealing the immensity of a star-strewn sky. We laid our saddlery and personal gear close together, for no matter how vast the space the Hawazim always camped on top of each other as if they found each other's proxim-ity comforting in the emptiness. Ahmad made a fire from the deadfall and palm-bast we had brought with us. I knew it

297

wouldn't last long, and after it'd finished we'd be using camel dung instead. 'Ali made bread – a couple of oval loaves kneaded by hand and baked in the sand under the ashes of the fire. We divided ourselves up into two messes and ate the bread served in camel's milk from the communal pot. Afterwards we drank tea and smoked our pipes, leaning back comfortably in soft sand.

'We were lucky today,' Ross said, blowing out smoke, 'the Divine Spirit was with us. But the problem ahead is going to be water. We started with our drippers less than half full – enough for three days. That means unless we find water the day after tomorrow we'll be in trouble.'

'What the hell are we going to do?' Daisy asked. 'We still have to get back from wherever we're going.'

'The Divine Spirit will guide us,' Ross said, smiling. 'Since we have water and firewood tonight I propose we make a small Shining – just the ten of us. If there is a solution we'll find it together.'

He groped in his saddlebag and brought out a bag of dried mandrake root and other herbs, which he laid carefully on his rug, together with a clean wooden bowl, and a small mortar and pestle. 'Will you join?' he asked us, using the antiquated language of the Shining.

All of us except Daisy answered, 'I will join!' She stared at the mess of dried bulbs and herbs on the rug, slightly bemused. 'I've read about this in your father's book,' she told Ross. 'Isn't this the ceremony where everyone gets off?'

Ross laughed. 'I don't think that's how my father put it,' he said. 'Actually it's more like communion with the universe and with each other – a way of plugging into nature . . . well we don't really have the words to describe it, you'll have to see for yourself.'

'It's a great honour to be invited,' I told her, 'especially as an outsider. Don't worry, it's not a drunken orgy – it's very peaceful. The drug can't make you do anything against your will.'

Daisy swallowed and looked at me doubtfully. 'Well,' she said, 'I suppose when in Rome . . .'

'So you'll join?' Ross asked.

She pouted and drew a deep breath. 'OK,' she said, 'what do I have to do?'

41

WHILE ROSS PULPED THE MANDRAKE and other herbs, mixed it with water and poured it into the sacramental bowl, the Hawazim produced a tiny orchestra of instruments from their saddlebags. There were two tablas, a stringed instrument with a cube-shaped sound box, called a *rababa*, and a whole range of pipes, including a four-hosed variety known as a *zummara*. Ross stood and picked up the bowl carefully. Someone fed bast into the fire and it flared, throwing misshapen shadows over the sand and making the eyes of the camels glow yellow in the darkness. We stood round the fire in a loose circle and there was silence except for the rhythmic sound of the camels chewing cud, and the low crackle of the fire. Above us Orion lay straddled across the velvet sky, with Sirius pulsating beneath. The Milky Way curled through the mesh of stars like gossamer, looking almost close enough to touch.

Ross had taken off his glasses, and his eyes were lagoons of blackness in the bearded face. He held up the bowl. 'Behold the Divine Water!' he said suddenly. 'We drink this in memory of the departed ones – all the souls of our ancestors back over the generations to the First Time. We drink this that we shall join as one – living and departed – in the Divine Spirit that never dies!'

'The Divine Spirit lives!' the others intoned. Daisy looked startled.

'As *amnir* I take the first draft of this Water!' Ross said. 'May the Divine Spirit guide me in the Shining and direct me to the way!'

'The Divine Spirit lives!'

Ross drank from the bowl – no more than a couple of mouthfuls – and passed it to Mansur, who took a gulp, his boss-eye glinting eerily in the flames. Slowly the bowl went round the circle, and when my turn came I took a draft, wincing at its familiar sourness. I passed the bowl to Daisy. She look at the orange liquid, hesitated, took a swig, and shuddered. 'Achh!' she said. At once the tiny band struck up, first the mesmeric thump of the tablas, then the quarter-tones of the pipes and *rababa* sounding beautiful and ethereal like an organ played *pianissimo*. The Hawazim began to sway, inclining their heads in time with the music, then cupping their hands around their mouths and exhaling a deep harmonic resonance that seemed to come right out of the earth. The men paused and suddenly the *amnir* stepped forwards into the circle of firelight, his eyes alive with wild colours, his arms thrown out. He stretched his head back and raised his hands, palms spread as if trying to catch the stars. 'I see the light!' he shouted out suddenly. 'I *am* the light!'

The words sank into my head like a stone in a pool, and eddies and ripples coursed through my blood, building up and up until they had become a tidal wave of pure emotion. I strained upwards to the stars and their light was a palpable force feeding my eyes. Yet another part of me was being carried along on those beams in a whoosh of motion, catapulted into the farthest reaches of the cosmos on the back of a river of fire. My consciousness flickered, fluctuating between my corporeal body, still rocking with the rhythm, and my astral body speeding through the night. I was object and subject, seer and seen, eyes and light, but also a third thing – a synthesis of the two opposites. I was Sammy Rashid, an individual, yet a small part of something so vast I couldn't imagine it, something I could never really be separated from. I was one with the other tribesmen, one with the whole human species, one with all the creation of plants and animals, the mountains, the rivers, the rocks and the seas. All the fabric of the universe was a single material fashioned into different shapes and forms, but all part of a single unifying current. I was the wind, I was the mountains, I was the sun. I was in the insects and the birds, the camels and the wolves, the flowers and the forests, the seas and the stars.

My conscious spirit, swaying in a huddle of humans and camels round a fire in the desert, was only an illusion of singularity, but beyond the barrier of darkness we were all part of a universal body and a universal mind. Time ceased to exist and the desert rolled before me like a book of pages whiffling in the wind, now a green land running with water and wandered by wild animals, now a wilderness as arid as the moon. I glimpsed fleeting images of dramas played out in that wilderness: half-humans hunting elephants with sharpened sticks for spears; horsemen riding hell-for-leather, chariot-wheels spinning, a great space ship crashing in the sands; camel riders trawling the plains with cowled faces; ancient aircraft taking off; veteran cars trundling across the desert; shining pyramids rising like huge silver funguses; a great beast with the body of a woman and the head of a lion; forked lightning, rain, wind and a volcanic mushroom cloud. The visions flashed faster and faster until they were only fragmentary images split off from some gigantic mandala like shards of a fractured mirror – my father taking me on his knee and saying, 'I'll come back for you Sammy, if it's the last thing I ever do'; my father's face, filled with remorse, at the window of a train at Aswan Station, my mother crying when she received his last letter; the Old Man in the alley saying 'We need you'; a spidery creature in the shadows of the Khan; Ibram's bloody corpse; Van Helsing dressed like a labourer at the old rest-house, Sanusi's tic working fearfully at the mention of Firebird, the old Bedouin at the monastery spitting at Brother Paul's feet; Father Grigori's hand shaking as he lit a cigarette; Andropov shrugging fleshy shoulders; Daisy disarming me with superhuman speed.

The string of images slipped through my mind like a coil, but before I could grasp any of them firmly they dissolved into dust, leaving me with a sense that all of them fitted into some vast pattern that it was beyond my ability to discern. I opened my eyes and saw the men still dancing, and the musicians bent over their instrument as if they had fused into them. I could no longer be sure if the music came out of the instruments, or out of the musicians' heads, or out of the earth, or out of all of those things at the same time. I saw Daisy – a blur of golden hair lashing wildly to her inner harmonies, with what seemed to be a gush of brilliant red energy streaming out of her. I blinked and for an instant I saw another figure standing behind her – a vast, diaphanous image of a woman, standing there serenely, emanating power, stretching as high as the stars. I stared at Daisy and our eyes met. For a split second there was a flash of raw power so tremendous that I almost fell flat. In that moment I looked right past the outer Daisy and into the depths of her being, and I knew exactly what it was that I'd missed. Daisy had Shining power! She'd kept it tightly in check, deliberately tried to hide it. It had been staring at me right from the beginning. Everything about her – the supernatural speed, the accuracy, the strength, the superb muscle control that allowed her to move as silently as a cat, the ability to come out with the right intuition at the right time, the hypnotic power that had persuaded me to help her breach the archives – told me that she was a psychic warrior of extraordinary ability.

And there was more. I felt a sudden and overwhelming certainty that Daisy had come to Egypt looking for me, and that her presence here among the Hawazim now was all part of a plan. Even if Daisy herself didn't know it, she was meant to be here and we'd been destined to meet because we were two halves of the same entity, like the two pieces of Ibram's map. We were each other, and together we made up a third thing that was more than the sum of its two parts. We needed each other. We belonged.

I felt a serpent of sensuality truckling along my backbone, gorging my blood with desire. Then I looked at Daisy again and there was another flash of power as our eyes met. When she

303

touched my leg the energy hit me like forked lightning. Her eyes were giant eyes and her smile a vast smile. 'Sammy,' she whispered. 'It's time!'

When we rose from the fire-hearth, no one paid any attention, and we staggered away down the soft dunes locked in each other's arms. In the starlight the dunes were pale, undulating, yielding feminine forms, and we crossed ridge after ridge, giggling like children, kissing, touching, feeling each other's bodies warm and glowing beneath our desert clothes. Daisy was already ripping off her *jibba* when we tripped and rolled wildly down a slip-slope, clutching frantically at each other as if we would roll off the edge of the world. We came to rest in pillows of deep sand at the bottom of the slope, and lay still for a second, listening to the eerie music that dripped faintly across the dunes. Then Daisy put her arms under my *jibba* and kissed me. Energy pulsed through my body like a raging flood, and I fell on her, pulling off her clothes and mine, scattering them around us on the desert floor. Her hands explored my chest, my thighs, my stomach and each touch set my body vibrating with indescribable ecstasy. We rolled back and forth in the soft sand, panting and groaning, our lips and bodies forming and breaking in endless oscillation. I tangled my hands in her hair, kissed her erect nipples, stroked her between the legs until she arched backwards, moaning with pleasure, and draped her legs over my shoulders. Then I was inside her and she screamed, and writhed, clinging on to me desperately, raking my back with her nails. The coupling went on and on for ever until we were no longer Sammy and Daisy, no longer male and female, but a single entity, melting, dissolving into each other until the night and the cosmos were no longer outside us, but within us, and at last the stars erupted into a blinding iridescence of light.

42

Next morning we had the camels going by fool's dawn. There was a haze in the air and a cool wind from the north, and the sun came up weakly like a bloodshot eye. 'Good,' Ross muttered to himself as he urged his mount forward, 'looks like the freak hot spell is over. The Divine Spirit be praised.'

'So, *amnir*,' I said, reining in beside him, 'did you learn anything in the Shining?' When he glanced at me his eyes behind the glasses were full of amusement.

'Yes,' he said. 'Did you?'

I glanced at Daisy and she reddened, and looked down shyly. 'I suppose I did,' I said. I considered telling them both I'd glimpsed that Daisy had the Shining power, but I rejected it. Ross had probably seen it already, and would reveal it in his own time. He placed his camel-stick in his left hand next to his headrope, and removed his glasses. 'It was a bad Shining,' he said, 'maybe there wasn't enough of the Divine Water, or maybe I mixed it badly, I don't know. I only got broken images, and there were . . . bad omens.' He replaced his glasses and tapped his camel lightly with his stick. I flicked my headrope to urge Rusasa to keep up. 'Does a tadpole-headed guy mean anything to you?' he asked. 'A guy in a black suit with legs like a spider, and a sort of crest of hair hanging backwards? The guy has a Sekhmet tattoo . . . here.' He pointed to his left wrist.

'Van Helsing,' I said, 'he's the CIA chief of staff in Cairo. Why, you think he could be the ghoul?'

'It's possible. But why would the ghoul get itself tattooed? It doesn't make sense.'

'What else did you see?'

'Just . . . well, I've got a bad feeling about this whole damn thing, Sammy. Something doesn't feel right.'

'What about the water?' Daisy asked anxiously.

'Ah, that's one problem I did solve. Ever heard of the Zerzura Club?'

Daisy kicked her camel's withers with her heels and it bucked up. 'Yeah,' she said, 'it was a bunch of desert explorers set up in the 1930s whose object was to find the lost oasis of Zerzura. They never found it, but I've read a report suggesting it was tied up with the Jason Scholars – the predecessors of MJ-12.'

'It was, but that's not really the point. The Zerzura Club used motorcars and light aircraft for their exploration, and they left water-dumps all over the desert in case they'd be needed in an emergency. Some of them are still there, and it happens there's one on our way to the Sea Without Water.'

Daisy's lips formed a roundel of surprise. 'The 1930s!' she gasped. 'That's more than sixty years ago. It's not possible!'

Ross laughed. 'Oh but it is. You see, years ago Mansur and I found one of the Club's dumps near Burj at-Tuyur. The water was still drinkable, and there were even tins of hard-tack biscuits that could still be eaten. All the tins were stamped with the British QM Department arrow, and the date 1937.'

'Good Lord!'

'The dump on our way is marked with a low cairn, and I don't need Ibram's map to find it.' He tapped his head with the hook of his camel-stick. 'It's all in here.'

At that instant, Ross's camel let out a bellow of rage and jerked its head wildly. Its great body stiffened, the eyes under the thick brow occipits bulging from its head. Ross gripped the headrope and pulled back but the camel went berserk, leaping into the air with its limbs working like oars. For a second Ross hung on gallantly, then he lost his seat and fell with a thump on to a bed of stones. The camel dashed away into the distance in a trail of dust, jumping like a fire-cracker until it keeled over, bursting both water bags. I rolled out of the saddle to help Ross. He was unconscious, his breathing heavy, and there was a cut on the side of his head where his skull had come into contact with a sharp stone. I hoisted him upright and Mansur dashed over with some water in a gourd, forcing it into Ross's mouth.

'What was it?' Daisy asked. 'What spooked the camel?'

Ahmad appeared with a stumpy grey snake and held it up to us by the tail, shaking his head. 'A puff-adder!' he said. 'A very bad omen!'

Suddenly Ross's eyelids flickered and he opened his eyes. 'Mansur?' he stuttered. 'What's happened? Why is it dark?'

Mansur and I looked at each other and I waved a hand over Ross's face. He didn't even blink.

'The Divine Spirit preserve us!' Ahmad said grimly, 'I said it was a bad omen. The *amnir*'s gone completely blind!'

43

W<small>E DISCUSSED SENDING</small> R<small>OSS BACK</small> to Bahrayn, but we all knew that without him we'd have little hope of finding the Benben Stone, or the water-dump he'd predicted we'd find. 'I've seen this kind of blindness before,' Ross said, 'it doesn't last for ever, but it takes some time to wear off. Until it does, the caravan must have a new leader. Sammy will take the lead from now on.'

'But *amnir*,' I protested, 'Mansur's the senior one.'

'I know,' Ross said, 'Mansur's one of the best fighters in the tribe, but this needs more than that. It needs a touch of the Shining power and you're the only one apart from me who has it. Don't forget, you are Nawayr – "The Little Light".'

After that I took the point, navigating on the dim beacon that I could feel flashing on the very edge of my consciousness. We rigged up a special camel-borne stretcher called a *shibriya* for Ross to ride in, and I towed it behind my own camel. For four more days we struggled on through the wilderness, seeing nothing but the sunlight sparkling on the stones, and the ghosts of wind-devils running helter-skelter across the empty plains. The second day was blessedly cool, but the freak hot spell was not finished and on the third the sun returned with a vengeance, leaching our bodies dry. After the day of the Shining, there were no more *hattias*, and the camels went hungry of fresh grazing.

They had to be fed on the barley we carried, and while it satisfied them it left their bellies dry; 'Like you or I eating a bag of biscuits,' Ahmad commented. The days were punctuated only by our few water-halts, and the ration dwindled from a full gourd each to half a gourd. Once we found a cairn in the desert, covered in tribal brands, and once a lone yardang – a surreal mushroom-shaped rock, fifty feet high. Another time Ahmad shot a huge monitor lizard which we ate that evening, eggs and all, and once Mansur found the tracks of an ostrich. 'Ali occupied himself in picking up Stone-Age hand-axes and scrapers from the desert floor. These only provided momentary diversions from the thirst that racked us almost constantly – a craving for liquid that over-whelmed every other thought.

By the fourth day the drippers were empty and we rode bent over our saddle-pommels, our mouths clogged with mucus and our lips so cracked and dry we could hardly speak. Halfway through the morning I halted my camel to stare at the horizon, where I could just make out the faintest shading of amber against the blue of the sky.

'What is it?' Ross asked from his *shibriya*.

'A kind of muzzy thing on the skyline,' I said, 'could be a cloud of dust.'

'No,' Ross said, with certainty. 'That's no cloud of dust, it's the Sea Without Water. We're almost there.'

Ross said that the water-dump lay just this side of the wall of dunes, and estimated that we'd get there before the time of the Afternoon Prayer. We perked up after that. There was no stop at midday, and we were too weak to walk. The camels carried us patiently, crooning and grumbling, their great legs working like pistons, their flat footpads crunching on and on. By early afternoon the dunes of the sand-sea had come into full focus – a vast wall of rippling silicon grains, flashing golden in the sun and blocking the western horizon. Not long afterwards I spotted a cairn, and turned the caravan slightly to the left towards it. It took almost an hour to get there and it seemed to last a lifetime.

Nobody spoke. We rode doubled over our saddles, each of us obsessed with only a single image – cool, clear water. When we finally came up to the cairn, though, I was impressed with the tribesmen's discipline. No one rushed madly to dig. Instead they couched their camels carefully on soft ground, hobbled and unloaded them, and only then walked casually over to the cairn. It was built of small blue granite boulders on one of which was an arrow painted in white paint. 'This must be it,' I growled through my parched lips, 'that arrow is the old British government Quarter-Master's mark.'

'Well,' 'Ali said, rolling up the sleeves of his *jibba*, 'we've got no shovels, so I guess we'll have to use our hands.'

We all got stuck into the digging – even Daisy. Our efforts were feeble, because our energy had been sapped by moisture-loss, but we were driven on by our thirst. Within half an hour my hand struck something hard and metallic and I cleared away the sand to find the top of a five-gallon jerrycan. 'The Divine Spirit be praised!' Mansur said. 'The Shining never lies!' I scrabbled in the sand frantically and the others weighed in, uncovering no less than ten jerrycans in a few minutes.

'Thanks to the Divine Spirit!' Ahmad said. 'We're saved.'

I hefted one of the cans out experimentally. It was heavy – as heavy as five gallons of water – and there was a reassuring slosh from the inside. Mansur helped me to lift it out of the pit. It was rusting on the outside and most of the paint had peeled off, but it appeared intact. I contemplated it for a moment, and the others gathered round expectantly. I wrestled with the hinged cap and found it stuck. Someone handed me a sharp stone and I struck the lip of the cap once. It flew back and there was a slight hiss of air. 'Ali produced a gourd and I smiled, lifted the jerrycan and poured. The water gurgled out cool and clear as the day it had been buried, more than sixty years ago. We mumbled thanks to the Divine Spirit with cracked lips, and squatted down on our haunches to partake of the holy sacrament of water. When everyone had drunk a gourdful we returned to the pit and began pulling out the rest of the cache, and only then did we realize that our celebrations had been premature. Of the nine other jerrycans in the dump, not one remained intact.

44

AT FIRST LIGHT, WHILE THE Hawazim made tea and crouched shivering round a desultory fire of smouldering camel dung, I climbed the face of the dune wall. The dune must have been four hundred feet high, a colossal barrier of sand rising to a razor-edged crest. The prevailing wind came from the north, which meant that the gentler incline – the slip-slope – lay on the opposite side. To get to the crest we would have to take the camels up a slope of about thirty-three degrees – the maximum angle at which sand can remain stable. I worked my way up slowly, zigzagging across the face, probing for pockets of drum-sand with my camel-stick. I wondered if we'd be able to get the camels up here, but that wasn't my main worry. The jerrycan had saved our lives – thanks to the Divine Spirit – but now it was almost finished, and we were hardly better off than we'd been yesterday. There would be no water in the sand-sea, and I doubted very much if there would be any at our destination. But we couldn't go back either – not unless we slaughtered our camels and drank the juice out of their bellies.

I sighed as I laboured up the dune-crest. Water equalled life, I thought – it was the eternal equation of the desert nomad's existence. Finally I made the top of the crest and for a moment I stood there, leaning on my stick, getting my breath back. As far as the eye could see in every direction was a tangle of high dunes, some arranged into long rambling walls, others forming oblongs, squares and crescents, like a vast Stone Age village of roofless shacks. I gasped. It really was like looking across a great ocean of frozen waves that scintillated pink, orange, ochre and in places even turquoise and aquamarine. The dunes were oriented the same way as the one we'd just climbed so that the sharp leeward slopes faced us, giving the impression of an impenetrable series of fortifications. They were beautiful, too, exquisitely sculpted by the winds over millennia into sweeping concaves and convexes, knife-blade edges and trailing sashes, radiant in the sunlight with a magnificence and a grandeur that sent a fizz of wonder through my veins. No pyramid, no ancient Egyptian temple, I thought, could ever emulate this sublime natural architecture – moulded by the winds out of the bed of a sea that had existed here in the dinosaur age.

I stood there spellbound for a few moments, watching the mobile wafts of sand that sprayed like spume over the rippling crests, constantly sharpening them. In another guise, the sand-sea was the wind made visible, just as iron-filings on the head of a magnet were the palpable expression of magnetic force. In all that massive expanse of sand, there seemed not a gram of comfort for thirsty men and camels, but then my eye alighted on something green growing on the windward slope of the dune, and I dashed down to examine it, whispering a silent prayer.

Five minutes later I was back on the crest, leaping down the face in great strides, leaving a pattern of small craters where my feet had plunged into the sand. I jogged straight towards the others, squatted next to Ross and poked at the remains of the fire with my stick.

'Well?' Ross asked.

'I can get us up,' I said, 'without falling in drum-sand. But on the other side of this dune there are rows and rows of others. It's like a maze.'

Ross pulled his saddlebag to him and fumbled for the two bits of Ibram's map. 'This thing's useless to us now,' he said. 'It's served its purpose – it showed us roughly in which part of the

Bahr the Benben Stone lay. But it's made to be used with a compass or sophisticated navigation equipment. Without the proper gear we can't use it in the sands.'

'There's been a lot of digging in the place,' Daisy said. 'Perhaps there'll even be some kind of track.'

I shook my head. 'I don't think so,' I said, 'if the site was obvious they could have located it from the air. They wouldn't have needed the map. That suggests it has been covered up and completely concealed.'

'Talking of the air,' Mansur said, looking up at the sky, 'we haven't seen our chopper for four days. It's odd that they left us alone so long.'

'Yeah,' I said, 'either they already know we're here, or they've given up on the map. I wouldn't stake my life on them giving up.'

'What will we do with the Benben Stone if we find it?' Daisy asked. 'I mean, it must weigh a ton.'

Ross removed his glasses and blew on the lenses. I guess it was out of habit, since they were useless to him now. 'Some people think the Stone was a meteorite that plunged into the desert thousands of years ago,' he said. 'It may have been made of meteoric iron, which was venerated in ancient times. If it was, it would probably have been cone-shaped, because the front part of a meteorite gets melted and tapers down when entering the earth's atmosphere. If the Stone *is* an iron meteorite, we'd be talking about something as high as a man with the weight of a truck. A crane could handle it, but we wouldn't get far with nine camels.'

'So what are we going to do?'

Ross put back his glasses and stared blankly towards the crest of the dune. 'I'll tell you that when we've found it,' he said.

'And if the map's no good, how *will* we find it?'

He tapped his head with his forefinger. 'I'll know the place when I get there. Until then, you'll have to trust me and Sammy to find a path through.'

'Mansur's one good eye flashed momentarily. '*Amnir*,' he

said, 'unless we get water we won't be going anywhere.'

I gave him a mischievous glance. 'Oh, the water,' I said, 'I almost forgot. How much is left in the jerrycan?'

'Enough for a couple of gourdfuls each. It won't last us a day.'

I considered it for a moment. 'No,' I said, 'but it'll last two hardy men two days. Here's what I suggest, Mansur. Pick the two fastest camels in the troop and send two men back with them to al-Bahrayn with all the water we have left. If they ride night and day they can make it in two days. They're to tell the rest of the *qom* to send a caravan here – to the cairn – with as much water and sour camel's milk as they can spare. It's to be here in six days' time.'

Mansur's face fell. 'Six days! But we might be dead by then!'

I grinned. 'Only the Divine Spirit knows that,' I said, 'but after all, we are the Ghosts of the Desert.' I dug my hand into the pocket of my *jibba* and brought out the mottled green fruit, as large as a baseball, that I'd found up on the dunes. There was a murmur from the other tribesmen.

'What is it?' Daisy asked.

'It's a sweet desert melon,' I said. 'They're very rare. Most desert melons are the bitter colocynth type – poisonous to humans – but the Divine Spirit has really smiled on us today. It must have rained here this year, because these things are growing on the slip-slopes. Now, we're not going to get water-fat on melon-pulp, but if we can find enough of them, we might just survive.'

45

THE SAND WAS LIKE ICE-WATER on our bare feet as we toiled up the leeward face of the dune. The camels groaned and their nostrils steamed, and often they pulled back on the head-ropes, digging their flat feet into the sand and threatening to send us tumbling down the slope. I coiled the rope round my hand and once round my body to give me more leverage, but every step was an intense effort of will. We drove, bullied and cajoled the camels on in fits and starts, but by the time we'd got halfway up the face we were all panting and bathed in sweat.

'Come on!' I bellowed from the front. 'Keep them moving or they'll sit down!' We heaved them on again, and I leaned into my headrope feeling it cutting into my shoulder. Every inch was a battle, but at last I was standing on the crest, waving my camel-stick triumphantly. I slithered down to help Mansur, who was next in line leading Ross stumbling through the soft sand. When he was safely at the top, we both sashayed down to help Ahmad. As each new camel arrived on the summit its owner would return to the column to help the next one, straining together on the headrope or driving from behind with threatening flicks of their camel-sticks. Daisy was the last in the caravan and by the time we got to her, her old she-camel had sat down. Ahmad fondled the beast's lips and she snapped at him lazily.

'Come on, Grandma!' he said. 'I know you're not as young

as you used to be, but don't let the tribe down!' All of us hauled, shouted and cursed, but the she-camel wouldn't budge.

'It's no good,' Mansur said at last, 'we'll have to unload her.'

We unslung the heavy woven saddlebags filled with grain, and unlaced the wooden saddle. Ahmad and I carried them on our shoulders to the top. A hundred kilos lighter, the old camel rose to her feet with trembling legs and allowed herself to be dragged to the summit. Finally, we threw ourselves down into the sand.

'Well, there it is!' I told Daisy, gesturing to the west, 'the Sea Without Water, the *Bahr Bela Ma*!' I glanced at Daisy and saw that her eyes were full of the same kind of wonder and confusion she'd displayed on our first day in the limestone desert.

'There's no way through,' she whispered shakily, 'this first dune almost finished us. We can't keep on doing that!'

The Hawazim heard her out in silence, and I saw some worried glances exchanged. Even Ahmad, Mansur and 'Ali had nothing to say for once. The three half-brothers looked towards Ross, waiting for his guidance. The *amnir* eased himself shakily to his feet, whipped off his useless glasses and began to clean the lenses on his shirt, taking a series of long, deep breaths. He replaced his glasses, and expelled air in a rush.

'There is a way,' he said, 'and I can find it. But Sammy must be my eyes.'

I nodded, strode over to my camel and took her by the head-rope. 'Come on!' I said. 'Let's move!'

The windward slope was scattered with the runners of desert melons I'd found earlier that morning, and we tied the camels together for the descent, and ran about collecting them, slicing some open and gobbling down the mellow pulp greedily, feeding the green rinds to the camels and saving the rest in our saddle bags for later. 'Ali and Ahmad collected armfuls of the green shoots and tied them in bundles on to our saddles so that the camels would have green vegetation to eat at the evening halt. The way down was a breeze after the climb, but Ross warned us to be alert for patches of drum-sand, which were more frequent on the slip-slopes. At the bottom there was a corridor of pea-gravel, like millions of tiny black droppings, and instead of broaching the next dune-face, Ross turned and led us up the avenue between the dunes. It seemed to be a cul-de-sac leading straight up to a wall of sand, but just when I was certain we were trapped, Ross – riding in the *shibriya* behind me – told me to swing suddenly to the west, and we found ourselves in yet another natural boulevard weaving through the sand skirts.

For the rest of the day and all through the next, Ross pushed me on unerringly, never faltering, never floundering, never turning back. Each time it seemed certain that he'd led us into a dead end, there'd be an exit waiting for us, unseen except by the *amnir*'s inner eye. Sometimes we were obliged to climb gentle slopes, pick our way gingerly between pits of drum-sand, dice with illusion as the silicon grains sparkled in the high sun. But I realized that we'd never have lasted even the first day if we'd tried to go straight across. I knew Ross was being guided by a beacon in his head, because I'd experienced the same thing myself when I'd led the boys through the *ghibli*, years ago and again, more faintly, earlier on this journey. But I also knew that my ability was puny compared with his. He was guiding us through what appeared to be an impenetrable morass of sand, through a place he'd never been in before, without map, compass or GPS, or even eyes, and without making a single false move. I saw the admiration and wonder in the faces of the other tribesmen as we struggled on, and I knew this feat would be talked about in hushed voices round campfires for centuries to come.

After the first day there were no more melons, and though we'd saved over fifty of the little green balls, their moisture content was small and never really satisfied us. On the second day, Ahmad spotted some fennec foxes scampering for their burrow, and he and Mansur dug them out. One of them gave Mansur a nasty bite on the hand before he bopped them on the head. That evening we camped in the lee of a great dune, and two of the tribesmen – Mamoon, and his brother Abd al-Hadi, went off to track down sand-rats. They came back with seven of the little rodents tied to their camel-sticks, and we roasted them in their skins, next to the diced foxes, on a smoky fire of camel dung. Daisy wrinkled her nose in revulsion at the tiny rat-carcases, but the smell of the roast flesh – even half-burned as it was – was so tempting to our half-starved bodies that she was soon eating ravenously with the rest of us.

'If I ever get out of this, I'm going to treat myself to a buffet at the Nile Hilton,' Daisy said through a mouthful of tough desert fox, 'lobster thermidor, fresh salad – definitely no rats or foxes!'

The food was pitifully little for the eight of us, and on the morning of the third day I awoke in biting cold with a hollowness in my stomach and a raging thirst that our few remaining melons couldn't satisfy. We didn't bother to light a fire – camel dung was the devil to light, and it wasn't worth the effort. Instead we just loaded the camels, moving slowly and ponderously like deep-sea divers, mumbling at each other through parched lips. To cap it all, a northerly wind started up as we set off, blasting a stream of fine particles into our faces. We clung on to the camels and bent into it, staggering like blind men through pillows of soft sand. The force of the storm seemed to get more and more powerful as the morning wore on, and each step into it became an agony. The sand-sea seemed to be mocking us, cackling and jeering, screaming abuse from a billion demonic throats. I saw Daisy staggering, pushing herself on with a pale, haggard face, her lips white and her teeth set hard in utter determination. I put my arm round her as we pulled our camels up a slope and down again.

'This is what madness must be like!' she rasped in my ear. 'The noise of it drives you crazy!'

When the storm stopped suddenly about midday, the silence was unexpected and eerie as though there was suddenly something missing. Ross urged me down a slip-slope and into a wide valley of apricot-coloured pillow-sand, whose surface had been swept clean and stippled into a rainbow of colours by the storm.

'Stop here!' Ross said, and I held up my camel-stick to halt the column and couched my camel.

319

'What's up?' I asked.

He gazed sightlessly around him, sniffing the chalky after-taste of the storm, while my eyes darted back and forth along the walls of the dunes which here looked like giant organ pipes. 'This is it,' he said with certainty, 'we're here.'

He couched his camel awkwardly and felt for the ground with his stick before stumbling off. I gaped around in astonishment. The place looked no different from the dozens like it we'd passed through on the way. I choked back a remark, and watched Ross staggering blindly towards the nearest slope. The rest of the company couched their camels and Daisy came up beside me.

'There's nothing here,' she said. If this was where the Germans and the others were digging, where's the detritus – camp rubbish, broken boxes, old fires, squashed tin cans?'

I bit my lip and glanced at Ross. He was feeling his way clumsily along the edge of the dune, leaving a pattern of foot-prints like the stitch-marks of a giant beetle. Suddenly he stopped, probed the sand with his stick, and began scraping it away with his hand. Daisy and I hurried over to him, and by the time we got there he'd already uncovered what looked like the massive stone lintel of a doorway that was still buried. It appeared to be carved from a single piece of granite that certainly wasn't from anywhere round here, polished smooth over millennia by the work of the sand. It was decorated in relief with a symbol whose outline had been eaten away by sand abrasion, but which was still recognizable. When I stooped to look at it, my heart started thumping madly. It was a heron with a human eye perched on a cone-shaped object – the same image we'd seen in Sanusi's book, now almost two weeks ago.

Ross ran a hand along the lintel, felt the reliefs, and took off his glasses. 'The Firebird tells us we're in the right place,' he said, smiling wearily through bloodshot eyes, 'welcome to the hidden mansion of the Benben Stone!'

46

A FEW MINUTES LATER THE others joined us and we worked with our hands and sticks in the burning sun to clear the doorway. In less than an hour we'd uncovered two massive granite uprights that must have weighed as much as the blocks in the Valley Temple at Giza, framing a door wide enough to admit a small motorcar. The door was made of a single piece of some heavy metal and seemed to be sealed airtight. It was covered from top to bottom in ancient Egyptian images and hieroglyphs, prominent among them the ferocious goddess Sekhmet, the wild jackal Anubis and the Eye of Ra. In the very centre of the door was a elliptical cartouche bearing a strange motif – two lion-headed sphinxes standing back to back, and carrying between them a conical object with a T-shaped protrusion on top, like a perch or a handle. The cartouche itself stood at the centre of a larger elliptic, which was made up of a number of small circles or dots.

'What's that?' Daisy asked. 'I've never seen anything like it.'

I examined the cartouche closely. 'The bell-shaped object is the omphalos,' I said, 'that's another form of the Benben Stone. The lions are probably the *Aker*-lions which guarded the entrances and exits of the ancient Egyptian *Duat*, which meant both the celestial realm and the Underworld. One was a mirror of the other. The beauty of the cartouche is that it folds meanings within meanings – on one level it's a kind of warning.'

Daisy gasped and stepped back. 'Look at this door!' she said. 'It must be thousands of years old, yet it's in perfect condition. And what's it made of?'

I ran my hand over it. 'Seems almost like lead,' I said, 'I didn't know the ancient Egyptians even worked in lead.'

'And what about the lintel and uprights? I'd say they're marble, and they're bigger than some of the blocks in the Great Pyramid. How the hell could they have dragged them across hundreds of miles of desert? It'd be virtually impossible even today!'

Ross felt the door thoughtfully. 'Lead's a soft metal,' he said, 'how could it have retained its shape so perfectly for so many centuries? Unless it just *looks* like lead.'

'What else could it be?'

'I don't know, but it's pretty damn strong whatever it is. The question is, how do we get in?' He braced a shoulder against the door and heaved. After a second, Ahmad, Mansur and a handful of the others joined him. The door didn't give a milli-metre. 'Well,' Ross said, 'it seems the Germans got in, and so did Ibram and Sanusi. If they did, we must be able to. Now, let's see . . .' He sniffed, adjusted his glasses and ran his fingers down the door, touching hieroglyphs and pressing the cartouche. Nothing happened. He took a step back suddenly and began to feel the dots in the larger elliptic surrounding the cartouche, counting them. 'Fifty!' he said, almost to himself. 'I knew it! They must have been testing our knowledge of advanced astronomy!'

'What do you mean?' I said.

Ross looked excited now. 'See these dots,' he said rapidly, 'there are fifty of them, arranged in an ellipse. A few years back I found a stela at Medinat Habu with an identical design. It signified the orbit of Sirius B around its sister-star Sirius A, which is complete once every fifty years.'

'But Sirius B's invisible isn't it?' Daisy asked. 'How could they have known . . .'

But Ross wasn't listening. Instead he was feeling a row

of hieroglyphs above the ellipse. 'Isis!' he said, pointing to a female deity with a fish-tail. 'In ancient Egyptian symbolism she signifies Sirius. Whoever built this place was testing our knowledge of astronomy by presenting the orbit of a star that can't be seen with the naked eye, and Isis is the key!' He pressed the Isis icon and there was a clunk as a hair-line crack appeared in the door, dividing it neatly in two. There was a second clunk as both halves of the door folded inwards with a hiss of air.

'Jesus!' Daisy gasped, and the Hawazim gaped in surprise. Some of them made the sign against the evil eye. The open door revealed a tunnel descending at a gentle angle into the belly of the earth, lit dimly by what appeared to be luminous strips. Daisy peered into it. 'Surely the ancient Gyps never had anything like this!' she said. 'Those doors must have been put in by Ibram.'

'No,' Ross said, 'I think they're original.'

'Why?' I asked.

'From what I've felt, I can remember that I've seen something like it before,' Ross answered. He turned towrads the Hawazim, whom I saw were hanging back diffidently. 'So who's going?' he enquired. 'I can't. I've got no eyes.'

No one answered, not even his cousins 'Ali, Ahmad and Mansur.

'Well,' Mansur said at last, his dead eye blinking rapidly, 'someone has to look after the camels.'

Ross smirked. 'Of course,' he said, 'and we'd better take full precautions. 'Ali – you set up the machine-gun in a commanding position just in case anyone approaches. Mansur, you and Ahmad rig up some kind of sun-shelter, then take the others to look for sip-wells or melons – anything we can use.'

They nodded, and Ross felt for me and Daisy, placing his hands on our shoulders. 'Well,' he said, 'looks like it's down to you two. You going or not?'

'All right,' we both said. Ahmad brought us two powerful flashlights from the camels, and at Ross's insistence, our

323

handguns. 'What about you?' I asked him, as we switched on the torches.

'I wish I could come,' he said, 'but in there I'll just be a burden to you. The Divine Spirit go with you. Good luck!'

47

THE TUNNEL WAS OVAL IN shape, made of the same bluish metal as the door, vaulted over our heads with curving walls covered in hieroglyphs and cartouches. The floor was a granite walkway notched to prevent slipping, thick enough to absorb the sound of our footsteps. The air was stale, and I couldn't make out where the dim green glow came from. There seemed to be strips of luminous tape somewhere up in the curve of the ceiling, but when I shone my torch-beam up there, they were gone. I advanced slowly down the corridor, tying my headcloth around my waist and peering at some of the tens of thousands of hieroglyph figures all painted in what seemed to be their original colours.

'This is fantastic,' I said, 'I've never seen hieroglyphs in relief on metal before. It's something entirely new!' I stopped to examine a particularly interesting portrait of Sekhmet – a grim-faced, terrifying figure with a lion's head, carrying the sacred sun disc and breathing fire. 'Whoever built this place was preoccupied with the idea of devastation,' I commented. I pointed to a stela portraying starving people with the ribs showing through their skin, and read the tiny hieroglyphs underneath. 'The people of the valley are starving,' I read aloud, 'and terror stalks the land.'

Suddenly there was an audible clunk as the outer door snapped shut without warning, extinguishing the daylight. We rushed back to it and knocked, and there were answering thumps from the other side, though the door remained solidly in place. A second later the green glow-strips went out.

'Great!' Daisy said. 'We're trapped! And the door looks airtight – we're going to asphyxiate too!' I caught the whirr and rumble of machinery from somewhere beneath the floor, and a moment later I sensed a faint stream of cool air. Then the glow-strips came on again, bathing the tunnel in eerie green light. 'There's some kind of air circulation system at work,' Daisy said, 'Ibram's team must have constructed it.'

'No,' I said, 'it would have cost millions. No, this is the original technology.'

'The ancient Egyptians didn't have stuff like this,' Daisy said. 'How can you be so certain?'

I said nothing, and we walked to the end of the tunnel and found it sealed by a second blue metal door. I examined it in the light of my torch and saw what appeared to be the marks of an axe or some other sharp, heavy instrument, which had cut into the surface of the metal but done no serious damage. 'I guess this is where Ibram or his predecessors got impatient!' I chuckled, traversing the door with my torch-beam. 'Let's see.' The centre of the door was marked with the *Aker*-lion cartouche just as the other had been, but this time the cartouche itself lay in the middle of ten separate ellipses, each one containing a circle or dot of a different size. One of the circles – the sixth in sequence from the centre – had a ring placed horizontally around it.

'That's Saturn!' Daisy said. 'It's easy enough.'

'Yes,' I said, 'but there are ten planets in this solar system, and ours has only nine. I'd guess we have to pick the odd one out.'

The two of us examined the planets carefully, identifying them by relative size as Mercury, Venus, Earth, Mars, Jupiter and the rest. 'What about this one?' Daisy asked, pointing to a very small icon that seemed to be followed by a fiery tail.

'By God, yes!' I said, 'that's Halley's Comet. It must be. It's a frequent visitor to our solar system but it's not a planet!' I pressed the comet icon and the door split in half with a thump and snapped open. 'It's easy stuff to us,' I commented, 'but a hundred years ago it would have flummoxed everyone, because it wasn't known then there were nine planets in the system. This club only admits beings with a certain degree of knowledge.'

We were standing before a small, cylindrical antechamber with walls that were bare except for a large stela embedded in one of them. The stela was covered in hieroglyphs, but in the centre there was a picture of a star-filled sky with a disc-shaped object suspended – an object which seemed to be trailing flames and smoke. Below the disc, apparently falling from it, was a cone enclosing a phoenix with a human eye – the Firebird – and below that was a landscape with bushes and trees. Animals such as lions and elephants, and shaven-headed human figures that looked like ancient-Egyptian priests were running about excitedly. We moved into the chamber cautiously and examined the stela.

'The cone must be the Benben Stone,' Daisy said, pointing at it, 'but what's the disc-shaped thing?'

I peered at it then gestured a knuckle at the stars that formed the background of the disc. 'That's Orion,' I said, 'and see this big star beneath it? That's Sirius. The disc looks almost like . . . it's meant to be a space-vehicle . . .'

'You mean a *spaceship*?' she asked, and I noticed there was a tremor in her voice.

I gave her a hard look. 'Why not? You said you'd seen bits of alien ships at Area 51.' I peered at the picture again. 'Look! The disc's trailing fire, like it was damaged or something, and if you look at the front here, you'll see that it's . . . well, broken up. The Benben Stone is falling out of the broken part.'

Daisy stared at the picture again. 'You mean the Stone is a part of the broken ship?'

'That's it,' I said, 'the Benben Stone was meant to be a meteor-ite – something inert. But what if it was more?' I jabbed a finger at the cone-shaped object. 'What if it's actually a fragment of alien technology, so advanced we can't even comprehend it?

327

Wouldn't that have made it the most valuable artifact in the whole of ancient Egyptian culture – so precious that it formed the centrepiece of the Firebird Project?'

'You mean as a religious icon?' she asked. 'Like the Black Stone in Mecca?'

'Maybe, but what if it was more than that? What if it had a *use* – I mean a practical use other than just an object of veneration?'

'What use?' Daisy enquired.

I frowned and looked around the small chamber, then back at the stela. Inset at the bottom, beneath the picture of the Benben Stone, was what appeared to be a stylized map sprinkled with animal-headed gods, Nile boats, serpents and sphinxes. A line like a road twisted and turned through the 'map', and the territory it traversed was divided up into twelve distinct units, each one intricately illustrated and detailed. I peered at the second unit. Inside it there was a tiny reproduction of the falling Benben Stone in the larger stela above.

'This is a location map of the whole complex,' I said. 'It seems to be based on the ancient Egyptian concept of the *Duat*, which was divided into twelve "Hours" or "Houses". The outer tunnel we just walked down was the First House and this is the Second House.' I moved my finger along the divisions on the map, and it came to rest on another tiny image of the Benben Stone, this time standing upright on what looked like a solid plinth. 'Here,' I said, counting off the divisions, 'the Stone itself is in the Fifth House, so we have to work our way through two more. In the *Duat*, the god Ra had to utter magic spells to pass from one Hour or House to the next. The puzzles we've had to solve must be the equivalent of the spells.'

Suddenly, as if it had allowed us enough time, the entire wall slid upwards noiselessly. Daisy sucked in a breath. 'Jesus Lord!' she said. 'Will you get a load of this!'

48

BEYOND THE SMALL CHAMBER LAY a gallery of thousands of pillars as vast as the trunks of giant trees. The pillars were made out of some reddish metal, I guessed, but might almost have been weathered sandstone. They were pitted and fluted, each of more or less uniform size, but sprouting excrescent nodes like odd metallic fungus-growths. The floor of the chamber became a walkway that curved gracefully through the great columns without any kind of support or safety barrier, like a magic path through a great forest. We took tentative steps forward and I glanced upwards and saw that the pillars disappeared into the darkness above us. Below us they vanished into a shadowy abyss. Smoke or steam wafted in strands out of the chasm and I thought I could hear the hum of invisible machinery from far below. The place was lit with scores of glow-strips that were constantly mobile, like the ones in the tunnel. I advanced a bit further and shone my torch on the nearest pillar. Close up the flutings looked like millions of tiny pipes fused together, and when I examined one of the fungal excrescences, I saw that it was made up of countless tiny parts like a series of micro-circuits, laid one against the other without any conscious design.

'One thing's for sure,' Daisy said, almost to herself, 'the ancient Egyptians of 2000 BC didn't build this – they could barely get it together to make a cooking-pot!'

I shrugged, and suddenly Daisy screamed. For an instant her eyes went wide with terror, and I looked up just in time to see a swarm of giant birds sweeping towards us out of the 'forest', shrieking like marabout storks. In fact that's what I imagined they were for a moment, until they swooped right over my head in a waft of wings, and I realized that they weren't birds at all, but more like giant bats or flying manta-rays. I drew my .380, but Daisy was already firing, her mouth twisted in fear and loathing. The shadows wheeled and swooped again, coming in so low that I thought I could feel the rush of air. Daisy pumped the trigger putting three or four rounds into one of the black things, but the creatures only banked, wheeled and dived again.

'Stop!' I yelled. 'Stop shooting!'

Daisy checked herself, tripped, and lost her balance. She stumbled over the edge of the walkway, dropping her SIG which went churning below her into the abyss. For a second I thought she would plummet after it, but then I saw she'd caught the edge of the walkway, and was dangling there gasping for breath. The dark shapes undulated back in amongst the columns and I rushed to help her, grasping her wrists and heaving her back.

'Christ! Christ!' Daisy repeated as first her torso emerged, then her legs. She sat on the floor catching sobbing breaths for a moment. 'Shit!' she wheezed. 'What the fuck *were* those things?'

'They weren't real,' I said, 'you shot bullet after bullet into them and they didn't blink. They weren't flesh and blood, just some kind of projection. It was just a cheap trick.'

'That cheap trick nearly cost me my life.'

'Think of it as a warning,' I said.

We followed the walkway as it meandered between the huge columns, advancing cautiously now, in single file, like climbers wary of hidden crevasses. The path seemed to go on endlessly, and the sense of awe grew as I started to grasp the incredible immensity of the place. Finally the walkway curved towards a door set in what looked like a sheer cliff made of the same reddish metal as the pillars, and scored with an intricate pattern of tracery like needle-marks on an infinitely fine tattoo. There were alcoves, bulging pillars, great baroque vaults and deep arches in the cliff, which made it look like the wall of a great cathedral. I shone my torch-beam at the door, and we made out another *Aker*-lion cartouche, this time set in the midst of two descending columns of hieroglyphic human figures in the familiar ancient Egyptian cameo poses. Against each figure there was a series of dots.

'Not planets this time,' I commented, 'looks like we're out of the sphere of astronomy altogether.'

Daisy held two fingers up to the columns and began counting off the number of dots. Against the first figure in the first column there were seven dots and against the corresponding figure in the second column twenty-three. The second figure in the first column had nine dots, the one below it eleven, the fourth figure twelve, the remaining three fourteen, fifteen and nineteen.

'It's not a mathematical progression is it?' I said doubtfully.

'No,' Daisy said. She pondered it for a moment. 'These numbers,' she said, 'seven and twenty-three . . . it's too much of a coincidence.'

'I can't see any connection,' I said.

'Seven's the atomic weight of the element lithium,' she said, 'and its counterpart in the second column is sodium with an atomic weight of twenty-three.'

'The periodic table!' I said. 'Sodium has a family resemblance to lithium – they're both alkali metals – but it's much heavier, which is why it was placed at the head of the second column.'

'Yeah, and let me think. In the periodic sequence lithium's followed by beryllium, isn't it? That has an atomic weight of nine. Then there's boron with eleven, then . . .'

'Carbon,' I said, 'with twelve.'

'Yeah. That's followed by nitrogen, which has an atomic weight of fourteen, oxygen which scores sixteen and fluorine which has a weight of nineteen. That's the first column. In the second we've got magnesium, aluminium, silicon and so on.'

'But there's a mistake,' I said, 'the atomic weight of oxygen is sixteen, but here it's given as fifteen.'

'You sure the others are right?' she asked.

We both studied them again carefully. 'Yes,' I said, 'they're all correct.'

'It's a deliberate mistake to see if we're on our toes,' she said, 'like the ten planets in the solar system. The relationship between the elements was discovered by Mendeleev in 1871, so no one could have got it right much more than a century and a quarter ago. The ancient Egyptians aren't supposed to have known about the elements, but whoever built this place certainly did.'

I pressed the oxygen symbol on the door and it split in half and sprang open. Inside there was an antechamber like the one in the Second House, with another stela on the wall, and we moved forward to examine it. This one showed the cone-shaped object from the previous stela – the Benben Stone – on the top of an obelisk, giving off some sort of radiance, represented by beams ending in tiny hands. Around the obelisk were groups of shaven-haired figures, some of whom were actually being touched by the beams of light. In the background stood a lion-headed sphinx and above it the night sky with the constellation Leo. I gazed at it, fascinated. '*This is the sealed thing . . . with fire about it*,' I recited, '*which contains the efflux of Osiris and it is put in Rostau. It has been hidden since it fell from him, and it is what fell from him on to the desert sand.*'

'What's that?' Daisy asked.

'Spell 1080 of the Coffin Texts,' I said.

'The what?'

'Coffin Texts – one of the major records we have of ancient Egyptian religious practice. That verse was always thought to refer to the Benben Stone. It suggests the Stone gave out some kind of divine fire or radiance – just like in this picture.'

'But the "fire" is actually touching some of the figures,' Daisy said, 'as if the Stone's power is influencing them in some way . . .'

'*Communicating* with them,' I said. 'Look – there's a Firebird squashed up inside the cone, just as there is in the first stela. It's like a chick inside an egg – as if there's a living creature in the Stone.'

'An artificial intelligence?' Daisy said, her voice filled with awe. 'Some kind of computer capable of communicating with human beings.' Her eyes shone as she looked at the picture. 'Imagine it! A computer that fell from a starship more than ten thousand years ago! If you had access to its memories, just think what intellectual riches there'd be! If the computer could really *talk* to people it could tell them the whole history of the galaxy – all the wisdom of a civilization millennia more advanced than ours – almost inconceivably advanced physics, chemistry, astronomy, medicine – think of the weapons applications alone! Worth a million times more than all the treasures of all the pharaohs who ever lived. Knowledge is power – it always has been. The mere *rumour* of the knowledge it contained might have been enough to invade a country for – even to sacrifice an army of 50,000 men.'

I was suddenly flushed with excitement as I realized this was no fantasy. It actually made sense. 'That's what MJ-12 were after,' I said, 'the power of the Stone was worth all the killing and all the expense. To them it would have been worth it thousands of times over!' I looked at the stela again carefully.

'Evidently we're in about 10,500 BC,' Daisy said, 'because the constellation Leo is in the ascendant, and that was the Age of Leo. We have a lion-headed sphinx, which may be the Great Sphinx at Giza with its original head.'

'Zep-Tepi,' I said, 'that's the time the Shemsu-Hor are supposed to have planned the Firebird Project . . .'

There was a hiss and the door snapped shut with unbelievable speed. Almost at once we heard a grumble of hidden mechanism and the chamber started to move downwards. 'It's an elevator!' Daisy said. We held on to the walls and watched each other speculatively until the thing came to a halt and the door slid open to reveal yet another antechamber and another stela.

'The Fourth Hour!' I said. 'Let's have a look at this!'

The central tableau of this stela was clearly the Giza plateau, with the three pyramids and the Great Sphinx whose head was now human. In the picture an ensemble of priests was gathered around the Great Pyramid, looking up at its apex, which seemed to be glowing with light rays that ended in tiny hands, like the ones on the previous stela. One of the rays extended into a starry sky in which the prominent constellations were once again Orion and Sirius. The pyramid itself was shown as giving off beams of light, but part of it had been hollowed out schematically to show a human being curled in an almost foetal position. Wires and cables seemed to run out of his head into the bowels of the pyramid, connecting with the glowing capstone, which held a squashed-up image of a phoenix inside it.

I scratched my stubble grimly. 'This is the culmination of the Firebird Project,' I said, 'the pyramids have been built, and the Benben is now the Great Pyramid's capstone. We've got a wired man inside the pyramid, connected to the Benben Stone. The Stone has rays emanating from it, one of them almost touching the star Sirius. This has got to be 2500 B C.'

I studied the stela again and began to read the hieroglyphs beneath it. Daisy watched me silently for what might have been twenty minutes. 'The text isn't clear,' I said finally, 'but it seems to be referring to the Great Pyramid as "the Instrument of Ascension".'

'Ascension of what?' Daisy said.

'In ancient Egyptian myth the pharaoh's "spirit" was supposed to ascend the stars to become Osiris – symbolized by Orion.'

'Why is the capstone giving out light?'

I pondered the hieroglyphs again. 'It says, "*when the Sound-Eye is placed in conjuction with the Instrument of Ascension, then the great design of the Horus-Followers is complete . . .*".'

'The Instrument of Ascension is the Great Pyramid,' said Daisy, 'but what's the "Sound-Eye"?'

'It's got to be the Stone – the capstone of the pyramid. Look

– in the picture both the capstone and the pyramid are giving out energy. Without the Stone the pyramid is inert, but the Stone, with its artificial intelligence, is like a smart cell that animates the mass of the pyramid, turning it into some sort of device.'

'Device?'

'It makes sense, don't you see!' I said. 'Scholars have always been puzzled by the accuracy of the pyramid. It has the kind of precision you only find in machines. That's because it *is* a machine, but a machine that doesn't come on line until it's fitted with the smart cell – the capstone. And look at this,' I said, pointing to a lower row of hieroglyphs, ' *"Only the Chosen One can use the Instrument to . . . reach . . . the stars . . . when the celestial bodies are in alignment . . ."'*.'

'Reach?' Daisy repeated dubiously.

'No the word isn't exactly *reach . . .* more like . . . *channel.* That's it! It actually says *the Chosen One can channel his spirit to the stars.*'

'Sounds like we're talking about some kind of message,' she said, 'radio-signals . . . channelling . . . crystals.'

'You've got it!' I said. 'The Great Pyramid and the capstone together were a vast crystal capable of channelling a message to the stars. Not a radio message, which takes thousands of years to get anywhere – that would be primitive junk to an advanced race. No, *a psionic* message, which travels at the speed of thought – virtually instantaneous!' Daisy was watching me doubtfully and I turned to her. 'Don't you get it We wondered if the Stone had some use and that was it! That was the object of the Firebird Project. The Shemsu-Hor and their descendants struggled over thousands of years to send a message to Sirius. The Nommos – the beings that started ancient Egyptian civilization – world civilization – weren't humans. They were stranded here on earth and their descendants struggled for thousands of years to get off a message to their home planet. To do it they needed four things – the Benben Stone, the Great Pyramid, a human agent capable of generating a psionic message – what we call an *illuminatus* – and the correct alignment of the stars.'

Daisy gulped. 'Wait a minute,' she said, 'even if it's true, what has it do with your ghoul?'

'The ghoul is an alien from Sirius,' I said, 'a Nommo. Since it escaped from Ross it has built up its strength again, and its efforts have been directed to finding the Benben Stone. There's only one reason it would want the Stone – to send a message to Sirius – to its home world. It's stranded here like the ancient Nommos and its plan is to to re-enact the ritual of the Firebird Project – to communicate across light-years, to let its race know that it's still alive. It had to have an *illuminatus* to operate the Stone, and that's why they've been hunting Ross over the past four years. That's probably why they wanted him in the first place. Ross is their Chosen One!' Another thought struck me suddenly. 'The new capstone!' I said. 'They're going to put a new capstone on the Great Pyramid at midnight on December 31st – the turn of the millennium. But it won't be a new capstone, it'll be the old capstone, resurrected after 4000 years!'

'The perfect cover,' Daisy said slowly, 'but they won't get away with it. First they don't have the Benben Stone, and second they don't have the *illuminatus* to control it. We're going to make damn sure they don't get them, either.'

49

THE WALL SUDDENLY LIFTED SILENTLY as the previous ones had done and we found ourselves in a vaulted tunnel whose arched roof lay hundreds of metres above our heads. At the far end was another door of the same bluish metal, but as we approached we saw that the door was buckled and the hieroglyphs on it burned away with what might have been some kind of acid. I pushed it open, but the antechamber inside had been vandalized in the same way, obscuring the picture and leaving only a few legible hieroglyphs round the edges. 'Can you make anything out?' Daisy asked.

'It's difficult,' I said, 'it gives a warning about "the Sound-Eye". It says: "*and the sages dwelt in the land of Wetjeset-Neter, where they set up the Sound-Eye as the centre of light that illuminated the island. But the Sound-Eye brought Sekhmet and darkness covered Wetjeset-Neter.*"'

'What's that all about?' Daisy asked.

I scratched my chin. 'I think we're getting warm. Since we entered this place I've been wondering why the hell they put the Benben Stone here, way out in the wilderness where no ancient Egyptian would ever go.'

'Me too,' said Daisy, 'it's like what we do today with atomic waste. And then there's the sealed doors of what looks like lead.'

'And there's nothing to tell us whether the Firebird Project succeeded,' I added. 'I mean we have no idea what happened back then.'

We were still pondering the inscription when the wall slid open suddenly and we found ourselves in a room bigger than the biggest aircraft-hangar I'd ever seen – it could easily have housed a fleet of jumbo-jets. The ceiling stood as high above our heads as the roof of the Empire State Building, and the walls, ceiling and floor seemed to be made of a milky crystal as white as alabaster. The strangest thing about the hall, though, was its shape. It was dodecahedral – with twelve perfectly matched walls set at angles to each other, each covered with blocks of hiero-glyphs in ivory, blood-red and blue. In the centre of the vast crystal floor was a sort of platform – a twelve-sided plinth under a canopy held in place by metal uprights. 'The Fifth House!' I said.

'My God!' Daisy said, staring round at the room. 'But this is where the Stone is meant to be!'

I walked slowly, reverently towards the centre of the room and looked at the dodecahedral plinth. As Daisy joined me, I squatted down to read the hieroglyphs that were inscribed on it.

'What does it say?' Daisy asked.

I didn't look at her. 'It says "the Sound-Eye", and look – there are marks inside here where a heavy object stood. But someone got here before us – the Benben Stone's gone!'

There was a second's pause and then suddenly I heard the distinct sound of hands clapping – a single pair of hands slapped together slowly and in unmistakable derision, amplified by the acoustics in the great chamber. 'Bravo!' a croaking voice said. 'How very brainy of you, my dear Rashid!'

My Beretta was already half-out when the shot cracked out and whizzed off the floor. I froze in mid-movement, then spun round to see a familiar spindly figure in a funereal black suit coming towards us – a figure with a pickled face, a bird-like fringe of hair on the back of his head and a tadpole head. It was Jan Van Helsing, and he was leading a troop of about twenty men in long black coats, all of them toting pump-action shotguns and submachine-guns. Two of the thugs supported the figure of Omar James Ross, while another two held their weapons to his head. Ross's eyes darted wonderingly around him, and I realized that he'd got his eyesight back, too late.

'Although I have to add,' Van Helsing said, turning to Ross, 'you took a little longer to get here than I'd anticipated, Mr Ross. Trouble with the old Divine Water was it?'

He moved forward until he was within a couple of metres of us then halted. 'Never mind,' he said, 'there are still six days to the millennium, and thanks to you and Miss Brooke we now have everything we need: the alignment of the stars, the Great Pyramid, the Benben Stone – *and* the *illuminatus*!'

50

THE OUTER DOOR OF THE Benben mansion snapped shut behind us, and for an instant I blinked in the blinding light. Two Chinook helicopters had landed in the valley between the dunes, and stood silently like brooding steel insects with a heat-haze rising from beneath their engine-cowlings. Mansur, Ahmad, Mamoon and 'Abd al-Hadi were kneeling next to the hobbled camels under a blazing sun, with their hands on their heads, and their rifles and daggers thrown into the sand in front of them. About ten more of Van Helsing's thugs were standing guard over them with pump-action shotguns. As we were shoved towards them I saw Mansur start up, his good eye flashing lividly in the light. There was a sickening crack as one of the black-suited guards hit him on the side of the head with the stock of his gun, sending him flying into the sand.

Ross bristled and turned angrily on Van Helsing. 'You want my cooperation,' he said, 'you leave my cousins alone!'

Van Helsing smiled and made a retching chuckle. 'Oh, I think you'll cooperate, Ross. You see, I took the liberty of having your wife and son brought to Cairo.'

'You're lying,' Ross said, 'they're in a place you won't find them!'

'They *were* in a safe place,' said Van Helsing, grinning his stupid fish-like grin, 'until they decided to visit Kharja Oasis. That's when we got them.'

He felt in his pocket and brought out an Agadez cross of the type worn by Tuareg nomads in the central Sahara. I recognized it at once. It was the one Ross's mother Maryam had worn – the one he'd presented to his wife Elena when they'd married four years ago.

Ross looked at the cross as if trying to assess its authenticity, then bowed his head. 'All right,' he said, 'but let the others go.'

Van Helsing smiled again and gestured to his guards, who pushed us over to where the four Hawazim were kneeling. They forced us down next to them, and threw our stilettos and my handgun into the sand with the other weapons.

'I should thank you again, Lieutenant Rashid,' Van Helsing said, 'without you we'd never have been able to track down Ross. We've been trying to get hold of him for four years, but every time we sent in a unit, he foresaw it and bugged out into the blue. I had a hunch you'd bring him right to us, and you did. This time his head-antennae didn't work – or maybe something warned him but he paid no attention. We had a bug set inside this place and as soon as it was tripped, we were on our way. We moved the Benben Stone days ago, of course. Thanks to Ibram and Sanusi we knew where it was and we didn't need any map. The whole map story was a set-up, Rashid, and you swallowed it hook, line and sinker. We even primed the front desk guy at the Mena to give you Ibram's case. We let you think we needed it so as you'd think you could get to the Benben Stone before us, otherwise you wouldn't have bothered. We made it seem like the map was what we wanted, when it was your *illuminatus* here. Actually the Stone is now safely under guard at the old museum rest-house at Giza – you saw it the time you spotted me dressed as a labourer – remember? Oh, you didn't know I'd seen you but I did. I could have had the Blue Berets take you then but I had a feeling you'd lead us to what we wanted. You see, I knew who and what you were right from the beginning, Rashid. Did you think I was so stupid as to miss that damn great hole in your right ear?'

'And I know who you are, Van Helsing,' I said, 'you're a dirty, shapeshifting *Nommo*!'

He cackled with laughter.

'You bastard!' Daisy said. 'You won't get away with this!'

Van Helsing retched. 'Oh, the famous Miss Dickless Tracy,' he said, 'who's going to stop me? You? Your daddy? He'll be so proud to know his daughter was killed in action, even if you're not really his daughter. I know all about you, too, Brooke – I know that's not your name, and I know you're not FBI, so please spare me the threats. You've been very useful to us in helping to mislead young Lieutenant Rashid here. By the way, I did enjoy throwing a spanner into the works of your little bonding episode by suggesting that you dumped on him. Cause a few lovers' tiffs, did it? You underestimated old Halaby, though, Rashid. Before we finished with him he was pleading to be allowed to tell us anything and everything. He was aware that the 1916 Firebird file was in the old archives, of course, and it was a damn good bet that you'd try to break in. Had to be in the next twenty-four hours, and after that it was a simple matter of ripping out the interesting material and having the river police watch the place. You covered your tracks well with your apartment, but Halaby was an old-timer who made it his business to find out things that weren't of immediate importance. He followed you home one day. When you were bumped by the police on the river you really had no place else to go, and we were waiting.'

I stared at him, dumbly I suppose, and Van Helsing turned and snapped at the black-coated figures by the helicopters. 'Start the motors!' he bawled. 'Let's get our *illuminatus* on his way!'

There was a roar as the choppers' engines started and their rotors began to spin lazily. The guards pushed Ross towards the door of the first Chinook and forced him up the ladder. 'What about the rest?' one of the guards asked Van Helsing.

'Kill them!' he said.

The rotors were spinning faster now, and the guards pumped their weapons. I looked at the desert around me – the lonely wilderness I'd grown to love – and a stream of visions suddenly pulped through my mind like an uncoiling puff adder. There was Andropov in the monastery telling us that the Sahara had turned to desert around 2500 BC, the Blij and Neuven ice-core samples showing there'd been an environmental cataclysm about the same time, 'Ali picking up stone axes in the desert, the mutilated inscription on the door of the Fifth House . . . '*and the sages dwelt in the land of Wetjeset-Neter, where they set up the Sound-Eye as the centre of light that illuminated the island. But the Sound-Eye brought Sekhmet and darkness covered Wetjeset-Neter.*' They say death concentrates the mind wonderfully, and with a sudden overwhelming gush of comprehension I saw in full focus the pattern I'd only glimpsed for the past days. Sekhmet meant devastation – that was the message Ibram had left for us. The Benben Stone had brought devastation and had been hidden out here in the deepest desert so that the same thing would never happen again.

'Stop!' I told Van Helsing. 'You don't know what you're doing! The Firebird Project failed. When they tried to use the Stone in 2500 BC it set off some kind of atmospheric reaction that converted the green Sahara into a desert, and brought down ancient Egyptian civilization! If you try to use it, the same thing will happen again!'

Van Helsing paused and sneered at me. 'So what?' he said. 'It's so much easier to colonize a devastated planet!' He grinned gloatingly. 'Nice thought to die with, isn't it? Bye-bye sucker!' He had just turned his back on me when the rat-tat-tat of a machine-gun punched out from somewhere above us and Van Helsing howled and jerked wildly as a couple of tracers smashed into his leg.

The guards threw themselves down, squinting to see where the fire was coming from, and in that instant Daisy moved with blinding speed. She grabbed my Beretta from the pile of weapons and fired, dropping the nearest guard with a single round. She rolled and fired again, and another burst of machine-gun fire blatted from a dune-top, cutting down two black-suited troopers as they dashed towards her. Ahmad, Mansur and the other Hawazim went for their rifles, and I snatched my stiletto. I saw Mansur blast a guard with his old .303 at almost point-blank range. The guard sailed back a metre and collapsed on the slope of a shallow dune. Another soldier grabbed Mansur round the neck and put a pistol to his head. In a second I was on him with my stiletto, slashing his neck from ear to ear until the blood splashed over my hands. Ahmad was firing from the hip now, advancing fearlessly towards the helicopters like an automaton, and the rest of the guards had given up the fight and were piling back into them. I looked round for Van Helsing and saw that he was still alive. He'd managed to drag himself to the ladder of one of the choppers and was hauling himself into the hold. 'Leave them!' I heard him bawl. 'Hit them with the missiles.'

The second aircraft wheeled around about a metre off the ground and lurched forward in a shroud of dust, coming straight at us. I could see the pilot in the cabin with his helmet and headphones on, and the missile-tubes bristling on the fuselage.

'Down!' I screamed, and everyone but Ahmad dropped flat in the sand. The Little Pot ran forward towards the metal beast, coolly dropped on one knee and lifted his rifle. I could almost see the pilot's finger poised on the missiles' 'Fire' button. Ahmad worked the bolt, took aim as though he had all the time in the world, and squeezed the trigger. There was a puff of smoke from the rifle, followed by a shuddering detonation as the chopper's fuel-tank went up. A singeing whoff of orange and black fumes lufted over our heads carrying a rain of grit, fragments of twisted fuselage and bits of flaming human bodies. The blazing skeleton of the aircraft dumped into the sand and I saw shadows flailing frantically inside the shattered frame. Daisy and I stood up, but I knew it was too late to save Ross. The other Chinook, with the *amnir* and Van Helsing aboard, was sweeping away in a long curve, gaining height steadily in a whirl of smoke and aviation fumes. It passed over us fast, and the last I saw of it was its shadow skimming over the dune-crests, heading east.

51

I T WAS ONLY AS I watched the Chinook disappearing into the distance that I realized what had really happened. I'd delivered Ross to his enemies packed, sealed and gift-wrapped. Van Helsing had never even needed the map. It had been a scam from the beginning, and he had sacrificed his own men just to convince us. That was how much he'd wanted Ross. The Old Man had saved me from perdition, given me a life, and this was how I'd repaid his trust – by putting the whole tribe in jeopardy. I sank down to my knees and dropped my stiletto, feeling tears coursing down my scorched cheeks. In a dreamworld, far off, I saw the fuselage of the Chinook still blazing, smelt the stink of burning aviation fuel, acrid smoke, grilled flesh, and took in the charred, mutilated bodies of Van Helsing's foot-soldiers scattered across the dunes. I watched numbly as Mansur and Ahmad worked their way through the shattered bodies, slitting the throats of those who were still alive. To them, I knew, it wasn't cruelty but compassion – they would have done the same for me. I stared as 'Ali came scooting down the dune-face dragging his light machine-gun, kicking up spouts of dust, and watched as the others embraced him. It was 'Ali who had saved us, but I had failed them all. In all the years I'd been with the Hawazim, I'd never felt such an outsider as now. I saw Daisy slap the dust off her *jibba*, sweep back her golden hair with a single movement of the hand, and look round for me. I saw her bounding over the sand towards me as if in slow motion. The next thing I knew was a savage slap in the face from the left and then another from the right, and Daisy shaking me: 'Sammy!' she was shouting, 'Sammy, you're in shock! Come on! For Christ sake, Sammy! We need you!'

It was the word 'need' that brought me out, blinking, and I suddenly became aware of a stinging face and a terrible, raging thirst. 'I fucked up . . .' I said, struggling to force the words out of my mucus-clogged mouth. Daisy slapped me again, even harder, with such force that I almost fell over.

'Jesus Christ!' she said, with an edge of hysteria in her voice. 'We all fucked up, Sammy. Don't dip out on me now!'

I rubbed my cheek and sat in the sand. Someone pushed a gourdful of water into my hand and I turned to see Mansur, grinning, his face burned raw from the Chinook blast. 'Spoils of war!' he said. 'They unloaded five jerrycans to water the troops, but they left in such a hurry, they forgot them! Now, don't drink too fast, brother – just sip.'

I didn't sip, I gulped greedily until Mansur grabbed my wrist and stopped me. I felt the liquid seeping down my body, filling my blood like the most powerful drug. Daisy drank a gourdful and when Mansur went off to water the others, she smiled at me weakly through cracked lips. 'Feel better now?' she asked.

'No,' I said, 'I led Ross into a trap. I should have seen it coming.'

'Bullshit, Sammy. I was as much part of it as you were. They set us up so carefully we had no way of knowing. They were determined to get Ross – they must have set us up from the beginning, right from the time they took Ibram's suitcase. They probably primed Abd al-Ali to give us the case with the map in it.'

'Well one thing's for sure, Van Helsing's not the alien.'

'How do you know?'

'Because Ross told me that when he shot the creature, it reverted to its original form. When Van Helsing was hit, he stayed Van Helsing. He's one of the Nommo's cronies, but he's not the Nommo himself.'

'Look Sammy, we've got six days to the millennium and whatever happens we've got to stop them sending that message. Like you said, if they try to use the Sound-Eye there'll be some kind of blow-back effect that'll probably wreck the whole biosphere. We should have realized Van Helsing already knew it. Someone defaced the stela on the door of the Fifth House – that was the message it contained. And that's not all. Van Helsing mentioned the word "colonize". Remember what Sanusi said in his rambling? That the ghouls came from another world and coveted the earth? "Be prepared!" he said. Our ghoul-boy's a scout and he's planning to bring an invasion-force in. These aliens are predators, we know that now. Do you fancy living on a planet that's a kind of private hunting reserve, with guys like Van Helsing as the game-wardens? Not me!'

I sat up. 'What the hell can we do? We're stuck out in the desert?'

'How long will it take us to get to civilization?'

'The nearest place we can find a telephone or a car is probably St Samuel's Monastery – on the edge of the Fayoum Oasis, but we only have six days. On these camels it's going to take us at least seven.'

52

IT TOOK US ONLY FIVE days to sight St Samuel's, but by the time we got there the camels were almost dead and so were we. The main body of Hawazim from al-Bahrayn had met us at the cairn marking the old water-dump outside the sand-sea, and but for them we wouldn't have survived. They brought with them confirmation that Ross's wife and son had disappeared on a trip to Kharja a couple of days ago. Mamoon and 'Abd al-Hadi returned south with the main caravan leaving only myself, Daisy, Mansur, Ahmad and 'Ali to approach the monastery. We dismounted as we came out of the desert on to the graded road, and the first thing we spied was a batch of earthenware waterpots, set up as an offering to thirsty travellers. We unpacked our gourds gratefully but all we found in each pot was a few inches of damp sediment. We led the limping camels through the almond and olive groves, right up to the cloister arch. There was a desolate air to the place that hadn't been apparent on my last visit here. The orchards had turned grey and brittle for lack of water, the pumps were silent, the feeder-channels dry, and the buildings seemed to be deserted. While Mansur and Ahmad took the camels off to find them drink and grazing, Daisy and I pushed open the gate and entered the cloister. Where there had last been monks wandering about lost in thought, there were now silent flagstones, and where there had been a garden bursting with blooms, there were now dead, woody stems and runnels of sand. 'It's like the place has been evacuated,' Daisy said.

'After sticking it out for nearly 2000 years?' I said, 'it doesn't make sense.'

A couple of Egyptian vultures perched in the upper branches of a eucalyptus tree eyed us with interest as we crossed the quadrangle. The heavy teak doors were closed but unlocked, and we went in, calling 'Peace be upon you!' as we searched the corridor and the lower offices for life. There was no one. A thick layer of dust covered floors and furniture, and bone-dry papers fluttered about. We were climbing the stairs towards the Patriarch's office, when Daisy suddenly stopped in her tracks. 'You hear that?' she asked.

I listened. From somewhere above us there came a faint but distinct sobbing sound. 'The Patriarch's office!' I said. We rushed up to the door and heaved it open. Father Grigori was lying on a rug in the corner of his spartan cell, curled up in a foetus-position, his face grey and bloodless, his eyes bulging out of his head, his body wracked with tremors. He stared at us blankly as we walked in, a dribble of saliva drooling from his mouth. Daisy found a pitcher of water and a steel mug in the corner of the room. I picked the tiny monk up and sat him upright on a chair, and Daisy fed him the water like a child. The Patriarch choked and coughed, then gulped down more. 'Where are they all, Father Grigori?' I asked. 'Where's everybody gone?'

'Pumps stopped,' he croaked, holding on to my arm tightly. 'No . . . water for the gardens . . . had to close down . . .' He gulped water again, this time clasping the cup with his shaky hand. 'Must have a . . . cigarette,' he stuttered. I opened the drawer of his desk and brought out a packet of Cleopatras and a lighter. I put one in his mouth and lit it for him.

'It's bad for your health!' I told him.

Half a smirk lit up the side of his face, and he breathed the smoke in deeply, letting it trickle back through his nostrils. 'Ah,' he whispered, 'that's good.' He took another swig of water.

'Where *is* everyone?' I asked again.

He took another mouthful of smoke and stared at us with wild eyes, his nicotine-stained fingers almost crushing the cigarette. 'Dead,' he said, 'or else *his* creatures, may God have mercy on them . . .'

'*Whose* creatures?' Daisy asked.

Grigori's eyes widened, almost starting from his head, and suddenly he dropped the cup, which crashed to the floor, slopping water over the stone flags. For a moment he seemed to be groping for something, then I realized that he was pointing behind us, his eyes brimmed with horror. I whipped my Beretta out of my pocket and Daisy wheeled round and brought up the big old 9mm Browning Mansur had given her. Framed in the doorway, dressed in a black T-shirt, a tweed jacket and black slacks, stood Professor Milisch Andropov, his slitted Mongolian eyes and his high cheekbones giving the impression that he was beaming at us.

Daisy lowered the weapon, and let out a sigh. 'Don't creep up like that!' she said. 'I didn't hear you coming.'

Andropov smiled at her and said nothing. For an instant I let the Beretta drop and looked from Andropov to Grigori. The cigarette had fallen from the Patriarch's grasp and his hand was still shaking as he hooked a crabbed finger towards Andropov. '*Him!*' he gasped, '*Him! Him!*' and, just as I finally understood what he meant, Andropov drew a .380 calibre snub-nose from his pocket and shot Grigori twice in the head.

53

THE PATRIARCH PITCHED SIDEWAYS OVER his chair with blood spurting from his head and before I could move Andropov had Daisy in an armlock with his pistol against her temple. He was a big man and I couldn't believe that he'd outmanoeuvred Daisy – the fastest operator I'd ever seen. But he had and there was nothing I could do. I let my Beretta fall and it clanked on the stone flags next to Grigori, who lay silent in a spreading pool of blood, his eyes staring lifelessly at the ceiling. Andropov relaxed and kicked Daisy's Browning away. There was a movement from outside as a monk appeared at the door, panting. It was Brother Paul – the guy who'd met us on our first visit – though now he looked dirty and dishevelled in his pill-box hat and black soutane. His eyes filled with shock as he took in the scene and he took two shaky steps into the room and knelt down to examine Grigori.

'He's dead,' he told Andropov, his face white with fear.

'As a doornail, my dear brother,' Andropov said. 'Now, pick up the weapons of these intruders, will you.'

Paul gagged, then lifted himself reluctantly and groped for our fallen weapons.

Andropov backed off. 'Well, well,' he said, 'look what the desert threw up. I never expected to see either of you again. Obviously Van Helsing has been shirking. No matter. You can't do anything. It's all in place now. We have the Stone, and we have the *illuminatus* – your good friend, Mr Omar James Ross, failed Egyptologist extraordinary. Thanks to both of you, I might add. You've done Majesty a great service.'

'You're MJ-12,' Daisy said.

Andropov ignored her, moving to the Patriarch's desk and bringing out a couple of pairs of handcuffs. 'I always thought these might come in handy,' he said. 'Cuff them, Brother Paul.'

Paul laid down our handguns on the desk and fumbled with the cuffs while Andropov covered us. When we were cuffed, he eased the cocking hammer of his .38 forward and put it away. 'You've caught me in the nick of time,' he said, grinning, 'I was just about to leave to see the grand finale of all our plans. I think it would be fitting if you would join me as my guests. We already have Ross's wife and child in custody, of course, but your presence might lend him a little . . . er . . . extra enthusiasm. And it's only right that you witness what you, above all people, have done so much to bring about – the historic reactivation of the Firebird Project.'

'You're sick, Andropov,' I said. 'It'll destroy the environment and bring down the whole of modern civilization.'

Andropov's eyes had taken on a dreamy look. 'Imagine being allied to a race like the Nommos,' he said, 'a race that could construct technology like the Benben Stone, ten thousand years ago.'

'And what about the rest of humanity?'

Andropov shrugged again. 'They are expendable,' he said, 'just grist to the mill.'

PART III

GIZA PLATEAU, CAIRO, EGYPT, DECEMBER 31ST 1999

54

THE JARRE CONCERT HAD ALREADY started when we arrived
at Giza, the eerie electronic music reverberating out of synthesizers and hundreds of human throats, accompanied by an
aurora of lights that lit up each of the three pyramids. A freezing
wind raised its head over the hilltop as our convoy threaded its
way through the crowds of half-hysterical onlookers – New Age
mystics, hippies, spiritualists, primal screamers, modern witches'
covens, ufologists, religious fanatics, ordinary tourists and even
expectant locals. There were people from every corner of the
world, members of every race, religious minority or weirdo sect
– maybe fifty thousand of them dancing, smoking dope, shouting
and carousing, thronging wild-eyed around the windows of our
car as we passed through the gates and headed up the short slope
to the entrance of the Great Pyramid. A cordon of Blue Berets
three-men deep had been placed round the base of the pyramid
to prevent anyone climbing up, and they closed round our vehicle
as the doors opened. The crowds cheered inanely as Andropov
emerged, and his men pushed us towards the entrance. We were
dressed in long black Arab cloaks with hoods Andropov had
taken from the monastery to disguise our handcuffs, and to anyone close enough to see anything it must have looked as though
we were all part of the night's theatricals.

We were ushered up the steps we'd been obliged to descend

ignominiously on our last visit, and when we got to the top I paused for a second, pretending to get my breath, and scanned the sea of faces. Below me was an ocean of humanity waving banners, yelling, jumping and caterwauling, pulsating with the unreasoning dark energy of the crowd. I gasped as I sensed all those individual spirits moulded into one vast reservoir of unconscious power, a power that could – if properly acknowledged and directed – have reached out to the most distant stars. I knew why they'd really come here, I thought. It was an attempt to find something more than the isolated, meaningless lives modern urban society condemned them to. It was a half-understood urge to find identity, to belong. The Hawazim already had that sense of belonging – they had no material security like this crowd did but they knew who they were and were perfectly at ease in their relationship with the Divine. As the guards shoved us into the tunnel, I felt an intense compassion for my species. They had come to see in the new millennium on an impulse they did not properly understand, yet none of them knew what was really going on tonight.

Van Helsing was waiting for us inside – a dark figure in a dark suit, his pock-marked face half shadowed in the rows of electric lights. The tadpole features registered surprise when he saw us. 'What are they doing here?' he asked Andropov.

Andropov's big Mongolian face creased into an inscrutable grin. 'The desert blew them in,' he said. 'You didn't do the job, my fine friend.'

For an instant Van Helsing's eyes flickered with fear, and I realized with astonishment that it was Andropov who was in authority here. 'I thought they deserved to take part in our little ceremony,' he went on. 'Is the *illuminatus* in place?'

'It's all ready,' Van Helsing said. He glanced at his watch. 'An hour till kick-off.' He led us half-crawling down the descending passage, and I noticed he was limping badly – no doubt from the gunshot wound 'Ali had given him in the thigh. We came to the divide where the ascending passage started and doubled up again to climb it. It was hard going with our hands cuffed behind us, and a relief to come into the Grand Gallery with its great corbelled vaulting, stretching twenty-six feet above the floor to a ceiling of granite slabs. Van Helsing halted and gasped for breath, and I guessed the wound in his leg was giving him trouble. He caught me looking at him, and scowled. 'I owe you ragheads for this, Rashid,' he said, 'and for a Chinook helicopter and a bunch of foot-soldiers.'

I felt the same irrational impulse to hit out at him that I'd always felt in his presence. 'You won't miss them,' I said, 'you already sold out your entire species to a pack of extra-terrestrial hyenas.'

'Shut up!' Andropov snapped, coming in after us. I noticed that he'd left his guards behind, but there were already four armed men in the gallery, dressed in shiny steel-blue protective suits with rubber gloves, over-boots and helmets that covered their entire faces except for plastic strips over the eyes. These guys must have been specially chosen, I thought, because they were all unusually big men – six and a half footers, built like locomotives. Andropov led us to a pile of open cartons at one end of the passage which I saw contained protective clothing of the same type the guards wore. 'Let's get kitted up,' he told Van Helsing.

'What, them too?' Van Helsing asked.

'Of course,' Andropov said, 'I don't want their filthy blood and germs all over the place if they have to be made a lesson of. They're here to give Ross a little extra fillip, but they're expendable of course.'

Van Helsing leered at me with pleasure, and ordered one of the guards to suit us up. The big man slung his submachine-gun over his shoulder and picked suits out of the cartons. They were one-piece things, impossible to get into with cuffed hands. 'Excuse me, sir,' the guard said, his voice grating, muffled by the helmet, 'we'll have to unlock the cuffs.'

Andropov paused halfway into his own suit and looked irritated for a moment. Then he felt in his pocket and slapped the key into the guard's hand. The big man unlocked Daisy's cuffs first and she let out a sigh, massaging her wrists. As the guard turned to me, I tensed myself for action. Andropov had forgotten my back-up – the *khanjar* strapped to my left arm – and Brother Paul hadn't been professional enough to detect it. I remembered what Ross used to say: 'wars have been won with less,' and began to take deep breaths, relaxing my muscles, preparing all the reflexes I'd spent my life sharpening for the last, desperate action that might change everything.

The cuffs sprang free and I paused. I was ready. My hand closed on the handle of my knife and I was about to whip it out with all the explosive power I could summon when a big, rubber-gloved hand closed like a vice round my right wrist. I looked up into eyes that bored into me from behind the distorting perspex – familiar eyes, I thought. A second later the big hand lifted and made a circle with fingers and thumb. It was a sign from *Yidshi*, the ancient hunting language of my tribe, and it meant 'Wait'. I watched the hand, fascinated, as its index and second fingers extended with the other two fingers and thumb tucked away. In *Yidshi* it meant 'friend'. I looked into the eyes again, took in the broad-shouldered weight-lifter's frame, and knew it was Hammoudi. I recalled distinctly having taught him a few phrases of *Yidshi* in case it ever came in. It had. I didn't know how he'd survived or how he'd got here, only that he was here and that we now had a chance.

I dismissed all questions from my mind and concentrated on donning my suit, over-boots and helmet as inconspicuously as possible. When we were all suited up except for our helmets, Van Helsing gestured to the guard to replace the handcuffs. Hammoudi put the cuffs on a couple of notches looser than they'd been originally, and I watched carefully as he closed Daisy's, noting how he inserted the clasp through the first ratchet, so that they only appeared to be locked. He did the same with mine, and handed Andropov the key.

'OK,' Andropov said, 'let's get on with it.'

The guards goaded us through the antechamber and into the

King's Chamber, and immediately I saw Ross. He was strapped and handcuffed into a tubular steel chair in the centre of an iron frame, from which a spaghetti of wires and tubes fanned out, disappearing into one of the shafts. He was wearing a protective suit but no helmet, and the wires terminated in dozens of electrodes attached to his head. Near the frame there was a table weighed down with computer terminals and electronics, with wires and cables running everywhere. The floor around was covered in strange artifacts I didn't recognize – pillars with pylon-like caps, strange twisted sculptures in white alabaster connected by cables, twelve-sided crystals set on plinths, glass globes with what looked like red and green worms crawling inside them, miniature pyramids covered with hieroglyphs, moulded steel boxes that could almost have been antique stereo speakers.

'The Divine Spirit greet you, *amnir*,' I said. Ross stared at me glassily and his lips moved, but no sound came out,

'He can see and hear you,' Andropov chortled, 'but he can't speak. Our drugs see to that.' He turned to Ross. 'Your friend Sammy Rashid is here to make sure you cooperate,' he said loudly, as if talking to a deaf mute, 'the girl too. If there's any resistance on your part, they'll die slowly before your eyes. If that doesn't convince you we have your wife and child standing by. I believe in saving the best till last. And remember, Ross, I can monitor your brainwaves on my encephalograph terminals, so I'll know if you're not giving it your best shot.'

The four guards shuffled in behind us and stood with their backs to the red granite walls. Van Helsing looked at his watch. 'Ten minutes to go,' he told Andropov. The Professor looked pleased. I gazed around at the chamber. At the back was the famous 'sarcophagus' with the fragment missing from one corner, the supposed resting-place of the Pharaoh Khufu.

Andropov saw me looking at it. 'There never was a body in there,' he said. 'The scholars who believed the pyramid was Khufu's tomb were quite wrong. It wasn't even built by Khufu. The pyramid was conceived and built with only one idea in mind

– to transmit a message to Sirius.' He took a step forward and pointed at the shaft through which the mass of cables disappeared. 'They used to think these were air shafts,' he said, 'but actually they were devices for measuring the alignment of the stars – in this case Sirius. The pyramid is built with superb precision and stands on a temporal nexus point. When the stars come into conjunction then the capstone and the pyramid together act as a boosting force for the psionic message generated by the "pilot". In ancient Egypt these individuals were specially bred over generations, but the psionic gene got scattered through the human population and Ross got it by chance. Of course there are other *illuminati* alive in this generation, but they're not that easy to isolate.'

'One minute to go!' Van Helsing said. He switched on the largest of the TV monitors and we all saw the technicians fitting the new capstone-sheath into place on the top of the pyramid. The sheath was hollow, of course – and made of some light alloy – but at the very apex of the cone, I guessed, the real Benben Stone had been concealed.

Andropov watched with fascination. 'It's all academic now, anyway,' he said, 'the Benben Stone is more remarkable than you people can even imagine. It is capable of opening rifts in space-time, of powering a starship through hyperspace. Its power is phenomenal. Last time they used it, in 2500 BC, it caused a massive energy blow-back that started a chain reaction in the atmosphere with devastating runaway potential. It destroyed the ecosystem of the whole of North Africa, turned a fertile land into a desert and brought down Egyptian civilization. The same is going to happen this time, but with even worse results, but what does that matter to the Nommos?'

'Time!' Van Helsing said, and on the screen we saw the capstone-sheath being slotted into place by the technicians.

'And now,' Andropov said, poising himself by a handle on one of the control consoles, 'the first message across the cosmos for four and a half thousand years!'

55

ANDROPOV WORKED THE HANDLE AND there was a surge of power and a hum like a billion bees swarming as the ancient energy cells began to wake up after four millennia. The cables and wires quivered, crackled and vibrated. Ross went rigid in his chair and he let out an ear-piercing shriek that was magnified by the perfect acoustics of the chamber. The oscillations on the computer-terminals went haywire, and Andropov lifted a fist in triumph. 'I thought so!' he said. 'You can't resist Mr Ross, because the Benben Stone is drawing out your psionic power.' He turned towards us and I saw that his face was shining. 'My people will hear me,' he said, 'they'll come.' It was only for a fraction of a second but it seemed to me his features began to liquefy and run like colours on a painting, his body shaking, trembling as if a thousand volts were going through it, until it became a cocoon of vibration, a vortex of eddies, a plethora of forms fading and melting into one another. It was as if his face was a tape fast-forwarding through scores of possible human features, and at the end of the tape I glimpsed something monstrous – an insect-like head with protruding jaws and a cranium projecting backwards. The ghoul at last. Then Andropov's face returned, still split with the leer of victory.

'There's just one thing I don't get,' I burst out, 'you could have had anything you wanted. Why murder innocent kids like the tailor's boy, or the other two I found in Cairo?'

The creature with Andropov's face looked at me through eyes as old as the universe. 'My species is predatory, like yours,' he said. 'We have ways of suppressing the hunting instinct just as you do, but when your friend here allowed me to escape into the desert I reverted to the old ways. I found I actually enjoyed it.'

Daisy was staring at him with shock written all over her, and even Van Helsing registered horror. Suddenly Ross screamed again and arched backwards, pivoting with such force that the cables taped to his head were wrenched out. Van Helsing moved towards him with his pistol ready, and in that second I broke out of the cuffs, slipped my *khanjar* from under my sleeve, grasped it by the top between finger and thumb and hurled it at him. All the power of all the hate I'd nurtured and bottled up since my days on the streets of Aswan was behind that throw. Time slowed to a crawl, and it seemed I could see the knife spinning ponderously like a propeller, gaining momentum, until it punched into Van Helsing's chest, making him stagger backwards against the red granite wall. Then time speeded up again into ultra-fast-forward, and I ducked just as Hammoudi snapped the pump-action shotgun into his hand like a child's toy, pumped the works once and squeezed the trigger. The sound blasted against my eardrums like a thunderclap and I reeled back as the shell caught one of the guards in the chest with such force that it bowled him three metres across the chamber and hurled him like a rag doll against the stonework in a shower of blood and entrails. Hammoudi whipped off his hood and almost at the same moment Andropov brought out his .38 snubnose and shot him. Hammoudi toppled and staggered against the wall as the two other guards moved in for the kill. He fired the shotgun one-handed into the face of the first and dropped the other with the pistol-grip in the groin.

I grabbed Andropov and tried to grapple the gun out of his hand, and I saw Daisy snap off her cuffs and leap across the room with the power and speed of an Olympic athlete towards Ross.

'Stop!' Andropov bawled. 'You fool! Don't you know it's too late? The message has been sent! Nothing can stop us now!'

Daisy wrenched my blade out of Van Helsing's chest and began to slash at the leather straps that held Ross. She eased his half-inert body out of the way, sat down in the chair and slapped the electrodes on her own head. I watched her in shock and Andropov stopped struggling.

'What the hell are you doing?' he said.

Daisy glared at him and suddenly the buzz and hum of energy increased in a crescendo, until the whole room seemed to be pulsating with it. Daisy's body seemed aglow with power, and for a moment I swear I saw, not Daisy, but the body of a giant woman, a vast, serene, diaphanous image as high as the stars. There was a deep boom as the chamber seemed to shake, then a blinding flash and a blast of energy as the instruments scattered about the room popped and erupted in smoke. The deafening buzz began to diminish and there was the whine of power running down. Andropov stared at Daisy in amazement and there was fear in his eyes. 'The *Guardians*!' he whispered. 'She's one of them!'

Suddenly he kicked me in the shins, knocked me out of the way and plunged into the antechamber. I jumped to my feet and ran after him, but he was already halfway down the Grand Gallery, knocking cardboard cartons out of his path. As he entered the ascending passage at the far end the lights cut, and when I arrived at the head of the passage I could hear only the clatter of his footsteps on the wooden ramps over the pyramid's hum. I doubled over and half-ran, half-stumbled through the darkness, until the entrance loomed out in front of me with the starlit sky showing beyond. I saw Andropov's figure in cameo as he pushed through the guards and turned abruptly, and in that moment I knew he was going to climb up to the apex of the pyramid. As I emerged into the light of the arc-lamps I saw the crowds below, a swaying, seething surge of movement and ecstatic sound, lost in a primeval reverie amid cracking, whizzing and crashing fireworks filling the sky with explosions of colour, and laser-beams slicing through the night to the tune of electronic music.

The Blue Berets at the door seemed adrift in the ecstatic atmosphere, and no one tried to stop me as I followed Andropov up the side of the pyramid. Lights were flashing brilliantly around the new golden capstone, showing me the shambling body in strobes as he climbed the successive courses of masonry. I struggled after him, breasting course after course, some no higher than my shins, others more than waist-high, so that I had to feel desperately for some kind of foothold to get myself over. Often I had to stop for breath on ledges that were no wider than my own foot, holding on to the massive blocks tightly to prevent giddiness and vertigo from overwhelming me as I gazed down on the writhing sea of humanity below. Andropov went on and on, crawling over the stones like a scarab beetle, already hundreds of feet above the crowds. Fireworks exploded throwing momentary splashes of light across the stonework, and the second and third pyramids appeared in the moonlight as vast, incandescent shadows.

At last I saw that Andropov had paused, perhaps two thirds of the way up, and I realized I was gaining on him. I scrambled over the courses panting heavily now, taking in the vast glowing sprawl of Cairo, a patchwork of light and shade, a glimmering gloss of streetlights hanging in the sky, pierced by tower-blocks and minarets in a dozen colours. Andropov was climbing more slowly, his energy sapped. By the time he reached the top I was only a few feet behind him, and as he pulled himself over the lip of the shelf on which the new capstone stood, I grabbed his leg. He snarled like a vicious animal and turned on me, launching a kick at my head. I dodged and almost lost my footing, then heaved myself over the lip and dived at him. The gun went off, the bullet skimming past my ear, but Andropov lost his balance and fell. I closed with him, trying to shake the gun out of his hand, but he was stronger and heavier than me and he forced himself on top and pressed the pistol into my ear.

'You meddling little worm!' he spat, his eyes wide with hate. 'You think you can destroy me? You think you can foil plans made by a species that has the patience of millennia? I should have ripped you to shreds when I saw you in the alley or in the house in Old Cairo. You remind me of Ibram. Oh, he wanted the power and privilege of having alien technology at his disposal, but when he found out what the Stone would do he got scared. He was going to rat on us, and that couldn't be allowed. That's why he had to die. And now it's your turn.'

I groped madly to get a purchase and suddenly my right hand closed on a loose iron bar – something left by the technicians who'd fixed the capstone-sheath in place. I took it, and felt power flooding through me. It was the most primitive tool imaginable, but with this club in my hand I was suddenly filled with confidence. I gave Andropov a smashing blow across the head and he fell backwards, lost his balance and slipped sideways off the ledge. For a moment he hung there, fighting for a hold, his big face growing diaphanous and distorted again, until I could see the ghost of the creature there.

'The message was sent,' he growled through gritted teeth, 'the Nommos are coming and there's nothing you or your precious *Guardians* can do about it!'

I looked him in the eyes, and stamped hard on both hands one after the other. 'That's for the tailor's boy!' I said. He screamed, let go of the masonry and dropped like a dead weight, plummeting headlong down the side of the pyramid, bouncing from course to course until he was out of sight.

56

DAISY WAS SITTING ON THE steps below the main entrance when I came down, with her arm round Ross. Hammoudi sat below her, smoking a Cleopatra while a medic bandaged up his thigh. An ambulance was making its way ponderously through the crowds to pick up the body of the man who'd been killed falling from the pyramid. I imagined the authorities would keep it hush-hush for the sake of the tourist trade. The music of synthesizers was still coiling through the atmosphere, the audience seething and surging blindly, but I noticed the numbers were dwindling now. It was the year 2000, and the new millennium had arrived.

I sat down heavily next to Hammoudi. 'I won't ask you any questions,' I told him, 'but thanks.'

He shrugged. 'It was your brother, Mansur,' he said, 'Ross gave him an emergency number for me, and he used it. Told me you'd been captured at the Fayoum by this oriental-looking guy. Didn't take long to work out it was Andropov. I had to put a couple of people down to get into the pyramid, but on the way I came across Elena and Ross's son. I liberated them. They're waiting for Ross round the corner at the Mena Palace.'

Ross was pale and looked half-comatose, but he sat up at the sound of his wife's name. 'It was that . . . blowback,' he stammered, 'almost killed me.'

'But the message went?' I asked.

'Yes,' he said, 'I couldn't stop it. The Benben Stone was designed to draw psionic power out of its operators. I sensed . . . it was incredible, there's a sort of creature inside the stone – an artificial intelligence millennia old, wise, sort of, but without any real temporal sense. It was almost as if I spoke to it . . .'

'The Stone's dead now,' Daisy said, 'I killed it. I had to, or it would have opened up a rift in space-time and caused the same kind of runaway chain reaction that happened last time.'

'Ibram knew what would happen when they used the Stone,' I said, 'that's why the alien had him murdered. Sanusi got cold feet too, and tried to warn us. Andropov must have been the Sayf ad-Din character Sanusi said had taken the amulet. One of his boys wore it and left it in the tunnel of the teashop to put us off the scent.'

Ross was staring at Daisy. 'I knew as soon as I met you that you had the power,' he said, 'but I decided to see how things panned out. Are you an *illuminatus*?'

'Yes,' she said, 'the woman who took me from the orphanage was well . . . a human projection . . . she was one of the *Guardians*. That's why I couldn't tell you who chose me for the assignment.'

'The side of the angels!' I said.

'I had a hunch the *Guardians* were behind this,' Ross said, 'I encountered them first four years ago, when I discovered a Nommo starship buried in the desert. The ship contained the body of the Pharaoh Akhnaton, who was also a Nommo – a ghoul. The *Guardians* helped to defeat him and sealed him up there. They're a kind of cosmic police-force of unbelievably advanced knowledge whose function is to make sure developing species aren't exploited by more advanced ones. My guess is that they built the Benben mansion in the desert and put the Stone there for safe-keeping until such time as we'd be wise enough to use it. But the ghoul got there first.'

Daisy looked at me and put her hands on my shoulders. 'The tests I told you about,' she said, 'were tests of my psionic power.

369

The *Guardians* knew that the Nommo lived and that he would make another attempt to reach the parent species. They knew the consequences might be disastrous for the earth, and they trained me to use my power. They didn't tell me anything about the ghoul or the Stone – their own rules prevent them influencing things directly. All I knew was that I had to contact Omar James Ross and Desmond Redfield's son.'

My face must have dropped a mile. I looked at her with absolute astonishment. 'You knew my father?'

'No, I never knew him. My mentor told me about him. He was an early recruit of the *Guardians* and he was sent here in the sixties in the cover of a USAF sergeant, to investigate the connection between Egypt and MJ-12. He had the psionic gene, and you inherited it.'

'But the letter! He told my mum that he was already married with three children.'

'Your father was liquidated by MJ-12 as a threat, and the letter was concocted by them. Desmond was never married to anyone else and never had any other children. MJ-12 got rid of all his records and managed to eliminate his memory from the face of the earth. That's why I didn't know your name or anything else about you.'

'But you never trusted me?'

'I had to be sure. MJ-12 has a long reach – you could easily have been a plant.'

I stood up, my mind awash with emotions that I couldn't control or even understand. I took Daisy by the hand and led her down the steps and into the jiving, ranting, electric crowd.

'It's not over yet,' Daisy said, 'the message was sent. There will be more visitors from Sirius.'

'Yeah, but it'll take them light-years to get here. That gives us plenty of time to prepare.'

The crowd around the base of the pyramid had all joined hands and were singing *The Age of Aquarius*. We stood on the last step and I put my arms around her, sought out her mouth with mine and kissed her. It was a kiss that seemed to last for ever, and when we finally broke I realized that the crowd was cheering and clapping.

'Hey,' she said, 'you don't even know my name.'

I smiled. 'To me,' I said, 'you'll always be Daisy.'

A barrage of fireworks exploded suddenly and she took my hand. Together we walked out into the crowd, our eyes fixed on the stars that scintillated in the endless night, until we were lost and adrift, another nameless pair of dark figures among thousands of wildly dancing shadows.